BOOTS AND THE LAW

Boots and the Law

A Story of Army JAG Service
In Fort Polk and Vietnam

Samuel T. Brick

iUniverse, Inc.
New York Bloomington Shanghai

Boots and the Law
A Story of Army JAG Service In Fort Polk and Vietnam

iUniverse books may be ordered through booksellers or by contacting:

iUniverse
1663 Liberty Drive
Bloomington, IN 47403
www.iuniverse.com
1-800-Authors (1-800-288-4677)

Because of the dynamic nature of the Internet, any Web addresses or links contained in this book may have changed since publication and may no longer be valid.

This is a work of fiction. All of the characters, names, incidents, organizations, and dialogue in this novel are either the products of the author's imagination or are used fictitiously.

ISBN: 978-0-595-48509-3 (pbk)
ISBN: 978-0-595-71918-1 (cloth)
ISBN: 978-0-595-60601-6 (ebk)

Printed in the United States of America

For Mary

Author's Note

This is a story of military service, the provision of military justice, strategic planning, and the Vietnam War. The vignettes and story-line that follow are fictional but are based, for the most part, on courts martial, legal proceedings, and incidents that happened in Vietnam, Fort Polk, or were experienced by the author during his active duty JAG service. The geography is as real as the author can make it. A list of maps found on Web sites and used by the author follows at the end. Any variance is the author's. The author has exercised literary license to instill an understanding for the reader of the struggles that occurred within the overall Vietnam conflict and the many civil and legal disciplinary problems that surfaced during the War. The story of Lanh, the VC leader and spy, also is fictional but is based on events that actually happened in the history of the Vietnamese people. It was inspired by Phan Xuan An, a spy for the north whose front was that of a Vietnamese journalist in Saigon. Phan died in September, 2005. The story of contract fraud is loosely based on the Sergeant Major of the Army's alleged consortium at the time, a matter of Congressional investigation that was never prosecuted in a court of law. That story is intended to provide the reader an understanding of how contract fraud could work rather than be a portrayal of an actual event. Names and characters in the following stories are the products of the author's imagination or are used fictitiously, and any resemblance to actual persons, living or dead, businesses, companies, or participants in the author's experiences are entirely coincidental.

Since Vietnam there have been substantial changes to the Uniform Code of Military Justice and its implementing Manual that continue with the changing environment of today's warfare. Among many other revisions to the military justice system, there now is a separate defense command, and of course, the judiciary remains independent. Direct commissions into JAG currently are at the grade of First Lieutenant.

My experiences at Fort Polk and in Vietnam taught me that strategy for victory in the court room depends on a reasoned approach for what will win. The strategy, as in warfare, should focus on a projected outcome. In Vietnam, the projected outcome for our war was a continued separation of Vietnam into two nations, a Southern democratic state enhanced with American military might and a North dominated by the communists. Something like the Korean peninsula. We were close at the Paris Peace Talks to obtaining just that. A better strategy initially might have been to work the promised elections after the French left and use diplomacy and our American penchant for independence and liberty to guide the Vietnamese Nation to becoming a world partner. But that's Monday morning quarterbacking. The Chinese hoards massing on the Vietnamese border and Khrushchev's boasting that all our children would be communists made such a strategy too dangerous for our leaders to swallow. Accordingly, we entered the fog of war, a combat scenario where you never know what will happen.

There is little mention of American women in the book. They served as Army employees in libraries, clubs, and other activities designed to take soldiers' minds away from the horrors of warfare; as nurses, civilian and military, who provided unknown comfort to dying and injured GI's giving part of themselves forever, there were over 6,000 female military nurses in Vietnam; with the Red Cross, a mainstay in overseas service, as any person serving overseas will attest; as clerks and secretaries for commands and units in Headquarters areas and in the field in many dangerous areas, there were over 500 Army clerks and secretaries in Vietnam; as beautiful wartime correspondents who must have surprised quite a few soldiers, marines, and airmen in the field with their presence, two lost their lives in combat action; and in many other functions. Eight American military women were killed. Seventeen American civilian women were killed. At the end of the book is a letter by LTC Annie Ruth Graham from Vietnam placed on the internet by her niece as a tribute. She was a veteran of World War II and Korea and wrote to her family and friends at Christmas, 1967, a month before the beginning of the Tet offensive. She died in August, 1968, at 52 years of age, and is memorialized on the Wall. She had two Bronze Star medals, and gave her life for the American soldier. She is just one example of the devotion and sacrifice of American women who served along with their male counterparts in combat situations. All women serving were volunteers. The draft did not include women and military directives forebade their membership in combat units.

The Vietnam War was terrible and so are all wars as any participant in combat will attest. People in the military don't like war. The military quietly follows its political leaders and this makes worse the horrors of an unpopular conflict. Warfare and its fog bred many of the criminal activities noted in the vignettes that follow. Some of the sentences for serious crimes, usually more lenient than one would suspect, are a consequence of military juries weighing the need for discipline while bearing in mind the environment in which our men were thrust.

PROLOGUE

▼

I was alone. A pounding in my chest, an alarm of impending pain, not just physical but including shame, and a flush to my face blurring my vision all made me understand I had to do something. I knew the bully was tough. He was a fighter and looked fierce. I couldn't walk away. There was no place to hide. What would I say? How could I get back to the warm comfort of social acceptance? I had to do something. He was within an inch of my face screaming at me, although what he yelled was hollow with an echo as if I were in a tube. I didn't know my fist was clenched. I didn't know I threw it out in a wild uncontrolled manner. I didn't know I hit him in the face. I only saw him scream out and run away to the other side of the play yard. I was six, he was seven.

It was the fall of my first grade at what used to be a girl's private Catholic school. I didn't attend kindergarten, staying at home instead with an independent, progressive mother. The first day of school, she deposited me at the door of the cloistered convent where only students, nuns, and certain lay teachers were permitted entry. She drove away in the family woody and I was helpless. The school's heavily-carved portal had a small pocket door near its top that a nun would thrust open with a bang to see who was there. She looked down from a round black bonnet framed with white lace. Her face had hair here and there, and with the bonnet cutting into her cheeks, was a pinched red. She had a fiendish smile as if I was Hansel and she had some candy. I was alone and she scared the hell out of me. I was afraid she would transform me.

I bolted from the door and scooted under a thick bush on the other side of the school yard where I hid and cried. So much for my first day of school. After awhile another little old lady with a similar round bonnet found me and yelled for me to get out. She heckled, "If I have to come in there and get you, I'm going to dress you up like a girl and parade you in front of the class."

That didn't sound like a good thing and reminded me there were other kids in the school. They couldn't get us all. Maybe it wasn't so bad after all. Besides, it gave me a way out. I could always say I only gave up when they wanted me to look like a girl. About ten minutes later I found myself in the back row of what for a six-year old was a huge classroom with lots of kids. They mostly were girls, all dressed in parochial school uniforms, sitting at attention in what seemed at first glance to be perfect rows of desks. I realized I was wearing the same clothes as the few boys. There was a soft-spoken, pale-faced little nun up front brandishing a long wooden stick. This one, again dressed in a black gown, had a squared headpiece covering all but her face and flowing down over her shoulders and back. She had a starched square white bib across her front and tight over her forehead. She said nothing about me being late; she just pointed with her stick to an empty desk in the back row. Did the nuns have hair or were their heads shaved? I suspect the word of my shenanigans got out and put me in the bully's cross hairs.

The nuns were my first drill sergeants and their bluster and threats sometimes followed by a sharp pop ensured military discipline in the class rooms. I suspect I was transformed but I held to a disposition of quick decision making and impulsive action. Real drill sergeants and a new profession where other people's lives many times hung in the balance brought me to an understanding that sometimes it's better to understand the consequences of your decisions before you act. With conscription, I understood my duty to serve. The duty was two years. Understanding my commitment made it easier to swallow. Little did I understand at the time that it would end up substantially more than what I first thought.

PART ONE
VIETNAM; FIRST
IMPRESSIONS

Arrival

A terrific hot blast hit me with full impact as I stepped from the frigid air conditioned contract airliner onto the ramp that led down to the Bien Hoa military airport. It was 1969, and at that time those in Vietnam called it the busiest airport in the world. It mostly was a South Vietnamese military, or ARVN, airfield but the allies also used it. There were palm trees and an open-faced terminal guarded by local police known as white mice. They stood around in dirty-white helmets cradling loaded M-16's . There was a heavy odor of jet fuel. There also were local farmers and indigenous folk cordoned off in one area with baskets of food, cages with live ducks, and all sorts of other items a relocated person might take to an unknown destination. I saw in another area a number of guys hanging onto tightly-packed duffle bags, queuing up to go home on the same plane that we came in on, now a "Freedom Bird." Charter planes did not stay long in Vietnam. I learned later that the VC, as part of their war on our morale, would target troops just completing a tour of duty as well as those just starting one. An MP directed me to a bus for the 90th Replacement Battalion. Its windows were covered with heavy chicken wire. Someone said it was to keep out grenades that might be tossed in the bus by terrorists passing by on little scooters. It took us on rural streets with lots of trees and framed by a concrete houses built in European style each surrounded by bullet-pocked walls and chain link fences. We then came to a highway with lots of those little scooters belching nasty fumes and many piled high with whole families as they putt-putted along. The bus seemed to keep its distance from the scooters. On one side of the street an ornate wagon with glass sides and decked in white was being pulled slowly by a little old French truck. A number of people all dressed in white walked behind in a procession. A young Buddhist monk in saffron flowing robes led the entourage. There was a group of musicians in the parade banging what looked like cymbals. It was a Vietnamese funeral procession, and as they walked along the side of the road with vehicles passing them by, they banged away the evil spirits.

The town of Bien Hoa, through which we drove, was hot, humid, squalid, smelly, and very French. White exhaust from the scooters and little trucks billowed everywhere. On each side of the street were two and three story buildings connected except for little pathways to the rear. The buildings were in every state of repair. Pieces of corrugated metal and canvas hung throughout. Bamboo shades and loose flattened sheets of tin-can aluminum covered store fronts on the street level. There were signs in French and Vietnamese with some English aimed at the troops. HUA THI PHOTOCOPIE, THAI-LAI Tailor, TAN VIET RES-

TAURANTE, NHA THUOC TAY PHARMACIE were but a few examples. There were open porches in front of some of the apartments. The dirt sidewalks were busy with people selling food and other stuff under jerry-rigged tarps. There were some with little tables on the walk ways hosting local men who appeared to be playing dominoes and more than anything else, just socializing. The side of the road was sprinkled with detritus from all imaginable functions. There were few automobiles. Those that were in this section predominantly were U.S. military. Scooters with over-sized baskets rigged on front served as trucks. A woman was carrying baskets almost as tall as herself that were hung on each side of a wooden pole across her back. Some women were dressed in old baggy pants with dirty blouses while others wore tunics, known as ao dais, over silk pants and white blouses. There were quite a few old men in the area mostly dressed in shabby pants and white shirts, collared and hanging down over the top of their pants. A little further along in a less dense area I saw an elderly woman squatting on a rut next to the road with her dress gathered around obviously relieving herself. I had no idea where I was going and I was the only officer on board.

We arrived at a heavily guarded entrance to Long Binh and an MP waved us in. We proceeded a short distance, came to a hill, and passed under a sign proclaiming the 90th Replacement Battalion under which in smaller letters appeared, "LTC J.J. Poole, AG Commanding." The bus stopped at the top of a hill. I wrestled my duffle bag, loaded with all my possessions for the next year, off the bus and looked down into the vast Long Binh compound. There were row upon row of buildings stretched out into the distance with busy streets, both paved and dirt, with a moderate flow of all types of military trucks and jeeps. I wondered if Long Binh would be my home and what might become of me. We entered into what looked like a reception building. It was heavily fortified by sand bags and had a welcome sign. Pairs of military police milled about. We reported to a waiting cadre of clerks whose job was to provide assignment orders, if in fact they had knowledge that we were supposed to be there. Helicopters dotted the sky and the area was dusty, sandy, and noisy. A line of choppers hovered over a large building about a mile or so away and one would dip down to its flat roof and then lift off, followed immediately by another. I learned later they were "dust offs" and a welcome sight for any wounded soldier. The white building had a red cross on its roof. According to the Geneva Convention that made the hospital immune from enemy targeting. I saw the first sign for a men's room since we landed. It was a large open area with vented windows near a high ceiling that did not quite do the job. A razed platform ran the length of one side on which was a row of maybe fifteen toilet seats perched over a cesspool. On the other side was a long trough for use as a urinal. It was slanted so the water running from the top end continuously flushed to the bottom. There were a few sinks by the door where I came in. Except for the exterior walls, it was an open area. I value my privacy but considering everything, I decided to get on with it especially as no one was around. I felt maybe I could do my business and evacuate the area before anyone came in. No such luck. As I sat with my pants around my ankles, an old Vietnamese mamma san with mop and bucket appeared out of nowhere. She proceeded to mop the concrete floor as if I wasn't there. I began to earn my combat pay as I entered the war zone.

The arrival clerks proceeded at their own leisurely pace in noting the presence of all who just arrived. They were updating each soldier's hand-carried 201 personnel files, properly recording the date the soldier arrived in Vietnam and was on his way to wherever or was available for assignment. They enclosed the newest set of in-country orders, if they had any. Computers were a thing of the future and the lines moved incrementally. I was looking for the shortest when I heard someone call for Captain Thompson. I saw a middle-aged warrant officer looking around so I went over and asked him, "Are you looking for a Gregg Thompson?"

He looked at the name tag on my Class B military blouse and said, "Welcome to Vietnam.

I'm Mr. McCormick, the warrant at the JAG office at Saigon Support Command. USARV assigned you there and I've got your orders. The boss asked me to bring you over to the office."

I grabbed my briefcase; he got my duffle bag; and we went outside to the office jeep. There was an enlisted driver in fatigues, covered by a helmet and nestling an M-16 next to his leg with the barrel pointed down. The driver introduced himself as a legal clerk at the JAG office.

Reporting In

Major Forsythe was seated at the staff judge advocate's desk for the Saigon Support Command according to the sign over his door. He was a nice looking guy sporting neatly combed hair and a not too long Roman face. He scowled at me when I reported with a salute. His fatigues were starched and pressed.

"Welcome to Saigon Support JAG," he motioned for me to sit and continued, "I'm glad you're here Thompson; we've been waiting for you. USARV called yesterday to say you were airborne. I'm on my thirteenth month in Nam and officially my tour's over. USARV, our JAG next higher command, asked me to stay for ninety more days because my replacement had to finish up some school he was attending, of all things hospital administration, and the new SJA fell off the wagon on his way over."

He didn't look happy. My take was that this was his first job in charge and he didn't want anything to happen to mess up his career. He was looking at papers as he talked. I immediately sensed not to get in his way. "Lieutenant Colonel Tom Cassidy will be your boss after he dries out a bit. He's in a medical facility in the Philippines. Apparently a quick trip to an airport bar during a delay between flights was more than he could take and he missed his connecting flight. He stayed at the bar a bit too long and fortunately was able to get some help from an Air Force JAG who happened by."

This was more than I needed to know. Forsythe continued, "We really need you as our case load is high and I understand you have some trial experience."

"Yes sir, but I mostly defended cases at Fort Polk. I was there about a year; went to the JAG school after that where I studied the rewrite of the military justice system. I also got to go to the Law in Vietnam course and the first military judge course. The Judge Advocate General certified me as a part-time judge under those changes. If possible, I'd like to sit on a few courts-martial while here."

"I know all about that. You need to sign in, get some billeting, and get your stuff in order. We have some surprises for you in the morning. See you first thing."

"What's first thing, sir?"

"How about 0700? And McCormick can show you where to sign in."

It was late afternoon. McCormick introduced me to a few members of the team as we walked out of the JAG offices. We started down the hall on the first floor of our metal building and I heard and felt a huge explosion. I winced and unconsciously ducked but saw that McCormick just kept on. He looked at me with a wry smile and said, "Afternoon monsoons."

We left the command building and trotted through a torrential rain to the personnel office across the court yard, me hunched over with duffle bag on my back and my brief case pressed tightly to my chest. I entered the personnel building sopping wet and followed a sign stating "In Processing." Upon entering a cavernous room with rows of desks, I saw a Spec Four framed in huge ear phones. He was on the front row and seemed to be day-dreaming so I sat at the chair facing his desk. The name tag stenciled on his fatigue shirt read Webster. He looked at me with a strange expression, "Sir, I need a copy of your orders and your 201 file."

I asked, "What are you listening to?"

"Janice Joplin singing Kosmic Blues. It gets me in the proper mood." I wasn't sure what that meant. Webster continued, "Your orders look in proper order and I see you've had all your shots."

I had enclosed a little yellow booklet, my shot record, in my 201 file.

While flipping through my thin little file, he asked, "Have you updated your next of kin and survivorship options?"

"I'm not married and think it's all in order."

"Do you have the Soldiers' Group Life Insurance and the beneficiaries specified for that? You know, if you don't specify somebody, the proceeds will go through your estate." He said this last bit of information as if that was something that would not be good.

"I did a bunch of legal assistance at Fort Polk and understand. I believe my papers are in order. I named my brother and sister as my beneficiaries, *per stirpes.*" I thought if I threw in a little Latin it would impress him.

"I know you, didn't know you were a lawyer. I was in the company right next to yours at basic at Bragg. We started about the same time. I remember you because you looked different from everybody else. I remember when we first came in; you had on slacks and a preppy shirt."

The Draft

The Draft Board finally got me at my third year in law school. I appealed for a II-S deferment until school was over and I completed the bar exam. When I graduated from the University of Pennsylvania in 1964, the new President Johnson, Robert McNamara, and Dean Rusk were trying to figure out what to do in Vietnam. The draft, while it had been ongoing since World War II, was just beginning to churn up bodies for Vietnam. My father told me he would pay for it if I continued on to law school but if I got a job, then his responsibility for my education was over. That made sense and I figured if I continued on, I could avoid the draft first with the educational deferment and then maybe get married and have a child so I'd have what the draft termed an "extreme hardship to dependents" deferment.

As the war progressed and body bags peppered the United States, the draft needed more men, school was almost out, and no one would marry me. The draft board extended my deferment a few months so I could graduate and take the bar exam. I eventually received an order to present myself for an Armed Forces Physical Examination. They were serious. I was the only one out of my law school to get drafted. Most had other deferments and a few actually joined.

The Draft Board examination was exactly what I expected—no privacy and lots of lines. We signed in, were ordered to strip down into our underwear, and got into line. The doctors were all in a row clip boards in hand. As we walked by, half naked, they would take a cursory glance to make sure we had two eyes and two ears. I believe their constant requests for us to move along were meant to make sure we could hear. A quick feel and cough were supposed to determine whether we had a hernia. They also made sure we had a heart beat. One examinee a few people ahead was wearing silk panties. He really didn't want to go. They miraculously found aberrations about some who were moved to different lines. A few must have had just one eye. I didn't see the guy with silk panties after we passed the line of doc's. At the last desk someone took my clipboard and informed me I was fine. I told him I had flat feet and a heart murmur and he said not to worry. He told me to go home pending further notification of the Board's decision.

I learned I passed the Maryland bar exam while helping my parents move. They decided to retire and move to the Caribbean since I, the baby, was leaving home. I received an Order for induction into the Armed Forces of the United States that told me to report to my local Selective Service Board in downtown Baltimore at noon on October 24, 1967. The last line in the Order stated willful failure to report would subject me to fine and imprisonment and to bring the Order with me. I had a big drink. Reports on the fighting in Vietnam garnered increased attention and I started jogging.

The Power of Admin Clerks

I barely recognized Spec Four Webster, the in-processing clerk, from Fort Bragg. I felt certain camaraderie with someone who went through the hell of basic just next to me and reminisced, "It's really a small world and I guess the Army is small as well. Do you remember our drill sergeant, a big bear of a man?"

He looked across the desk at me, now a captain, and must have felt the same emotion, "Yea, I remember him and from what I saw, I'm glad he was yours and not mine."

"He actually wasn't all that bad. A lot of bluster. We called him Smoky Bear or The Smoke but not to his face. Just before we graduated he collected five bucks from all the trainees for a going away party. The thing is it never happened. After the ceremony we all were looking for him or for where the party was going to be but he was nowhere to be seen."

Webster smiled, "I'm not surprised. How did you get from Fort Bragg to legal assistance at Tigerland?"

"I went to Polk as my next training assignment and after about a month they pulled me out and put me in the JAG office. I got a commission and they asked me to stay. Now I'm here. While at law school I toyed with JAG. I even went to the Pentagon and visited the JAG career management office. The four-year commitment scared me off. Actually, I didn't think I was the military type so career management seemed unnecessary. I figured I could handle the draft and two years but after Fort Polk and Tigerland, those four-years didn't look so bad."

Webster fiddled with his pencil, looked across at me and said, "I know what you mean. I went to the University of Delaware and after graduation my Draft Board sent me the notice. I spoke to some friends who told me almost everyone who gets drafted goes to Vietnam as a grunt so I signed up for a three-year tour with a promise to be a personnel clerk and here I am."

I went on that not too many JAGs wanted to go to Polk and Tigerland but since I was already there, I stayed and got into the routine of prosecuting and defending courts-martial. The draft and Tigerland kept us pretty busy with AWOLs and desertions. Eventually, I received orders for Vietnam but since I hadn't gone to the JAG School in Charlottesville, Virginia, for a basic course in military law, the JAG personnel office in the pentagon gave me the option of attending military schooling first. With a year of JAG under my belt, and the fact that the war might be over by the time I finished the basic course, I opted for the home of the University of Virginia and all its glory. While there, since I had some court work at Fort Polk and apparently some respect, I was selected to attend the first military judge course. It was designed to certify judges so the JAG Corps could implement the recently enacted major changes to the military justice system. I was probably the least experienced and most junior lawyer in the course, but I didn't tell Webster that.

Webster looked through my files and was trashing some duplicates and other stuff as personnel weenies do and said, "I can't find your leave record."

It scared me a little and I answered too quickly, "It should be there. I've taken leave. I thought I saw it there."

He had a sly grin as he repeated, "I can't find any leave records. It doesn't look like you took leave after JAG school and jungle training."

"I went to see my parents in Vieques, Puerto Rico."

He interrupted, raised his hand palm forward and firmly stated, "Sir, we need to reconstitute your leave record."

I finally got it and after answering a few questions as to my whereabouts the past two years, my new friend put me in possession of a new record that reflected very little leave. The power of enlisted clerks never ceases to amaze me. He told me of the requirement to change my dollars for military payment certificates to cut down black market activities and to get my ration card so I could purchase some booze and cigarettes. He said I had to go to finance to arrange for pay and suggested an allotment that would pay approximately 10% interest on funds from combat pay to be available when if I got back to the states. He said I had to return to the 90th for transient billeting until a permanent place suitable for an O-3 was available.

The medical clerk gave me a big fat malaria pill and said I had to take one every month in country, and if I forgot, malaria would make me sick and stay with me for the rest of my life, sneaking up when least expected. He said the pill might mess up my stomach and to take it on a full stomach.

My First Night In Country

The landlord for my new hooch at the 90th, an enlisted guy, showed me where things were. I had a steel bed with a thin mattress over metal springs with a metal locker behind on the second floor of a long open-sided and screened building. The bed was in a line of similar beds each separated by a chair. Everything was painted dark Army-green. Not much privacy but this was better than my own tent in the jungle. The landlord showed me the bunker I should go to when we were under rocket attack. It was a hut at the end of the building next to mine and round-topped with sand bags all over its top and sides. It had a wall its height about two feet in front of the entrance door. The wall, a protective barrier, also was fully sand-bagged. You could get into the bunker from either side of the barrier and hopefully a rocket wouldn't follow suit.

He related as I peered inside the bunker, "Find a good place to sit Captain. The further back, the better it is. A couple of weeks ago some officer who just got in-country was killed from lucky shrapnel from by a VC rocket. Lucky for the VC. He was in a hooch on the second floor just two buildings down."

"Thanks for that welcoming message."

He looked down at his clip board and told me, "Make sure you have your helmet and a flack vest. You'll need 'em. You should be here about three weeks and then Headquarters Company will assign you a little safer spot. The VC get a special joy out of targeting our folks just coming and just going."

I found the 90th chow hall and being pretty tired after my trip and a typical Army meal, I returned to my bunk where I pulled out the latest Playboy I purchased on my way over. My stomach started to bother me either from the Army food or the malaria pill. After a few trips to the can I fell asleep.

I awakened sometime in the middle of the night from a deep sleep. I was dreaming of swimming in the multiple blue-shaded, gin-clear waters of the Caribbean with a beautiful girl whose hard nipples and areolae were visible through her bikini top when I heard thundering feet and a siren. I woke up with a hard on. I didn't know where I was but looked around and realized it was Vietnam. It quickly abated. Most of my room mates were moving in a determined pace down the center aisle. They were in all states of dress and most with their helmets on. Several wore flack jackets. I figured I'd better get going so I quickly put on my new fatigues and boots. My boots had a steel arch to keep bamboo sticks from puncturing my feet so, as the quartermaster NCO told me, I wouldn't have a bad day. I grabbed my helmet and started for the bunker. I was the last one out who was going out. I heard someone's tape player broadcasting Daddy's Home by Shep and the Limelights. I saw a few people, maybe ten of the sixty or so of my room mates on that second floor barracks, still in their bunks. I got to the foul-smelling, fully-occupied bunker in quick order. I found a small space on a wooden bench right by the entry way and settled in when another siren whined. The guy next to me said it was the all clear signal and everyone went back to bed. I have never been able to understand how the MPs could figure out it was all clear. Unless they were just messing with us, I suspected the sirens blew when rockets were launched into a certain area or someone saw someone or something that looked dangerous. As we returned to our bunks I could see a few flares on the other side of the Long Binh compound. Maybe they showed the VC on the run. Or maybe it was some guy in a guard tower who got bored, wanted some excitement, and hit an alarm. After I was back in my cot and attempting to get to sleep, I heard and felt a large WUMP. I expected another siren but there was none and no one seemed to notice. I fell asleep and this time dreamt about crawling under barbed wire at AIT in Fort Polk.

I went to my bunker when the siren sounded maybe for two or three nights after that and then for the rest of my time in the transient billets, I just rolled over. Flares were always going off at the perimeter around Long Binh; most of the time you could hear the thump-thumps of helicopters; and there were large WUMP's all night at the 90th Replacement billets. One guy slept fully dressed to include flack jacket and laced jungle boots. Someone said he was a dentist. He was always first out the door at the siren's wail. I fortunately never heard or felt any successful hits while at the 90th. It was good to leave the 90th but I didn't have a clue as to the fog of war I was about to enter.

PART TWO
COMMISSIONING INTO
ARMY JAG

Basic Training and the Bar

I finished basic training at Fort Bragg in January. My company got leave for Christmas so no leave was authorized before our next duty station. I was a "US" and my serial number was US 51669657. Others were RA's and their serial numbers had an RA in front. The US's were draftees and were in the Army of the United States. I thought that was cool. The RA's were Regular Army. There was a difference between being an RA lower enlisted guy and being a lifer. Many RA's like Spec Four Webster, went into the Regular Army and agreed to an additional year's commitment to get a specific military occupational specialty such as clerk typist, supply clerk, chaplain's assistant, or some other position that might have less of a chance for immediate combat than the draftees who everybody knew were jungle bound. Others would sign up for an extra year to get an assignment to Europe, Korea, or some area other than Vietnam. That didn't guarantee that their second tour wouldn't be Nam and many times it was. We repeatedly were encouraged to go airborne and a few did. That, however, didn't change the two-year service requirement. Basic is mostly a blur. We got yelled at and learned to strip down, clean, and shoot M-16's, 45 caliber pistols, and 50 caliber machine guns. We threw real hand grenades, shot light anti-tank LAW's, and low-crawled under two foot high chicken wire with red tracer bullets streaking over us. One guy started to stand up during this exercise and the drill sergeants went crazy. He went to the psych ward and we never saw him again. It was a dangerous way to get out of the Army. We learned basic combat hand signals and how to maneuver under fire. There was a story of a guy a few companies down who stabbed a pencil into his eye to get a discharge. The rumor was that the Army would keep him even with one eye but I thought the whole thing a bit much. I still wondered at the amount of personal drive it must take to put your eye out. Anyone doing that would be a great candidate from the draft dodgers of the nation for their Medal of Honor.

We camped out a bit, sharpened our marksmanship skills, and marched around to a cadence provided by singing drill sergeants.

"*I wanna be an airborne ranger,*
"*I wanna go to Viet Nam.*"

Fort Bragg Basic Training

About half way through basic I was permitted to call home.

My mother excited to hear me said, "You got something in the mail from the Court of Appeals down in Annapolis. I hope you don't mind, but I opened it and it's pretty important. You are invited to a swearing in ceremony to the Maryland Bar on Friday, November 17th. Too bad it's not closer to Thanksgiving."

I told her, "Thanks, I don't mind you opening my mail but please forward anything personal. I don't know whether I can get away or not. They're pretty tough about that sort of thing but I'll ask. You know we are not coming home Thanksgiving. It's Christmas instead and I think we get a week then. Nothing is set in stone. Everything's something you have to earn."

She asked me, "What can I do to help?"

"I think you'd better leave that to me," I was worried about having my mother helping me out and how my drill sergeant would react, "I'll let you know."

We discussed some other pleasantries about what was going on but all I could think about was the importance of being sworn into the Bar. I couldn't practice law or really be a lawyer until I was formally sworn in. I asked the first sergeant if I could have the weekend of the 17th off. It was two weeks away. He said no but told me he'd mention it to the company commander. I was pissed and dejected. About a day or so later the Smoke ordered me to stand by after formation. He said I could leave for the weekend to be a lawyer and I had fifteen minutes to make the necessary arrangements. I immediately took off and called home.

The Thursday before my leave everybody in the unit got haircuts. This was something we did every three weeks. The platoon marched to the barber shack in the middle of the training area. We waited in line outside and went in, one at a time, as one of our brethren left sheared. The shack housed two barber chairs, a large mirror behind, and didn't have a Field and Stream magazine. It was a quick thing. The barber would move the electric hair clippers back and forth across our head until nothing was left. As he ran the clippers over my head, he seemed to clip away my brains. After about two minutes, he put out his hand for the $4 fee. The following morning, completely shorn, I caught a plane out of Fayetteville, North Carolina, to Washington National where my parents were waiting. The honorable judges of the Maryland Court of Appeals swore me into the Maryland Bar after which I celebrated with my parents at the City Dock in Annapolis with Bloody Mary's and Maryland crab cakes. My mother confided that while I was studying for the bar she made a novena to St. Jude. I thanked her and said it worked. Only later did I understand that St. Jude is the patron saint of lost causes.

Advanced Infantry Training at Tigerland

When I arrived at Fort Polk's advanced infantry training, I was sent to a holding company so they could figure out where I should train for jungle warfare. The company clerk sent me to a small lounge where I seemed to wait forever. I didn't have anything to read and the magazines in the room, Time and a few sports journals, didn't provide much comfort. I sat on an imitation leather couch and read the latest edition of Time. It reported on the rising American death toll from an ongoing North Vietnamese and VC offensive that started at the Vietnamese New Year holiday. It focused on the uncanny abilities of the VC. There were stories on the fighting in Saigon and other major South Vietnamese cities and problems facing the marines in a venerable old city called Hue. The room had a small curtained window. Outside there were a bunch of guys playing touch football. They were just back from Vietnam. Tigerland was looming over me, the war seemed to be going south, and these guys seemed extremely happy to be back. I thought if lucky, that could be me in a year's time. I was depressed, a bit scared, and homesick. Having some time by myself in that little room to think about it, I made the decision to pursue a JAG commission. I thought if I was going to Vietnam, I might as well go as an officer and do something I was trained to do; after all I now was a Maryland lawyer.

AIT was a bitch. We got up in the dark, low-crawled all over the place, and constantly ran from one location to another. Tigerland was designed to teach us about the jungle and the problems the infantry had in Vietnam. These things were drilled into us as matters of life or death. We learned about nasty shit-covered bamboo spikes the VC would hide under vegetation on our trails so wounds on our feet would fester and render us incapacitated or worse. They showed us mockups of little toe popper land mines. They demonstrated wire triggers to detonators for explosives that could blow off our feet or if the VC were lucky our legs. They told us not to use the same trail day after day and not to bunch up. What they called a pecker checker taught us some basic medical procedures. We learned how to tie off arteries so if someone had an arm or leg blown off they wouldn't bleed to death and have to be taken in a zip up body bag to "the dump." The cadre showed us how to paint our faces and use foliage to hide. They taught us how to call in a fire mission. It was scary and not fun. Most of our instructors were just back from Nam; our second lieutenants were on their way. The officers were learning from the seasoned NCOs as well. The NCOs were vets of the jungle and serious about what they had to say. Everyone listened. We trained six days a week. When we moved from place to place, the drill sergeant would sing various jogging cadences. He sang a line almost always about going airborne and the troops would repeat it while jogging along:

"One, two;

"Three, four;

"Marchers answer "THREE, FOUR;

"If I die on the old drop zone;

"Box me up and send me home:

"Pin my wings up on my chest; and

"Tell my girl I done my best."

On Sundays, if our work was done and we were not in trouble, we could go to church and the movies or the PX. Mess hall was a little later on Sunday mornings and a bit more relaxed. If we were in trouble, we were assigned mess duty or work detail. I went to church those Sundays I could and prayed hard for deliverance from Tigerland and its aftermath. At morning formation after about a month of pure hell, the drill sergeant boomed out, "Thompson, get your gear out of the barracks, strip your bed, and report to the first sergeant."

Top was a rough old southern boy who joked when I reported, "Thompson, you're sittin' in high cotton."

Nothing in my life at that time was funny or soft so I asked, "What's that mean Top?"

"We got orders for you this morning assigning you to Company D, Special Troops, with duty at the JAG office. It's on the other side of post and you can catch the bus that comes by battalion headquarters. We all know you applied for a JAG commission. They want to get a good look."

This, I later found out, was to be an "observation tour." My prayers were answered and I thanked Him profusely.

Fort Polk JAG

The Fort Polk JAG office was in an old two-story converted wooden barracks building. There were ten JAG officers, six enlisted personnel, and ten civilian employees. The staff judge advocate, Lieutenant Colonel Leonard Hoff, was a round-faced, rumpled-looking, easy going lieutenant colonel who looked like Tom Bosley while playing Howard Cunningham in Happy Days. When I reported I could see several certificates on his walls, one stating he was a member of the Bar of the State of Indiana. He greeted me, "Gregg, we're happy to have you with us. I'm Len Hoff and I understand you are here for a designated period and either you will be returned to Tigerland to start another AIT program, be reassigned permanently to this office as a legal clerk, but that's not in stone, or you will get commissioned into JAG. It's up to you and how you get along here in the office and whether my deputy and I believe you can perform well as a JAG officer."

"Thank you for the opportunity, sir."

He seemed to change his demeanor and gave me a serious look while he said, "I'm assigning you first to legal assistance. It's an important part of the office and if you have any problems whatsoever, don't hesitate to come see me."

He was the highest ranking officer I had met since being in the Army. Other than the building being on fire, I wasn't going to bother him. Hoff introduced me to his deputy, Major Ben Toffle, and left me with him. Toffle was a no non-sense martinet. He was of average height but looked hard and constantly glared. He had a short waxed crew cut and appeared fit and pretty tough. He was wearing jump wings.

Toffle grimaced while looking at me. "Shine your boots, get your uniform in order and get a set of crisp Class B khakis. Polish your brass and your shoes and I'll see you when you look like a soldier."

He took me to the JA sergeant major who he ordered, "Get this recruit in shape so he can do something worthwhile."

The sergeant major escorted me to the legal assistance office and showed me an Army green metal desk with a faint oil smell. He told me it was mine. There was a lop-sided metal chair with a torn vinyl seat leaking cotton stuffing pushed under. I looked in the desk drawers and they were empty except for some dust bunnies, crumbs, and a few left over paper clips, the debris of some flakey unknown predecessor. The drawers squeaked and rattled as I yanked them out. I had a phone. This was my first desk as a practicing attorney. It was better than a ditch in the jungle with a shelter-half roof which is what the Tigerland folks said I would get in Vietnam. Someone put a pile of military books and legal pamphlets on the top corner. These centered on the provision of legal assistance in the Army and generally what military lawyers do. I got to work.

Legal Assistance

Captain Ted Plumber, the head of the legal assistance branch was a peculiar little JAG captain who'd march around his section and tick off parts of whatever he was doing by moving his fingers out one at a time. He stood up straight in an attempt to gain an extra inch to his relatively short frame. His face was bunched up with round little glasses perched on a stubby nose. He seemed always to give lists of things to do or how to do them in numbered increments. Ted appeared efficient but after some observation seemed more to plod. He was anally neat and everything in his pale green office with its wooden barracks walls was stark and in its place by the numbers. He wore an Army garrison cap, an envelope shaped flat thing that had gold piping around its edges with the officer's insignia of grade on its right front. The garrison cap is affectionately known in the Army as the "cunt cap." He'd wear it straight on and pushed down over his head so it looked for him a bit large. Plumber knew Army Regulations well and was not talkative, at least not to me. I learned legal assistance officers prepared lots of wills and powers of attorney, normally ministerial functions that were no big deal in law school. Plumber did this well. In law school we spent more time on estate planning, something proscribed in legal assistance, except maybe for the base commander. Each soldier was encouraged to have a will, with special emphasis for those going into the combat zone.

Plumber looked down at me and said, "It's our responsibility to provide legal advice. The local lawyers do the court work. They file for the divorces and write up the separation agreements. All the regulations allow us to do is give legal advice regarding problems the soldiers face when being away for extended periods. Make sure you read Army Regulation 27-3 that tells us exactly what we can and can not do. We also are supposed to get each soldier a will. For those soldiers from Louisiana, we have special procedures for that. Check with Mr. Feuille, our civilian attorney from Louisiana who takes care of those. As an extra function, we review findings of investigations into military losses of property and equipment. If, for example, a soldier loses a weapon, an investigation ensues with findings that might require the soldier to pay for the lost property."

He pointed his pen at me and directed, "You will be responsible for working on these. I put Army Regulation 735-5 on Reports of Survey on your desk. Give me a short note with the appropriate citations and your recommendation for each case. Make it part of the formal JAG action. I'll review and sign it should your product be acceptable."

I wasn't sure what he meant by product but understood I had to make the determination whether the soldier was not just simply stupid and not have to pay, or was really stupid and then be liable. He continued with his fore finger raised for emphasis. "Under no circumstance let a soldier execute a general power of attorney. The soldiers will push on this but it's against our policy. If pressured, send the soldier to me."

A general power of attorney authorized the person receiving it to do anything the soldier could do if he were present. Soldiers would get married right before coming on active duty and request this broad authority for their new spouses. Each would profess his wife would never do anything not in their mutual interest. Full of emotion and homesickness and burdened by the worries of impending combat, the soldier heard and believed the words of the popular song, Soldier Boy:

"Soldier Boy, Oh my little Soldier Boy

"You were my first love;

"And you'll be my last love;

"I will never make you blue;

"I'll be true to you."

The problems to which the general powers gave rise were devastating. Once the soldier's side of the bed was empty, many spouses who got this authority stripped the absent soldier of everything he owned and had her boyfriend of the moment fill the empty space. She would finance the affair through her general power. He would definitely be blue when he looked at his bank statement. We overcame this with another remedy. These were the special powers of attorney. They give specific direction with limited functions—sign income tax returns, move household goods, pay bills, register and repair cars, etc. It was a little more work to determine the soldier's specific requirements but it removed temptation from the designated "attorney" and saved the soldier heartbreak and us substantial domestic relations legal work. We were very busy in legal assistance and JAGs from other sections in the office assisted us pursuant to Major Toffle's extra-duty roster.

Commissioning

All the JAG officers were married except one who was leaving Fort Polk when I arrived. For the most part, they lived in married officer quarters in a newly built company grade community. I lived in enlisted barracks in the Company D Special Troops area. Major Toffle told me the observation tour would be about a month and he would make the determination as to whether I would be commissioned or not. Toffle's boots had a mirror shine and his uniform stayed crisp all day. His brass buckle was so highly polished it sparkled in the dark. Each night I worked hours spitting on and polishing my boots to get a mirrored shine. I never succeeded and he kept after me. I asked a few guys at Company D how to do it and they said you had to be airborne to know. I remembered the drill sergeant's cadence from basic that was especially poignant in Louisiana. After the one-two stuff:

"Coon skin and alligator hide;

"Make a pair of jump boots just the right size;

"Shin em up, lace em up, put em on your feet;

"Spit-shined jump boots just can't be beat!"

Toffle seemed more concerned about my military appearance than my ability to practice law. He was single but living with a woman off post. He referred to her as his "House Mouse." The major had airborne wings and wondered aloud why I didn't. I was never sure whether he was kidding or serious. He had a glint to his eyes that seemed to hide a smile. I reciprocated by not showing fear but rather by making the confrontations fun. I noticed the captains in the office stayed their distance.

Company D, Special Troops, was comprised of the clerks, cooks, and other administrative personnel who staffed the post. There were not many trees in the company area and the buildings were all of the same barracks style nestled in dirt and sand with painted signs establishing each place. There was little grass, at least on the ground. Special Troops was a catch-all for folks who worked on post and were not part of a regimental command. The post hosted a boxing team and the boxers lived in our open barracks. They were exempt from making the morning formations and from company details. The company commander, First Lieutenant Bob Turner, was a frequent visitor of the JAG office. He was not airborne and not planning a military career. He fit in well with the JAG officers.

First Lieutenant Turner was responsible for disciplinary issues with the headquarters command troops. Fort Polk was in the middle of nowhere so the off-duty bored troops found some relief with the drugs that permeated the nation in the late 60's. The supervisor of the guy in trouble would request his ass and Bob had to mediate and render the appropriate measures. The JAGs helped him do that. If he came down too hard, the senior NCOs, whom he also commanded, would whisper into their bosses' ears that he was not up to the job and the word would get back to the post commander who would find another Special Troop commander. If he didn't provide sufficient discipline then the officer who might be offended would complain and again, Bob would be the whipping boy. Accordingly, he walked a thin line and that he did it well was attested to by his longevity in the job. The dusty and sand-strewn command area was not neat like in the basic and AIT areas. We were on the other side of Fort Polk from Tigerland in more ways than just location.

My observation tour went by quickly. I remembered when a young kid my uncle's admonishment at a Christmas dinner that children were to be seen and not heard. I started seeing legal assistance clients and preparing wills and powers of attorney. I met most of the personnel in the office and found out what they did. There were people who worked on all types of claims, from household goods damage in government moves to civilian automobile accidents involving government vehicles off post. They had claims for training incidents that caused problems to neighboring property and claims by victims of military crimes. It seemed everyone wanted a piece of the action. Government contractors had their own set of claims. Those fell in another JAG section that reviewed contracts the post entered into for repairs, maintenance, and everything else that kept the base going. There was a section that handled administrative matters such as whether the post commander could accept an invitation to speak at a Lions Club luncheon during a seminar they were having about support for the war in Vietnam.

I was reviewing a report of survey that found a staff sergeant with duty as a mechanic at a battalion motor pool liable in the amount of $357 for losing a set of wrenches when Major Toffle came by. He asked, "What are you doing?"

I told him, "I've got a report of survey. Apparently, a sergeant left a wrench set out over night. It was on a large metal table in an open motor pool. It was pretty stupid and I believe the surveying officer's recommendation that he be held for pecuniary liability is correct. If the sergeant had left the wrenches inside the garage but not in their locker cabinet, it might just have been stupid, but not really stupid like leaving them loose on a table out in the open."

Toffle said, "That seems appropriate. I agree. How about coming over to my office?"

It was near the end of the duty day and this was the first time he had done this; normally, if he wanted to see me, he'd send someone to get me. This was particularly strange because LTC Hoff was in Alexandria for a civilian Bar Association event and Toffle was in charge. I wondered what I'd done wrong and unconsciously looked at my shoes.

Sergeant Major Adkins, the chief enlisted person in the office, shot me a look as I followed the major by Adkins' desk. I couldn't tell whether it was an evil grin or a smile.

I slowly entered his office.

He grabbed a paper in the middle of his desk and standing beside it looked at me. "Again the Army screwed up! I just got a message from the Pentagon and they tell me you're officer material. If you agree to four-years of active duty, I'm supposed to offer you a commission as a captain in the Army of the United States and then swear you in."

He gave me the message. It was an official Order from the Department of the Army and my name was set out as the recipient. I couldn't talk. My emotions filled my chest and my vision blurred. After the threat of hell in the jungle, after being the recipient of NCO indignities in basic training, and after serving as the lowest guy in what seemed the entire Army, that message evaporated what had been a huge weight. I was about to jump from being a private, E-2, to an officer, O-3. Toffle stared at me. I felt like when I was thrown in the deep area at age five and told to swim. I wanted to go hide and be by myself for a few minutes. My throat constricted and I nodded a bit.

I croaked, "Let's get on with it."

He looked me straight in the eye. "Raise your right hand."

It shot up before I could think.

Then without any written aid Major Toffle straightened up, as if he were at attention, and told me to repeat after him:

"I, Gregg Thompson, having been appointed an officer in the Army of the United States, in the grade of captain, do solemnly swear that I will support and defend the Constitution of the United States against all enemies, foreign or domestic, that I will bear true faith and allegiance to the same; that I take this obligation freely, without any mental reservations or purpose of evasion; and that I will well and faithfully discharge the duties of the office upon which I am about to enter; So help me God."

I did.

Toffle congratulated me, shook my hand, and told me LTC Hoff would be home at 1900 and wanted me to come to his house for dinner. Wow! I'd made it. I said, "Sir, I don't have anything to wear."

"Don't worry about it. You're fine. Let's go to the Club for a celebratory drink." He seemed a different person and not so bad. He smiled at me and pinned some captain's bars on my uniform shirt collar and paraded me around the office. Everyone congratulated me and the sergeant major reminded me of the military tradition where a newly commissioned officer is supposed to pay a dollar to the first enlisted person who renders him a salute. I felt in my pocket and fortunately had a dollar. Toffle said I would need to go through certain administrative procedures the next day. He assumed I would stay at Fort Polk and I didn't know any better. I straightened up my desk a bit not knowing what else to do, and we headed for Toffle's shiny Cadillac. I had been riding the bus. Adkins was waiting by the door and smiling rendered me a crisp salute. I returned it and paid him the dollar. It was a neat feeling and this first salute by a guy I really respected gave me a bit of a thrill. Seems stupid but it did.

Toffle introduced me to a few staff officers at the club and we sat down at a table by the bar. I had a scotch with just a splash. I had not been drinking for a while so attempted to be careful. After a few drinks, it was time to go to Colonel Hoff's house and I needed some dinner; already I was a bit woozy.

Lieutenant Colonel Hoff lived with his wife in an area on post reserved for the more senior officers. There were no children at home. Mrs. Hoff was pleasant and hospitable. Both congratulated me and Hoff asked what I drank. Toffle said we both were drinking scotch. The colonel gave me a tumbler filled with ice and scotch and not much else. Fortunately, Mrs. Hoff had some nibbles on the table. Another couple, a captain from the justice branch and his wife, joined us. LTC Hoff introduced me although I had met Captain Meyer in the office. He had always been "Sir," and now Meyer told me to call him Stan. His wife, Melissa, said she saw me at the PX and thought I might be the new lawyer in the office in line for a commission. About half way through the scotch, Hoff got serious. He said he wanted me on his team at Fort Polk and to work with Captain Meyer in the justice section primarily as a defense counsel. He said I still would do reports of surveys and help out in legal assistance with everyone else. I was so happy to be commissioned and from the scotch that I said "Yes sir." I didn't understand I might have had other options which could have taken me out of Fort Polk.

Mrs. Hoff put on a fantastic dinner, but I don't remember most of it. I do remember some discussion about where I would stay that night. Toffle wanted me to get a room in the BOQ, the bachelor officer quarters, but I told him all my stuff was at Company D and I really should go there. I remember through a fog of alcohol placing my cap with its new captain bars at the end of my bed as I passed out. Someone told me later that at company formation the next morning the platoon sergeant reported all were present and accounted for except two boxers and a captain. That apparently got a pretty big chuckle from those present.

Part Three
My First Case

Pvt Ronnie Placide

I came to realize that maybe LTC Hoff had more in mind in keeping me at Fort Polk than just having another company grade officer around. He was getting a young law school graduate whom he observed for about a month. He was getting a lawyer who never tried a case and who hadn't been to the JAG basic class that taught the vagaries of military law. His job was to get convictions on those cases he recommended to his immediate boss, the General Court-Martial convening authority. He didn't want any acquittals. The defense counsel's job is to represent his client as a legally-certified attorney and do all necessary within the law and the ethics of the legal profession to help his client. The defense counsel under his marriage to the law was to get the acquittals of those same soldiers his boss was trying to put in jail. If the staff judge advocate had a particularly adept or experienced defense counsel, he had an easy decision. He would assign that officer as a prosecutor. Accordingly, the less experienced JAGs were given the defense cases. I asked about this and the response was the prosecutor's job was more difficult than the defense counsel's and necessitated a more experienced officer, someone who knew the system a little better. The prosecutor, the trial counsel in courts-martial, had to conduct the trial, work within the command in gathering witnesses and preparing evidence, and generally make the prosecution case. I never really understood this distinction because I, as defense counsel, also had to gather evidence and witnesses, and know the military in which my client was being prosecuted. In the JAG Corps today, defense counsels no longer are in this position. Today, they're in a separate command with separate rating levels within that defense command and are selected from experienced military lawyers by the Office of The Judge Advocate General. In 1968, prosecuting and defending lawyers sometimes shared the same offices and had the same rater.

LTC Hoff had to play this game carefully. If he assigned a wet-behind-the-ears lawyer, like me, as a defense counsel on a significant case, he faced the issue of inadequate representation when the case was reviewed on appeal. He then would look bad within the JAG community that overall sought fairness within the military justice system, and he might have to face his rater, the two-star post commander if the case were overturned. My first case was a big soft ball.

Private Ronnie Placide turned himself in at Headquarters Company, 3d Basic Combat Training Battalion, at 2015 hours on Thursday evening, March 21st, 1968.

"Sarge, I'm reporting in. I was a member of C Company but can't find it."

He was in civilian clothes, his hair a bit long for the military, and he looked lost. "Sarge, I've been absent for a bit but want to finish up my two-year gig. I got drafted but had some problems at home and had to leave for a bit."

Sergeant First Class Butler, the duty NCO, called the battalion duty officer, 1st Lieutenant Ed Bullion, who came right over to the headquarters company orderly room. Ronnie saluted him as he entered the room.

Bullion looked at Placide and asked, "Who are you and what are you doing?"

Butler interrupted, "Sir, C Company moved and this guy says he wants to soldier."

Ronnie said, "Private Placide, sir. I left Fort Polk in January, 1967, because I had serious problems at home. It was just after getting back from Christmas leave."

Bullion called the JAG duty officer who told him to call the MPs. After about an hour, Chief Warrant Officer Paul King, from the Fort Polk Criminal Investigation Command, the CID, arrived. The first thing he did was walk up to Placide and say, "You're under arrest for desertion in time of war. You have the right to remain silent. Anything you say will be used against you and you can get a JAG lawyer to help you. The penalty for desertion in time of war, which you did, is death. I suggest you don't say anything."

King then looked over at 1LT Bullion. "Sir, I would like to place this deserter in the stockade. With your permission I will do just that."

Bullion responded, "Mr. King, I don't think I have the authority to authorize that and I certainly am not going to bother the company or battalion commanders with this tonight. I think it appropriate for you to keep him in the CID orderly room tonight. In the morning I believe we can work out exactly where he can be kept pending what will become of him. After all, he turned himself in and doesn't appear to want to run off."

On Wednesday, March 27, a few days later, Major Toffle called me to his office. He gave me the file and said, "Gregg, this is a simple little desertion. The guy was homesick and quit the Army and was gone for over a year until his guilt got the better of him and he came back. Do you think you can handle representing this kid?"

I replied, "Yes sir. I'm ready."

I looked at the file and was surprised at the charge. Notwithstanding the fact that Placide was gone over a year, he turned himself in and clearly said he wanted to finish his tour. He was not wearing his uniform when he came back but obviously impressed 1LT Bullion. I wanted to know why he left and what Ronnie had to say. I also needed to talk to Bullion. Ronnie was in pretrial confinement and this was the first time I got to see the Fort Polk stockade. Stan Meyer, who helped celebrate my promotion at LTC Hoff's house, was going to prosecute. He told me he read Placide the charges and an Article 32 investigating officer was appointed. The Article 32 officer examines the evidence for its veracity, examines the form of the charges, and makes recommendations as to disposition of the matter to the convening authority, at Fort Polk the post commander. It's similar to a grand jury determination.

I presented my orders appointing me defense counsel to the MP at the stockade front desk and told him I wanted to meet my client, Private Placide. He said he'd heard there was a new JAG and orders were not necessary for me to see my client. I thanked him and someone brought Placide to a meeting room at the front of the stockade. Ronnie was slight of build, thin, and of medium height. He had a baby face the color of dead grass with light brown hair now in a close military cut. He had on a wrinkled fatigue uniform with no name tag or insignia. His boots were a mess and he smelled like a musty long-vacated room.

"I'm a lawyer and member of the Maryland Bar, but I was just commissioned in JAG and this is my first case. I worked in the JAG office a bit and feel comfortable taking your case." I wanted to be up front.

He looked me in the eye and said, "It's ok, sir. I know you'll do good."

"Whatever you tell me regarding the case is privileged information and I wouldn't reveal it to anyone without your permission. Are you Catholic?"

"Yea, but I don't always do church."

I continued, "Well it's like confession. I can't tell anybody what you tell me regarding your leaving post just as a priest can't say what you confess to him in the confessional."

Ronnie looked knowingly at me. "Sir, I didn't think it was that big a thing for me to come back. I knew I had to serve some time, but can I get the death penalty?"

I answered fast, "It's not on the table."

His voice cracked and he said quietly, "The man who took me the night I got back said a firing squad could shoot me, sir."

I told him, "That's not possible. Have any other lawyers come to see you?"

"Some captain come by two days ago, introduced his self and said he's the lawyer tryin' to put me in jail. I don't remember his name. He said someone else would help me and to shut up. He give me stuff to sign and I signed it. I dunno know what it was. You must be the guy to help me."

I asked, "Did he say anything about a death penalty?"

"No sir."

"For you to get a death penalty, the case would need to be forwarded by the convening authority as a death penalty case and your's wasn't. The other lawyer would have to tell you if it was a death case. Besides, for the death penalty, it has to be desertion 'in time of war,' and Congress hadn't declared war that I know of. If you want, you can have a civilian lawyer represent you but you'd have to pay for it."

Ronnie Placide looked down and said, "I don't have no money no how sir, so I guess you're it."

"Since you've been in the stockade, has anyone else asked you anything about being AWOL or to sign anything?"

"The guy in civilian clothes who took me to the police station said real quick like I could have a lawyer and then asked me why I left and what I did after. He wrote up some paper and tole me to sign it since it would make me look bad if I didn't. He's the guy who said they could shoot me."

"Did you get a copy?"

"No sir. After I signed he left me alone and next thing some MPs come and take me here."

"What happened, why did you leave Fort Polk in the first place?"

Ronnie Placide related the following story:

"I got drafted just after high school. I finished ok and was workin' at the Texaco gas station in Bunkie, when I got my draft notice. I was livin' with my Ma. Pa

run away when I was 8 and Ma looked after me and my two sisters. They are a little younger than me. Ma did ok. She worked at the All Star Motel cleanin' rooms and I watched the young ones while she was workin'. Every once in a while Gran would come by from Alexandria but pretty much complained the whole time. Ma got a raise after awhile to night clerk so she was home days. When I got drafted Ma told me to send home some of my pay til my sisters got married. I came to Camp Polk in early November and didn't get home til Christmas. When I got home, Ma was sick and not getting' paid. She said they was gonna let her go if she didn't get back to work real quick. The All Star folks was sorry about it but needed someone to do the work. We didn't have much of a Christmas. I boiled up some sweet potatoes and peas and got some chickin' from the church. Ma went to the hospital but they would'nt see her cuz she couldn't pay and as they tole her, she weren't sick enough. I called Gran before I come back and she said she'd come down but could only stay a bit. I got back to camp and after a day or two called home. Gran was there and said Ma was real sick and could I come. I asked my drill sergeant who tole me it was too bad but that we had a war to fight. I called agin but the phone was out. I called the Tinsleys next door who said Gran left and Ma was alone with the girls and they was runnin' wild. I asked if they could get Ma to come to the phone and they tried but she wouldn't come. I worried a bunch and thought I'd better git home. I sneaked out that night and hitched a ride outside Leesville back to Bunkie to take care of stuff at home. I wore my uniform home but left most of my gear in my locker in the barracks. I thought I'd only be gone a few days. Ma was real sick and the girls didn't have much to eat. I went over to the church and they helped a bit. I then went by the Texaco and asked if they needed some help. The guy there, Bill Courie, liked me so he hired me on right then. He gave me some money and tole me I had to make it up. After awhile I got the house fixed up and Ma started feelin' a bit better. She called about her job at the All Star but they said it was gone. She stayed in bed most of the time and the girls went to school. Time flew by and I started workin' another job with a concrete pourer that give me a bit more money. One time a guy come by lookin' for me but Ma told him I didn't live there. Before I knew it summer was over and it was Halloween time. The concrete guy said there was not much work left so he let me go. I told Ma she had to get work cus I had to go back to camp. She finally got a job at the clothes store in Crowley for the holidays and they needed some extra help in the store room so they hired me on. We worked through the holidays and Ma got lots better. She stayed on at the store but Bill called me from the Texaco and told me his wife was real sick. He asked if I could help out a bit til she got better. She paid the bills and kept the papers for the station and tax time was around so Bill was in trouble. I got on there and finally left a couple of weeks ago when Mrs. Courie got better. Ma is ok now and still workin' at the store so I come back to camp."

I asked him, "Do you still have the uniform you wore when going home."

"It's in my closet; I didn't think to bring it back. Most of my stuff's at home."
Ronnie looked down as if he were embarrassed.

"Did you ever call your old company to tell them where you were?"

"No sir."

I softened my tone and slouched a bit in my chair. I asked, "Is you mother ok now and can she come to trial?"

"She's ok sir, but has to take care of the girls and might not be able to make it."

"What about Bill and the Tinsleys, can they come?"

He looked like he was trying to make himself small. "I dunno know, sir. But I'll bet if a lyiar from the Army asked them to, they would come."

I smiled and said, "Private Placide, it's lawyer."

I got Ronnie's address in Bunkie, directions to his house, and as much information about Bill and the Tinsleys as I could. I told him if he needed me for anything, for him to call or leave a message with the MPs at the stockade. I gave him a handwritten note with my name and phone number at the office and he folded it and put it in his pocket. He said he was ok; he was catching up on some rest. I reiterated that there was no death penalty involved and the most he could get was two years at Leavenworth. I told him not to talk about his case to anyone and I'd be back in the next few days.

I went that afternoon to Headquarters Company, 3d Basic Combat Training Battalion, looking for Lieutenant Bullion. They sent me to Company D where Bullion was the Executive Officer. I asked him about Ronnie.

Bullion answered, "Sir, I didn't know what to expect when I got the duty officer call and went over to the company. But Private Placide couldn't have been better. He stood up and saluted me when I came into the orderly room. He didn't have on a uniform but stood straight and looked me in the eye. He looked and acted like a soldier. I was surprised and his attitude made me want to help him."

"What's the deal with pretrial confinement? I understand you told the CID agent he had to wait until the morning." I moved some papers around in my file.

He answered, "The guy was a total jerk. He came in all full of himself and tried to scare this poor kid. He talked about the death penalty and I knew Placide was no Eddie Slovak. Besides, I heard that there were certain procedures regarding pretrial confinement that I didn't want to mess up."

I asked him, "Would you be willing to testify on his behalf? I need to show that he turned himself in and exercised some military bearing. Maybe you can help on that."

He quickly responded, "No problem, sir. Let me know when and where and I'll be there."

I got back to my office and there were two other absent without leave cases on my desk, each with general court-martial orders appointing me defense counsel. I also had a message from Toffle that he wanted to see me as soon as I got in. I immediately reported.

Toffle said, "The Army might be willing to do something about Placide."

"I don't understand, sir."

"There might be a deal on the table but Stan Meyer will discuss that with you."

"Sir, I need to go to Bunkie on the Placide case. How do I arrange for transportation and is it ok for me to just take off for a day or so? I may need to get some witnesses over there and have no idea as to the procedures."

Toffle twirled his chair so his back was to me as he looked out the window behind his desk and said, "The Sergeant Major will take care of all that. Just tell him what you want and he'll give you the proper format for a request for travel orders and witnesses. In the meantime I'd like you to take care of matter regarding a staff sergeant who was waving a rifle around at his quarters off post during an argument with his wife last night. I understand the damn thing went off. The wife called the guy's company commander and he called me. It's a civilian matter since it's off post but it might be better to scare the guy a bit so he won't do it again. Do you think you can handle it?"

I answered the back of his head, "Yes sir."

I now knew what LTC Hoff meant when he said they were busy.

SSG Conroy; Off the Record

Spec Four Billy Young, one of our legal clerks, signed out the staff car and took me to see Staff Sergeant Conroy. Conroy lived out in the country on a hard-packed dirt road not too far from the main road between Fort Polk and DeRidder. It was a dark wooden structure, one story, with a pitched roof and a screened porch across the front. There were some propane tanks, a broken up dog kennel, and a bunch of junk lying around. A rusty old pickup truck was parked in the front with a Fort Polk red sticker. Red ones were for enlisted personnel; officers had blue stickers. Billy told me he vaguely knew the guy. I went up and before I knocked I saw what looked like a bullet hole in the screen door.

A guy comes out with no shoes, dirty jeans, and a dirty grey tee shirt. He had short hair. I showed him my ID to give my visit some official status and introduced myself as Captain Thompson from the post JAG office. "Are you Staff Sergeant Conroy?"

He looked grim, "Yes sir, are you here to take me to the stockade?"

We stood on his steps and, with that opening, I replied, "Not at this time." I knew I couldn't do that but felt a little more authoritative. I continued, "Your CO is pretty upset and worried about you shooting a rifle when arguing with your wife."

He said while standing in front of the screen door so I couldn't see the bullet hole, "It was an accident, sir."

I could see into the porch. There was a ripped up old day bed, some broken chairs, and quite a bit of trash. I told him, "Sergeant Conroy, you're no longer a kid and married life has a lot of responsibilities. As an NCO those responsibilities are special and very demanding. If you're not getting along with your wife, the chaplain can help. If you're not church going, the medical corps has some social workers who might be of assistance."

"I'm ok, sir."

"Where's your wife now?"

"She's over at her sister's, not too far away."

"If you get physical with your wife again the police might put you in jail and then not only will you get busted and lose your strips but you also have a good chance of losing your job. If the company commander hears you still have a problem, he'll most likely request orders for you for Vietnam so he, the company commander, won't have a problem." I was stretching things a bit but was on a roll.

He seemed to know he was going to skate. "Sir, I'll never load the gun in the house again and promise I'll never swing it at my wife again."

Now I was learning a bit more than I wanted.

"Are you sure your wife's ok?"

"Sir, when I swung, I missed."

"How I can I make sure this won't happen again?"

"My wife and I have a pretty wild relationship, sir. I love her and I'm gonna go over to her sister's and apologize and bring her back home."

"Sarge, before you go, do me a favor. Take a bath and shave. Put on some clean clothes. Go to the store and get some flowers and take them with you. See if your wife wants to go out to dinner."

He looked at me a bit strange but responded, "That sounds like a good idea."

I asked him to call me the following week and let me know how it went. He thanked me and I left. He never called and we never had any other phone calls about Billy Conroy.

I now had three general court cases, the responsibility for the office for reviewing all reports of survey at Fork Polk recommending remuneration, helping out in legal assistance, and being Major Toffle's go-to guy. I had been a JAG officer for three weeks.

Private Placide's Proceedings

Private Placide and I entered the office of LTC Carney Poole, a rugged old infantry officer who was serving in the G-2 section of the post headquarters. I asked what that entailed and the sergeant major told me it was an intelligence function for the command which at Fort Polk mostly concerned security. The post commander, at LTC Hoff's recommendation, appointed Poole the Article 32 investigating officer. We were about to have our grand jury. Poole's hair was full and hard cut. He looked wind-burned and his face was shadowed and drawn. It was 0930. He sized us up as we entered the room. Ronnie and I marched over to his desk and reported. Ronnie's salute was sharper than mine. Poole didn't return our salutes and told us to sit down. Not a great start. Stan Meyer was in the room making last minute adjustments to his legal weapons. CWO Paul King, the arresting CID agent, sat next to him wearing a mean look.

I had gone to Bunkie and taken a picture of Ronnie's closet with his uniform on a hanger. I intended to present it. The Bunkie witnesses didn't add much in the manner of whether there was guilt or innocence and actually may have given the prosecution some evidence that indeed, Ronnie wasn't on duty, so I didn't call them. The prosecution was required to prove the period of Ronnie's absence. I had requested Lieutenant Bullion, the officer who first saw Ronnie when he turned himself in, to come over and say a few things. He was in Poole's outer office. Poole started the Article 32 investigation and gave me a copy of his appointing orders. He asked if the accused had seen and been presented the charges and I said he had. He then looked over to Stan and asked him to begin.

Stan showed me an extract from the morning report for C Company, 3d Basic Combat Training Battalion, Ronnie's old unit, for both Saturday, January 14, 1967, and for Monday, February 15, 1967. The January 14 entry named Private Ronnie Placide as not present for duty and absent without authority. It was authenticated on March 25, 1968 by a signature of the current C Company commander. The February extract documented that Ronnie was dropped from the company roles as a deserter. It again was authenticated by the C Company commander in March, 1968. I saw these before as part of the original file. I looked at LTC Poole and said, "Sir, I object to these documents."

Poole looked like he smelled gas. "On what grounds?"

"Hearsay, sir. The current C Company commander who authenticated the entries wasn't present at Fort Polk in 1967. The second entry dropping Private Placide from the roles doesn't comport with Army Regulations because it should have been made thirty days after the first entry of absence without authority, not thirty-two days later and that variance makes it irregular." These were weak objections but I thought I should let Stan know we would fight.

Poole looked over at Stan who pontificated, "The extracts are official C Company entries whether they comported with AR's or not and, as such, can be accepted into evidence. If there are any irregularities, they only go to probative value."

I immediately said, "Sir, the entries were made in contemplation of this hearing, and if irregular, should not be treated as official Army records."

Poole seemed a bit flustered but said, "OK, I'll let them in." I held up asking him if he knew what probative value meant.

Stan then introduced CWO King who was sworn and told LTC Poole his name, grade, and duty assignment. King said he was the duty officer for the CID command at Fort Polk on the evening of March 21, 1968. He said the duty officer at the 2d Battalion called him that night and said he had a deserter in custody. He said he went to the command and apprehended the subject, Private Ronnie Placide and then, with a flourish, pointed to Ronnie and said he was the person he apprehended. Stan asked, "Did Private Placide make a written statement?"

Mr. King responded, "Yes sir."

Stan showed him what appeared as the statement and asked, "Did you advise Private Placide of his Miranda rights prior to him writing the statement and is this it?"

"Yes sir, I told him his rights and that's the statement."

Stan then showed me the statement and started to give it to Poole. The statement, signed by Ronnie, admitted to being away, to having deserted the Army, and to being apprehended by Mr. King. I got up and said before Stan gave the paper to LTC Pool, "I object sir, on the grounds that the statement was not Private Placide's; that it was not written by him; and besides, Private Placide was not adequately informed of his rights."

Poole looked at Stan for some help and Stan said, "The statement was signed by Private Placide and, if you need me to, I can get some other evidence as to it's being Placide's."

I said, "Sir, maybe I can clear this up by asking a few questions of Mr. King."

Poole asked if there was anything else Stan wanted from Mr. King and, if not, maybe I could cross examine him.

I fiddled with some papers in front of me and looked over directly at the CID agent. "Mr. King, on March 21st when you were the CID night duty officer, you said someone called you regarding Private Placide. Who was that?"

King answered, "I believe it was the 3d Battalion duty officer."

"Do you remember his name?"

"No." It seemed his absence of military custom in addressing me as "Sir," was intentional.

"What did he tell you when he called, Mr. King?"

"He said they had a deserter who had just come back and they needed someone to pick him up and put him in jail."

"So what did you do?"

"I went over to the Headquarters Company to apprehend the deserter."

"Well if the duty officer had the person, why did you have to apprehend him?"

"I had to take him to the stockade and lock him up or he might have gone off again." "Did you actually take Private Placide to the stockade?" By now I was standing in front of where he sat.

"No sir. The lieutenant there didn't want to turn him over for confinement. He said he just wanted me to hold the kid until the morning when the battalion commander could decide what to do with him."

I recognized his return to addressing me properly. "So, in fact you didn't apprehend him, did you?"

"Well I arrested him and read him his rights and put him in the CID orderly room under lock and key for the night. I think he slept on the couch."

"But Mr. King, you didn't leave post to go get him, did you?"

"No sir, I guess not."

"Did you ask him any questions?"

"I asked him when he left and what he did."

"Did you advise him of his rights before that?"

"Yes sir, when I arrested him I read him the Miranda warning card before I got him into my car."

"Did you handcuff him?"

"Yes."

"So what did he tell you?"

"It's all in the statement."

"Did you write the statement?"

"Well yes, I wrote it but it was pretty much what was going down and what Private Placide told me."

"So you gave him a written statement that you wrote and typed and you requested him to sign it."

"Yes sir. It was based on what the deserter said."

"So you're telling Colonel Poole that the accused, Private Ronnie Placide, used the word 'apprehended'?"

"Probably not."

"How much time elapsed between when you gave Private Placide the statement you wrote and requested him to sign and when he actually signed it?"

"I don't understand you."

"How much time did it take for Private Placide to sign the statement?"

"He went right ahead and signed it."

"Thank you Mr. King."

I then looked over at LTC Poole and said, "Sir, I renew my objection and the reasons are obvious; it was not Private Placide's statement but what Mr. King wanted Private Placide to say. Lieutenant Bullion was the duty officer the evening of 21 March and is outside and ready to testify that he never called Mr. King. Bullion called the MP Desk Sergeant not Mr. King."

"I'll take the statement under advisement and I understand and believe it was written by Mr. King. Does the prosecution have anything else?"

Stan hesitated and then declined. He really wanted to make a statement.

Poole looked over at me, "Do you have anything further Captain Thompson?"

"I would like to call 1LT Bullion, sir," I answered.

"Well call him and Captain Meyer can swear him in."

After Bullion saluted Colonel Poole and swore his oath, he identified himself as the duty officer for 3rd Battalion the night of 21 March, after which I asked him, "Did you get a call that night from the Headquarters Company regarding Private Placide?"

"Yes Sir. The Duty NCO, Sergeant First Class Butler, called and said that a guy came to the orderly room and said he couldn't find C Company. He told me C Company relocated about six months ago to the other side of the battalion because its head shed was being renovated. Sergeant Butler told me the guy said he had been absent without leave since January, 1967, and wanted to come back to duty and finish up his tour. He said he didn't know what to do with him."

"So what did you do?"

He continued, "I went over to Headquarters Company to see what was going on. As I entered the building this kid in civilian clothes jumped to attention and saluted me saying, 'Good evening, sir.' SFC Butler was on duty and he introduced Private Placide and told me that Private Placide had just turned himself in after being AWOL since January a year ago. Private Placide was very respectful and said he was sorry but he had no choice and now was ready to soldier."

"What did you do?"

"I wasn't sure what to do with Private Placide so I called the JAG duty officer. He told me to call the MPs, that they'd get on it in the morning. I then called the MP desk and they said they would send over a CID agent. I stayed there and talked with Private Placide who told me about his mother being sick at home and his father being gone. He sounded pretty mature and sincere. Anyway, the CID guy arrived all in a huff and said, 'Where is the filthy deserter?' I was a bit surprised at his attitude but I haven't had much experience with CID agents. He sounded as if he'd had a drink or two."

I asked Bullion if Mr. King was the CID guy and he said he was. I then asked him to describe what Mr. King did with Private Poole.

"The first thing he said was deserters could get the death penalty in time of war, and they were having one hell of a war in Vietnam. His words were a bit slurred but almost exactly that. Anyway, he told the private he was under arrest, and he immediately handcuffed him. He then asked me if he could place Private Placide in pretrial confinement. I said I didn't think I had that authority and I wasn't going to bother the battalion commander that evening. I was certain Private Placide wasn't going anywhere; after all he had turned himself in. Anyway, I told Mr. King we would get in touch with him in the morning and maybe he could keep the private over at the CID office for the evening. He said ok and took Private Placide away."

"Did you see or hear Mr. King advise Private Placide of his rights to a lawyer or anything like that?"

"No, and I followed King and Private Placide out of the building to the CID car. I was parked just next to Mr. King's car. I watched them and saw Mr. King give Private Placide something but I never heard him say anything about lawyers."

I smiled at him and asked, "Would you want Private Placide in a unit you were commanding?"

"Yes sir; I don't think he'll go AWOL again. I also know if he had serious problems at home, I'd either give him some time to straighten them out or send him to the chaplain for help."

I thanked Lieutenant Bullion and asked Stan if he had any questions. Stan declined. I then showed Stan the blown up photo of Placide's closet with his uniform hanging up in his house in Bunkie. I also had some pictures just of Ronnie's house that made the Fort Polk barracks look like the Waldorf Astoria. Stan glanced at the pictures and waved his hand in a dismissive attitude. I gave them to LTC Poole as defense exhibits.

Stan then addressed LTC Poole. "Sir, this is a case of extended absence without leave. The accused, Private Placide, left post in January, 1967, and stayed away until late March, 1968. He never called. He never asked for help. He stayed at home while others went to Vietnam and died. There is no excuse. The leave was of such a period as to be a clear case of desertion. The company morning reports are sufficient for conviction by themselves. There are no mitigating factors other than that the accused turned himself in and that he did should not mitigate the strong presumption of desertion by the extended absence. As to the confession, even if Private Placide didn't type it up, he signed it and that's pretty strong proof it's his. There is sufficient evidence for desertion and you should recommend a general court-martial."

I argued that Private Placide clearly had no intent to stay away. He turned himself in and wanted to finish up his period of conscripted service. I stated his uniform was in his closet which showed his intent to return and, in fact, he did return. The only reason he didn't go to his old unit is that it moved but he knew enough of the military to go back to his Headquarters Company. I also indicated his military bearing to Lieutenant Bullion. I did not mention, nor did Stan bring up the fact, that Ronnie didn't wear his uniform back to Fort Polk and that he never called the company to say where he was or what he was doing. Stan also apparently didn't know that someone, probably the FBI, came looking for Ronnie at his house and was told he didn't live there.

LTC Poole said that he would have his report ready in a few days. He then dismissed us all and Ronnie went back to the stockade.

In about a week, Stan came by my desk and asked if we could discuss the Placide case. I told him I would prefer to see what LTC Poole was going to recommend first. Stan said he had the Article 32 report of investigation and that Poole recommended a general court-martial. He gave it to me and I scanned it looking at the bottom line for recommendations. Poole recommended trial by general court-martial and that the charges be changed to absence without leave. This was a victory.

Stan looked at me. "Gregg, obviously this is not a case of desertion. It still is pretty serious being away for over a year. Maybe we can get a plea. LTC Hoff has approved me offering eighteen months, a DD, and total forfeitures for a plea."

"I'm not sure I understand." I was jockeying for more time to think about it.

"Well for Placide's plea of guilty to AWOL for over a year, the command will not approve any sentence in excess of eighteen months confinement, a dishonorable discharge, and total forfeitures."

"Thanks Stan. I'm glad you understand there's no desertion. If you could have seen this kid's house you would have realized he had it better in the Army. I have three witnesses from Bunkie, ILT Bullion, Placide's former drill sergeant and some pretty strong reasons for leaving. I can substantiate his problems while gone with a sick mother losing her job and two little sisters who depended on him. I've got his employer who says he was great and a neighbor who will testify to the terrible problems the family had especially when Private Placide first got home. He came back on his own and wants to soldier. Eighteen months and a DD seem pretty strong for a kid who came back on his own."

"Gregg, I know this is your first case. You have to understand that being gone over a year is really serious and eighteen months is a gift."

"I don't think so Stan. They're many cases where AWOLs over a year get substantially less than what you're offering. I think we'll take our chances with the Court. Then you can see what a first time lawyer can do."

"What about a BCD, nine months, and total forfeitures?"

I thought that we might be able to beat that with a court and 1LT Bullion's testimony. The way the deal works is if the Court gives a lesser sentence, then that's what takes effect. If the court gives a harsher sentence, the deal kicks in.

"That's a little bit better. I'll recommend it to Private Placide."

I saw Ronnie in the stockade and told him what Stan offered.

He answered, "You mean if I go to jail for nine months, I don't have to serve no more?"

"Yes, but you'd get a Bad Conduct Discharge that would eliminate some Federal benefits and besides, you told me you wanted to complete your tour."

"For nine months, I'm outta here, and I don't get no benefits no how."

I told Ronnie we might be able to beat the deal, that he could get less than nine months and might be retained in the military but the jail time wouldn't count to his two-year required service.

He said, "Don't do that. Maybe less than nine months is not so bad but if I can get outta here, let's do it."

I thought maybe I could explain why Ronnie went AWOL but that opened the door for the court to retain him. I explained this to Ronnie and the risk we would have by giving too much extenuation and mitigation. He asked where he would go to prison and I told him, Leavenworth. I also told him he might get some time off for good behavior and he might get credit for the time he spent in pretrial confinement. He responded, "That's all fine but no retained or whatever in the Army."

I had to be careful because if I didn't do everything I could to get the least sentence for Ronnie, the appeal every criminal discharge from the military automatically gets might raise an issue of inadequate counsel. That wouldn't be good for my first case. I explained all this to Ronnie and he said he understood but still wanted out. The only thing now of real concern was the criminal discharge that if adjudged would carry with it a pernicious blot on Ronnie's record for the rest of his life. Most applications for employment require a statement as to whether the applicant was convicted of a criminal offense and many ask whether he has been discharged from the military with less than an honorable discharge. After explaining all this to Ronnie he said he wanted the deal and wanted out of the Army, bad discharge or not. The stockade obviously dampened his fervor for performing his military duty.

After Ronnie, Stan signed the deal. In my first General Court-Martial, I called one witness in extenuation and mitigation, the Texaco manager, Bill Courie. He testified Ronnie was a pretty good worker but surprised me and added sometimes he didn't show up for work. He said he'd still hire him back if he got out of the military and that he was a nice kid. Ronnie made a sworn written statement I had prepared stating the reasons he left and why he was gone for so long. The court found Ronnie guilty of AWOL for one year, three months, and five days and gave him a dishonorable discharge and a year in prison. Pursuant to the deal, the general court-martial convening authority only approved so much of the sentence that included a bad conduct discharge and nine months confinement at Leavenworth. Ronnie served five months after which he was released to civilian life where he went back to Bunkie and started a house painting service, mostly the inside of new houses, for builders in Alexandria, Louisiana.

PART FOUR
FORT POLK AT ITS BEST

Tommy Lamude; Life in the Stockade

I was at the stockade going over the post trial procedures for Harry Burke, a kid who got a BCD and ten months for nine months' AWOL when one of the stockade guards came over and asked if I could talk to some kid who was threatening suicide. I said ok, bring him in. I then met Tommy Lamude. Tommy was convicted by a special court-martial for possession and use of marijuana and given two months' confinement. He was serving it at the Fort Polk stockade and already had done five weeks. Tommy said he'd enough and was going to kill himself. I said go ahead but what's your problem. I never had any training on this and was over my head but didn't know it. He said the stockade was terrible; that he couldn't sleep at night because a group of three or four guys would single out some weak kid at night and go to his bunk, pull his covers off and then hold him down. Each would fuck him in turn. He said he saw one guy sucking them off while the others laughed. Tommy said he found an iron pipe that he kept in his bed to fight them if they came his way. Tommy told me there were no private cells unless someone got in trouble. If in trouble the guards would throw you in a cell by yourself and you couldn't talk to anybody. All the prisoners otherwise slept in an open bay in double-decked bunks.

I was pretty astounded and asked Tommy, "Have you really seen this?"

"Yea, it's dark but I saw it and I heard it too."

"Do other prisoners know about this?" I'm sure my face expressed some doubt.

"I don't know how they couldn't. They try to keep quiet but there's lots of rustling and noise."

"Have you said anything to the guards?"

He grimaced at the thought, "No sir. These guys would kill me if I did and I thought maybe the suicide thing would get me outta here."

"How often does this happen?"

"Not every night. Maybe three times a week."

"How long has it been going on?"

"For about two weeks now. A bunch of guys came in from Tigerland about three weeks ago and it started not long after that."

"Who's doing this?"

"First of all, I can't see exactly who they are because it's dark and they're in the shadows. But I couldn't tell you anyway, they would kill me for sure."

I let up a bit. "OK, I'll see what I can do."

Tommy left and I asked to speak to Captain Perry, the MP in charge of the stockade. Perry said that Private Lamude was a trouble maker and constant complainer and he wouldn't believe anything Lamude said. I said it was a pretty astounding allegation. He responded that suicide was pretty astounding too. He told me the guards do bed checks each hour and that they check randomly and in pairs. He said they haven't reported anything out of line. I said maybe there's a lookout. He looked at me and said he had control of his stockade and there weren't any problems. I thanked him and left.

When I got back to the office I knocked on Major Toffle's door. He told me to enter and I recounted Tommy's story. His response was, "Bullshit."

"He seemed pretty convincing to me."

"He's probably a closet queer."

"I don't think so. He might be working me for something else, maybe a change in confinement, but he seemed pretty convincing."

He looked at me hard and said, "You've been a defense counsel too long. You're beginning to believe them."

I had been a lawyer for only a few months at the time and felt maybe he was right but it was a big chance to take. I asked him, "If he's lying, isn't that making a false official statement and by itself a punishable offense."

Toffle looked me in the eye and asked, "In what way was this official?"

"Well he asked to see me and told me about crimes going on."

"First, he didn't ask to see you. He said he was going to kill himself and then you, a defense counsel, went to see him about the suicide and asked him why. He didn't say he was accusing anybody in particular and there is no signed statement. We'd have a tough time making a case out of that."

"You're probably right. But if there's really a gang running rampant in the stockade, there may be more serious problems coming. After all, I remember a sociology class in college where the professor said rape's a control thing. Maybe these dudes are trying to get control. Who knows what will occur if they do."

"You're dreaming. But I'll tell you what I'll do. I'll call Captain Perry and tell him we're concerned and suggest he put an undercover person in the stockade for a week or so to see what's going on. But first I want a signed official statement from Lamude so if there's nothing going on we can go after him for an Article 107 violation, a false official statement. If he gives us a statement, Perry can isolate him or transfer him to another stockade. If he refuses to make the statement, that's it. How does that sound?"

Captain Perry got the statement from Tommy Lamude and transferred him to the stockade at Fort Benning where he was supposed to finish up his time. Perry put an undercover MP in the stockade barracks who after the second night reported something definitely was going on but at the other end of the barracks. He said he couldn't see who was involved but he could see lots of movement and he heard some muffled yelling. He was afraid to do anything else since he was alone. Perry then ran a full undercover investigation and caught four inmates in the act of subduing another prisoner. The four were placed in isolation. Further investigation implicated them in numerous offenses of assault, sodomy and rape. Since I got the thing going I was not part of the prosecution or defense at what were several subsequent general courts-martial at Fort Polk. The four received lengthy prison sentences at Leavenworth and I heard Tommy Lamude was sent to the Fort Benning hospital after being beaten up. Although he got an investigation going of the Fort Benning prison guards for some kind of extortion, it was not substantiated and Tommy was released back to duty where he was given an administrative general discharge because of his past drug usage.

I heard not too long after Lamude's threats of suicide that some trainee took his rifle, ran out into the middle of the company area and started shooting at the barracks. The company area was off in a hollow by a curve of a road that led out to the rest of the training battalion. It was isolated and beautiful in a serene setting nestled under hundreds of tall loblolly pines. The kid only had two clips of ammo so there wasn't a substantial amount of shooting. When he was down to just a few bullets left, with some training officers and NCOs stealthily attempting to corner him, he sat down on the steps of a barracks building, put his rifle between his legs with the barrel in his mouth, and pulled the trigger. The M-14 blew his brains out the back of his head and all over the barracks door killing him instantly. Nobody else was injured in the incident. Our office participated in the subsequent report of investigation but I was not involved. I went over to look at the crime scene anyway. It was empty of trainees and company personnel. There was an eerie silence. The event really scared me. Since then, I take talk of suicide very seriously and get the psych people involved. I now understood clearly that military service, especially combat and basic training have substantial psychological pressure riling up unbelievable emotions in many different ways.

SSG Chris Nettles; Rape or a Passing Fancy

I was not lead counsel but appointed to the defense team for a tough rape case involving a trainee's wife. Laverne Easel, came to Fort Polk to see her husband at Tigerland when he had Sunday free time. She stayed at the Exchange run Post Lodge. It was similar to an Econo Lodge; simple but cheap and clean. Only those authorized Post Exchange privileges and their guests were allowed to stay at the lodge. Laverne arrived early Saturday afternoon, signed in, and toured the post. She couldn't see her husband until midmorning on Sunday and ended up at the NCO Club Saturday evening where she enjoyed drinks and dinner.

A band was playing at the NCO club. There was a dark bar in the back with a small dance floor. After dinner at a bar booth, Laverne ordered a gimlet, a gin and lime concoction. She said she had three or four before the evening was over. Other witnesses stated she slurred her speech and was wobbly later that night. A group of girls from Leesville befriended her. They partied and danced with each other, with a number of different NCOs, and with a few local guys who came for the event. According to the statements collected by the CID who investigated the rape, Laverne was especially friendly with one or two guys. She was wearing a short skirt and a white blouse with its top three buttons unbuttoned partially revealing a lacy bra and Laverne's cleavage. Since everybody was in informal civilian clothes, the only way to determine whether someone was military was by his haircut. Almost everyone had short hair so that didn't help. The club was integrated and some of the statements compiled by the CID expressed resentment that Laverne danced more intimately than she should with an African American male who later was identified as Staff Sergeant Chris Nettles. It was almost that she deserved what she got. One of the statements said Nettles was dressed at the club in Levis, a polo shirt, and loafers.

A guest at the Post Lodge called the night clerk early Sunday morning to report a disturbance on the first floor. The caller stated it came from near the back entrance. The clerk investigated and found a broken window. He saw a light on under Laverne's door and knocked to see if she heard anything. He heard her crying and became concerned when she didn't answer the door. He went back to his desk and called her room. When she answered, he asked if she was all right. She blurted out she'd been raped by an intruder.

After the MPs responded, they called in the night duty CID agent, Chuck Ames, who took her statement. She first told him about going to the NCO Club and then related the following story. "I heard a knock at my door after I'd gone to bed. I went over to see who it was and this guy with panty hose pulled over his head pushes into the room. I don't know the exact time, but it was after midnight. I was on the first floor. He knocked me to the floor when he pushed in and then closed the door. I remember he closed it quietly. He held a big knife down the side of his leg, and said he'd cut me up good if I didn't blow and fuck him. He raised it up and swung it over me. He must have hit me because my forearm's cut. I was still on the floor and he held me down with his foot while he took his pants off. They were light chinos. He didn't just let them down, but he took them all the way off. He wasn't wearing any underpants and his thing was hard. I got on my knees and starting giving him a blow job. He grabbed the back of my head with one hand and held the knife against my back with the other. After I sucked on him a minute or two, he grabbed my hair and pulled me up and pushed me over to the bed. All I had on was a short nightie so he got on me and did it. I was really scared so I let him. I don't remember him turning off the light but when it was over, the light in the room was out. He dressed fast and left. He was a light-skinned black guy, not too big and not too small."

Ames asked, "What else was he wearing besides light chino pants?"

"He wasn't wearing underpants. He had on sneakers and I can't remember his shirt. I think it had a collar."

"Did you recognize him from any of the guys at the club?"

"I couldn't tell what he looked like. He looked real scary with his face all squished in. I could see he was light-skinned and pretty average size."

There was no DNA evidence available to assist the police in 1968. A nurse examined Laverne later Sunday morning and opined she had sex but there was no evidence of a forced entry.

Mr. Ames and his partner found Sergeant Nettles at the S-1 section of the Third Training Brigade Monday afternoon. Ames told Nettle's boss they were investigating an incident at the NCO Club from the previous Saturday evening and wanted to get a statement from Sergeant Nettles. Nettles met with them in the S-1 conference room and told them he had danced with Laverne at the club but didn't know her previously and had not seen her since. They asked where he went after the dance and he said for a ride around the area by himself. On Wednesday morning, his supervisor told him to report to the CID office for further discussion regarding the Saturday night incident. He did and Ames asked to see if he had any recent cuts or abrasions. Nettles pulled up his pants leg and showed them a cut just below his knee. Mr. Ames then advised him he was suspected of rape and read him a Miranda warning.

After Nettles acknowledged he received the warning, Ames' partner asked how he got the cut. Nettles first denied seeing Laverne after the dance and being involved in any rape. He then told them he scratched his leg on some barbed wire in a field near his trailer while out for a walk. He couldn't tell them exactly where the barbed wire was other than it was not a fence, but just hidden in some bushes he was walking through. The CID agents took several photos of his cut leg. The 3d Training Brigade Headquarters Company Commander later that afternoon swore out charges against Nettles for having sexual intercourse by force with a female not his wife, one Laverne Easel, without her consent, in violation of Article 20 of the Uniform Code of Military Justice, a felony rape. Chuck Ames arrested him Wednesday evening at the 3d Training Brigade while he was still at work.

Nettles couldn't produce anyone who could say they saw him after the dance or while walking through the field. Every other African American male at the club was contacted and had a tight alibi. The CID reported that he was cut by glass when he entered the guest house through a window near the back door. Laverne's room was the second from the end and if her curtains were open, someone could see which room was hers. There were no useful incriminating fingerprints on the window and no blood on the window or the floor. You couldn't tell from photos of the cut whether it was made by glass or barbed wire and there was no doctor's statement. A photo showed a jagged nasty six inch long scrape well crusted over. The CID searched for the panty hose but the agents were unable to find them in Nettles' trailer or anywhere else. They didn't find any chino pants in the trailer but did find a pair of sneakers. Laverne was not able to say whether they were the ones worn by the rapist. They found some hunting knives but the victim couldn't identify any as being used in the attack. The CID inventory also included five pair of clean Army underpants.

Nettles had no civilian or military police record. He worked in the records management section of the S-1 office and his supervisor said he did a good job. He refused to take a polygraph examination as to whether he was telling the truth. He said polygraphs were part of his "persecution" as a result of his dancing with a white girl at the club.

I discussed court strategy with the lead counsel. "How much and how harshly should we cross examine Laverne? Do you think she'll break and confess to making it all up or will she be strong and get the court's sympathy? Is it worth attempting to get her to admit she led him on? Should we hit her with an out-of-the-blue question to rattle her? Maybe ask her if he was circumcised? How deeply should we get into the actual sex act? Do we get her to admit she was submissive in order to show she didn't give enough resistance? What about the oral sex? After all she said he forced her to do that. But it could go both ways. That she admitted she gave him oral sex so readily may make her look bad but it also could influence the court to think she was really scared. We should ask why she was at the club in the first place dancing while her husband was training just a short distance away. Maybe ask how much she had to drink. Why didn't she give just minimal resistance? That may be the hook the court can hang its hat on. Why couldn't she more particularly identify the knife? If that made her afraid, she must have gotten a good look at it. Why was the hotel room not more messed up? What was the relationship she had with her husband? Did she have sex with others while absent from her husband?"

"Gregg, I'm thinking also about whether the window was broken because it was painted shut and an occupant at the Inn lost a key and had to break it to get in, or did the rapist break it? I'm concerned why she didn't report the rape immediately by calling the front desk or running out and screaming. She had to wait until someone called her. In the meantime, if there was a rapist, he got away. It seems she may have been remorseful because she was unfaithful, and then got caught. We also need to send an investigator to Laverne's home town to get an idea of her reputation, but we have to be careful not to sully her name. But the main thing is, if she was dancing with Nettles just before the club closed, she certainly should be able to identify him later, even with panty hose over his face. She might even recognize his smell. It just doesn't compute."

We spent hours debating how much we wanted to attack Laverne, but the consensus was that the prosecution had insufficient evidence to get a conviction in any event and harassing Laverne would only alienate the Court.

The case went to trial before a military court made up of a colonel, two lieutenant colonels, two majors, and a captain, all stationed at Fort Polk. The lieutenant colonel military judge was from Fort Hood. Laverne reiterated her statement of the rape for the court and cross examination failed to break her of the account. She remained firm in her account. The prosecution built its case on Nettles' cut leg, the fact he was at the club and danced with the victim, that he was the same size and race as the perpetrator, and that his whereabouts were not substantiated at the time the crime occurred. They had to use circumstantial evidence. They used the nurse's testimony that there was sex, and lots of photos, reports, and expert testimony as to the broken window, the amount of curtain that had to be open for visibility inside the room, that fear of a knife could be mortal fear especially when accompanied by a perpetrator whose face was grotesquely flattened by a silk stocking, and testimony of the activities at the club. They introduced a close-up photo of the cut on Laverne's arm that made it look bigger than the scratch it was. They couldn't put Nettles at the scene of the crime, but all the technical stuff made it seem he was. They didn't mention the underpants.

We didn't attack Laverne for making a false statement but attempted to muddy the waters by pressing there was no real proof of the crime and she didn't complain until the night clerk heard her crying and called her room. We argued she was out for a fling and picked someone up whom she later met in her room. We argued the sex was consensual because there was inadequate resistance and there was no proof of actual force or rough sexual activity. We said all the evidence was circumstantial and Laverne couldn't identify Nettles even though she was with him earlier in the night. We highlighted the rapist was wearing different clothes than Nettles at the dance just a few hours before and that the prosecution never proved Chris Nettles was at the lodge. We suggested the scratch on Laverne's arm was self-inflicted. We finally argued a lone woman, dressed only in a nightie, would never open a hotel door in the middle of the night to an unknown person without keeping the chain latched.

The court, after four hour's deliberation, found Nettles guilty of rape. They sentenced him to eighteen year's confinement at hard labor and to be discharged from the Army with a dishonorable discharge. Nettles professed his innocence throughout the trial and its sentencing phase.

I heard later the Court of Military Appeals reversed the conviction based primarily on inadequate evidence. It found all the prosecution had to convict was a cut on the defendant's knee not connected to the crime other than through conjecture, a weak motivation for a criminal act, a lack of an alibi, and that the accused danced with the victim a few hours before the alleged rape. The Court ruled the prosecution failed to establish a crime actually occurred. The Court implied the victim had to offer more resistance than she did and inferred a lack of evidence, other than the victim's lurid testimony, to a crime of rape. The Court found reasonable doubt throughout the entire record and noted the accused was never placed at the scene of the crime. We had done our job.

The Court also stated it was unclear from the record of trial whether the court knew about Nettles' refusal to take the polygraph exam—the appellate court apparently believed the military jury knew about it. When the case was over-turned the SJA had been reassigned, the Post Commander who convened the court was retired, and all those who had served on the court had either retired, been separated, or were reassigned. There were no recriminations. Laverne's whereabouts was unknown. Her husband was in Vietnam and said he didn't care where she was; their marriage was over. Everybody interested in the case was gone. Sergeant Nettles had served ten months in prison by the time the military appeals court over-turned the conviction. Instead of a return to duty, Nettles accepted a settlement for back pay with an honorable discharge.

Life in Louisiana

My BOQ room got small very quickly. The fellow who shared a bath with me introduced me to a friend and suggested we all rent a house. I was foregoing my housing allowance by staying at the BOQ and really wanted some independence from the military so I jumped at the opportunity. We found a house in DeRidder and furnished it with some stuff the Army shipped from my home in Baltimore and some stuff my room mates got. It worked out pretty well. Terry, who shared my bathroom in the BOQ, didn't stay long. He received orders for Vietnam, left in somewhat of a hurry, and we never heard from him again. Bob Sorbonne, the guy Terry introduced me to, turned out to be a great roommate. He loved to bar-beque and we cooked on our back porch almost every night. We adopted a stray mongrel that we named, "Little Girl." Little Girl fell in love with a stray dog in the area and a couple of months after she took up with us had six puppies. She berthed them as far under the house as she could. I was worried about their wel-fare in such a precarious place so I climbed under the house, watchful of snakes from the creek out back along with tarantulas and scorpions. I saw a tarantula the size of a small mouse in our front yard one afternoon. It scared the hell out of me just looking at it. Someone told me they could jump a distance of six feet. I got some gasoline, and poured it on, and then quickly lit up a match and incinerated the beast. It's lucky I didn't incinerate myself. Tarantulas definitely were out there and I didn't like them. Everybody talked about scorpions. I looked in my boots every morning but never found one. I had a few drinks and goosed up with liquid courage I took a cardboard box with me under the house and never seeing anything untoward retrieved the pups using the box and brought them into the kitchen. Except for one, they were active and playful. I think Little Girl was happy I made them part of the family. The quiet one never really made it. She soon died. Maybe a scorpion bit her. I had a heavy ornament on the wall above the puppy box and while feeding them one evening, I brushed it and it fell striking a pure white little male. He yelped, screamed, and cried. I felt terrible and babied him for days. He eventually became the strongest of the litter and was first to be adopted. All the puppies were adopted by folks from post, both military and civilian.

When I left Fort Polk, I had to leave Little Girl. It was sad as she was a super loyal little dog. She would go nuts when we came home after a day at work. That's the only time she peed on the floor. She did it in her excitement and it wasn't anything to scold her for. When we were at home, she accompanied us everywhere and if we picked her up she would reach her snout out to lick us in the face. I loved her and knew that Ben did too. I took her to the home of one of the ladies who cleaned our offices. She had three or four kids who seemed happy playing with her. I sneaked away and as I looked in my rear view mirror through watery eyes I could see her playing with the kids. I knew she would be looking for me to take her back home. I felt terrible. Moves in the Army are tough.

Saturday mornings at Fort Polk usually found me on base at the Old Club. The officer's club opened its bar at 1000 hours Saturday morning and served Bloody Mary's and Mimosas for $1 each. This was known as Sick Call. Ben had a girl friend he would visit every Saturday morning. I'm not sure whether she was married or not; he would always say, don't ask. Anyway, he never brought her around. Saturday morning was a great time for a visit to Sick Call and it got the weekend off on a good start. A substantial number of unmarried or unaccompanied senior staff from the Post would attend. I got to know a lot of these officers and am certain this didn't hurt my job as defense counsel. It was a relatively small community and Sick Call was an institution in itself. The pressure of the war especially was strong with almost everybody either having just come from or just about to go to the jungles of Vietnam.

Death of a Chaplain

One Sunday morning I was at mass on post and the chaplain, a priest, requested us to pray for all those lost in Vietnam especially for Father Aloysius McGonical, killed the past week in Hue. It hit me like a thunder strike. Father McGonical taught me biology at Loyola High School just outside Baltimore. The last thing I remember of him was his walking at a fast pace around the campus of Loyola High School reading his breviary. You could see him doing that almost every day.

I also remembered Father McGonical's toughness. He wouldn't put up with anything from our unruly and nasty class. There were rules and they had to be obeyed. He would take books and throw them at us. One time when a particularly obstreperous student was raising some devilment in the class, Father McGonical called him over and said, "Hey Bud, kneel down." The kid did and the priest kicked him hard in the chest. No one complained. The bastard had it coming. He taught us biology and we all anticipated his lecture on reproduction. But it not what we expected; it was like all his others—the specifics were set forth and there was no room for giggling or questions. Things in biology had a certainty about them. It was very clear. Here I was in Louisiana and I couldn't believe I heard Father McGonical's name as being lost in Vietnam. I didn't even know he had gone. I went into the sacristy after mass. I could barely speak and my chest was full. "Father, you prayed for Father McGonical. Was he a Jesuit?"

"Yes. He was a chaplain. He was an Army major and he had heard they didn't have a chaplain in Hue, an area of terrible fighting during Hue. Against orders he made his way up there and in the middle of a fire-fight walked down a path to a group of marines split off from their company. A VC sniper shot him in the forehead while he was walking out in the open."

I said through a breaking voice, "He taught me in high school."

The priest told me he was sorry. I didn't know him and he was new to the chapel. I couldn't answer and left. That's all I could think about the rest of that week.

Father McGonical has been a cult hero ever since for my class at Loyola. In all our reunions we tell stories about him. It's amazing the influence he had on that group of young men. He was one of the toughest guys I have ever known. He was short and built hard. He had a tough face with round glasses and spoke in almost a gangster manner. He was a loner. I found out later he was thrown out of Gonzaga High School over in Washington because he got into a fist fight with a student and beat him up pretty badly. I'm sure if anyone complained about his kicking the kid in the chest at Loyola, McGonical would have suffered a similar fate. But no one said anything. I'm also sure those in authority at both of those schools would never know the influence that man had on the students with whom he came in contact. He was the first man I ever knew who didn't give students that little opening that a bunch of smart-ass high school kids would do whatever they could to drive a wedge through. He was celibate and I'm sure that took its toll. He most likely was struggling to live the unnatural priestly life which surely affected his demeanor. There's no doubt he would always be where the action was heaviest and he was needed most. He was a man of God and a man for others. He had to be the best person to comfort those going into battle and those dying on the battlefield. The dying would know with absolute certainty they were going to heaven. He may not have told them about the seventy-seven virgins but he would have let them know, as combat soldiers and marines giving their lives for their country, it was in the natural scheme of things that they would enter heaven with their heads high and with the angels sounding bugles. I know when he was shot dead by the North Vietnamese in Hue the trumpets in heaven resounded with great blasts. Whenever I feel a need to be tough, he's there for me. The weird thing is, of all the priests, mentors and teachers I've had, Father McGonical is the least likely to have had such an effect on me. He never befriended me or anyone else that I know of. But, in retrospect, he was more than just being there. He was tough, firm, and consistent. I knew each afternoon I could see him somewhere on the Loyola High School grounds reading his breviary and that if I fucked up he would let me have it. A young teenage kid growing up in Baltimore in the late '50's needed just that tough consistency.

Private Kirk Youngblood; Philosophical Decisions

On a beautiful sunny training day at Fort Polk Colonel Hugh Randall Ross III was enjoying his second cup of coffee in his office as the Commander of the First Basic Combat Training Brigade. Colonel Ross was of short to medium height, and somewhat portly. He had a thin white mustache and neatly trimmed white hair around the sides of his head and in the back. Ross was mostly bald. His face was of a kind man. He realized he would not make general. He thought the Army made a mistake about that, but there always was that outside chance. Nevertheless, he was happy with his career as it was winding slowly down. His office was fairly large and painted a lively rose his secretary had selected. His S-4, his logistics officer, procured him a large wooden desk, normally reserved for general officers and he inherited a general officer credenza that nuzzled up against an interior wall. It now held a loaded coffee pot on top and a stocked liquor cabinet below. There was a large picture over the credenza of Stonewall Jackson on his horse leading an attack through some woods at Antietam. The window behind the desk looked out onto the brigade parade field where each week Colonel Ross graduated 500 or more young men from a basic training program that he felt was his own. The office was sunny and cheerful.

Colonel Ross commanded a great staff and his biggest pressure was to maintain discipline both with his NCOs and trainees. His battalion commanders did most of the hard work. He got the training guidelines from the Army Training and Doctrine Command and passed them on for implementation. He knew there would be some problems and he felt if he came down hard in military justice matters, its deterrence would suffice. A low rate of criminal infractions made him look like a good leader. Ross' secretary, Elaine, along with her official responsibilities, took care of his personal requirements such as paying bills, getting his uniform cleaned, ordering lunch from the Old Club, and shopping for presents for his wife and his subordinates. Ross thought he should have an aid or two as did officers of his grade and position in years past and was disappointed at the lack of respect in today's Army. He was leaning back in his chair gazing out his window around 1000 hours when Elaine buzzed him on the intercom. She said officiously, "Sir, there's a Mr. Youngblood in the outer office who would like to see you. Do you have a minute or two?"

Ross was fully confident in Elaine's functioning as his gate keeper so he responded, "Of course, please send him in."

Private Kirk Youngblood left his basic combat training company after breakfast that morning, hailed a cab, and went into Leesville, the closest town to Fort Polk. Using his father's credit card that he kept since entering college, he purchased a three-piece suit, a light-blue silk shirt, a rep dark-striped tie, and a pair of tasseled loafers.

Kirk graduated from the University of Michigan immediately after which he was drafted into the Army. His father was a veterinarian with a successful practice involving both domestic and farm animals. His mother taught geometry at the local high school. Kirk played forward for his high school basketball team but was not good enough to play at Michigan. He joined the DEKE house at Michigan, the same house to which then Congressman Gerald Ford had been a member. Kirk was a basketball star for the fraternity team that won the interfraternity championships when he was a junior and senior. He was elected house treasurer in his senior year which was especially important because a fire destroyed the DEKE house that year. Kirk was a bit of a hero during the fire. He went into the smoking building to save the fraternity mascot which was trapped in a room on the second floor. His selection for the draft was a bit of a surprise and interrupted his plans to attend vet school and go into a joint practice with his dad. He was tall and had medium-length hair, carefully parted on the side. His bearing and look, especially with his newly purchased clothes, was that of a trim, young Ivy League stockbroker. Elaine escorted him into Colonel Ross' office, introduced him to the colonel, and asked if he would like a cup of coffee. Kirk said, "Thank you that would be very nice."

Colonel Ross was cordial and seemed pleased with his visitor. "What can I do for you this morning?"

Kirk took a sip of the coffee and reaching into his vest pocket he produced his military identification card. He leaned across the highly-polished conference table where the two were sitting and pushed the card over and said, "Sir, thank you for seeing me. By giving you my military identification card, I hereby resign from the Army."

Colonel Ross' eyes now focused on the card and he looked again at Kirk and said, "What do you mean? What's going on?"

Kirk sipped some coffee. "Sir, now that you have my ID card, I no longer am in the Army. Thank you for taking it back. I appreciate your hospitality but no longer can perform as a member of the Army."

Ross looked at the card turning it over and over and looking up asked Kirk, "It appears you are a private, maybe a trainee. Are you a member of my command?"

"No longer, sir. I was in Company C of the 2nd Combat Training Battalion but I cannot in good faith train anymore. I am opposed to killing people."

Ross called Elaine into the office. "Elaine, I think we have a problem. Will you please escort Mr., or is it Private, Youngblood into my waiting room for a minute or two."

After they left, Ross grabbed his hot line and pushed the button for an automatic call to the Commander of the 2nd Battalion. He asked in an emotionally loud and somewhat shaky voice, "John, do you have a Youngblood in your command?"

LTC John Howard responded, "Sir, I'm not certain, can I get right back to you, why the question?"

Ross yelled. "I have a Youngblood, Kirk something or other, in my outer office. He says he was in Company C but he no longer can be in the Army. What the hell is going on down there?"

"I will be right back to you, sir."

Colonel Ross thought to himself it was a good day gone bad. A minute later Howard called and Elaine put him through immediately. "He's in Company C and I understand from Captain Ryan that he does a pretty good job. He's not reported missing. Are you sure you have Youngblood?"

"I have his ID card and he says he's out of the Army."

Howard told his boss again he'd be right back. He then called Captain Ryan, C Company commander, "Charlie, the Old Man's up my ass. It's something about a Youngblood who's in your company. Colonel Ross says he's in his outer office. Do you know anything about this?"

Captain Charlie Ryan pulled out a folder and ran his finger down the list of his trainees. "Sir, he's in Lieutenant O'Malley's platoon. They're training in the field, spent last night out there. It will take a little while to contact them. Young-blood is supposed to be in the field."

"If you like command Charlie, you'd better make it a little while less than thirty minutes. You can call me at Colonel Ross' office. Out!"

Howard then yelled over his shoulder to his military clerk-secretary as he marched out of the office, "I think we have a problem."

He then got in his staff car and raced over to Brigade headquarters. When he got there he ran up to Colonel Ross' suite of offices where he saw the well-dressed Kirk Youngblood, whom he had never seen before, calmly perusing a Life magazine in the waiting area.

Youngblood looked up and said "Good morning, sir."

Howard asked, "Are you Private Kirk Youngblood of my Company C?"

Kirk responded, "Sir, I am Mr. Youngblood and I used to be in Company C of the 2nd Battalion but I'm no longer in the military. Colonel Ross took my ID card."

Howard looked over at Elaine and said, "Can I go in?"

Elaine responded, "You'd better."

LTC Howard knocked on the door and walked in. Colonel Ross was at his desk turning the ID card over and over in one hand. Howard said, "Sir, it looks like he's mine but I haven't yet heard back from Charlie Ryan who's commanding C company. He should call any minute."

"What do you suggest I do with him?"

Howard replied, "How about a call to Len Hoff?"

"Do we really need to bother the Judge? Has it come to that?"

"It looks that way, sir. But to be sure we'd better wait for Charlie's call. The guy outside could be an imposter. I don't believe it but we'd better be sure. Youngblood's platoon's in the field and Charlie's on the way out there now. I believe he's going to chew on somebody for not noticing the guy is gone."

Elaine buzzed the colonel and said over the speaker, "Sir, Captain Ryan is on the phone for Colonel Howard."

Howard put the phone on speaker and told Captain Ryan that he and Colonel Ross could hear him. Ryan reported, "Sir, Youngblood isn't where he's supposed to be. Lieutenant O'Malley said he saw him at breakfast and he was in his tent overnight but no one has seen him since. No one saw him leave and no one noticed his absence until I asked for him."

"Charlie, that's really unacceptable. I will talk with you later about personnel accountability. Come by my office in about an hour. Out here."

Howard looked at Colonel Ross and said, "Sir. I think we need to call JAG."

Ross called LTC Hoff who told him to order Youngblood back to his company. Hoff said to give the ID card to LTC Howard who can get it to Youngblood later. If he refuses to go, Hoff told the colonel to call the MPs. If he says ok, then let LTC Howard take him. Ross hung up and asked Elaine to send Private Youngblood into his office. When he came in, Ross looked at him and said, "It seems that indeed you are Private Kirk Youngblood and that you are a member of C Company in the First Brigade. Your handing your ID card over to me doesn't remove you from the Army or relieve you of your military commitment and responsibility. As a trainee, you need to be training and I now order you back to duty. You are to go immediately with Colonel Howard who will take you back to the company area. Captain Ryan will see you to your platoon in the field."

"I am terribly sorry sir, but my conscious will not permit me to partake in the kind of activities going on in your training. I cannot shoot anymore with the object being to better my skills at killing people. I do not consider myself any longer a part of the Army."

Ross looked at Howard. "John, he's all yours. Have Elaine call the MPs and call Len back and tell him what happened. He'll provide you further guidance. If you need me, you know where to find me as apparently do most of the people in the command."

Howard took Youngblood into the outer office and called the MPs.

Colonel Ross went over to his credenza, grabbed a bottle of Dewar's Scotch whiskey and a crystal glass from the cupboard and poured himself a good belt. It was almost lunch time.

Youngblood's Court Martial

Major Toffle came by and threw Youngblood's court-martial file on my desk. He said, "This one's yours. Your client refused an order by the Commander of the First Combat Training Brigade, a colonel, to go back to duty. The accused is claiming he's a conscientious objector."

I read the file and late that afternoon went to the stockade to see Private Youngblood. I told him I was his lawyer and all the rest of the introductory stuff. He seemed surprised the Army would give him a lawyer. He said he thought he was getting an attorney from the ACLU, the American Civil Liberties Union. I knew from my times at Sick Call the conservative military officer community at Fort Polk considered the ACLU a communist and traitorous group. I didn't think an ACLU lawyer would be the best thing for a jury made up of senior officers and maybe some enlisted personnel. I told Youngblood this and he said it was ok. He related the events pretty much as laid out in the court-martial file except, when he was in the field, his drill sergeant authorized him to go back to the company office to take care of some personal problems. He said he got a ride to the company in the mess sergeant's deuce and a half.

Private Youngblood's status was the key to the defense. If in fact he was a conscientious objector, the Army had procedures to discharge him. I would argue that Colonel Ross' order wasn't lawful because Youngblood let him know he couldn't obey the order since he considered it in violation of his moral parameters. The issue was complicated however, because to have an effective Army, you can't stop everything just because someone at the moment says it's against his beliefs. Colonel Ross could not order a member of the Amish community to train to fight a war. But that person first must show he's part of the Amish community and he believes their religious tenants forbidding killing other humans no matter what. This normally is done prior to entering the military. The prosecution in all likelihood could establish that at the time of the order, Youngblood had not established his conscientious objector status. Although the military prefers conscientious status to be declared and awarded prior to entry into training, the procedures permit a person to firm up their objections after entry in the military. Youngblood's situation obviously was the latter circumstance especially with his leaving his company when it was having weapons training firing at cut outs of Vietnamese civilian men and women, in peasant garb, identified by the drill instructors as "Fuckin' commie VC."

Army regulations require an investigation that the objector is sincere in his beliefs. This is determined by the applicant's past and present activities and thoughts and how the applicant conducted himself. My job was not to prepare and present Youngblood's CO application. My job was to defend him at his court-martial. That he refused an order to train based on his convictions would be a strong motivation for the court to return an acquittal. The problem was that Youngblood didn't file a formal application until after charges were entered against him and he hadn't given his chain of command proper notification of his status when he refused to train. He just left the area for, "personal reasons." His attempt at resigning was a good sign of his sincerity but it failed to comport with Army discipline and good order. That much was clear.

Youngblood's mother contacted the ACLU and they sent an attorney from Lake Charles, about 70 miles south of Fort Polk. He called me and then came up to see me and Private Youngblood. He didn't look like the devil. Actually, he seemed like a pretty decent fellow. I thought he just might change some of the old guard's perceptions of this group of what they thought in Louisiana at that time were antichrists. He said he would be at the trial but I should take the lead for the court-martial. He would handle the CO application which was not administered at Fort Polk but by a board convened at Headquarters, Department of the Army, in the Pentagon.

Kirk Youngblood stayed in pretrial confinement for about five weeks before we could get the trial going. I made my defense and the trial counsel worked hard to keep it from the jury. The trial judge stated the conscientious objector issue could be a matter of extenuation and mitigation but the primary issue as to the lawfulness of the order was Colonel Ross' right to tell Private Youngblood to go back to his company and train. It's clear Ross had authority to tell Youngblood to go back to the company. It would be up to his company commander, Captain Ryan, as to whether he would immediately be sent for training duty or whether he'd send him to a chaplain or psychologist. The latter, of course, was mooted by Youngblood refusing to return to his company at all. Ross' order, I argued, pre-empted anything Captain Ryan might have intended.

The trial took a full day. Instead of parading Colonel Ross and Lieutenant Colonel Howard into the court to establish what Ross said and how Youngblood reacted, we stipulated to those facts. On defense, Youngblood pled not guilty and stated his reasons for not returning to the company. He made a big deal of his epiphany occurring when the sergeants made the company fire at cut outs of Vietnamese civilian women. Stan attempted to rebut Kirk's sincerity by introducing an MP guard who testified that, while Kirk was waiting outside during the pretrial Article 32 Investigation, he would sit by a tree and squash ants as they crawled along side him. The guard felt this strange behavior for someone opposed to killing. I noted that killing ants is substantially different from killing people. The court quickly found Kirk guilty.

On extenuation and mitigation, Private Youngblood gave sworn testimony as to his general unfamiliarity with the Army and about his moral convictions. He said he was opposed to all wars, not just the Vietnam War. He talked about his college days and his plans to help animals. Kirk told the Court he applied for conscientious objector status and was confident it would be granted. His testimony was refined, respectful, and sincere. The court appeared interested. Colonel Ross appeared pursuant to Stan's request. Ross stated that during the Youngblood's visit to his office he was deferential and that he bore no ill will towards the trainee. Colonel Ross did say he would rather that Private Youngblood had used the chain of command instead of running to his office for something his company commander easily could have taken care of had he been asked. Two NCOs from Youngblood's company testified they talked to him about war. They stated Kirk did what he was told while with the company and everybody seemed to like him. They testified, the day before Youngblood left, the company was at the range firing M-14's at targets with painted on likenesses of Vietcong men and women.

When we were finished presenting our evidence in the extenuation and mitigation phase, Stan, the trial counsel, in a sangfroid manner waived his closing argument as to what he, and by implication, the command wanted for a sentence. He would wait for our statement and then rebut it with his own version of the horrors of war and combat that Private Youngblood patently was avoiding with his feeble objector argument finishing with those being the final words for the Court along with his obviously suggested harsh sentence. I looked at my co counsel, the ACLU attorney from Lake Charles, and suggested that we not say anything. By doing that I told the ACLU guy, Stan was precluded from any closing statement. Our case was amply set forth through Youngblood's own testimony, the last thing the Court had heard up to that time. I passed on closing and Stan got up to present his argument. I objected and the judge affirmed the objection. Stan asked to approach the bench and it was clear he didn't realize his mistake. The judge told him, "You waived your opening statement. Your next chance is to rebut whatever the defense says. Since they didn't say anything, you have nothing to rebut and your case is over."

The court came back and sentenced Kirk to ten months' confinement with total forfeitures for ten months. They didn't sentence him to a punitive discharge. This was a major victory. The court obviously felt Kirk was sincere in his beliefs and left the discharge up to Headquarters, Department of the Army, pursuant to his CO application. He would never have a criminal discharge on his record. Kirk's application was approved six weeks after the trial and he was discharged from the Army as a conscientious objector. The Army excused him from serving the remainder of his sentence but left the guilty verdict unchanged. Kirk went on to vet school when he got home and after graduation moved to Minnesota where he became an inspector for Hormel meats in its Spam division.

Return to AIT

I went back to Tigerland one afternoon to visit my old advanced infantry training company. About nine months had gone by since I was supposed to be "sittin' in high cotton." The first sergeant was there but everyone else I knew had gone.

He greeted me. "Gregg, good to see you. I'm surprised you're still at Fort Polk." Things really change quickly in the training brigades especially with a war going on. "I heard some pretty good things about you over at JAG."

"Thanks Top, I'm doing what I was trained to do at law school. Are any of the guys who were here when I was still around?"

"Well Nam eats up most of what we put out but I don't know what happens to them once they go. The battalion chief told me Charlie Francis and Rick Hughes didn't make it. He said they were mine. I believe you were here when they were. He didn't know whether they were KIA or just shot up pretty bad. He said he had less than a 50% survival rate among the young lieutenants that came through the battalion before shipping off to Nam and that wasn't good." Top glanced out the window to the side of his desk at a view of loblolly pines interspersed with paths marked with whitewashed stones and continued, "He was looking for some suggestions as to how we could get the young officers better trained. Do you remember them?"

"I don't remember the names but I might recognize their faces if I saw them." He glanced around his small office in the wooden company headquarters building and said, "Well, I don't have any pictures. We have too many who come through for that. What about you? Any plans for going overseas?"

"I guess it's in the mill Top, but nothing formal so far." I felt honored by Top's informality and obvious regard for me. I wished him luck and left for the Old Club where I had a big drink.

PFC Joey Locklear; Angola to Vietnam

Soon after my thoughts about "sittin' in high cotton," LTC Hoff invited me to his office. He told me in about a month or so I was getting orders for Vietnam. I guess Top prepared me for the inevitable but it was still a shock, like losing a close relative. My whole life was changed.

My last big case at Fort Polk was not a court-martial at all. The Army has procedures for everything. If someone in the Army is convicted by a civilian court for a felony and given a sentence of a specified lengthy period, usually over a year, the person's most recent command can convene an administrative discharge board to administer a discharge for "other than honorable conditions." The respondent service member must be notified of the action but doesn't have to be present. Most prisons won't release the respondent prisoner any way. The discharge is based on what Army Regulations call, "serious acts or omissions that depart from military norms." That might leave a lot to consider but these are usually pro forma matters.

Private First Class Joey Locklear finished advanced infantry training at Tigerland and worked in the supply depot at Fort Polk pending a training slot at the Fort Benning Airborne School. He and two of his new coworkers had a weekend off so decided to go to New Orleans to party. Joey had just met these two dudes and they convinced him to come with them for what they promised would be the time of his life. Joey didn't know the guys were slime balls from Mississippi who were given a choice by a Booneville half-drunk judge of joining the Army or doing five at Parchment Farm. They got caught fencing a stolen TV by a vigilant former Klu Klux Klaner who was running a seedy pawn shop when he saw the owner's initials carved on the bottom of the TV.

They got a pass from the first sergeant, rented a car from the PX, and took off. They were going through Southern Louisiana on I-10 when Joey's two friends told him that, after the car rental, they didn't have enough money to really experience New Orleans the way they wanted. The girls there were a bit pricier than the locals in Leesville. It was late Friday night, about 2330. Joey's buddies said they knew how to get some bucks fast. They pulled off the interstate and drove into Crowley. One of the guys grabbed a pistol from under the passenger-side front seat and the other got a wool cap that he slid down over his head. The one with the gun got an Army undershirt out of a laundry bag he was using as a suitcase and wrapped it around his face and over the top of his head. Joey, realizing his buddies had a plan the entire time, said, "What's goin' on?"

"There's a convenience store just ahead that's ripe for the takin'."

Joey cried out, "Whoa, who said anything about this?"

Wool cap head mumbled back through a cutout for his mouth, "Dude, we got some comin' and youse in it all da way."

Joey was in the back seat. The two up front told him if he didn't want to join in they would let him out and he could hitch hike back to camp or get to New Orleans on his own. Joey didn't know anyone in Crowley and few in Louisiana for that matter so he thought a minute and said, "I'll drive but I'm not going in the store."

All agreed and Joey got in the driver's seat and drove up to the store. They waited outside for about five minutes until no cars or customers were in sight. The two went; one pulled a pistol and the other grabbed $312 out of the cash register while the compliant clerk stood by with his hands, as he was told to do, reaching for the ceiling. The robbers ran out, jumped in the rental car and Joey immediately took off throwing up stones and dust as he sped out of the unpaved parking area onto a local road on the outskirts of Crowley. Fran and Billy Boudreau, an elderly local couple coming home later than usual from visiting Fran's disabled sister in Lafayette, were pulling up to the store for some cigarettes as Joey was racing out. Some dirt and stones hit their two-year old and just polished Buick and Fran especially was pissed.

"Billy, I think something not quite right's going on. Why would that white boy be drivin' those two colored and why are they racing away?"

"I dunno know Fran, did you get a good look at the car?"

Fran smiled, "I got the make and license plate."

"Which way are they going, can you see?"

"Looks to me they're headed back to the highway."

About 20 minutes later Joey was stopped speeding East on I-10 by a Sheriff's Deputy for Lafayette Parish and two State Police cruisers. A helicopter quickly appeared after they hovered overhead. The police found and recovered the $312 stolen cash. They retrieved the woolen cap from under the front passenger seat and found an army shirt bundled up on the floor in the back. They got the gun out of the glove compartment. It wasn't loaded and they didn't find any bullets. The police arrested all three for armed robbery. It was easy for the district attorney in Crowley, seat of government for Acadia Parish, to get five years for Joey and ten for the other two for armed robbery. The three were sent to serve their time in Angola, one of the toughest and largest prisons in the United States.

About a year later when Joey's commander sent him the notice the Army was giving him an administrative discharge for conduct not in accord with Army standards, he sensed a way out. Joey thought if he could be retained in the Army, maybe the State of Louisiana would let him off for the remainder of his sentence so he could return to military service. This would be a second cousin to what the Booneville judge did to his buddies.

Instead of signing the routine appearance waiver and succumbing to what normally was an administrative military action, Joey requested counsel and to appear before the Board. His parents had been working for his release all along and they got the normally intransigent Angola warden to let Joey out for the hearing. Joey looked younger than twenty-two. He had been at Angola for eight months, having served the first part of his time in the Lafayette jail. The warden was protecting Joey from some of the more evil elements at Angola but couldn't keep it up for Joey's full five. Toffle appointed me Joey's counsel.

The command appointed First Lieutenant Richard Jackson, an assistant personnel officer in the S-1 section, as recorder for the board. He wasn't a lawyer. His job was to act both as the board administrator and advocate for the command. If the defense counsel raised legal issues the recorder couldn't answer, the President of the board was supposed to recess and go to the JAG office for its advice. In this sense, the hearing was a bit lopsided in favor of the defense but that depended on the aggressiveness of the defense counsel. The Board was comprised of Lieutenant Colonel Charlie Culpepper, Major Don Burch, Captain

Terry King, and the non-voting recorder, Lieutenant Jackson, all officers at Fort Polk, Culpepper and King recently having served in Vietnam.

I requested the Angola warden to attend as a witness but he declined, sending instead a prison guard and member of his social services staff to accompany Private Locklear. I tried to get Joey's former commander in Tigerland but he was in Europe and the command wouldn't release him to testify. Instead, he sent a letter saying he knew Joey and favorably endorsed his request for jump school. The letter went on to state Joey was one of his better trainees and he let everyone know he wanted to go to Vietnam. His old CO, for some reason, didn't want to go on record that he would endorse the return to the Army of a convicted felon and convict. His letter was better than nothing and I decided it would help. I obtained a copy of the trial transcript that established Joey's guilt and clearly indicated he was a reluctant participant. That Joey got half of what his codefendants were sentenced to proved that the Judge, who gave the sentence, understood his lesser culpability. Joey's parents would attend.

The night before the administrative hearing, there was a cocktail party at the Old Club for the post provost marshal, an MP Officer, who was promoted that afternoon to colonel. I worked through lunch to get the defense for the Locklear administrative hearing finally organized. After I felt I had done all I could for Joey, I stopped over to the club to congratulate the new Colonel Stallworth. I had a congratulatory drink and then another. They served meatballs in a chili sauce and grape jelly mixture; finger-sized soggy egg rolls with bland mustard on the side; a tray full of cheese cut up into tiny squares nestled with four types of crackers; some celery, carrots and broccoli pieces with a creamy moccasin-colored sauce; some pigs in a blanket; and some over-cooked liver wrapped in under-cooked bacon. It was the Fort Polk Old Club's number two offering. I was pretty hungry and had a bit of everything. The club's number one offering had all the above with shrimp and a medium hot cocktail sauce along with alligator fritters, a local specialty. The number one party menu was available to any officer but it was poor form to order it unless you were a general officer or were retiring. I enjoyed the number two offering as I had yet another drink and with some more meatballs, no need for dinner. Major Burch was at the party and I saw him coming over my way. He grabbed my arm and said, "I understand we're going to have quite a show tomorrow."

I was taken aback and answered, "I don't understand sir. I have an administrative board on a very important matter."

He came back, "There you are again, Gregg, always the consummate defense counsel. I'm on the Locklear Board."

I knew he was and he seemed a bit tipsy but I didn't want to mess things up so I said, "Sir, I look forward to presenting an interesting case but don't think it appropriate to get into the particulars at this time. If I did, then you might be challenged by Lieutenant Jackson and I don't want to miss your experience and fairness." I didn't want to let the opportunity get away altogether.

Before I knew it, I was one of the few left at the party. After all, Stallworth was a regular at Sick Call and, as a defense counsel, his friendship could make a difference. Maybe. I left with lots of bonhomie and made my way home to DeRidder where I quickly fell asleep. I awoke the next morning with a horrendous headache. Stallworth, I then remembered, served the house military club bourbon, not Jack Daniels Black. I was late to the office and they forwarded Mrs. Locklear's phone call. The Locklears were in Lake Charles on their way up to post and wanted directions. Fortunately the trial was scheduled for 1300 so I had a few hours to get myself in order. I called and asked Mrs. Locklear to stop by our house. It was on their way. I wanted to talk to them before the hearing so this would serve its purpose. Just a little bit of an excuse. They were about to leave and would be there in forty-five minutes.

I cleaned up and got into my uniform before the Locklear's arrived. Joey was to meet us with the Angola witnesses at the post courtroom I reserved for the board. I didn't know when his parents had seen him other than in a prison setting last. The Locklear's arrived and told me that when they got up they called Angola from their motel in Lake Charles and learned Joey left around 0830. Joey should arrive at Fort Polk before noon which would provide an opportunity for him and his parents to have lunch together. Mrs. Locklear said I didn't look too well. I told her I had a terrible headache but not why. She immediately became concerned and started to tell me all her remedies. They actually sounded pretty good but I didn't have the appropriate stuff for some and for others didn't think a drink before a hearing very professional. Anyway, she ended up massaging my head, especially my temples on which she exerted substantial pressure. For a minute I thought my head would pop but the headache seemed to lessen. Mrs. Locklear knew the reason for my malady and I'm sure she had some personal experience as how to treat it. In an off-hand manner, Mr. Locklear said if we won the case, Joey might be the first American born in Vietnam to return to fight the communists.

This was the first I had heard of any of that. I spoke to Joey a number of times but never in person, always over the phone. He never said anything about this. I knew Joey wanted to go to Vietnam but never understood the connection. Wow! This would be something on which the board could hang its hat. I asked the particulars and Mrs. Locklear told me Joey was born in 1948 when she and her husband were working at a rubber plantation for the French in Indochina. She said Joey lived the first three years of his life in what now is Vietnam. I asked Mr. Locklear where he worked and he responded he retired from Michelin. I told Mrs. Locklear I needed her to testify.

Lieutenant Jackson opened the proceedings in the Fort Polk Court Room and entered Joey's company morning report of the Monday morning after his arrest. It showed he was marked absent as not returning from pass. He then presented a copy of the company morning report for a month later that showed Joey was dropped from the roles because he was incarcerated in a civilian penal institution. He then entered a copy of Joey's conviction, certified by the clerk of court for Acadia Parish. I had no objection to the entries. I started by introducing Private Locklear to the Board and then by introducing his parents who were seated in the first row. I then asked the guards from Angola to come into the courtroom; they had been waiting outside, and I introduced them. Everyone was together and I attempted to lessen the formality of the process. I then made a short opening statement in which I laid out Joey's case.

I began. "PFC Locklear was not drafted in the Army. He joined. He did a great job in basic and AIT and worked hard because he knew he was going to Vietnam. He actually wanted to go. He was selected for jump school, but when he finished his training no slots were available. He was placed in a holding company at a supply depot and spent his days loading trucks. Even that he did well. He basically was alone. No one else at the depot was waiting for jump school. The two soldiers he worked with were losers but Joey knew he had to get along. If he got into trouble, he would lose his slot. He got a weekend off. His two new friends also had a pass and they discussed what they would do. They decided to go to New Orleans. On the way Joey made a bad decision. So bad that in the short moment it took him to decide to stay in the car, in that little slice of time, his life was ruined. You, members of the Board who have taken an oath to find justice, can put Joey back into a life that will matter. You have that power. What you will hear will show that justice demands Joey's retention."

I told the board that his military record, although short, was impeccable except for the one aberration. The board had his 201 personnel file before it. I pointed out that he was recommended by his commander for jump school and he wanted to go and after that go to Vietnam. I told the board that Angola was a terrible place and said Joey's been punished enough for his reluctant participation in the robbery. I said witnesses from Angola would testify that Joey had no problems in the Army or at Angola. I said Angola eventually would kill Joey but if they retained him, in all likelihood he would be returned to the Army so the case has become a matter of life and death and that I was sure they all would agree that death was a disproportionate sentence for his participation in the crime. I stopped for a minute to let that sink in. Then I told the board that Joey was born in Indo China in what now is Vietnam and if the board so determined, he would be the first American born in Vietnam who would return there to fight for its independence against communism. I ended up saying again that the case was a matter of life and death.

I presented my witnesses and the commander's statement and Joey testified about the crime and how he tried to get out of it but felt hemmed in. He said he was sorry not just because he got caught but because he knew he hurt people. The prison social services lady testified and said in response to questioning by LTC Culpepper that if Joey were retained in the Army, in all likelihood he would be released back to Army jurisdiction. She explained how that worked and said her recommendation would be to release him. She said she had spoken to the warden about the case and he seemed amenable to such a scenario. When we finished our presentation, Culpepper looked over at Lieutenant Jackson and asked if he had any further comment. He said he didn't and personally would not object to Private Locklear's retention.

I asked the guard if Joey could stay to hear the board's findings and then for dinner after. He said they could wait maybe an hour but then they had to get back. Not like a court-martial, the board doesn't have to return a verdict at the hearing. Notwithstanding, in about 30 minutes as we milled about the court room parking lot, Lieutenant Jackson came outside and asked me if Joey were retained would he get back pay. I told him I didn't know but thought that should not stop a life or death situation. I said, if necessary, Joey would sign something declining pay for the time he was confined. I found out later that Jackson called Toffle who told him Locklear's status in civilian confinement is leave without pay so the issue was moot.

The members of the board came out of the court room. LTC Jackson went over to Joey and said, "The Board is recommending your retention. We are going out on a limb on this and you'd better not make us look bad."

"That's not going to happen, sir. I learned my lesson."

Each of the members of the board then came over and shook Joey's hands, and then mine. They uniformly thanked Mr. and Mrs. Locklear for coming.

The Army retained Private First Class Joey Locklear on active duty, Louisiana released him from Angola, and Joey returned to the Army. He retook advanced infantry training but this time he didn't opt for airborne school. He got orders for Vietnam and, while serving with the 25th Infantry Division, known as Tropic Lightning, received a Bronze Star for valor in Cambodia in 1970. He also received a purple heart as a result of a shrapnel wound from a North Vietnamese grenade in his thigh. When Joey came back to the United States he finished college at the University of Utah and got a job as an account executive for a printing company.

Toffle's Demise

Near the end of my tour at Fort Polk, there was an unpleasant situation at the JAG office. Toffle got into trouble. I knew he drank considerably and not always just after work. One day when LTC Hoff was away and Toffle was Acting SJA, we had to forward a court-martial package to The Judge Advocate General's office to meet the deadline for our administrative review. That a court-martial convicts a person is a first step in the prosecution process but there's tremendous pressure on the SJA and the convening authority to complete their reviews and get the file to higher headquarters so they can commence the formal appellate process that automatically follows. Such efforts go unnoticed by most critics of military justice but the process is under strict time lines and well-orientated to the rights of the accused until all reviews and appeals are finalized. In the case at hand, Stan, now the chief of military justice, completed his review, LTC Hoff accepted the review and took it to the post commander who accepted Hoff's recommendation and signed a formal decision memorandum, and the transmittal papers were prepared to go to Army JAG. The SJA had to sign the forwarding documents and we were one day ahead of our deadline. Stan had to go to court and knew I had a special relationship with Toffle. He asked that I take the papers to Toffle's quarters where he was hosting a military judge scheduled the next day for a general court-martial not involving me. Stan may have known more than that but he said no more. I said I'd take care of it.

Toffle was living off-post at his girl friend's house. I knew them both and I considered them a couple just like the married officers. LTC Hoff treated the situation that way and I followed suit. I actually thought they may have been married but didn't make a big deal about it. Some hard-nosed military guys would rather shock the busy body than give him a glimpse at his personal life. I wasn't sure about Toffle's marriage status and didn't really care. It was my first visit to his girl friend's house and I got there around 1430. Toffle introduced me to a venerable colonel, our military judge for the next day. He was introduced as being airborne, having been a glider pilot in World War II, and having flown over Normandy on "D-Day." The guy had a bad leg and I didn't ask how. The war stories were flying fast and furious. Both were still enjoying their liquid lunch. Toffle's voice was slurred and the colonel was relaxed. I figured there was no discretion involved in a transmittal document so I asked for Toffle's signature and he signed the paper, his name for Hoff's.

My work accomplished, I wanted to get back to the office but Toffle wasn't ready to release me. He said airborne troops had to know how to kill with knives. They were the silent type. They could jump quietly in at night and with knives dispatch the enemy outposts before anyone knew they were there. He went into the kitchen and collected all the knives he could find. He told me to sit down. Then the two airborne troops took turns seeing who could stick the knife closest to the center of the wall across the room. He asked me to take a picture down from the wall and that gave them a substantial killing area. After all, the knives were not weighted. A few stuck digging out some wall board and it became my job to retrieve those and the ones on the floor and return them to the combatants. The wall was looking a bit rough. Toffle and the judge were in hysterics and I felt uncomfortable in such esteemed company. Eventually, I was permitted my leave and got back to the JAG office. Maybe two weeks later LTC Hoff called his officers together and told us MAJ Toffle was being relieved. I never was sure what happened but in the puzzled queries there was something about Toffle overextending his authority while LTC Hoff was away. Toffle was assigned to a training battalion for duty as executive officer pending a discharge board. I never found out what happened and never saw him again.

Departure from Fort Polk

I often worked past the standard close of the duty day at the Fort Polk JAG office. I didn't have children or a spouse waiting at home and in such an out of the way place there was no pressure for me to get home. One evening a mess sergeant at one of the training companies stopped by the office to see me about a civilian issue involving his next door neighbor. Sure. Apparently the next door neighbor didn't file an income tax return for the year before and was worried about what might happen. I explained the process and told the mess sergeant that the best thing to do was to file the thing as soon as possible and pay what was owing to stop penalties and interest charges. I told him that a six month delay may not get him jail time but he should be prepared for a penalty. After our session about his "neighbor," the mess sergeant invited me to his house for a Cajun fish fry. It was one of the most fun experiences I had in Louisiana.

When Cajun folks ask you to accept their hospitality and you do so with no reservations, you are treated as one of them. Someone caught a mess of catfish and my host laid newspapers all over his kitchen counters. I was out in the country and not terrible far from Fort Polk but there was no semblance of the military. There was a large pot of oil on the stove where an unlimited supply of fresh cat fish, a few at a time, took a short bath in the boiling oil and then jumped onto the newspapers to drain. A bucket of ice with some Dixie beer stood in the middle of about eight people, men and women mostly from the neighborhood and a local church, who would grab a fish, pick it apart mostly with their fingers, and wash it down with some of Louisiana's finest. It was a little bit reminiscent of my days in Baltimore sitting at a long wooden table covered with newspapers picking crabs and drinking Boh. In Louisiana we stood and picked the fish. The neighbors I met never said anything about tax problems. It was wonderful and a memory I will always cherish.

My going away party was a happy and sad occasion, both for the same reason, leaving Fort Polk. Quite a few from the post came down to my house in DeRidder to say goodbye. I purchased a whole pig from a local who brought it live to the back of my office after work and shot it in the back of its head with a 22 caliber pistol. He helped me stuff it in the trunk of my car. I took it to a restaurant I saw each day on my trip back and forth from DeRidder. They had a huge smoker and were happy to prepare the hog for my party. The party with the smoked hog was fun and enjoyed by all. Quite a bit was left and I divided it up with a couple of civilian secretaries from the office. I couldn't take it with me. Almost the entire JAG office was there. The wife of the incoming deputy SJA (Toffle's replacement) signed a scroll Ben put out: "May the Blue Bird of Happiness put filet mignon and wild rice in your "C" rations, Joyce." Joyce later became a well-known Washington chef and was for awhile the pastry chef at the White House.

The day after my party I drove out of Louisiana. A few years later, while exchanging Christmas cards with a few of my fellow trial lawyers, I learned an attendee from the party got trichinosis from the pig.

PART FIVE
SAIGON SUPPORT
COMMAND

Wilbur R. Enoch; Hero Gone AWOL

When McCormick dropped me off at the JAG office after my first night in Nam, I reported again to the Acting SJA, Major Barry Forsythe. Three hundred and sixty-three days to go. Forsythe asked, "Did you get settled in ok?"

"Yes sir, I'm ready to go. Since I just got out of JAG School I thought maybe I could teach the required classes on the changes to the military justice system." I wanted some diversity in what I was doing and didn't want to be married to a desk for a whole year.

"I don't think that's required in a combat zone but I'll check it out." I got the impression he was very careful about such requirements and felt that's a pretty good thing for the top lawyer.

I asked him, "Do you mind sir if I sit on some special courts as a judge? I was certified after attending the first judge course in Charlottesville. I know I can't do it in this command but might be able to help out some other folks."

"If you can find the time, it's ok with me, but if you have any extra time, let me know first." Not a good sign. He introduced me around the office and showed me to my little cubicle.

I shared it with Phil Smith, a JAG captain from Colorado. He married right before coming to Vietnam and the separation was straining his new relationship. His morale was down and he had no R&R in sight. Our little office was designed for one person and large enough for only two desks, a file cabinet, and one side chair between the desks that served as a table. It would be impossible in the office for me to see witnesses or defendants in private. On the wall to the right of my desk was the hand-written docket for our General Court-Martial cases.

Forsythe appointed me trial counsel in a court martial involving Wilbur R. Enoch, a member of the 551st Transportation Company (Terminal Service), 71st Transportation Battalion (Terminal). Enoch was 18 years old and joined the Army to get out of town. He was from Hastain, Missouri, near the Lake of the Ozarks and the Harry Truman reservoir. He was an only child and his mother died when he was six of ovarian cancer. His father, an auto parts salesperson at a local Pep Boys store, raised him until he remarried when Wilbur was 16. His stepmother worked as a waitress in a local diner serving the evening shift. The stepmother moved into the Enoch home and Wilbur attended high school. Wilbur was a good looking kid but very shy. He played trumpet in the school band and preferred to watch TV than study. No one was home to bug him and he liked it that way. One night he awakened from a dead sleep and his stepmother was sitting on his bed with her hand on Wilbur's naked and hard penis. Wilbur was embarrassed and pretended to be asleep. After awhile she put her mouth on him and Wilbur came and she left. Wilbur felt terribly guilty. The very next day he got a lock for his bedroom door and started going after girls in his classes at school. At first he tried a direct approach and would walk up to a girl and say she was cute and he wanted to take her out. That didn't work even when he went after freshman girls. Most laughed at him and made him feel inferior. He then tried to get a reputation. Sports were out; he was too late in school to start football and he never had played basketball. He knew a couple of guys who did drugs and befriended them. They started coming over to the Enoch house after school. Wilbur's stepmother left for work just before school got out and his father didn't get home until after dinner. The kids smoked weed and eventually invited some girls to party. He and his buddies smoked and had sex with two girls in particular. They would experiment and tried to get other girls to come over as well. Some did and the house became an ongoing after-school event. He was running low on funds because his allowance wouldn't support the drugs for the girls so a friend asked him if he wanted to sell some weed. He started selling lower classmen his $5 bags and remarkably was not caught.

Enoch worked at the lake during the summer and got a new group of clients. He saw one of his buddies get busted for possession and thrown in jail where he stayed until school started. It was Wilbur's last year and he decided to cut back and be more careful. He liked the extra income and how the girls would treat him when he bought them the stuff so he found a pretty good supplier and recruited some friends to sell for him. He started making more than he ever imagined and the girls around the house became more beautiful and willing. He saved his money in a lock box he kept in his closet. He drove a used 1964 Mustang convertible he got from what he told his father were his summer earnings. Wilbur graduated from school in the bottom third of his class and was getting ready to renew his operations on the lake when he learned that one of his sellers was busted attempting to sell to some eighth graders who were coming to the high school in the fall. Using a fake name and address, he moved his drug funds into a bank in Clinton. He told his supplier since school was out he had to terminate his operations. He cleaned out his house of all drug and sex paraphernalia and gave each of his sellers $500. He told all his friends that the party was over; he was going in the Army. The police came to his house about a week later with a search warrant. His mother was home at the time and aghast that Wilbur might be doing something untoward. She had no idea. They found nothing incriminating and he denied any wrong doing. He took his pre induction physical and asked the recruiter if he could go early.

Wilbur left in July for basic training at Fort Benning. He did well and received orders to Fort Eustis for advanced transportation training. His first assignment when he graduated was to Vietnam. He arrived in November 1967, and his first job was to fill huge thick fuel bladders with diesel and then rig them for delivery to armored units in the jungle. He did this until just after Christmas when he was reassigned as a driver. He was supposed to drive tank trucks filled with gasoline from the Long Binh depots to various units throughout the Corps area. He heard rumors floating around that the North Vietnamese were reinforcing the VC and a large attack was imminent. The target was supposed to be Khe Sanh, an airstrip near the DMZ with North Vietnam, a marine base, out in the middle of nowhere. The rumors were that substantial artillery was being moved south along with a number of NVA divisions. Toward the end of January the Vietnamese holiday of Tet approached and the South Vietnamese entered into a voluntary cease fire of about a week to honor the New Year. Enoch's convoy started north in late January up highway one under an MP escort. He could see rice paddies and huge water buffalo working the fields together under large wooden yokes. The farmers worked, holiday or not. There were little villages here and there, some sporting Esso or Texaco signs, and of course, there were many little food stands rigged under canopies of dirty canvas and sporting home made tables with chairs of various kinds that looked like they came from some town's dump. Highway One was paved and that made the trip fast.

Route 1 Village

The problem with going fast is that sometimes you run into nasty situations with little time for a planned response. The convoy was moving at 50 mph with an MP jeep rigged with a 50 caliber machine gun to its front and with other MP jeeps skirting up and down its left side. Wilbur was keeping pace and daydreaming about Asian pussy when the truck behind him exploded. Wilbur heard a thump just before the explosion. The enemy was close. The blast seemed to propel Wilbur's truck forward but he didn't feel or see any damage. He pulled to the side of the road and stopped. He saw the MPs moving up to the front of the convoy to address the attack. Wilbur grabbed his M-16 and a pack he had filled with ammo and five hand grenades and jumped from his truck and ran away from the stopped convoy. Any of those tank trucks filled with raw gasoline if hit by a bullet or shrapnel could explode and spew fire that would burn anyone in the vicinity. In effect they were traveling bombs with a high chance of exploding in any fire fight. He heard weapons fire and in a low crouch ran about twenty yards to a low wall that ran up the side of the road in front of a marshy rice field. He jumped over the wall and saw two other drivers low crawling to the wall. One was shot and fell half way there and the other ran back to the trucks for cover. Wilbur heard automatic rifle fire near the front of the convoy. Eventually the MPs started a return fire but it seemed meager in comparison to what was coming in. They were aiming at the trucks and another truck blew up with an immense explosion causing black clouds to join the black smoke from the already damaged truck near Wilbur. Wilbur decided he'd better get the injured driver out of the roadway. He left his stuff and scooted along behind the wall until he was about 15 yards from the injured driver. He heard a barrage from the MPs and ran the short distance to his friend who he grabbed under the arms and dragged back to the wall for cover.

It was Gene Grey, a kid from Pennsylvania. Gene had blood all over the lower part of his body and his pant legs were wet and speckled with dark maroon colors. Gene was unconscious. Wilbur made sure Gene had good cover and then retrieved his bag and rifle. He ran in a crouch along the wall to where he heard the shooting coming into the convoy. Smoke and the smell of burning fuel and bodies permeated the area. As he moved along he could see three MPs with an M-60 machine gun set up at the front of the convoy just to the side of a five-ton truck. They were shooting across the road toward the wall he was using as protection. He realized the enemy was in front of him and he was coming up on its flank. There was a lot of foliage on the paddy side of the wall so he had cover. He crawled a bit further and made his way over the ground through some twisted barbed wire and broken glass. He stayed as close to the wall as a leech sucking blood in the swamps. He glimpsed some movement about thirty yards ahead. He couldn't tell how many there were but they had mortar and periodically he could hear its WUMPF. He grabbed three grenades from his bag and set them up in front of him. He then loaded his M-16 and put it on automatic. The MPs let off a blast towards the wall and then turned the weapon to the front. Wilbur, in turn, activated and threw each grenade at the enemy's flank. They were firing into the MPs when the grenades started going off. He grabbed his rifle and emptied its load with one short burst at the area where he had seen movement. He loaded it again and switched the setting to semi-automatic. He threw yet another grenade and saw that he had only one left. He looked up and saw some pajama-clad Vietnamese running in a low crouch into the rice paddy. There were about 20 men, stealthily moving across the rice field in increments—a group of five would move quickly and then set down and then another group would do the same. He anticipated their moves and started firing with some success as they moved away. He was reloading when an MP jumped the wall and said it was over, they had left.

The MP looked at Wilbur and asked if he was all right. Wilbur didn't realize it but he had blood all over his side. Some was Gene Grey's but he was shot above his elbow. An Apache gunship came over in about five minutes and started raking the rice paddy with automatic fire. A large explosion on the far side of the paddy produced a rapidly expanding black cloud. A medevac arrived in another ten minutes and set down on the highway just to the front of the convoy. It took away Gene Grey and two others, one an MP with a bullet wound in his upper shoulder and the other a mechanic who had multiple shrapnel wounds all over his body. The mechanic's flak jacket saved his life but he still was hurt pretty bad. The MP Captain thanked Wilbur for his quick thinking and help. A corpsman wrapped up his arm and put him in a second medevac with two other injured drivers, one with pretty bad burns on his face, arms and chest.

The MP Captain in charge of the convoy recommended Wilbur for a Silver Star but USARV downgraded it to a Bronze Star for valor. Wilbur also got a Purple Heart for the flesh wound to his arm. The action was considered part of the Tet offensive. He went back to duty driving tank trucks in late February and served the remainder of his first tour without incident. He got to like the camaraderie of the military especially in combat and decided to reenlist and stay in Vietnam but this time for an easier job. He lost six friends in attacks on convoys and thought it was just a matter of time before his gasoline-loaded tanker was hit. Every time out was a crap shoot. He did have a reputation and wanted it to continue. He signed up as a clerk for a unit in a little camp just outside Long Binh near Saigon.

Wilbur went to Bangkok on R&R near the end of his first tour and thought he had fallen in love with a beautiful young Thai girl he met at a bar. When he came into the narrow little bar it was pitch black. The music was ultra loud and he pushed through a crowd to the middle of the bar where he ordered a beer. He hadn't had sex in a long time. He felt some fingers running up his thigh reaching his crotch and he could see a smiling young girl in the twilight of the cash register's small lamp. She grabbed him gently and asked if he wanted some company. He ordered her a Bangkok tea and told her not to let go. She didn't for that and the next two days. It cost him $295 for the three days he was with her and he wanted it to last forever. When he woke up at his hotel on the fourth day she was gone and he had no idea where. He went back to the little bar where he fell in love and asked for her by name. The bouncer told him to see the mama san in the back. He pushed his way through the crowd where he found a little room near the rear exit sign with a table lamp dimmed by a heavy red velvet shade. A woman sat at a makeup table and asked what he wanted. She didn't look as old as he thought a mama san would. He asked for Pearl, the girl he had stayed with the previous three nights. She told him Pearl was occupied for the next few days. She had a full schedule and was one of the best girls there. She might arrange something in a month's time. Wilbur was heart broken but he understood. He went to his hotel and slept away the remainder of his time on R&R. He came back to Long Binh a wiser man.

Wilbur's first pass into Saigon from his new clerk position found him in a Chinese restaurant downtown. It was a medium-priced place and he felt out of place in his dirty enlisted fatigues. The military there were mostly captains and majors and they were in the minority. The restaurant was filled primarily with Vietnamese. Each table had a cloth with a lazy susan in the middle that the Vietnamese would swirl around examining all the various Chinese delicacies from which they would pick with their chop sticks. One woman with a small child about three tables away kept looking at him. He returned her glance and she smiled back coquettishly. She was sitting around a table with five other Vietnamese.

Wilbur signaled the waitress and asked, "There's a beautiful young lady at the table over there. It looks like she is with her family. I would like to meet her. What do you suggest?"

"She Vietnamese and not boom boom girl."

Wilbur said, "I understand that but she is very pretty, and she smiled at me."

"Not good idea. You alone and it look bad for her."

"If I were Vietnamese, what would I do?"

"You not Vietnamese." The waitress lingered.

"But if I were." I pushed 200 piasters across the table to the waitress.

She placed her hand on the money. "Give me a note. I will take to the papa san. Ask if you can send his table bottle of mao-tai."

"What's mao-tai?"

"Chinese liquor."

He wrote a short note in English and gave it to the waitress who took it to the oldest man at the girl's table. She said something to him and the whole table looked over. The old man nodded and smiled.

The waitress brought the table a bottle of something that they passed around. The girl continued to glance in his direction. Eventually a young man from the table came over and invited Wilbur to join the group.

Saigon Alley

Wilbur bowed to each person and sat down. He met the love of his life, Binh Toh. Binh is a Vietnamese word for peace. Binh was beautiful with flowing black hair and wore a sheer purple ao dai with painted lilacs on its front. It hung seductively over Binh's silk pants. She had a soft face with eager bright eyes and full sensuous lips. Wilbur arranged to meet with Binh the next day so she could show him around Saigon. That following evening, Wilbur's last on his authorized absence from his unit, they visited a night club. They caught a motorized rickshaw that drove them down some Saigon boulevards as they sat hip to hip and entered some small streets in a densely populated area. Eventually they got off and walked through a maze of small dark and narrow alleys to a little courtyard. Binh's narrow three story house sat at the edge of the courtyard. The first two floors were fully occupied by an extended family sleeping all over the place, some on couches and others on the floor. Binh held Wilbur's hand and pulled him through the area stepping over sleeping children and not saying anything. They went up some stairs and then further up a circular iron staircase into what looked like a small loft at the top, third floor, of the house. Quianh, Binh's baby, was asleep in a little bed in the corner. It was covered with mosquito netting. The windows were open admitting a cool night breeze perfumed by a mélange of smells of sweet flowers and smoldering incense with hints of odors from the Saigon River. Binh pulled Wilbur to her thin floor mattress and with a flourish surrounded her sleeping space with mosquito netting tacked to the ceiling. She then carefully unbuttoned Wilbur's shirt and kissed his chest licking his nipples while she reached for his hardness. She unzipped his pants and moved down his body where she took him in her mouth. He let her do it a minute then afraid he couldn't hold himself pulled her up and found her naked and wet. He entered her and quickly climaxed. Wilbur was smitten. Binh made love to him again that night and this time she came as well. They stayed together living in Binh's loft with Quianh and among her family. About a week later Wilbur returned to his unit to get some personal stuff. He was placed on restriction and administered non judicial punishment.

Wilbur ended up going AWOL six times. After the nonjudicial punishment he got a special court-martial for his next foray and then another. The first charge I saw was for six days absence without leave. He came back and the following day took off again for almost two months after which he came back for two days. It seemed he would come back to pick up his pay and change some dollars into MPC and go to the PX. He then split for a month and a half when upon his return he stayed around for five weeks while the command generated general court-martial charges. He then split for another two and half months. When he returned the last time the command put him in pretrial confinement at LBJ, the Long Binh Jail.

LBJ was not a fun place. It was overcrowded and the scene of a vicious prison riot about ten months before in which one prisoner was clubbed to death with a shovel, the warden and deputy were beaten severely while attempting to bring the riot under control, and 63 MPs and 52 inmates suffered major injuries. It was not a place you wanted to be and was designed to be a worse venue then combat. Other than the general population which were contained within razor-topped barbed wire fencing, the more serious inmates were kept in metal Conex shipping containers welded together to form a multi-cell metal building. Temperatures in the Conex containers reached the hell for which the place was designed. Signs were placed around the perimeter of the jail looking out prohibiting picture taking. Since there was little press coverage of last year's prison riot the signs appeared unnecessary.

AWOL in Vietnam did not have a support structure of friends and family similar to what might be available back home. Jobs for AWOL servicemen in Vietnam were unavailable. Accordingly survival depended on supporting one's self through a Vietnamese girl friend and ultimately the black market. The

AWOL GI could go to the PX and this made him popular with his girl friend and her family. He also could support himself by changing money and selling drugs to troops on pass in Saigon. The CID, the government's detectives, knew all this and investigated Enoch. They found out about his girl friend and determined he purchased money orders in excess of the $200 authorized in any one month. The CID couldn't tell whether the girl friend's family was involved with the VC or not. It was not something you could find out by going to your local police force. Half the local police sympathized with the VC. The finance clerks kept pretty good records of their MPC transactions. They didn't have lists of AWOL soldiers to check against and basically anybody with a right to the MPCs could buy them. This appeared to be a good case for my first prosecution. I thought Saigon could be a fun place to hide if one was so inclined and apparently Wilbur Enoch was so inclined. I was going to make sure the papa sans in Saigon would need to get someone else to work their black markets.

Around lunch time, I saw Phil in the area outside my office. He looked at me and said, "Hey Gregg do you want to go to the PX? Fred Hopps needs to go as well. I have the jeep and need a new razor. We can get a bite after." Fred was one of the other captains in the office.

It turns out Fred was going to defend Enoch. When I got in the jeep I noticed there was no ignition key.

Phil saw me look. "We secure the vehicle with a chain and master security lock. The key to that is kept on a peg by the exit door."

"Why don't we just use an ignition key?"

Fred piped in. "In combat, military vehicles have to be ready for quick action by anybody and the ignition key would mess things up."

I thought to myself that it would be nice in combat if everyone had a key for the chain and master lock.

The PX was full of everything you would ever need to live comfortably in a combat support area and then some. Signs warning of severe prosecution for black market activities took the place of the usual shoplifting warnings. There was a full supply of toiletries and junk food. Cigarettes were cheap at $2 a carton. I bought some Marlboros. There were the usual trinkets and cheap gift stuff with lots of tape recorders, speakers, head phones, and other music paraphernalia. They had every camera imaginable with countless accessories. They had a few civilian shirts and pants. I guess they were for use during leave or R&R. There were racks and racks of girlie magazines with soldiers standing in front and opening the centerfolds for all to see. They also had paperback books. There was plenty of booze—beer, cordials, whiskeys, gin, whatever. The military calls alco-

holic beverages and PX stuff Class VI supplies. I had a ration card and its alloca-
tion of three bottles of booze each month was all I needed. In the PX in Vietnam
everything was cheap. I picked up a few other things to make life a bit more comfortable in my transient billet and we went to lunch.

There were mess halls all over Long Binh. You were supposed to use the din-
ing facility assigned to your company or headquarters and we did that on occasion but we also wandered. Each guy had his particular favorite, and of course,
with the one-year tour for everybody including mess sergeants, mess hall ratings
always were in flux. We visited the mess hall for a transportation command that
was supposed to serve a pretty good lunch. It was not so good. The hamburgers
were like greasy cardboard squares and the lettuce on the salads was wilted with a
nasty sharp taste. Fred apologized and said the cook must have DEROSed. He
explained that DEROS was the acronym for a soldier's date of estimated return
from overseas, in this case Vietnam. I knew from my tour at Fort Polk that if you
were short, you were leaving soon. I realized DEROS must mean the same thing.
I was not short. Phil had 197 days and Fred 125. Neither was short but each day
everyone knew his exact count and loved to talk about it, especially when he was
closer to DEROS than you. It seemed to provide some pecking order in the general scheme of things. When you would meet someone in the early part of the
conversation he would ask, what's your DEROS? I would answer 360 or something like that and he would laugh, look down at me, and say his was 100. I had
quite some time before I would ask someone about their DEROS. On the way
back to the office I told Fred I was trial counsel in the Enoch case and saw he was
defending. I didn't tell him it was my first prosecution. He said he hadn't seen
Enoch yet but planned to go over to LBJ in the next few days and would speak to
me when he got back.

Enoch's Court Martial

A couple of days later while Phil was out of the office, Fred stopped by and asked
if I had a few minutes to speak about Enoch. I had drawn up the charges and figured young PFC Enoch was facing four years—six months for the AWOL less
than thirty days, six months for the violation of the Black Market regulation, and
a year for each AWOL over thirty days. Wilbur's decorations were not in the file
and I smelled blood. Fred sat down in Phil's chair, leaned back, and said, "Greg,
the Enoch case is a tough one."

I jumped back, "Tough! Christ Fred, the guy's a yo yo! He keeps bouncing
back and forth. He causes more trouble than he's worth and all they got him for

his stay in Saigon was one money order violation. I'll bet if we look further they'll be more."

"Greg, Wilbur's on his second tour. He extended from the first and got a job in the orderly room. His first was driving tank trucks back and forth between Long Binh and Cu Chi. He saw quite a few buddies' bite the dust and every day was a crap shoot. If a rocket hit his truck, he was a crispy critter."

I still was astounded. "Fred, he joined quite a few others who did very well and completed their tours. That he signed up for another year is nice but it doesn't exonerate him from running off at every chance. Besides, his history is not all that great—he does have two previous convictions."

"What do you think you can do for him with a guilty plea?"

I answered more confidently than I should have, "Actually, the prosecution should not be all that tough. I have the morning reports as to his AWOLs and the money order stuff is a matter of record. Everyone knows that to survive in Saigon when AWOL, you must get into some pretty nefarious activities. Drugs, prostitution, petty thievery are all part of it. Obviously, there is some money laundering. Where did he sleep? Where did he eat? What did he do all day? Did he have a girl friend? But what the hell, I can take three years to the Old Man and see what he thinks."

"Well he did have a girl friend. Apparently she had a child, not his—some other GI's, and he felt homesick with the family setting and couldn't resist it. I don't think three years will do it Gregg. None of that stuff about prostitution or petty thievery will be admissible. There's lots of conjecture but you don't have any fire. Further, his company doesn't look all that great in letting him loose the first three times he split. There must have been some thought behind that."

"You mean the fact they didn't put him in pretrial should benefit him, I don't think so."

"Gregg, the guy isn't all bad. He did a year of tough service and fell in love. That will be very strong mitigation for a war-time court most of whom probably envy him. Admittedly, he hasn't performed well the second year."

"Performed! He's hardly been here." I tried to appear offended.

"Well, three years in jail's not going to do it. We will demand proof and you may have to call back Captain Harney who authenticated the last two absences. He has DEROSed you know."

"Those records are sufficient in their own right."

"Well normally they are, but we have a witness that will swear Wilbur came back on the 29th of January, not the 31st and that takes away the efficacy of the morning reports. It may force you to call Harney back. That should be fun."

"Let me think about it. Maybe I can amend the charges."

Fred left and my thoughts of blood all over the place evaporated. Now I knew the travails of prosecution. I didn't think the Army would return Harney from where ever to prosecute a slime ball like Enoch for a relatively short term AWOL. I looked in on Major Forsythe and asked if he had a minute. When I related what had happened, he suggested that I may have been a bit hard nosed. He said he could take an eighteen month confinement to the convening authority and it would be an acceptable deal all around. I asked him if it would matter if we had some more money order violations. He said that didn't matter at all. The court knew when you went AWOL in Vietnam you had to support yourself in the black market and it only went to aggravation of the AWOL. They knew he wasn't serving daily Mass at the Cathedral in Saigon. I thanked him and left.

Great! I didn't want to lose face with Fred Hopps; maybe I would have other cases with him. And besides, I didn't want to look like an ass. So I did nothing but get the charges authenticated, read them to Enoch, and initiate the Article 32 proceedings. I scheduled the 32 and pretended I was in the process of bringing Harney back from the states. I included his name in a list of witnesses Fred requested thinking if we proceeded on a not guilt plea maybe I could get Forsythe to bring him back. At least that was my rationale.

Fred, Phil, I, and several others from the office continued to dine together and attend movies around the Long Binh camp but we never discussed our pending cases. Finally, Fred stopped by my little cubicle with a file under his arm. I could see he was ready to deal. He sat down at Phil's desk and asked if I had thought further about what to do on the Enoch case. He said, "You didn't amend the charges and surely you're not going to bring Harney back from Germany."

I didn't realize he was in Germany, thinking that I could get him back from CONUS in short order if the need was really paramount. "I spoke to Major Forsythe and he thinks he can sell two years to the convening authority."

"I don't know," Fred came back, "I was thinking eighteen months. He could go to Leavenworth and serve probably twelve and then go home."

"What the hell, if he can get someone here in Vietnam to attest to his good service the first year, I'll recommend 18 months."

Fred said he would discuss it with his client and see about a witness in extenuation. A few days later, Fred gave me a statement from the battalion XO who endorsed the recommendation for Enoch for a Silver Star. The recommendation was denied after Wilbur took off the first time but apparently he got a Bronze Star for valor even with the AWOLs. How he did that while flagged is anyone's guess. I learned Wilbur got into a firefight during Tet and did a pretty good job stopping a VC company moving on a tanker convoy. Enoch's citation read in part, "His quick thinking and actions thwarted an attack on an outnumbered convoy thereby preventing damage to the convoy and substantial injuries as well as ensuring the delivery of much-needed fuel to the 25th Infantry Division for use during the Tet Offensive."

Fred told me Enoch agreed to the deal.

The convening authority approved the guilty plea to all charges for eighteen months with a dishonorable discharge and total forfeitures. We went to trial in early July, and after hearing a sob story from the battalion XO as to Enoch's hero-ics, and hearing Enoch's unsworn statement about his girlfriend, I gave a tepid explanation of what guys did while AWOL in Vietnam. Fred then put on a pretty good closing argument speaking to valiant service and a lovesick young boy away from home in a combat zone. He talked about the Purple Heart and bleeding for one's country. The court came back with a BCD and a year's confinement. Fred beat the deal and my first case as a prosecutor was a bust. Apparently the court was homesick and they didn't want to waste their time listening to a raw captain telling them what people did in Saigon.

Wilbur was shipped to Leavenworth without getting to say goodbye to Binh or her family. He vowed to himself that he would return when he got out of the Army. When he left Binh the last time her house had a refrigerator, a TV on each floor, and a stereo system with two foot high Sansui speakers. Binh's father had a full bar and took over as papa san to a small drug distribution network that Wil-bur set up in downtown Saigon. Unbeknownst to Wilbur, Binh's brother was a VC leader. Wilbur's constant funds for the family's support and his drug network helped finance an underground VC unit in Saigon and shipped additional funds to Hanoi. Once Binh learned Wilbur was in prison, she set out seeking his replacement.

Quarters in Long Binh

I finally got out of the transient billets and was assigned to a two-story wooden structure with rooms that went the width of the building with screened doors on each side. Walkways were on both sides of the building on both floors. There were no windows, just screens. At night I could see flares light up the perimeter of the camp and could hear the constant comings and goings of helicopters. There was a communal latrine down the hall near stairs that came up in the middle of the building. Mama san's would make your bed and clean your room each day for $2.50 a week. They would shine your boots, wash, starch, and iron your fatigues for another $2. You had to give them the wash powder and starch, readily available from the PX. They spoke no English but could communicate when they needed something. They would qualify things as "Number One" or "Number Ten" meaning really great or horrible. They didn't seem to know any variables between those numbers. My room mate was a Red Cross employee stationed in Vietnam to facilitate soldiers going home on emergency leave and for other Red Cross stuff. He was middle-aged and not very talkative which was fine with me. I told him I was surprised at the prices for the mama sans and he said not to overpay because it would screw up their economy. He related if it were up to the rich American GI's, the mama sans for the officers might make more than the bank officers did in downtown Saigon. Again, there were bath room issues with the mama sans.

Our showers were in the latrine area in the middle of the building and that's where the mama sans would hang out and work on the fatigues in the middle of the day. Normally it was not much of a problem because you were at work all day long. But if for some reason you were at the barracks and had to go during the day, the mama sans would smile at you while washing and pressing clothes in the latrine. They would sit on their haunches in the showers chewing bettle nut and spit the juice on the shower floor. I saw them one day washing a set of fatigues on that same floor by hand. It was better if I hadn't known.

One evening I was reading in my bunk and had an eerie sense someone was staring at me. It was hot and humid as usual and I was naked but for my underpants so I felt a bit self conscious. I looked over my book around the room and then up to the top of my locker on which was perched a mouse-sized roach peering down at me. Before I knew it the damn thing flew right at my face. I jumped to the side, book flying in the air and landed on the floor. The thing was behind the head of my bed on the floor getting ready to take off at me again. It must have been deciding wind vectors. I grabbed the latest edition of the Stars and Stripes to hit it and after a quick look thought maybe I should call in some artillery. Since I had no idea what my coordinates were and besides, as a lawyer I had no idea how to do so, I grabbed the biggest book I had at the time, The Manual for Courts Martial, 1968 Ed. It was too big and inflexible to swing as a weapon so I went for my combat boots. After quite a battle and bruising my knee on the side of the bed, I finally beat the damned thing to death with my left steel-reinforced combat boot. So went my first combat action in Vietnam. Even though injured, I decided it was not enough to report to the First Aid Station. Even though I'd heard of some folks getting a Purple Heart for less, I decided it might be bad Karma for me to test my luck so early in my tour. Maybe if I had only twenty days to DEROS ...

Marcus Jackson; Involuntary Manslaughter

Apparently Forsythe didn't think I'd done such a great job on the Enoch trial. He assigned me again as defense counsel. It, however, was not just any case. It was an involuntary manslaughter charge which was surprising since murder one easily could have been on the table.

Racial tension in Vietnam was a magnification of what was occurring in the United States at the time. The draft was depositing its catch of young American males in Southeast Asia. Since many African American males in 1969, for various social logical reasons, didn't attend institutions of higher learning and get an educational deferral, they were captured by the draft and hauled off into military service in higher percentages of their race than those of their European American brethren. Integration in the late 60's was in its infancy and the military, always slow to change anything, was slow to adjust to racial change. That is not to say that they didn't try. The Army was supposed to be integrated in the Korean conflict but there were many problems in that combat zone. Martin Luther King's assassination in 1968 and the riots that followed opened a preference for overt action by blacks for perceived or real wrongs. It took a while longer for Dr. King's peaceful strategy to grease the integration process in America. With blacks more responsive to racial issues, they looked to each other for support. In Vietnam substantial protocols among African Americans for greeting one another provided moral support but set them apart from whites. Intricate hand gestures were reserved to blacks; the military salute was not something offered readily. This, either intentionally or unintentionally, caused resentment among whites. Such conduct was more evident in the support areas such as Long Binh and headquarters areas in the rear. It didn't work in the jungle where soldiers had to depend on each other. This was a matter of life and death where you couldn't see and couldn't hear the many perils hidden in the thick mass of vines, slime, high grasses, banana plants, and rotten foliage that was everywhere. If a soldier, white or black, couldn't be depended on in the jungle, he didn't last. Both black and white soldiers, officers and enlisted, were depended on for all their military skills in Vietnam and this joint need forged a respect between races that was hardened by jungle warfare. Not just in Vietnam, but in all wars where people of different color fight, race isn't an issue where the fighting takes place. What became difficult for many blacks is that after fighting together with whites for their country in Vietnam, they returned to the United States to find the nation no different from when they left. In 1969 and 1970, they still couldn't get a meal at a diner in Virginia.

Private (E-2) Marcus Jackson and Private First Class Thomas Owings were assigned to menial jobs at the U.S. Army Depot in Long Binh. They loaded trucks going into the field and unloaded trucks coming from ships or planes bringing supplies and materials from America, Australia, and allies in the Pacific. They worked six days a week, twelve hours a day. They were not taught to and did not operate equipment. Their days off would vary. Sometimes they got guard duty which broke the monotony. In the evenings they would join other black soldiers, smoke weed, and drink Schlitz beer. They were bored and not happy with the fortunes of their life. They had seen, been a part of, or heard about riots throughout the U.S. and the year before in the LBJ prison. They staked out a place they considered their own in the Troop Command area where they could smoke and drink without anyone bothering them. The unit officers and NCOs could smell the acrid weed burning but the men reported for duty on schedule and did their jobs so they looked the other way. They did what they were told, maybe not happily and maybe not immediately, but if the supervisors were patient the work would get done and besides, hand grenades were readily available. Privates Jackson and Owings had an attitude. Most knew it and stayed out of their way.

Spec Four Bobby Kichener didn't know it. On May 19, 1969, Ho Chi Minh's birthday, Bobby drove his 5-ton truck from Vung Tau to Long Binh with its load of mobile generators wary of heightened enemy action because of the North Vietnamese hero's anniversary. The convoy had a double MP escort and made the trip with only two incidents. A rocket was fired at the second vehicle in the convoy and overshot its target. The MPs didn't find the shooter and the convoy continued. At an area with dense grasses, palm trees, some old rock walls, and scrub trees on both sides of the road the convoy started to take heavy weapons fire, probably a 50 caliber machine gun. Kichener, one of the better drivers, saw the fire before he hit the ambush zone and pulled his vehicle across the highway to stop what was behind him and provide a protective barrier. The trucks ahead accelerated through the ambush with the only disruptive damage being a shot-away air hose and a severed diesel fuel line. The convoy was held up about forty minutes while the MPs cleared away the ambush site and minor repairs were made to the damaged vehicles. There were four VC casualties and no captured weapons. One driver suffered a nasty burn attempting to fix the air hose.

Bobby was happy to get back to Long Binh. He had 147 days left before his DEROS. A monsoon hit hard after Bobby saw to the unloading of his truck. He went to the Troop Command chow hall for dinner before returning the truck to his motor pool. After dinner he stopped at the command enlisted club for a few beers and then proceeded to get the truck signed in. On the way to the loading area he had to navigate through an area filled with thick oozing mud. He found a jerry-rigged board walk that led by the Jackson/Owings area. He was looking down and slowly finding a board here and there to keep from sinking in the nasty mud when Owings yelled at him, "Yo White Boy. Why don'tcha find someplace else to relieve yoself?"

Bobby, with just enough beer to be bold and a bit belligerent came back, "This looks like the perfect place to squeeze my thing. I think I just might do it here."

Bobby then grabbed at his crotch in a taunting manner and Marcus Jackson told him, "You are in trouble honky and you don't know it."

At that Marcus, having consumed at least six Schlitz beers, along with Owings and two other black soldiers who were smoking weed ran the short distance from the front of their billet and struck Bobby on the face and wherever they could. Marcus struck him hard in the stomach. Bobby bent over, convulsed, and collapsed in a muddy puddle. Someone kicked Bobby in the side a number of times. When Marcus hit him in the stomach, Bobby regurgitated some of his just finished fried chicken and dumplings. Bobby came up from the puddle for a breath of air and inhaled some of the vomit. A piece of chicken caught in his wind pipe and caused him to lose consciousness and die.

Major Forsythe presented me Private Marcus Jackson's file. He said they were planning to try Jackson's case with a PFC Owings who also was involved in the death but the defense made a motion to split and the military judge granted it. Mike King was going to defend PFC Owings and that trial was going first and within the next day or so. King, a senior JAG captain, was the shark of the office. He was close to DEROS and while in Vietnam gained a reputation defending a number of the participants in the LBJ riot, obtaining meager sentences and getting some acquittals. One of his murder cases involved the court-martial of a warrant officer who killed his Vietnamese girlfriend when he surprised her one day while she was earning some extra money from a marine. King got the court to acquit his client under the theory that the murder occurred during an uncontrolled heat of passion. According to King, the heat of passion continued after the warrant left his girl friend's hooch to get his weapon out of the arms room. This took him at least a half hour. Such conduct normally is a clear indication of premeditation. When he returned the marine had already left. The warrant officer, according to King still not understanding what he was doing, shot and killed the girl. The court's acquittal in this case came to be known as the "mere gook rule."

The next morning I visited Private Jackson at the LBJ where he was in pretrial confinement. Jackson was being held in one of the metal Conex containers. It was hot, noisy, and nasty. I was not permitted in to see it. The guards brought Jackson to a conference room, a sad looking space next to the prison admin area. The room had dark metal walls with a door hung onto hinges soldered to the wall, a small wooden table, two straight-back chairs, and a little screened window cut out with left over traces of acetylene burn marks on the metal wall. The window looked out at the muddy entrance to the jail. Waiting for Jackson, I heard an off-hand remark from one of the clerks in the admin area that Jackson was the nigger who killed the white driver and was in the tin can. Some beginning. Marcus was a big, nice-looking, kid. He came bleary-eyed, sweaty, and dirty.

"Sir, I'm sorry that white boy died. I didn't mean to do no killin'. I only hit him one time but he fell and I understand his dinner come up and choked him."

"You are being charged with involuntary manslaughter and intent to kill is not necessary."

"Sir, all of us was sittin' out there drinkin' and smokin'. The monsoons is really bad and the whole place stinks. We got a bad job and the Army's treatin' us like slaves. All we's do is load trucks and labor stuff. I is Eleven Bravo, an infantryman, and I wants to fight. I trained for that, got my profession. I gots some friends whose marines. They in the field where's I want to be. Sir, can Capt'n King defends me?"

I thought he had a pretty good attitude but understood it might be influenced by facing charges for homicide. "I can ask about Captain King but don't think he'll be made available." I didn't tell him it was my first homicide case and that I'd just recently arrived in Vietnam. I think he knew. I went over with him what happened and it pretty much paralleled what the CID reported in the file. "The medical report is that Spec Four Kichener died by getting some vomit caught in his windpipe after he was struck in the stomach. You're right about him vomiting and breathing in his vomit. It was a terrible thing and unusual but precipitated by the attack. There is no evidence in the file that you or anyone planned to kill Kichener. The charge of involuntary manslaughter seems correct and actually more beneficial to you than what might have been charged. The Army is especially sensitive about racial issues. The LBJ riots of a year ago really set things off and four or five blacks ganging up on a white guy doesn't look too good."

Jackson asked, "What can I get for an involuntary killin'?"

"A DD and ten. You have the right to have some enlisted on the court but if you ask for them, they will be senior and I understand the senior enlisted often

are tougher than the officers. I would recommend against that but it's your decision. I have to tell you about it."

I could see he blanched by the realization that he might go to prison for ten
years. "Will they be all white?"

"I don't know. They're not that many senior black enlisted around that I
know of."

"Don't want no enlisted, sir."

"I'll ask about Captain King."

I was visiting the USARV Headquarters about a week later when word came
that Mike King had done it again. The court convicted Owings but retained him
and gave him a year's confinement and a $100 fine each month for a year. When
I got back to the Saigon Support Command Headquarters, Mike was ebullient
but did not speak to me about trial strategy. I had a different military court, the
same judge, and the one who landed the killing blow to defend. King liked being
the top gun. I took Marcus Jackson's request for Mike King as counsel to Major
Forsythe who, as I predicted, said Mike was unavailable. He didn't give me any
reason even though I waited a moment before my next request. I understood
Mike had made allegations in his trial that Marcus was the instigator of the attack
and therefore couldn't defend him. I just wanted to hear it from Forsythe. I asked
him about a deal and he said tersely the command didn't deal on homicide cases.
It was not a collegial visit. The command obviously was embarrassed about the
Owings sentence but found some excuse from the fact that Marcus produced the
hit which precipitated the regurgitation and ultimate death. They were going to
atone for Bobby Kichener's blood with my client's lengthy incarceration. Forsythe was leaving within the next few days and the new SJA was sobering up. Mr.
McCormick, the warrant administrator who met me at the reception station,
whispered that Forsythe was waiting for the end of my trial before he DEROSed.
He said the Old Man, the general who commanded Saigon Support Command,
gave Forsythe a rough time on the Owings sentence. Before lunch, I saw the
major in Captain Shields' little cubicle leaning over Shields and banging his
pointed finger on some paper. Shields was Marcus Jackson's trial counsel.

That afternoon some of the guys in the office wanted to go to a club on the
other side of post where apparently they had a pretty good band. We had dinner
at the hospital mess and piled into the jeep about 2000 hours. The five of us
drove across Long Binh to a club sponsored by the Post Exchange. It got pretty
wild inside after an hour or so. The place was packed with soldiers and civilian
contractors sitting at little tables and standing around in the large room with a
stage up front. There was a long bar on one side with street arrows behind giving

the distances to certain cities in the United States. NYC 8376 miles, and so on. Beer was on sale for fifty cents a can. I didn't see any women other than those on the stage, a group of young Philippine girls with a small band singing stuff from the Top 40's. They did Hey Jude, Born to be Wild, Chain of Fools and lots of other stuff. When they did Fear's mainstay towards the end of their program, everybody joined in at the top of their lungs:

"We gotta get out of this place,
"If it's the last thing we ever do.
"We gotta get out of this place,
"'cause girl, there's a better life for me and you."

We left in a pretty good mood with lots of thoughts of home and the opposite sex. I saw one "round eye" when at USARV headquarters. Seeing a "round eye" was a big deal. She was a legal secretary and not a candidate for any of the girlie magazines on the PX racks but pretty popular nonetheless. It gave some perspective to the Vietnamese girls we saw all the time. The guys talked about the few American women who were in Vietnam with the Red Cross and some contractor women. Nurses were isolated and stayed busy in the hospitals. We didn't see them in Long Binh. Mike King told us a story of a married Army colonel at the USARV headquarters who had an affair with a good looking civilian "round eye". She was a civil service secretary to a general officer. The colonel was sent home and the woman reassigned to Vung Tau where she clerked for a noncommissioned officer.

I spoke to Jackson a few more times. We discussed his pleading guilty and working out an acceptable stipulation of the events and circumstances that might be favorable. Our thoughts were he could look repentant and we would control the picture the jury would hear. I told him not to say anything about the Army treating him like a slave; it would only piss off what I found out was to be a court composed entirely of white officers. Jackson agreed and I took the idea to Shields, the prosecutor, and presented him with our stipulation. It said nothing of Marcus being the one to hit Bobby Kichener in the stomach. We only stipulated that he was one of the four to gang up on Bobby and he only hit him once. Shields read the stipulation and about half way through said, "I don't think so. Gregg, you've got to be kidding. I'm going to put Owings on the stand along with two bystanders who'll say Jackson was the instigator and struck the killing blow."

"I guess that means you don't like our stipulation. Very well, you'll need to prove it."

He had given me a list of witnesses previously but even though I thought he might, I didn't realize he was going after Marcus as the instigator of the attack.

From what Marcus told me, Owings was the first off his chair to go after Bobby and the first to hit him. I figured I'd better go see these witnesses again because Marcus' case would depend on a strong cross examination and I didn't want any surprises. Before I moved out, however, I went back to see Marcus.

"Have you talked to Thomas Owings since his trial?"

"Captain Thompson, I haven't talked to anyone 'cept you since I been in jail."

"What about the prison staff?"

Jackson said, "Oh, they yell at me once a while but no real conversin'. I did talk to guy in cell next to me. He axed what was I in for and I told him murder'in a white boy. He said that was bad and axed if I do it but I tell him I would never do that, I am a church going man." He then smiled at me.

"Do you know where Owings is?"

"I heard he was let out after his court."

"What about the others who were involved in the attack. Where are they?"

"They run as soon as the dude looked bad. I stayed and tried to help him. Thomas walked over to the company and popped another beer. A white dude who was pissin' in a tube sticking out of the ground by a building not too far come runnin' up. When the MPs arrived he pointed to Thomas and me as the culprits."

"But Marcus, where are they now and who are they?"

"They'se gone. I don't want to say who they are. But they'se gone."

I thanked Marcus and went to the admin area. I asked to speak to PFC Owings, a witness in a pending court-martial of which I was defense counsel. They said Owings was under house arrest at his company area.

I went to the Depot area and found PFC Owings. He was in the C Company orderly room sitting back with his feet on the desk next to the company clerk. I asked if we could talk somewhere in private. He nodded and made it an effort to get up.

"PFC Owings, I am Captain Gregg Thompson, Marcus Jackson's lawyer."

"Yea, I heard of you."

"Excuse me. You still are in the Army. It should be 'yes sir'. Is that correct?"

Owings with surprise responded, "OK, yes sir."

"Good, now Marcus told me what he remembers happened to Bobby Kichener. What's your version of what happened?"

"Should I have my lawyer here? *Sir.*"

"Well that's up to you. But as I understand, your court-martial is over and you would only have a lawyer for appeal purposes. The trial counsel in Marcus' case gave me your name as a witness for the prosecution and that means I have a right to talk with you." I didn't tell him that he didn't have to talk to me.

"OK captain, what do you want?"

"First, what happened?"

Owings leaned back in his chair and looked up at the ceiling as he responded, "Well this dude come saunterin' into our area walkin' likes he owns the place. We's been drinkin' some and its real hot and muggy like it gets after the rains. So we's been workin' all day at this shit job and the dude disrespects Marcus."

I asked, "How did he disrespect Marcus?"

"He grabs his crotch and points his thing at Marcus."

"He pointed it at Marcus or did he motion to whoever was with you?"

"Naw, it was just at Marcus. We was standin' around and Marcus yells something at him and he grabs his crotch and Marcus takes off at him. That's how it went down."

"So, Private Owings, you didn't participate?"

"Well I did follow Marcus up to where the dude was and I hit at him and glanced a blow off his shoulder. That's why I got a year."

"PFC Owings, who asked you to testify against Private Jackson and when did they ask you?"

"A couple of days after my trial, Captain King and Captain Shields, the lawyers come to see me. They say it might go easier for me if I told the court in Marcus' case what happened. I didn't testify in my case and gave an unsworn statement later in the trial. Captain Shields said he might get me out of LBJ prior to leavin' for prison if I did a good job testifying and the time would count on my sentence cuz I's restricted."

"Did Captain Shields help you decide what you were going to say in court?" I looked at him hard.

"He like you. He axed what happen and then axed if I were sure about it. That's all the events and who went first and all that stuff. Since I was drinkin' a bit, he helped me out in the way the event played out. But that's what happened."

"What's your relationship with Private Jackson?'

Owings sat up straight, "What's you mean 'relationship'?"

"Was he a buddy, your friend, or just someone who you knew casually because he worked with you?"

"Naw, Marcus my buddy. We met over here but both us are Eleven Bravos, that's what he calls it, and we drink together almost every night."

"Did you know that what you say might cause Private Jackson more time than what you got?"

"I don't think so. That court find me wrong and they gave me a year for hittin' the dude. Marcus hit him and he died from that hit. At least that's what Captain King said."

"Thanks Private Owings. I'll see you in court." I then left.

That night a group of us from the JAG office went to the 24th Evacuation Hospital mess for dinner and a movie after. After a pretty good meal we walked along a corridor that led through some open areas to a hall where they showed just-released movies two or three times a week. About forty post-triage patients were laid out in lines in one of the open areas waiting medical treatment. These were the ones that the triage folks determined would live. The military developed triage into an art during Vietnam. Bloody arms were wrapped up and immobilized, some with plastic air-filled casts; legs were messed up pretty bad, splinted, and with just enough treatment to stabilize the wounds; a few soldiers still in their battle fatigues had chest and stomach wounds; and there were what looked like a number of head traumas. Lots of IV bags hung from mobile hangers with tubes attached to the wounded providing pain killing medicines to alleviate pain. I saw maybe one medic among the group. We could hear choppers coming and going at the hospital helipad. There must have been one hell of a battle somewhere. I felt weak after walking by and my head started swimming. I was cold and the top of my head damp. I went to a stairway around a corner and put my head between my legs for a minute or two before I got up. Not looking back at the injured but with my stomach now a mess, I walked down the corridor to the hall with the movie. We watched Jack Lemmon in April Fools and I went back to my room down and beat.

The next morning I looked up the witnesses on Shields' list thinking it was put together with Forsythe's help. Two white dirt bags pretty much confirmed what Owings said. I asked each privately if the trial counsel promised them anything for their testimony. One said no; the other told me to ask the captain. I then went to find the others in the group that attacked Bobby.

I stopped first at the Company C orderly room to try to determine who else was involved. Owings wasn't there. The clerk, an African American, said, "That Thomas Owings is one bad dude. He started it all."

I asked, "How do you know that and where is he now?"

"He's over at the barracks taking his afternoon nap. That's what I heard."

"What about the other two who were involved in the attack, do you know who and where they are?"

"I'm not sure but I heard a couple of black guys in the field may have been visiting and been with Owings and Jackson at the time."

"Do you know their names and unit?"

"No, it's all rumor anyway."

"What about Marcus, what's his reputation?"

The clerk softened a little and said, "He's a pretty good guy, sir. He's quiet and does his work. He's never been in trouble before that I know of."

"Is there someone you know who might testify for him?"

"He worked for Sergeant Bill Randolph and he might say something good."

"Anyone else you know who might be able to help Marcus. They're trying to paint him as the instigator, the bad guy in the whole thing?"

He looked down and whispered quietly, "Go see Aaron Parks over at Company E. Don't tell him I said anything."

I went to Company C and the first sergeant told me Parks was at Camp Camelot helping to offload some barges that had just come in. I thanked the clerk and started over to Camp Camelot. It's down Highway 1A towards Saigon. The terminal is just across the Newport Bridge and then down around to the foundation for the bridge and about a half mile down a well-packed dirt road. It was about three miles up river from Saigon, and relatively new. There was heavy security. To get in, I had to convince the MP at the gate I was on official duty.

Saigon River with Transports Waiting for Space in Terminal

I found Spec Four Parks taking a break from loading trucks destined for Cu Chi and the 25th Infantry Division. They were carrying Class IV items, primarily lumber and cement. He had a green undershirt tied around his neck, no shirt on, and looked like he rolled in sand. I asked if he was Specialist Parks and could spare a minute. He said he could. I then introduced myself, "I'm Captain Gregg Thompson, the defense counsel for Private Marcus Jackson. He needs your help."

He sat a little straighter from where he had been sprawled out. "What can I do for you Captain?"

"First, do you know Marcus Jackson and Thomas Owings?"

Parks looked carefully at me, "Yea, I know them, captain. They're the colored guys who killed the trucker."

"So you know what happened. Did you see anything?"

"I saw it all. I was taking a piss over next to the area Owings thought was his own. Nobody, especially no white guys, went over that way when he was hanging out. He and a couple of his buddies. They were always looking for trouble but Owings had the big mouth and was the leader."

"What about Jackson?"

Parks replied, "Marcus; he's a pretty good guy. A terrific worker and he don't say too much. He normally didn't hang with those guys. He's not their leader if that's what you mean. But he was there the night it happened."

"Can you tell me what you saw?"

"Well it was real muddy and this guy comes out of the mess hall and looks around a bit. He sees there's lots of mud and his truck's on the other side of the company area. So he follows some boards over the mud and is going by the black guys when he grabs his crotch and waves it at Owings. Owings is a hot head and jumps up and runs for the guy, through the mud and everything. It looked like he was possessed or something. I remember he didn't have his shirt on and the mud and water were splashing up as he ran. It happened pretty quick. Two other guys run out as well and Marcus, I guess joined in the melee."

"What do you mean, you guess?"

"I saw him hesitate at first but his buddies ran out fast and he was left alone so I guess he just followed them. The white guy was down after being hit and kicked a bunch and I saw Marcus go up to him, lean down, and hit him in the stomach like he had to be a part of the gang and then back away. The guy started choking and trying to spit. Two of the guys, I don't know them; I think they were from some other unit; anyway, they run away and Marcus leans over the guy and tries to help him. Thomas pushes Marcus down in the mud and says leave him alone but Marcus starts shaking the guy and trying to get him to breathe. I zip myself up and run over to help but the guy is turning blue and passes out. I yell for someone to help and Owings takes off but Marcus stays there to do what he can. It happened pretty fast. A bunch of guys come around, and after what seemed forever, a medic comes in an ambulance and the MPs follow right behind. Marcus got the medics to look at the trucker's throat but it was too late. I told the MPs what happened and Owings started it all. They went over to his hooch and arrested him then came back and arrested Jackson. I gave them a statement later that night."

"Did you testify in the Owings case?"

"No sir, no one asked me to. No."

"Have any other lawyers spoken to you about testifying in Marcus' case?"

"You're the first one to come by. I've been in the field doing some convoy escort stuff but generally, I've been here."

I thanked Spec Four Parks and asked if he would testify in Marcus' trial and tell the court what he told me. He said he needed to talk with the first sergeant but that thought it would be ok. I told him I would speak to the first sergeant and would be in touch.

I got one of Marcus' supervisors to testify that he was dependable and responsible and that he wanted him back on the job. I called his mom and asked if she could come to the trial. She declined. The whereabouts of his father were not known. The mother sent a letter saying Marcus was a good boy and never got in trouble.

We went to court on schedule. I got Marcus cleaned up and in a starched and proper uniform. His boots had the high shine I've never been able to replicate. He looked sharp. The prosecution started with the dirt bags. Both were in filthy sun-bleached fatigues with scuffed up boots and looked like they hadn't had a bath in weeks. On cross, one admitted he was up for possession of drugs but Captain Shield's told him if he testified he would only get a letter in the CO's desk drawer. The other was pretty surly and didn't offer much. Owings followed Shields' lead in such a manner that his being coached was obvious. I still hammered at him especially with his preferential treatment since being convicted. He hadn't worked since his trial and he made the decision to testify in Marcus' case after his trial and right before he was let out of LBJ. The Court seemed especially interested when I pounded on the fact that all Owings did after his trial was wait around in the company area. Shield's introduced Bobby's autopsy report and had a doctor testify as to the causality of the hit and Bobby's death.

I asked for a directed verdict after the prosecution rested but the military judge denied my motion. I put Parks on the stand knowing his testimony would implicate Marcus but after the judge's ruling I knew that the prosecution had made its case. Parks was super, not too pushy, just matter of fact with lots of concern. He noted Marcus was not the bad guy and avoided pointing his finger at Owings but I got across that he felt Owings was the instigator. He clearly repudiated Owings statement that Marcus was the first to go after Bobby Kichener. He also made Marcus look good in attempting to care for Bobby after he realized Bobby was seriously injured. I got the medic who came to the scene and he said Marcus never left Kichener and tried to help him. I held my other two witnesses, Sergeant Randolph, Marcus' supervisor, and the company clerk for extenuation and mitigation in order for them to testify Marcus had never been in trouble and was a pretty good guy.

The judge advised the court they did not have to find intent to kill to find involuntary manslaughter. He said all it had to do for a guilty finding was to find the accused committed an offense against the victim and that offense led to or was a cause of the victim's death. He also instructed that striking the victim against his will could be such an offense. The court returned in about an hour with a guilty verdict. The extenuation and mitigation phase of the trial started immediately after the verdict. I introduced the letter from Marcus' mother and had Marcus' boss and the company clerk testify. Marcus then testified under oath as to what happened. He admitted he hit Bobby and was terribly sorry. He said he didn't like hanging around with PFC Owings but nothing else was going on. He came off well but I knew courts didn't give too great a credence to an accused being sorry after getting caught and convicted. Shields asked for ten years and a dishonorable discharge. I asked for retention and strong consideration for a light sentence. I was worried but felt I had done all I could. Again the court was not out very long, maybe 90 minutes.

I stood next to Marcus and the President of the Court, its most senior member, a colonel, read the sentence. "This court in secret session with two-thirds of its members concurring hereby sentences you for killing Specialist Four Bobby Kichener without intent to confinement at hard labor for twelve months, forfeiture of $100 pay per month for twelve months, and reduction to the lowest enlisted grade."

I listened for the type of discharge and there was none. It was the same sentence Owings got. Owings sentence was never mentioned in Marcus' trial but the court had to have known. It was a big win for me and bigger for Marcus Jackson who was facing ten years in prison.

Owings was given an administrative discharge from the military after serving nine months at Leavenworth. Marcus Jackson served six months and was returned to Vietnam in late 1970 where he was assigned to the 25th Infantry Division as an 11 Bravo. While searching for weapons and NVA supplies in Cambodia, he was struck by remnants of a rocket propelled grenade and lost his left eye. Marcus was sent home the second time with a Bronze Star Medal for valor and a Purple Heart.

Extra War Zone Duty

Staff officers at Headquarters, Saigon Support Command, performed inspection duty for the troops standing guard at the various towers surrounding Long Binh. In our area, the compound was secured by a new fence and a perimeter complex involving an area of concertina wire in front of an eight foot wall of black dirt interspersed with machine gun bunkers and backed by lookout towers. The concertina wire had tin cans with metal objects hung at various places so they would rattle when shaken. Someone attempting to low crawl through the wire had to avoid moving it. Once warned by the tin jingle, those in the towers and the machine gun bunkers could see what was going on. The VC frequently attempted to breach Long Binh security in the early years of its development, but in our newly enhanced security line there were few incidents. My job was to inspect four towers in that sector. I was to ensure the guards were there, alert, and that they knew their jobs. A number of JAGs bitched they were legal professionals and this wasn't part of their duty. They didn't complain, however, about receiving combat pay.

An MP briefed me on the night's password and countersign. It changed daily. The pass word for my inspection night was "Cincinnati" and the countersign was "Reds". I had a jeep and driver that took me out to the towers, maybe fifty feet high, with an enclosed shack at the top. If an attack occurred, it was not too safe a place to be. A simple charge at the tower footing would give the shack's occupants a bad evening and any occupant would make an easy target while climbing up or attempting to get down. On the other hand, it posed a deadly threat to anyone attempting to get through the wire and over the dirt berm. If I were assigned a guard position in one of those towers, I would ensure I kept awake and alert on my watch. Surprisingly, there were incidents of guards falling asleep on duty in the towers; I didn't want to find any or surprise someone armed and possibly aiming their weapons down at me. Besides, I'm afraid of heights. I don't mind being in a closed airplane a mile or two in the sky but fifty feet straight up dangling on a ladder at night is pretty scary. It might be even more so in daylight and I guess that's why they say don't look down.

I arrived on foot at the bottom of the command bunker. It looked out to the dirt wall and fence line. I had on a steel helmet and a protective bullet-proof vest and was wearing a combat belt with a canteen and first aid kit. I had an empty holstered 45 with two loaded clips on my belt. I started climbing up the tower and made sure to hit my helmet on a rung whenever possible. I was not quiet and a bit scared. Eventually, about twenty feet off the ground someone leaned out at the top and yelled down, "Who's there."

I held on tight and responded, "I'm Captain Thompson, the Inspector of the Guard."

"What's the password?"

My mind went blank. A town, Ohio, what the hell was it. Where's the rung. I swung my arm around it and looked up trying to keep my helmet on. Toledo? I yelled, "Toledo."

The tone from above me changed, "Nope, that ain't it captain. Try again."

Finally it came to me as I gripped the steel ladder a bit tighter. "Cincinnati."

"OK, that's it. Nice try captain. But we know the password."

They thought I was testing them. Phew. "And the countersign?"

"Reds. Come on up Captain."

"Thanks."

I climbed the rest of the way up and never looked down but already worried about my descent. The ladder reached to the rear of the shack so you had to swing off across an open space into an open doorway. The open space was wide enough for me to fall through even with all the gear on. Nothing was below except a hard ground fifty feet or more straight down. But a fall would not be straight. I probably would bang into the tower structure along the way; not that I was thinking about the possibility of falling or anything. When I tumbled awkwardly into the shack, the guys up there looked alert and sharp. I told them I was a lawyer and this was my first time in a guard tower. They seemed to know and showed me around. They demonstrated their field radio worked by calling the Command Post. They let me look through the star-light scope. There was a small village nearby and they monitored the goings on there. During Tet 1968, a bunch of NVA staged in a small hamlet just outside the base perimeter called Widows' Village. They waited for their surprise attack on the II Field Force Headquarters located at the other side of post from where I was. The widows were surviving spouses of South Vietnamese soldiers and received a small pension from the Vietnamese government. They earned extra money filling sand bags for soldiers at Long Binh and hosted the NVA when they needed someplace near the post to stay. While the guards held up the North Vietnamese attack on their perimeter with machine gun and rifle fire, Company B of the 4th Battalion, 39th Infantry, and a recon platoon of another 9th Infantry Division battalion, came to their aid with a combat assault just inside the Long Binh perimeter near the II Field Force headquarters. The 9th was headquartered at Bearcat, not far away. These units went through the Widow's Village I could see through the star-light scope in a hard fought battle clearing it out. Fifty NVA were killed and the 9th lost four of its own. The Village was decimated.

It paid to monitor the goings on of those houses close to the perimeter. I saw the greenish image of an old papa san walking down a path through the scope and had a good look at some nearby shacks. I then looked down at the concertina wire and focused in on each little piece of trash amidst the razor wire. There were no sappers or VC. But they were out there. With our new perimeter security system and the decimation of their forces at Tet the previous year the few remaining VC and the North Vietnamese infiltrators resorted to shooting rockets into Long Binh. They were playing with us, letting us know they were there and that we didn't control the night. The guard towers were supposed to look out for such shenanigans and also for any military activity by the NVA, more active throughout South Vietnam after Tet.

Getting down actually was not as bad as going up, except for getting on the ladder. Swinging myself out over that open space to catch the correct rung made my heart pump a little quicker. My other three climbs were uneventful. I made a good bit of noise on each ladder and all the guards appeared happy I was there, interested, and that someone cared. I remembered the password and with each climb became more comfortable. I was glad it was dark and I couldn't see down. Only the command bunker had a starlight scope. One of the bunkers had a faulty screen in the front opening that worried its occupants. It couldn't stop an incoming rocket. They all wanted starlight scopes. They all were alert and competent. I made note of their requests in my inspection report and didn't report on forgetting the pass word. I don't think anyone knew except me. I felt safe when it was over primarily because it was over but also because I saw and felt confident with my security system.

Billy Hucks; Are We Winning?

I received a letter from my mother that a second cousin from Columbia, South Carolina, would be in Saigon for a short period in the next couple of weeks. She suggested I show him around if I thought it safe. I didn't know him but had heard of the family on my grandfather's side. She wrote he was Billy Hucks and was a third mate on a merchant ship transporting supplies to Saigon. I checked with a friend from the 4th Transportation Command. He told me Hucks' ship would be in town in about ten days. I had been to Saigon a few times but it always made me uneasy. There were stories of GI's resting their arms on open windows of vehicles stopped in heavy traffic or at stop lights when a Vietnamese on a bicycle or scooter would ride beside the vehicle and swipe his hand down the resting arm taking the GI's watch as he zoomed by. The thief then would race off into heavy traffic and through the warrens of the crowded city never to be seen again. There was substantial traffic all over Saigon.

I requested the office jeep and went down to the port to find my cousin. I met Billy and he was surprised and excited about a chance to get off the ship. He was confined for security purposes but I told him it was safe and if he could get off I could show him a bit of Saigon and take him to a Chinese restaurant McCormick told me about. Billy introduced me to his Master. I asked if he and Billy could accompany me for dinner in town. He declined but allowed that Billy could go. Billy had heard of our side of the family but didn't know I was a lawyer and in Vietnam.

When we got to the jeep Billy said, "OK Gregg, let's cut the crap about dinner and get some booze and pussy. The guys on the ship say Tu Do Street is where the action is."

"Well Billy, you can certainly find some trouble on Tu Do Street. I told my boss I was just using the jeep to go to dinner but a cocktail before can't be too great a diversion. I sort of thought we could get a nice dinner in Cholon."

"Maybe later. Let's get a drink and see what the girls have to offer."

I started to wonder what I had gotten myself into but decided to ride with the punches at least for awhile. I looked at a little map I had of Saigon and figured how to get to Tu Do Street. I was a little apprehensive because I had no weapons and the place was packed. We found this nasty little street loaded with strip joints and skinny little bars. I parked the jeep and locked it, checking by pulling the chain to make sure it was all secure. I was chained it to a thick stake embedded in a little cut between two heavy pieces of concrete. When we started off on the wide sidewalk this old papa san came over and said "Dai We, I got good girl, Number 1 all the way."

"Not right now old man."

"You want young boy?"

I ignored him and we walked down the street. It was noisy with music coming from the bars and bouncers outside the doors soliciting people to come in. As we were walking, Billy saw a little table with an umbrella over it just outside a bar. Behind the table sat a middle-aged Vietnamese in a nice looking white shirt who was conducting some kind of business. The bouncer from the bar stood next to the table. I didn't at first see the sign that said "Change Money-Best Rates in Saigon."

Billy went over and pulled out a wad of green backs. He was in line behind a GI who was conducting some business. I followed him over and pulled him away saying, "Billy, it's unlawful to have dollars in Saigon. We use piasters or MPC."

He said, "Well here I am and I'm getting rid of some of the dollars so I won't be so much unlawful Mr. Lawyer. What the fuck is MPV?"

"It's MPC and it's local military scrip but if you change dollars you can get a good rate. Dollars especially are valuable."

He went over to the man. "What do I get for $50."

"How about 21,000 p?"

Billy looked at me and I told him it was a nice but expensive exchange. I told him to ask for 500 more. He asked for 700 more and ended up getting 21,300. I figured dinner was on him. I told Billy, "Now we need to go someplace else and fast. Everyone in that bar saw what you did and they'll pick your pocket or harass the hell out of you until you spend some of it on them."

He put the piasters and about $100 in his pants pocket and buttoned a flap over the pocket. Billy said, "They teach you that at the Merchant Marine Academy."

We walked about three-quarters of a block further and he found a bar he found promising. It had a picture of a naked girl bending over in neon lights, moving up and down. When we walked in, several girls swarmed all over the both of us. I felt someone grab me; I was hoping it wasn't the young boy the Papa San asked about. Then some young girl, heavily made up, winked and pushed up against me. I told her not tonight honey. I looked over and Billy already was sliding into a booth across from the bar with a girl right behind. She yelled something in Vietnamese at the bar tender and in a minute another girl brought drinks to his booth. I ordered a beer and stood at the bar listening to the Shirelles singing over the bar's loud Hi Fi system, Dedicated to the One I Love. The girls let me alone and glanced out the door for new prey. When someone entered, they would swarm like bees over a discarded half-eaten, rotting piece of fruit. The place was moderately crowded, almost entirely with GI's sitting at the bar or in booths along the wall. I was a bit embarrassed because I had on fatigues and anyone could see I was an officer. After about 15 minutes, Billy got out of the booth and said, "OK, now that's taken care of, let's go to dinner."

"With all that "p" you're buying."

"OK with me. I still have 16,500 piasters."

When we got to the jeep, it looked like some one had fiddled with the chain. The jeep otherwise was not disturbed. I found the restaurant in Cholon and again, secured the jeep, this time on an iron bar just outside the restaurant. Billy asked while we were having our dinner of deep fried squid with plum sauce and cao lau, a pork and shrimp dish with wide noodles and sesame cake, "What do you think about how long you're gonna be here? It seems we should be clearing out pretty soon."

I replied, "What do you mean. We have things under control. There's still some fighting we need to clean up in the jungle and throughout the delta. Also there are some problems up country. It's no longer just the VC. They've been hurt pretty badly. The regulars from the North are taking their place. The North Vietnamese Army continues to send supplies and troops down the Ho Chi Minh trail but we're hitting them hard and before long, they'll either run out of gas or tire of the effort."

"That's not what I hear. It's my understanding the North is just beginning and they have unlimited resources from Russia and China. I hear we can't stop them even with our napalm and B-52 carpet bombing. The papers report when we take out a bridge, the next day another's up and the supplies keep coming."

I said proudly, "Well we beat the shit out of them at Tet and it was their biggest effort to date. Christ, they sent everything they had and still couldn't get control over anything."

My cousin continued, "Well last year Cronkite said we should negotiate a settlement. He said we were mired in a stalemate and the honorable thing was to negotiate or something like that."

"I don't think Walter understood what we won at Tet. First of all, when the VC took control of anything they'd kill all the civilians who opposed them or even supported the South. Just like Stalin. In Hue the communists sought out the civilian bureaucracy for the city and killed them all throwing their bodies in ditches. They put all the Catholics they could find in a church and murdered them all. These were civilians, not people under arms. We kicked these assholes out of Hue and the other cities they tried to take over which included most of the major cities in the south."

"The press doesn't dwell too much on that. They showed TV footage of the American bloodshed in Hue and what the fighting did to our guys. It was terrible. The marines really took it on the chin."

I told him about Father McGonical, my high school teacher who was killed at Hue. "Actually the marines did pretty well. They minimized their losses with substantial artillery fire and pinpoint bombing. The ARVN commander at Hue before Tet apparently saw or knew about the NVA troops coming and he put up token resistance. He may have been in cahoots with the NVA for all I know. He said later he was attempting to trap them but they took over the ancient Citadel, a two square mile complex of an Imperial Palace surrounded by a thick wall and then played havoc with the local populace. The marines through determined and persistent house-to-house fighting that went from street to street eventually kicked the commies out. They were unbelievable. You don't want to get into a fight with a bunch of American marines. The NVA used civilian hostages as shields, killing many before running back into the jungle. Many Buddhists supported the NVA but after the marines were done, they split or took a new tack. We drove the enemy out of well-entrenched fortifications where they had Buddhist support and committed atrocities. The thing is the commie true colors came out at Hue and a lot of Vietnamese seeing what they would do if they took overall control came over to support us and the South. The press didn't report much of that."

"Bullshit. I hear the South lost heart after Tet. A lot of ARVN soldiers think Westmoreland knew about it and let the NVA troops into Saigon right before the attacks. The press reported he also had advance notice and didn't reinforce his security or pay attention to all his electronic eavesdropping supposedly surrounding Saigon and the American bases. Or is that just a ploy, there really are no surveillance devices. Anyway, his general in charge of securing the area moved troops from the Cambodian border before the attacks because he suspected something was going on."

"Well the military won in Saigon. The Marine guards at the American Embassy along with a few MPs killed nineteen sappers who blew up the barriers outside the Embassy and stopped a major attack that outnumbered them. We also kicked the VC out of the radio station and with ARVN help secured the Presidential Palace and the ARVN military headquarters. The VC set up in Cholon and we kicked them out of there as well as the race track, a cemetery, and wherever else they thought they could hide. They didn't control anything very long. You also don't hear about the ARVN troops kicking VC ass at their military academy and the Pasteur Institute in Dalat. The staffers at MACV even got into the action."

"They needed reinforcements but the communists took over Cholon for quite a while."

"Billy, they had control for a short period. We're having dinner in Cholon now. We have driven the enemy out and it's safe. We have control."

"You said you were a lawyer."

I told him, "You know probably the more important victory at Tet was Khe Sanh"

"Khe Sanh was a tough fight. So, big deal." He started to look tired.

"More than just big deal. Khe Sanh was just like Dien Bien Phu with the French. It would have been a psychological win. It was isolated by being far from its supply points and had a number of fire bases and listening posts surrounding it. The same general who outlasted the French at Dien Bien Phu, an old guy named Giap, is the person who planned the Tet offensive. He used massive artillery followed up by attacks from waves of hidden infantry against the French. He knocked out the supporting bases, one by one until he hit the main base and the French surrendered. But at Khe Sanh, the Americans learned from the French mistakes at Dien Bien Phu, and even with the weather against them, we continued supplies and B-52 air attacks, many dropping napalm and bombs almost on top of their spotters. The North Vietnamese finally were trounced and had to pull back. It let Brother Giap know he wasn't playing with the French. His war was with the United States. His loss there let him know he couldn't win a military victory against determined American forces, many draftees like me."

"So we won at Hue, Saigon and Khe Sanh, and I admit, that's pretty impressive. Have the North Vietnamese gone away, Gregg?"

"No, now they're the ones doing the primary fighting in the south, not so much the VC. But it's hit and run and not many all out enemy battles. But more important, we have control over the major cities and we'll get the NVA before too long. If the fuckin' press would leave us alone, we could wrap it up."

He glanced out at the darkened street and said, "And you still don't own the night or the jungles do you?"

"We're getting there. If we had some political will in Washington like our military will as demonstrated at Tet, we probably could go into North Vietnam and snuff out the enemy headquarters, their supplies, and hopefully Uncle Ho, himself."

He said, "And bring in the Chinese. That's all we need. Cronkite was correct, we're mired."

"We might be mired, but our guys won already. Hell, we beat the shit out of them wherever they fought and we're winning against the terrorists."

My cousin then hit a nerve. "It seems you're not just winning the war against the VC but the South Vietnam civilian population as well. What about Mai Lai? Didn't some Army fuckups shoot up a village and kill a bunch of women and children. I'm sure the Vietnamese love that."

"I'm not really all that up on Mai Lai. I've been here while it's been breaking and I'm certain if such an atrocity as Time magazine described really occurred just after Tet, it pales in comparison to what the North Vietnamese did at Hue and what they've done throughout the south."

"Gregg, you say lots of people in the south now support the effort because of what the commies did, but it looks like American troops have committed some pretty nasty things themselves. And I understand the South Vietnamese Army are no saints either. Some general shot a purported VC right on the streets. You could see his brains being blown out. I still think we're mired. Anyway, I've had enough of this foreign food and think it's time for some more pussy."

"Billy, any war is terrible. The thing is we can win this thing militarily. Even without going into the North, eventually we'll stop the harassment by the VC."

"And at what cost Gregg? What's it worth to us? Anyway Gregg, enough. Where's the pussy?"

He made me think and I was tired. "I don't know Billy, but I've got to get back."

I took him to his ship and said my good bys. He gave me the rest of the "p" and told me to get it back to him in dollars when I came to visit Columbia. I told him, "Billy, it's been great meeting you. I'm not sure when I can get to Columbia. Hell, I've never even been to Charleston. I'll be here awhile so when you get back on your next trip, it's my treat."

"For an Army guy, Columbia's great. There's Fort Jackson and for a bachelor the girls at USC can't be beat. Besides, my mom's got a great house in Forest Lake right near the camp. Get stationed in South Carolina, they love the military there. You'd fit right in. And after this trip, the merchant union has me off for awhile and then I hope to hit an African run. I don't think I'll be coming back here."

I said goodbye and told him to watch out for the girls in Morocco. I was a little more apprehensive on my drive back to Long Binh than I thought I would be. I started to think maybe I was becoming a little militant.

I visited the unit historian and checked what he had for the statistics for Tet. They reported the combined North Vietnamese and Viet Cong offensive killed 1536 U.S. troops and wounded 7764 others. Eleven were missing in action. The South Vietnamese Army lost 2788 killed and had 7764 wounded with 587 gone missing. The figures for the enemy were estimated at 45,000 killed and wounded. The U.S. and South Vietnamese took 6991 of the enemy prisoner. It was the greatest offensive the North had as of that time and showed the enemy's resolve to join the North and South into one communist state. The U.S. military was fantastic in its quick and competent reaction to the fighting. The U.S. rejected the NVA's offensive and the NVA failed to achieve its military and political objectives. There was no chance for U.S. political involvement. It happened too fast.

Private First Class Ed Bond; Premeditated Murder

Major Forsythe gave me a new file and said he would be leaving soon. The SJA, LTC Tom Cassidy, was on his way. Forsythe said I was trial counsel on a premeditated murder charge. An ammo clerk killed a fellow worker who was asleep in his bunk. Phil Smith would defend.

Ed Bond was born into a family of six that lived in a lower middle class neighborhood in Atlanta. He had two brothers and two sisters. His mother worked most of the day in a deli making sandwiches and cutting meat. She would go into work once the kids were off to school and come home in the late afternoon, usually around 5 P.M. She sliced her hands and fingers numerous times but never lost a finger. When she wasn't home, Rebecca, the oldest girl, at nine, took care of Rachel, her little sister, who was five. The two boys, Philip and Sam, were eleven and eight, respectively, and able to take care of themselves. The father worked in a metal fabricator works and when Ed was born was doing double shifts fabricating machine parts for use in a new cannery. The family was fairly well off with a three bedroom house and a Ford Fairlane station wagon. They made regular payments on both. Ed was a surprise and upset the family equilibrium. Philip and Sam shared one bedroom and the girls the other. The parents had a bathroom next to their room and Ed moved in with them. They couldn't afford a new house.

On Ed's third birthday his mother moved Philip, now fourteen, into an area in the basement the Dad had cleared out. It was an imposition for him to come up to the second floor to go to the bathroom and the basement was a bit damp, but the arrangement worked. The parents put Ed into the room with Sam, now eleven. The Dad said Ed was too old to stay with in the parent's room; it was time to get out. The boys weren't happy with the new arrangement and took it out on Ed. It was his fault and if he'd never been born, everything would have been ok. Rebecca and Rachel followed suit and blamed everything on little Ed. The kids teased him unmercifully and the parents didn't come to Ed's aid even when he came crying. Sam especially was mean. He would hit Ed on his upper arms with a knuckle causing bruising, trip him when he wasn't looking, drop things on him, and steal his food. Ed got mad and had numerous temper tantrums but the kids learned to ignore them and the parents sent him to bed crying.

When Ed turned five, Sam was almost 14 and hated Ed. He continued to hurt him and while Sam never caused any serious injuries, he frequently terrorized Ed with physical beatings and mental torment. Their mother thought everything was fine and got away from it all in her deli job. Ed never obtained any help from either parent when he complained and the girls lived their own lives. One night while Sam was sleeping Ed took an iron rabbit the father had made and brought home from his shop for use as a door stop and swung it down as hard as he could on Sam's head. Sam never awakened. It was a horrible tragedy for the family and Ed had to go to a doctor twice a week and demonstrate how to play with other children and tell what he saw in abstract pictures. Ed's mother had to quit her love in life, her job. She blamed Ed and never showed much affection after the tragedy; she just tolerated him. Ed now was in his own room and Philip joined the marines.

When Ed entered high school, he garnered a reputation as someone who would never give in. He just wouldn't bend and would do anything to win. In the 7th grade he bit a kid's ear so violently that the kid had to have surgery for its repair. In the 8th grade he was on the bottom in a fight with a bigger boy pounding on him. He grabbed an iron pipe and hit the kid in the head knocking him out. Fortunately the kid lived. No one bothered Ed after that.

In high school Ed had few friends. His mother went back to work and Ed came and went as he pleased. She didn't attend Ed's graduation after which he spoke to a marine recruiter and said he wanted to sign up. Philip found out and called the recruiter. The marines rejected him. Ed then volunteered for the Army and ended up as a PFC in a logistics position in Vietnam with the 54th Ordnance Company (Ammo) (Direct Support/General Support) 3d Ordnance Battalion (Ammo).

Ed developed a friendship with a coworker, Spec Four Arthur Brook. He and Arthur completed a tour of extra duty that entailed two days of four hours on and four hours off guard duty and had a day off to recuperate from the exhausting duty before going back to work. They prepared ammunition requisitions and managed ammo distribution. On the day off, they played some small stakes stud poker with some other off duty guys. Arthur got Ed to fold two pair when he held a pair of kings. Arthur took in $2.40. Another hand went by in which Arthur ended up with a full house and Ed had two pair, queens and tens. Arthur increased his bet to make the pot worth $3.25, most of it Ed's money, before the call revealed Arthur's win. Ed was out of money and pissed. He called Arthur a cheat and a lot of other nasty things. Arthur ignored Ed's accusations, said he had enough, and went to bed.

Bond wrote a note and put it on his bedside table.

"I am sorry for what I have to do but I've had enough of Arthur's crap. I love my sister, Rachel, and I wish her well. Ed."

Ed then went to the 54th Ordnance Company Arms Room, signed out an M14 rifle, requisitioned some bullets, loaded the gun, walked back from the arms room to the barracks, where a few people, to include Auther Brook, were lying in their bunks, walked over to Brook's bunk, and shot the sleeping Arthur Brook twice in the head killing him instantly. It was 1700 hours. Ed then went over to his bunk and lay down while holding his rifle next to him. Those who were awakened by the shots called the MPs.

I thought it would be an easy case of premeditated murder. The MPs found the note and the CID determined it was in Ed Bond's handwriting. I got the Arm's Room sign out sheet with Bond's name on it. It contained the date and time he checked out the weapon. The MP first on the scene said Bond gave him the rifle when asked to. It had been recently fired. Two brass jackets were found near Brook's bunk and the firing pin marks matched Bond's M-14. I had witnesses to the argument at the poker game and to Bond taking out the weapon. I had the investigating CID agent's testimony as to the weapon and the MP's testimony as to the note and the scene in general to include the smoking M-14. I had a witness who woke up at the rifle's blast and smelled cordite. He would testify he saw Bond walk over to his bunk with rifle in hand after the shots and lay down. It was an open barracks and there was smoke in it. I had photos of the bloody corpse and an autopsy report that the shot was the cause of death. I didn't have a witness who saw the shooting and Bond refused to make any statements. The Article 32 Investigation proceeded without any input by the defense and I gave Phil a list of my witnesses and what I intended to introduce. Phil requested to bring Bond's mother to testify from his home in Kentucky. I didn't object. The 54th Commanding Officer, Captain Joe Pang, called and told me Phil Smith, requested him to testify at the trial. I asked about what and he said Phil just asked him to be there. Pang had sworn out the charges against Bond. In the military justice system, someone has to initiate the proceedings and this normally is done by the unit commander. He formally swears out specific violations of the UCMJ written on a charge sheet but anyone subject to the Code can swear out charges against anybody else subject to the Code.

We went to court and Bond pled not guilty to premeditated murder but guilty to the lesser included offense of voluntary manslaughter. After I put on my case, Bond testified in his defense. "It was an accident. I didn't intend to shoot Arthur. I just wanted to scare him. He had been giving me some guff and just beat me at poker. Nothing to do no killing for. Simple stuff. Arthur was my buddy."

Phil asked, "Just how did it happen?"

"I got my weapon to clean it and get it in good shape after our guard duty. I didn't have nothin' else to do so I figured this was as good a time as any to clean it up. Well I see Arthur lying in bed and I goes over to his bunk playing with him a bit. I thought I could scare him and maybe he would lay off me a while. Well, I'm waving the rifle around and it goes off and hits Arthur in the head. It was an accident."

Phil asked a bunch of stuff about how Ed never was in trouble before and then looked at me and said, "Your witness."

"PFC Bond, the autopsy report shows that there were two shots that hit Specialist Four Brook in the head. If you were just waving it around, how did you shoot twice, both killing shots to the head?"

"Sir, it's hard to believe but it was an accident. I know I pointed it at Arthur but not to shoot him. I just was trying to scare him."

"A note was left beside your bed stating you were sorry for what you were about to do. Was that your note?"

"Yes sir, that was mine. It meant I was sorry about using the M-14 to scare Brook. I was sorry and mad, but nothing mad enough to kill for."

"After you shot him what did you do?"

"I was in shock, sir. I went over to my bed and lay down." I didn't ask him anything else.

Phil called Bond's CO, Joe Pang. "What kind of soldier was PFC Ed Bond?"

Pang testified, "He was above average. I was his senior rater once and he had a good enlisted efficiency report."

"Did you know him personally?"

"Well I knew him as a member of my team. He seemed like a pretty good kid."

"What did you think when you heard about the shooting?"

"I was surprised, especially because I thought PFC Brook and PFC Bond were good friends."

Phil motioned with his hand that it was my turn. I asked, "Did you swear out the court-martial charges for premeditated murder against PFC Bond?"

Pang answered my cross examination, "Yes sir, I did."

"Why did you charge him with premeditated murder?"

"From reviewing the file your office sent over, it looked like Bond thought about killing Brooks before he did it." Phil jumped up and objected but it was too late. The judge over ruled the objection telling Phil he had opened that door. Phil's use of Pang back-fired. It was a risky play.

In closing, Phil made a fairly convincing argument that Bond didn't intentionally kill Brook. He told the court to examine the incongruity of Bond intentionally killing his work mate and close friend and he pushed reasonable doubt on Bond's intentions to such an extent that I couldn't be sure the VC didn't kill Brook. In my closing rebuttal I hammered hard on the note, Bond signing out the weapon, and each of the two shots hitting Brook in the head. The court came back in two hours with its finding of guilty to the charge of premeditated murder.

Bond's mother cried out loud at the finding and was in tears and unable to testify in the extenuation and mitigation phase of the trial. The judge wanted to give her some time to compose herself but she just waved at him handkerchief in hand. The court, having found Bond guilty of premeditated murder, could only give him life imprisonment; their discretion for punishment with such a finding is life or death and the case was not tried as a capital or death case. I said nothing in the punishment phase. The court had some discretion regarding the type of discharge. They gave Bond a bad conduct rather than dishonorable discharge, the lesser of the two. The mother who had come to Vietnam must have helped a bit with her emotional outburst in what was an inconsequential issue for a sentence of life imprisonment. I was told that life at that time meant Bond had to serve twenty years in prison before he would be eligible for parole. As Bond was led out of the courtroom in hand cuffs his mother refused to look at him. Ed Bond didn't show any emotion. He just walked past his sobbing mother who had her head down with her back to him.

Full Docket

In mid July all hell broke loose. The SJA gave me three cases to prosecute. One was for a major who first conspired with a Vietnamese to sell a jeep, and then exceeded his ration of purchasing dollar instruments in a month. We also charged him for unlawfully fraternizing with an enlisted male but I thought with better investigation, we might have gotten more out of that relationship. He was a real beaut. My second case was for four specifications of money laundering. My last case was a sodomy involving a private (E-2) forcing a PFC to have oral sex over a three month period and then attempting to extort $200 by stating he would tell everybody his victim liked to give blow jobs. Only when the accused wanted money did the victim, a mental category IV, go to the MPs. Cat IVs were allowed in the military as a test and to help in the push for a larger Army to fight the war. The Cat IVs basically were slow.

I worked out a deal on the money laundering case with Bill Combs, a new defense counsel in the office. The accused already had a previous special court-martial for the same thing. The idea of MACV Directive 37-6 for which he was accused of disobeying was to keep dollars from reaching the North Vietnamese and to keep the Vietnamese economy stable. GIs could go into Saigon and the rest of Vietnam and spend piasters or what the troops called "p". As my cousin Billy Hucks found out, the rate was 118 "p" for $1 MPC but on the open market a soldier could get 4300 "p" for twenty military payment certificates and for $20 a supercharged amount of 8600 "p". Lenny Parr made a bundle on his money transactions. Coming into the country each soldier had to hand over what dollars he brought with him to finance clerks in return for an equal amount of MPC. The MPC were currency within the military community. Vietnamese wanted the MPC as it was relatively stable and the Vietnamese could get soldiers to buy them PX items they otherwise couldn't get. A lot of soldiers returning from a rest and recuperation tour out of country would try to sneak in green backs so they could get the premium exchange rate. Most were caught. Some like Billy Hucks were in country one way or another for short periods and brought dollars with them. They usually made quite a bit of money. It was a problem for the command and MACV periodically changed the color and form of the MPCs, exchanging them for the military in a closely restricted manner. Those caught with the old stuff would suck wind.

Parr agreed to a year, total forfeitures, and a dishonorable discharge for a guilty plea on the black market case. The court gave him ten months and a BCD with $100 forfeiture of pay per month for ten months. He would only get pay until discharged so the forfeitures were not a big deal. Bill Combs argued Parr had been in the jungle and didn't realize the severity of his violations. The money amounts weren't large and the accused wasn't an AWOL problem. The frequency of the violations impressed the court and they based their sentence and discharge from the military on that.

The sodomy case involved a confession after the victim, PFC Harry Schaeffer, went to his commanding officer and complained that Private Charlie Long was trying to extort $200 from him. The CO, 1LT Bill Wells, asked Harry, "How is he threatening you?"

"Sir, Private Long takes me in the back entrance of the hooch and makes me go under the stairs. He tells me if I don't suck him off he'll beat me up."

"He does what?" Wells looked astounded.

"He makes me give him blow jobs."

The lieutenant asked, "How long has this been going on?"

"About three month's, sir."

"Where does the $200 come in?"

Harry replied, "He told me last night that if I didn't give him the money he would tell everybody in the company about it and they would all make me do the same thing."

1LT Wells called the CID who interviewed Harry and then asked Charlie to come in for some questioning. The CID told Charlie that Harry complained he was forcing Harry to give him $200. They didn't tell him about the sodomy. They advised Charlie of his rights to counsel and proceeded to ask him about the

$200 extortion. Eventually Charlie admitted to telling Harry he would beat him up if he didn't give him the money. The CID then shifted their interrogation to the sodomy charge. After more questioning, Charlie admitted to the repeated instances of sodomy. They then arrested him for both extortion and sodomy.

In a pretrial hearing on a motion regarding Charlie's confession, the military judge refused to allow me to enter into evidence any admissions by Charlie to the CID about the sodomy. The extortion testimony was permissible. It meant that I needed Harry to testify to the blow jobs and it would be his word against Charlie's denial by pleading not guilty. Harry wasn't too smart and his testimony would be weak. The defense would attempt to break Harry down by saying and implying he was imagining the whole thing.

The defense's problem was Charlie's confession to the extortion with an implication that something else was going on and I would have Harry speak to the particulars and frequency of the conduct. The defense also would not be able to allow Charlie to testify because if Charlie denied the actions, I could get his prior statements into evidence. The thing was the entire situation was so bazaar that a court might just believe Charlie's version. He was big and looked like an all American guy. Harry, on the other hand, never stood up straight and was pasty-faced. I asked Bill Combs, Charlie's defense counsel, about a deal and he figured the less the court heard about the entire thing the better off his client would be. Bill and I agreed on a deal and Bill recommended Charlie plead guilty to everything for a dishonorable discharge, a year and a half confinement, and total forfeitures. The court gave him a BCD and five years. Charlie beat the court's sentence and I got my conviction. Harry was sent home for medical (psychological) reasons while Charlie went to Leavenworth where he ended up serving a year. Harry's service for the Army was a minus in the government's test program for Category IV admissions to military service. After the war, to enlist in the Army you had to be a high school graduate with a mid-range scholastic average.

Green Beret Murder

While the major's trial was pending and my other cases were ongoing, our office had to provide a defense counsel for a Green Beret warrant officer. He was assigned to the Vietnam Special Forces command and was charged with participating in a conspiracy to murder a Vietnamese double agent. Since I was the command prosecutor and had a full docket, I wasn't tagged. Phil Smith, who was working mostly as defense counsel, got the assignment. The case involved the commander of the Special Forces command in Vietnam and a number of Green

Beret officers out of the Nha Trang Special Forces headquarters. The killing became a major event with national press coverage.

Sergeant Buddy Harlow was a weak undercover operative in the hinterlands of Vietnam with responsibility for the recruitment and operation of Vietnamese spies. His job was to obtain an accurate flow of human intelligence especially of North Vietnamese Army operations in Cambodia. Harlow's spies were to report on enemy activities—supply dumps, encampments and movements, rest areas, and the like. Vietnamese intelligence agencies were of no use because the commands believed they were infiltrated by NVA agents. Besides, the Cambodian intrusion was a U.S. operation not sanctioned by the Vietnamese government even though it was being launched from Vietnam. Buddy had some experience in the intelligence field but was having difficulty recruiting any worthwhile spies. He recruited two Vietnamese whom he thought had access to North Vietnamese information. Both were former VC with roots in the North but were turned under the Hoi Chanh program, which would release VC from confinement and prosecution if they agreed to support the South. He was paying them well but had garnered little valuable intelligence product.

While doing some administrative work and attempting to understand some intercepted documents, Buddy met a Vietnamese interpreter, Ly Cong Huong. Huong proved to be a good interpreter and impressed Buddy with his sophistication and intelligence. Huong was upper class and out of place in Buddy's normal sphere of operations. His other two agents were farmers. Buddy was under terrific pressure to get something going so he courted Huong and brought him into his fold. There was no time for lie detectors and the normal back ground checks for new spies.

Huong seemed too good to be true and Buddy became a bit suspicious when a patrol was ambushed with his spy being one of a very few people who knew about the mission. Then Buddy came across a picture surreptitiously taken by South Vietnamese spies in North Vietnam that showed someone with an uncanny resemblance to Huong in North Vietnam in conversation with the leader of the North Vietnamese intelligence command. Buddy reported the possible problem to his boss who got Huong to take a polygraph under the presumption that the Special Forces were looking at him for a new job. The lie detector started to jump erratically when Huong started discussing members of his family entering the NVA and his previous occupation with the Special Forces in another area of Vietnam. During a lull in the polygraph the intelligence folks checked and couldn't find any such previous employment. The lie detection continued and more deceit was evident, especially when the interpreter was asked about ties with the North.

He obviously was lying. A couple of agents then questioned him with sodium pentothal. Huong spoke while under the drug of previous work he had done with another U.S. intelligence cell. Huong never admitted to being an NVA agent. They determined Huong was a double agent.

The issue became what to do; they had an asset that they might use again knowing who they were dealing with or they might use him for disinformation. The Special Forces were operating throughout the country in what was known as Operation Phoenix, a joint CIA-military operation where communist leaders would be identified in small villages and towns and then assassinated. The new commander of the green berets in Vietnam, Colonel Jordan Farrell, a Spartan like West Pointer, convened a meeting to discuss the options. His deputy and his intelligence chief along with those most familiar with Huong's case attended. Farrell's decision was to eliminate Huong but first to check with the CIA to see if they had any suggestions. The CIA agreed to the military's proposition. Colonel Farrell approved a plan which immediately was set in action. Huong was drugged, rolled in chains, taken out into the South China Sea in a small boat, shot in the head, tied to a couple of heavy tire rims, and then dumped into the water. The military assassins reported back that they accomplished the mission. Shortly thereafter, the CIA sent a message to the Special Forces Headquarters telling them not to proceed; they had further information involving members of the Ly family and killing Huong might undermine those activities.

The CIA chief of operations at the Saigon Embassy became concerned with what was going on and visited General Abrams, the overall military commander in Vietnam. The CIA chief said he thought the Army had just killed a double agent. Abrams requested Colonel Farrell to come see him. Farrell didn't get the usual approvals when he put his plan in action. He didn't want to appear weak to his new subordinates and knew his immediate boss didn't approve of the Special Forces anyway. Farrell never contacted the MACV intelligence offices about the assassination so he thought he might be in trouble. When General Abrams asked him about the operation, he lied that the agent was sent into Cambodia on a mission. Farrell then circled his wagons and closed ranks in his tight organization so no information about the operation would be released. Not long after, Buddy Harlow got scared and started seeing ghosts. He heard what he thought were green berets coming after him. He went to a CIA office up country and turned himself in "seeking asylum." He recounted the assassination and the word got back to Abrams who was pissed probably more for being lied to than for the unaccounted for actions of the green berets.

Abrams sent his best CID agents to investigate. The agents already had been to the Special Forces headquarters investigating numerous complaints of what was considered a rogue organization even before Farrell came on board as its new commander. They investigated alleged illegal sales of U.S. military equipment to various Vietnamese, most likely VC, by some renegade green berets. During their investigation for General Abram's, Farrell's people kept a close eye on what they were doing. Farrell's group purloined the CID agent's files and bugged their rooms. General Abrams understanding that the Green Berets were out of control decided to try all the participants in the assassination for murder and to keep the prosecution secret.

The Army started the proceedings by swearing the lawyers to secrecy. They defended their action on the sensitivity of the case and its possible impact on the intelligence community. The defendants were put in LBJ in its hard spots except for Colonel Farrell who was placed under house arrest in a colonel's trailer. One of the accused wrote a lawyer from his home town and asked him to help. The lawyer tried to find out what was going on but the military stonewalled. He finally released his client's story to the U.S. press. The Army first tried to cover the matter up but the press eventually found about the murder and it made the network evening news.

The defense theory was risky and unusual. It involved something that might have been wrong but since the government uniformly was not enforcing the crime, it became unenforceable through disuse. The defense was more forceful if it could prove that the government was doing what was proscribed. Accordingly, the defense lawyers asked for substantial information regarding the Phoenix program and other U.S. intelligence activities. My office mate Phil Smith even asked for information regarding the death of Che Guevara. It was not long after that the so-called adults in Washington took charge and terminated the proceedings much to the MACV commander's dismay. Colonel Farrell was loved by the Special Forces. He was one of them and lived a Spartan existence in Vietnam. Abrams sent him home and replaced him with a non Special Forces Army officer who brought with him a personal trainer and masseuse. It was a sharp and not welcome change for the Special Forces command which was now required to live within the rules of the Army, Vietnam or not.

The Black Market Major

When I reviewed the depraved black market Major case, I knew it would be tough. Bill Combs was defending. I looked up Ted McManus, the CID agent who wrote up the investigation. I needed to find and speak to the Vietnamese who reported that Major Ted Westerfauel was attempting to sell him a jeep. That was the most important charge, and according to the file, the Vietnamese was my only witness. The other stuff was nasty but the jeep was jail time for the major. If the sale was allowed to proceed the jeep undoubtedly would have gone to some VC leader or maybe even an NVA unit. The Vietnamese was the coconspirator and the conspiracy, although perfected with action by both conspirators, had not moved to its goal, at least we had the jeep in question back in our inventory. Westerfauel was living well obviously in excess of his salary. He must have been selling something. We just had to prove it. Jeeps occasionally were lost and unit property officers routinely wrote off losses to combat action. In war, combat is cited as the reason for the loss of all kinds of military items. From alter linens to general purpose vehicles, property book holders exercise substantial license in reporting combat losses. Ted picked me up in his vehicle and we headed into Saigon to find the key to a successful prosecution. Ted didn't emanate confidence and this worried me a bit.

Saigon Traffic

The Saigon streets were wide and tree-lined and earned the moniker as Paris of the Far East. Exhaust fumes were a persistent and pungent layer that drifted over the city. Primarily the smoke came from a myriad of motorcycle trucks, bikes, taxis, and delivery vehicles putt-putting all over the place. Going into Cholon, a predominantly Chinese part of Saigon on the West bank of the Saigon River, the Binh Tay market was a major attraction and the traffic was wicked. A poor hand-icapped Chinese who became quite an entrepreneur developed Binh Tay. He recycled garbage and purchased businesses in the area until he formed a major market system. He is memorialized in front of today's market by a sculpture of bronze lions and dragons spitting water into a fountain in which his brass replica stands proudly. Farmers still come into Cholon and bring their produce to Binh Tay to sell to Chinese and Vietnamese. It was a good place for the VC to buy many things, including a jeep.

Ted drove me into Cholon and we stopped in the middle of a block on a dusty little street with a curb about two feet high. I got out and walked in the street next to a gutter layered with mud and loaded with trash. I squeezed along parked cars so the passing traffic wouldn't run me down and came to a narrow set of stairs leading to an elevated side walk. Scooters and bikes zoomed by splashing left-over puddles from a just passed rain squall. It seemed the entire population of Saigon was in Binh Tay. We pushed our way through a mass of people to a little store nestled between a small ceramics shop with a display of unfired pots and bowls and a motor cycle parts store. A few old people were sitting at tables up the walkway. They were sipping tea and looked embalmed with their taut skinny old faces. Ted led me into the store. It had dried parts of exotic animals on a scatolog-ical display and smelled of musty old dead leaves with a hint of formaldehyde. The wooden floor was dirty and the store dark and nasty. A desiccated snake head peered out of a box telling me with its fake eyes of its wicked past. Ted intro-duced me to Huc Pham who was standing behind an old wooden counter. His English was barely passable. I would say something and he would nod assent but it was not clear he understood anything.

"Mr. Pham, did Major Westerfauel say he could get you a jeep?"

Pham nodded. "You wanna buy jeep?"

"No, but where could you get jeep if I did?"

"I got number one jeep. Only 600 MPC for you. Maybe 350 dolla'."

"Mr. Pham, I don't want to buy a jeep. Do you know Major Westerfauel?"

"Oh yes. He good man."

"How do you know him?"

"He take me to Long Binh and show beaucoup jeep; most no lock. He buy me drink at bar."

"Would you get US jeep from Major?"

"Oh yes, Major get me only best jeep. U.S. Very good. All number one."

"How many jeeps have you sold?"

"I sell you jeep for $375, but only dollars. MPC different price. Much more."

"Where's the jeep?"

"You give me $250 now and I get jeep in three days and then you give rest."

"Mr. Pham, where does jeep come from? I need to know whether it's a good jeep."

"Major only bring number one. No key needed"

"OK Mr. Pham, thank you. I'll need to talk to my friend about this."

I then went to the other side of the room and whispered to Ted, "Is this guy for real? Did you actually get his statement?"

Ted looked at me like I just got in country. He said, "He made a statement and it's pretty obvious the major's working with him."

"Maybe, but to get him to testify in court will be quite a feat. And even if he does, the court might take what he says with a big grain of salt."

Ted said, "If we could get a buyer, then it might work. What about setting up a sting?"

I told him, "It's too late for that. The major's already under charges. If you did that earlier, it might have worked."

"Whatever."

"OK, let me take a different tact."

I went across the room to Pham. "Mr. Pham, I am going to put Major Westerfauel in jail for attempting to steal a jeep from US government. I want you to testify in court. Can you do that? I will bring you to base and you can tell many American officers what the major does with jeeps."

"Yes. Yes. I like do that. Come by tomorrow and I tell you good time."

"Thank you Mr. Pham. I will be back tomorrow."

We left and stopped at a Chinese restaurant Ted said was one of the better ones in Saigon. It was crowded but we were seated quickly by an eager Vietnamese maitre d' and given a menu with English subtitles. It didn't taste so good to me.

The next day I brought an interpreter with me so I could clarify exactly what we wanted to do. Ted couldn't make it. When we got to the shop Mr. Pham wasn't there; instead there was an attractive middle-aged woman dressed in her Ao Dai. The shop still smelled nasty. The old folks were still playing dominoes outside. We asked for Pham and the interpreter talked a lot to the woman. She answered a bit and he related to me that Pham was arrested by the Vietnamese police after we left the day before and taken to a Vietnamese jail in Saigon. I asked the interpreter for what and he initiated another barrage of Vietnamese which went back and forth and finally the woman behind the counter shrugged. The interpreter looked at me and shrugged. I asked our interpreter if we could go there. He said no problem. Obviously Pham was being watched by someone affiliated with the major or whoever was involved with his sale of Army vehicles. We got to the jail and the interpreter got us through the tough part—locating Pham in what must have been over 2500 incarcerated Vietnamese in a place that looked like it was designed to hold 200.

A guard led Pham to a small conference room with a big mirror and a window out into the prison. I greeted him "Mr. Pham, remember me, I want you to come to military court and talk about the major selling American jeeps in Binh Tay. Can you help me?"

The interpreter did her part. It seemed a lot longer than what I said but I don't know Vietnamese. He listened and replied and she said to us, "Mr. Pham said he would be willing to testify in the American court especially if it will help him get out of Vietnamese prison."

"I'll do what I can. Why were you arrested and what can you say about the major?"

The interpreter again after the two translations, mine and then his, said, "He told me that whenever he needs a jeep he tells a papa san who works as a bus driver at Long Binh and the papa san then tells the major. In maybe two days, maybe four, the major tells the papa san he has a jeep for pickup at the Huc Hoa Restaurant. Pham goes to the restaurant and the major or someone else gives him a jeep and he gives the major or the delivery person money and they di di mau. Police came for Pham yesterday afternoon and arrested him for selling poison. Pham said he didn't sell poison; he only helped with a very old Vietnamese herbal remedy."

I said, "I'm sorry about your arrest. How much would you give the major for a jeep?"

Again through the translator, "It varies sometimes $250 and sometime $300. Always dollars. The major doesn't want MPC."

"Where can we find the papa san?"

The translator didn't ask Pham. Instead he immediately replied, "He's gone. He quit his job when he heard the major was in trouble and went up country."

"Ok, thank him. Tell him I'll arrange for his release from jail to testify for us and will try to get him out. Court is in four days."

I went with the interpreter to the prison warden's office and asked to speak with him. After a short wait, maybe even too short, they seemed to know what was going on, a large well-dressed Vietnamese came out of a nearby office. He said if we could arrange a car, he could allow Pham to leave the prison for one day to testify. He said to have a driver come to the prison at 0830 the day of the trial. I responded we could do that, thanked him, and left. I later arranged for an MP to pick Pham up and bring him to the court room. Trial was scheduled to start at 1030 so if he got there by 11, we would be all right. I emphasized that the MP had to be at the jail at 0830.

Trial commenced and I put on my witness for the fraternization part of the case, a young soldier who testified he had a close relationship with the major. He said that they dined together in Saigon a number of times and enjoyed each other's company. I showed him a silver Zippo lighter with his initials and the major's initials engraved on the back with the words "Fondly forever," and asked him if it was his. He said it was and that the major gave it to him as a sign of their friendship. I didn't delve into the relationship any further because I knew he would deny anything sexual and also knew the court wasn't stupid. The violation of the regulation was pro forma. I had the records. I then called Mr. Pham and looked around for my Vietnamese witness but didn't see him.

I asked the judge for a short recess. He complied and I went outside the court, looked all around, and saw no one. It was 1145. I called Ted and he was out. I called the MP office and they said they dispatched the driver who was supposed to get Mr. Pham early in the morning and he hadn't returned. The interpreter was there and I asked if he could call the prison to see if Pham had left. He asked what number. I had no idea. I knew where and what it was but in Vietnam, there were no phone books that I knew of. It was time to come back to court so when the proceeding started, I asked to approach the bench. The judge asked if I was ready. I told him my problem and from what I could fathom my witness was on his way and I had the interpreter ready. He said we needed to proceed but could recess until after lunch. I didn't eat lunch but stayed on the phone attempting to find Ted or anybody who knew what was going on. I even called the MPs to see if they knew of any incidents on the highway between Long Binh and Saigon. The MP said it was all clear. At 1300 the court reconvened and still no Pham. I requested a further recess until the next morning and the judge said he had transportation scheduled to Guam and it wasn't possible. I told him I had no further witnesses and requested a continuance. The judge looked to Bill Combs who objected. He said the major had suffered long enough. The judge denied me any further delay.

I was surprised Bill didn't move for a motion for a directed verdict for that part of my case but in retrospect thought maybe he considered that if the court had to make a finding of not guilty on that charge they might look at the other charges and think the judge felt they were sufficiently proven. I rested. Bill put on several character witnesses and the major refrained from testifying as was his prerogative. The court was out about forty-five minutes and came back with a conviction for the fraternization and excess purchase of MPC, relatively minor charges. I was pissed. The extenuation and mitigation portion was comprised of a gaggle of witnesses who paraded into the courtroom and told how great a guy Major Westerfauel was. The court gave him a thousand dollar fine and a reprimand. My only satisfaction was that I knew his career was over. He was sent home within two weeks of the end of the trial.

The My Canh

I found a place I liked for Friday evening dinner. That's if I could get transportation.

It served a killer bouillabaisse. The My Canh was built on a barge anchored on the Saigon River and was serviced by a narrow gangway from a busy downtown Saigon Street. It was close to the American Embassy and had a history. Up to June, 1965, it was frequented by Americans, French, and well-off Vietnamese. The folks at the Embassy especially enjoyed its French and Vietnamese cuisine. At 1900 on June 25, 1965, a Friday night, the place was packed with dinner customers. A bomb, probably a claymore, set in the water just on the river side of the barge at deck height exploded propelling a heavy load of lead shot at table height taking out anything in its way. The explosion immediately killed several people and wounded many others. After the blast, customers and staff, many walking wounded and others being carried, piled onto the narrow gangway to exit the restaurant. As they were scurrying off, another bomb, this one from a bicycle on shore next to the boat, exploded toward the gangway killing and wounding even more. The combination of the two bombs begot a devastating result. Thirty people were killed, including nine Americans of which five were military. After the attack the restaurant remained closed for a brief period and then reopened but never to its previous popularity. In the fall of 1969, I was usually the only soldier there. The bouillabaisse varied a bit week to week and was good, especially with a glass of Alsatian Riesling, except for my last visit when the soup had an overly fishy and unpleasant taste. The My Canh wasn't attacked again during the war.

Freddy Walker; Combat Pressures

PFC Freddy Walker found himself on a hill with his platoon somewhere in the middle of the jungle. He came by helicopter and his platoon walked in a spread out fashion with the lieutenant and radioman 70 yards back. They carried rations for four days and resupply was as necessary. The lieutenant said he wasn't sure how long they'd be out. Freddie was from Detroit and hadn't been away from home until drafted by the Army just a little more than five months before. He hadn't made many friends and was in country for twenty-seven days. Freddy was a loner. There were troops on the hill above and below him. They were all dug in and had been for longer than they should have. The Lieutenant reported an NVA battalion was moving in the area and expected it to pass, sooner rather than later.

Moving Out on Patrol   *M'60's*

This would be Freddy's first combat action. He never killed anyone but felt he could. After all they were trying to kill him. He dug in when they got to the ambush site, he filled some sand bags with dirt and rocks, camouflaged his little bunker, and made it as comfortable as he could while constantly adjusting the branches and grasses he hung around his little place. He got a mirror from his pack and painted his face. The green and black paint with his brown color and the camouflage spots made him hard to see. He rubbed some mud on his M-60 so it wouldn't reflect and shine. He set the machine gun on a swivel and determined its range of fire. SGT Terry told him they would do four hour shifts at night.

The second day his anticipation was high; the enemy supposedly was close. He thought whom he might kill. Did the gook believe in communism or was he just a farm boy forced to take up arms? Did he have a grandmother? Was he married? Did he go to church? Where did he live? What did his house look like? They were supposed to be NVA so he probably was from the North. How did he join? Did he hate me? What did he eat? What's a communist anyway? Later he thought the enemy stopped to rest but would be there any minute. He thought he heard them. He tried talking to the guy in the bunker next to him but the guy told him to shut up. He started looking at the sky for choppers and Freedom Birds. He began to wonder about the entire operation but still kept watch. He moved around so much he had to replace most of the foliage. He thought he saw someone or something running through the tall grasses and dodging behind trees. He felt a snake but couldn't see it. Something was there and rubbing him. There was something moving in his shirt. The third day he felt bugs all over his body and in the bunker. He couldn't see any but he knew they were there. He thought the guy in the bunker next to him was VC. He certainly looked like an NVA troop. He told SGT Terry and he laughed. He told Terry he wanted to go home but Terry told him to stand firm. Every movement in the high grasses was a low crawling communist. He got some new rations but they were the same crap. He had nothing to read from his pack and hyperventilated. He was hot and cold. He was scared and wanted his grandmother.

The morning of the fourth day he knew something had to happen. Freddy had never fired the M-60 at anyone. He wanted to shoot the damn thing to make sure he could. He kept moving it around and aiming it pretending that a rock just inside some elephant grass was a VC. He sighted it maybe thirty times each hour. This time he put some pressure on the trigger but not enough. He thought he saw someone in the brush but couldn't be sure. He asked the guy in the bunker at his top right. Freddy awakened him. The guy said if it moves shoot. Someone in the area to his right whispered they're not here. Finally Freddy thought the rock was NVA. It was a helmet. Didn't the sergeant say they were almost here? He put a little more pressure on the trigger. He could be a hero by firing first. And just a little more. Out of no where the gun went off and kept firing. It started moving on its own and blew the rock apart. It started up the hill until he was shooting out its side at his dug in neighbor. He turned as the gun moved further up to the area above Freddy and then down the other side in an almost 360 degree arc. His finger was glued to the trigger and it kept shooting until Terry jumped him from behind and knocked him off the gun. The lieutenant crawled up to the nest and said, "What the fuck was that all about? Are you crazy or something? Is anyone hurt?"

Terry yelled out, "Let's have a report. Start at number six. Number six, report."

The report continued around the hill with each bunker responding in turn. Miraculously no one was killed. One guy got some cuts from a rock that ricocheted and hit him in the forehead. The sergeant calmed Freddy down and the lieutenant finally moved the platoon away from the ambush site. He sent Freddie back to company headquarters and said he was filing charges. Freddy told him he was sorry but couldn't remember exactly what happened. The lieutenant yelled it was attempted murder, that's what happened.

The new SJA, LTC Tom Cassidy, asked his legal clerk to get me. I went to his office and he gave me Freddy's file. He said, "Gregg, this one's for you."

I responded, "Do you want me to prosecute or defend?"

He gave me a parlous glance, "Heavens no, definitely not prosecute. The kid's obviously psycho. I want you to defend him. Get him to a doc and get a psychiatric workup. You also might want to get to his unit—take him with you—and get the particulars so you can tell the doc. Get some statements. You're defense on this one. Let me know if you have any problems."

"Yes sir."

What a change from Forsythe.

I made arrangements for Freddy's psyche exam and went over to the company to see him. Surprisingly, he was not in LBJ but instead under house arrest in the company area. For charges of attempted murder, this was a new one for me. I asked to speak to Captain Charlie Magruder when I got there. "Charlie, Gregg Thompson. I'm defending PFC Walker in his court-martial. I would like to talk to him but first can you tell me a bit about him and your version of what happened."

"Sure. I wasn't there but Walker seemed to have lost it. Lieutenant Hollis had his platoon set up for an ambush that never materialized. Either the info was wrong or the NVA got spooked. Anyway, Hollis had the platoon at the site too long. I've already spoken to him, but he's lucky the NVA didn't turn and hit him on the flank, high ground or not. You never stay in the same place that long. They were there four days—eating, pooping, getting supplies, and generally making themselves known and any ambush obvious. General Giap and Uncle Ho probably knew in Hanoi they were there. Jane Fonda probably wanted to visit and tell 'em all to go home. I was back in Saigon for a logistics meeting for the battalion commander or I would have ordered them out of there after maybe a day. I might have given them two days at the very most. Four days in ambush; not hardly. We really were lucky. I need to keep a close eye on Hollis. Green is an understatement."

"OK, but what about Freddy Walker?"

"Walker fucked up. Apparently this was his first action and he went a little off the wall. Lucky no one was killed. One guy got a stitch or two, I understand from an exploding rock. Sergeant Terry told me he was trying to get Hollis to move out of the ambush and that most of the men were probably asleep in their holes when Freddy let loose."

I asked, "Did Walker try to kill the lieutenant?"

Magruder looked at me with concern. "I don't think so. Hollis was in a command bunker near the top of the hill and apparently dug in deep when the shooting started his way. He filled out the attempted murder charges and gave them to battalion because I wasn't back yet. The battalion CO got all worked up and endorsed the charges without talking to me. I'm in a bit of a bind because I don't want to undermine the Old Man. But Walker also probably needs to get out of here. If a protracted delay causes him some combat stress, he's not going to make it through a real fire fight. Besides, in a fight, if the guys see him firing around like he did on the hill, they'll shoot him."

I said, "So that's why he's not in pretrial at LBJ?"

Captain Magruder, the Company Commander, in command form, said, "It would be cruel to put him in a place like that. If he can't handle a few days in a hole out in the open, what do you think would happen to him in a Conex container?"

"Good point Charlie. Any chance you can testify about your theory of what happened?"

"I need some cover from the Battalion CO but if you get a psych report that shows some kind of personality disorder to handle protracted stress, I'll give you the protracted stress."

"Thanks. Let me talk to Walker, Charlie, and maybe we can stop this at pretrial."

"I certainly hope so. And thanks, Gregg."

I met Freddie Walker and he seemed like a nice kid. He was raised by his grandmother because his mother had been in jail most of his life. His mother was into heavy drugs and stole stuff to support her habit. He didn't know who his father was. He was close to the grandmother and his uncle worked for General Motors and supported the grandmother, him, and a bunch of others. The uncle worked lots of overtime and it kept him out of the house. The grandmother was taking care of a few other kids but none were Freddy's siblings. He said he didn't remember what happened on the hill. I told him I wanted a doctor to evaluate Freddy and needed to speak with the lieutenant and Sergeant Terry.

Freddy saw Captain Bill Handy, an Army psychologist. As soon as I heard the exam was over, I went over to the psych office to find out what Handy determined. Handy told me Freddie had an acute personality disorder based on an inability to handle simple stress. He said sleep deprivation, poor leadership, low morale, and poor unit cohesion all worked to aggravate the condition. He said the "event" with the M-60 could have been forecast had Freddy been evaluated beforehand. He opined that considering the stress, Freddy was unsuitable for further combat and wasn't responsible for his actions with the M-60. I asked him to send a report to Freddy's battalion CO with a copy to me. He said he would do that.

About a week later I got the copy of Handy's diagnosis. It reported basically what Handy told me in his office. I called the battalion executive officer to see what they were going to do. He said it was a bunch of bull shit and the battalion CO had enough of coddling poor performers. I was a bit shocked and said, "I guess that means you're not going to withdraw the charges and not going to start paperwork for a medical transfer."

The XO said, "That's not going to happen."

I thanked him and started my preparation for the Article 32 investigation. First, in accordance with LTC Cassidy's direction, I started the arrangements to go to the unit. They were still were in the field on patrol and separated from their headquarters. I contacted Captain Magruder, the company commander, and requested to see Lieutenant Hollis. I said I would go to the field if necessary and I also needed to speak to a few other platoon members. He said they would be coming into a small outpost in two days and if I didn't get them then it would be another two weeks before they would be accessible for a visit. I asked him if he could help me set up the trip. He gave me his executive officer and directed him to get us transportation and a driver. Magruder said the rest was up to me. I told the office sergeant major what I needed and he arranged everything but told me he couldn't get an MP as a guard in time for the trip. He said Walker had to have a guard. I was perplexed and the sergeant major said, "You be the guard."

"That's crazy, Sergeant Major, I'm his defense counsel."

"So what, sir, there's nothing in the regs about a defense counsel being a guard."

"I don't even know what a guard's supposed to do."

"Christ Captain Thompson, he's supposed to make sure the kid doesn't run away. I'll get you a weapon."

"I already have a forty-five." He had me hooked and I didn't realize it. I went on, "You know if I have any trouble that takes me out of being Walker's DC."

"He's your client now, sir. I understand he really isn't in any trouble. He's been on house arrest and for attempted murder. Come on Captain."

"Thanks a lot, Sergeant Major. I guess I'll have to do it."

When we walked over to the jeep to drive away from Freddy's company I looked him in the eye and said, "PFC Walker, I'm not only your defense counsel now but to do my job best I've had to put myself in a position to be your guard. This is pretty weird and I must to tell you that if you attempt to escape or do anything untoward, I'll have to resign from being your lawyer. Do you understand?"

"What's untoward Capt'n?"

"Freddy, if you do anything wrong, I have to report it and then I can't be your defense counsel anymore. Now as your lawyer I can't tell anything you tell me in confidence but if you do something wrong on this trip, I'll have to report it and we'll be through. Also if you try to run off, and I don't think you will, but if you do, I'll shoot you in the ass. I'm not such a great shot but I can shoot a bit and will aim for your ass. Let's go and enough of this, OK?"

"Yes sir."

I had no doubt that Freddie completely understood. I didn't like being my client's guard but, after all, there was a war going on. We took off from the company area and I noticed the driver had an extra M-16 in the jeep. We all had helmets and flack vests. I had my forty-five. I'm not sure whether the extra weapon was for Freddy or me. I suspect it was for Freddie. We reached the company in a stand down mode and found the lieutenant looking over some maps. I asked the driver to keep an eye on Freddy and went to see the lieutenant in private. He asked me to help get him out of the mess he made for himself. I realized Charlie Magruder got through to him. I said I'd do my best. He related what happened and admitted he was angry. He said the firing went right over him and all he thought about was going home in a body bag after being killed by friendly fire. I spoke to a few others who called Freddie a loner and a bit odd before the firing ever began. They were not upset and most thought he was nuts. A few said they were glad it happened because they wanted to get off that hill before they were hit by mortar fire or worse. There was no one who admitted to being Freddy's friend. On the drive back to Long Binh, we saw some Apache attack helicopters firing at an area along a tree line about 500 meters to the side of the road we were traveling. There was an open field between us and I worried that when the Apaches left the commies would take off our way. The driver sped up a bit and got us out of there. I guess the Apaches did their job. The VC were an elusive bunch.

The Article 32 investigating officer heard from Lieutenant Hollis and the psychologist. The lieutenant admitted he held the ambush site too long and that there was substantial stress with the troops. I didn't bring up that most were asleep. The Article 32 officer thanked us and prepared his report recommending that the charges be dismissed. The convening authority, with LTC Cassidy's favorable recommendation, complied. Cassidy thanked me and said I did a good job.

The Army discharged Freddy honorably for medical reasons. He returned home where he received several awards for quick and sympathetic responses while employed as an emergency 911 operator for the Detroit police department.

Mr. David Boone; In Time of War

LTC Cassidy sent for me again. He gave me two files and told me to prosecute both. He said they'd be tough and was counting on me. This was my first pep talk since becoming a JAG. I took the files back to my office and soon realized why. One was for premeditated murder, my second since being in country, and the other involved the prosecution of a civilian employee of the Exchange Service who was heavy into the black market. The civilian, an American, ran a small PX close to Long Binh but in the middle of a dangerous area that had experienced substantial combat. The murder was a multiple stabbing of a soldier who was in a fight with a third party. Many witnesses were standing around watching the fight. Everyone froze when the defendant started stabbing the victim who had his opponent held on the ground. The victim bled to death from the multiple stab wounds.

At the time it was unclear whether we had jurisdiction to try civilians in Vietnam. Article 2 of the Uniform Code of Military Justice states that, in time of war, persons serving with or accompanying an armed force, in the field, are subject to military criminal jurisdiction. The big issue was whether it was time of war as contemplated in the law. There definitely was a war going on and the civilian defendant, David Boone, was accompanying an armed force in the field. His actions involved a criminal enterprise with soldiers who made up part of that armed force. The problem was the war was not declared by Congress. The most senior judge in Vietnam had the case by himself—there was no court; he was alone, and he was not afraid to make decisions.

I argued Mr. Boone was in the field. He was at Bearcat, the home of many military units, to include some marines and airborne troops as well as support, MP, transportation, communication, and maintenance units. His hooch had been attacked by rocket fire and bullet marks pocketed the outside wall. His quarters and the PX were surrounded by sand bags. Army intelligence reported that in the area there were substantial NVA and allied military movement. There constantly was a VC threat. Sappers were caught almost every weekend attempting to breach the Bearcat perimeter. Boone opened the store, the Camp Martin Fox Post Exchange, on a regular basis.

Boone visited Saigon frequently and saw quite a few of his friends playing the black market, enriching themselves in the process. They smuggled dollars and valuables into the country and sold them to Vietnamese at huge profits. They wondered why Boone wasn't rich. They suggested American cigarettes could make someone a bundle and didn't the PX have an unlimited supply?

Boone recruited a couple of NCOs to help him get a market going for the cigarettes he was prepared to supply. He ordered more Salems than he needed and started storing the excess in his warehouse. He got his NCO buddies to work with some South Vietnamese in Vung Tau who ran an R&R Center for soldiers of the South Vietnamese Army. Boone took 600 cartons of Salems, worth $840, from his excess stash and got his NCO buddies to transport them in the unit truck, borrowed for the caper, to the Vung Tau beach resort. They made the sale to a Vietnamese entrepreneur who got a bunch of young Vietnamese girls to sell the cigarettes on the beach and all around the little resort. The MPs checked the local Vung Tau PX to see if Salems were walking out of there and found that PX not the source. The MPs then called PX headquarters to see if they lost a major supply and the PX said no. They checked their records and suggested the CID, who took over the investigation, check out the Camp Martin Fox exchange. PX headquarters told the CID the Bearcat manager had ordered an unusually large amount of Salems for its rather small operation. He ordered more than any other PX in the country, even the main PX in Long Binh.

The CID investigated and found a .25 caliber pistol in Boone's hooch. It was against MACV Regulations for Defense Department civilians, to include PX employees, to have privately-owned weapons. Boone's records were a mess but established no criminal wrong doing. He obviously was disorganized but that isn't criminal. He denied he did anything wrong and said some NCOs broke into his warehouse awhile back and stole some Salems. Further investigation found a military quarter-ton truck that had on its log a trip to Vung Tau and the identity of the operator. When confronted with Boone's allegations, the NCO truck driver spilled the beans and the entire conspiracy was exposed. Boone refused to discuss anything with the CID, consistently stating that they had no business in his store and no jurisdiction over his person. The CID looked at the entire picture and came to the conclusion Boone was guilty.

Selling goods to an Armed Force in the field by itself probably is insufficient to be accompanying that force for purposes of military criminal jurisdiction. Accordingly, I introduced records establishing Boone's use of the mess halls, his occupation of military quarters, MP security for the PX and Boone, and his authorization for military medical care. I argued we are at war and related the Tet offensive just past as well as testimony from the S-3, the operations chief for the local unit. The major stated Bearcat was involved in the greater Saigon protective force and he numerated several current military operations. I argued Article 2 of the UCMJ didn't say the war had to be a "Congressionally-declared" war and if the Congress meant that, they would have said it. It just said during time of war, and clearly, we were in a war with substantial combat losses. The judge agreed and ruled we had jurisdiction to try Mr. Boone.

Once I got over the motion to dismiss, it was easy to prove the conspiracy and theft. The co conspirator made a good witness and the CID organized records at the warehouse to establish Boone's intent and the cigarette deficit. Boone refused to testify. The judge found him guilty of the conspiracy and larceny of the cigarettes as well of violating the MACV weapons regulation. He sentenced him to a year in prison and to pay a fine of $5000. He included that in the event the fine was not paid Boone had to serve another year.

Saigon Support Command Court Room   *Vung Tau Restaurant*

After sentencing, the MPs immediately took Mr. Boone to a holding cell but LTC Cassidy intervened and got the convening authority, the commander of Saigon Support Command, to release him to the Exchange Service pending review and appeal. Boone spent maybe two hours behind bars. Cassidy knew of another Vietnam civilian prosecution that had been argued before the U.S. Supreme Court but was not yet decided. When I got back to my office the phones were going crazy. I answered a call from the director of the Vietnam

Exchange Service. He told me he didn't want Boone in jail; he just wanted a conviction so the Exchange could fire him. I was shocked and disappointed. Basically, we did the PX' dirty work.

Under Article 64 of the UCMJ, after every court-martial a judge advocate reviews the case for legal sufficiency. At the time, if a sentence of more than six month's confinement were adjudged, the staff judge advocate for the commanding officer who convened the case had to prepare a legal brief as to whether the court's action was legally correct. The SJA also could make recommendations as to what parts of the court's findings and sentence the convening authority would approve. For people who say the military courts are not fair, this is an area where justice can be meted out when error is apparent. The military system wants to get it right. This bit of automatic instant replay by the official in the booth is not available to the civilian criminal courts.

Cassidy was smart and fair. He also knew the druthers of the Exchange Service and knew the chances of the case being overturned for lack of jurisdiction were high. He got the convening authority to approve only that part of the sentence that called for a fine of $2500 and for Boone to be confined at hard labor until the fine was paid but not for more than a year. Cassidy figured Boone would pay the fine to stay out of jail and if the case were overturned all would not be lost. The PX with the conviction and convening authority's action fired Boone and sent him home. Not long after the trial, the Supreme Court announced its decision that there had to be a Congressionally-declared war for the military to exercise its jurisdiction over civilians. Boone paid the fine. The Supreme Court in its ruling said military courts were not competent to administer justice sufficiently to merit the military prosecuting civilians. I guess they didn't care about military and naval personnel. We did.

Cornelius White; Murder at Cam Ranh Bay

In the murder case I anticipated a spirited argument against premeditation which would leave murder two on the table. If the killer acts out of passion or in a moment of rage, a jury or the court in the military could determine murder two or even manslaughter. Under military law, the court can only give a sentence of life or death for premeditated murder and unless the trial is referred as a capital trial, death is off the table. Cornelius White's trial wasn't referred as capital but the charge was murder one.

If you like swaying palm trees lining beaches on a crystal blue body of water gently caressing its sandy edges, Cam Ranh Bay is the place for you. The Bay is made of a peninsula that runs to the south with the South China Sea on its outside and an inlet to its inside until it faces another peninsula jutting up from the south coast. The two look at each other over an opening that forms a well protected harbor. Sand dunes line the northern peninsula on the bay side and dunes line the South China Sea. The mountainous topography throughout gives character to what already is an exquisite area. The bay is surrounded by five large mountains and there are mountainous islands to the north and numerous little hilly islands just off the coast. Nha Trang, a coastal resort once popular with the French and also boasting beautiful beaches, is just to the north. The port at Cam Ranh Bay has a long history with use by the Russian fleet in 1905 before its significant defeat by the Japanese in the Battle of Tsushima and use by the Japanese in 1942 for their invasion of Malaysia. In 1944, the US Navy destroyed the Japanese infrastructure and military forces abandoned the bay until 1964 when the Navy came back to examine its use as a major port in support of the South Vietnamese. At that time the VC were using Vung Ro Bay, just to the south, as a clandestine port to bring in supplies from the north. The U.S. decided to control the area by developing Cam Ranh Bay.

As the war progressed, the value of the bay became evident and the Army developed it into a major port. The Army also used what became a major Air Force base on the outside peninsula to provide air supply to troops in the field where ground support was unavailable or impractical. Early in the war helicopters did this but they were inefficient for the required heavy loads and their use removed them from other functions such as troop movements, medevac operations, and fire support. The Army started using C-130's, a heavy duty slow flying plane that used a relatively short runway, to carry and deploy 10,000 and 15,000 pound bombs. They could carry two of these at a time. Army riggers would fit them with specially-designed chutes to improve accuracy. Because of the bombing success, the Army decided to use the C-130's for pin point jungle supply drops and for the supply of units outside normal supply lines. The riggers would load crates for high altitude drops in areas where there were anti aircraft guns precluding low flights. They also loaded for low level drops in areas where they couldn't land. The rigger art and the C-130's became a major part of the Army's overall supply effort which in turn permitted the placement of troops and small encampments so military planners could control isolated areas and observe enemy movement.

Spec Four Cornelius White was a rigger with the 109th Quartermaster Company (Air Delivery) attached in Vietnam to the 278th Supply and Service Battalion. This unit was instrumental in supporting the marines at Khe Sang during its seventy-seven day siege. They were called the RISKS and without them surely the marines wouldn't have made it. White was stationed at Cam Ranh Bay. Corne-lius was born in Detroit, but was raised by his mother's sister in Chicago. His mother died in child birth and his father was unknown. His aunt worked for Northwest Airlines as a ticket agent. She had two other children, both older than Cornelius and both girls. Cornelius always was small for his age but made up for it by exhibiting a tough-guy demeanor. He would fight at the drop of a hat and would do anything to win. His aunt referred to him as a trouble maker. He was suspended from high school several times for fighting. White enlisted in the Army just out of high school and after basic was assigned to Quartermaster School at Fort Lee. He went to rigger school after that from which he immedi-ately was assigned to Vietnam.

The 109th company area was nestled in the hills overlooking the bay and the riggers lived in hooch's built on sand. They shared the area with several other units of the 278th. There was a small club that provided some comfort to the rig-gers. The hooch's were set up in rows facing each other and there were day rooms, orderly rooms and other support buildings throughout the area. Piss tubes were inserted in the sand at convenient places mainly in the barracks area. Troops coming from the field would drift in and out, the main attraction being the beach and the South China Sea. Troops could swim and relax on the beach staying with those stationed there in whatever empty bunks they could find and they could drink and smoke. A few toughs from the 11th Armored Cavalry Regiment oper-ating in the general area wanted some beach time and a bit of relaxation so they hitched a ride on a Chinook for an overnight out of the jungle. They had a friend who let them stay with him just next to the rigger company area.

After swimming all day, they went to the rigger club and started drinking Black Label at twenty-five cents a pop. Some of the riggers were cooling off after work and the two groups started comparing experiences. With the Blackhorse troops losing friends in frequent sorties with the NVA, any derogation to their importance was a slight to their KIAs and was a fight waiting to happen. They appreciated the riggers efforts in getting them fuel, ammo, and grub especially if dropped when they were in the middle of nowhere but felt their combat was more important than just rigger support. The riggers questioned the value of the 11th holding little areas in the jungle that nobody wanted anyway. The Black Label fueled their emotions and the discussions became heated. They no longer were waiting; a fight was happening and the club manager told them to take it outside.

A large group left and a fist fight quickly started next to the rigger company area. Two soldiers, PFC Charlie Marshall from the 11th Cav and Spec Five Hector Lopez from the riggers, were wrestling after exchanging punches and Charlie started to get the better of Hector. Specialist White was watching. He saw Charlie wrestle Hector to the sandy ground and start hitting him in the face. The sand on Hector's face caused an oozing rash with each of Charlie's punches. White ran to his barracks and back again and immediately commenced stabbing Charlie in the back and side turning the knife as he did taking chunks of flesh. His knife plunged into Charlie puncturing his lungs and kidneys. He cut with deep slicing strokes into Charlie's neck and back. Before anyone realized the extent of what was going on and before Charlie could react, Cornelius had taken six deep carving strikes. By the time someone got the courage to get moving and stop him, Cornelius' hand and arm were full of blood and he had stabbed Charlie thirteen times. Charlie let Hector go and went into shock. He tried but couldn't get around to see the still stabbing Cornelius White. By the time he was restrained, he had stabbed Charlie seventeen times and both Charlie and Hector were covered with Charlie's life blood that now was draining into the sandy ground. Charlie lost consciousness on the sand. When a medic finally got to the scene, Private First Class Charlie Marshall was dead and Cornelius White was covered in his blood.

I received the file resplendent with gory photos and a full autopsy report giving the cause of death as exsanguination by multiple stab wounds. The CID report also gave the name of several witnesses to the fight and two brief statements. White refused to make a statement and was in the Long Binh Jail. Phil Smith was going to defend. The CID and LTC Cassidy, the SJA, recommended non capital murder one and the convening authority bought it. I knew Phil was going to lay waste with a passion of the moment argument that would bring the verdict down to murder two and maybe bring up a defense of another on behalf of Hector. I didn't believe Charlie Marshall deserved that so my work was cut out.

The file had little on premeditation so I had to find it. Further, Phil was screaming about the pictures in the file. He told me he would object to their admission in evidence as of little probative value and that they were prejudicial because they were gruesome and inflammatory. He said he would object even if we ever got to extenuation and mitigation. Phil was an optimist. I didn't say anything because it was my position that they showed White's clear intent to not just interrupt a fight but to exercise deliberate and deadly force. White caused the gore; now he could stew in it. I was mainly worried about the defense of another angle that might bring the charges down to involuntary manslaughter. I had to investigate.

My first thought was to go to the scene to see what I could find. I didn't believe I had any obligation to invite Phil along. He was doing his own thing. So far, I had a killing for sure and it was easy to prove it was perpetrated by the accused. I had two statements by witnesses to the fight that said Cornelius did it. Both also said Cornelius was covered with blood but I had no pictures of that or for that matter of the scene. My only pictures were of the cut up torso. I knew there was a fight and Charlie had Hector down and was hitting him and then Cornelius jumped in and started "hitting" Charlie in the back, the sides, and the neck. One witness stated he thought Cornelius was trying to get Charlie off Hector. I also had the knife; it was small and for all intents and purposes no more than a pocket knife. It had the name "Barlow" stamped on a metal hinge. I guess they called it a rigger's knife so Barlow could make big bucks producing what you might buy at the Five and Dime for a buck. It had two blades and was covered with dried blood. I tried to open it and couldn't. I thought the dried blood had glued it shut. I then looked for some magic button or latch that would release the blade from its resting place. There was nothing so I went back to work and exerted a bit more energy in grabbing one of the blades between my thumb and forefinger while holding the knife tightly in the other hand. I didn't want to wash away any caked blood that might be holding it shut; I might mess up the evidentiary value. Once my thumb and finger hurt from the pressure it popped open. The effort to open the knife might help prove premeditation. It was not something that could be grabbed in the passion of the moment but was similar to loading a gun. It took time, effort, and thought; some planning—get this thing open and have at it. But I had to prove that. It could be that Cornelius had the knife in his pocket, pulled it out, had some quick way to open it and went after Charlie. So far it was weak and as it stood murder two might even be hard to prove.

I hitched a ride up the coast from Tan Son Nhut into Cam Ranh Bay in a twin engine Army C-7 Caribou. To avoid any ground action we flew southeast and over Vung Tau out to sea and then turned to the northeast and up the coast. I had a seat on the left side of the small passenger plane and could see the beauty of the beaches that defined the coast. As we passed Phan Thiet there were palm trees reaching out over the water and further along wide red sand dunes coming right up to the beach with mountainous islands perched along the coast. Further along, we reached the outside of Phan Rang and the pilot told us over the intercom this was primarily a South Vietnamese Air Force base but that we had some units there. We then came to Cam Ranh Bay, circled out to the north, and then back for a landing at the air base on the peninsula.

Cam Ranh Bay

As we came in the area looked hot and sandy. I could see military activity with planes, trucks, and every imaginable vehicle loading and unloading. I asked the pilot when he was going back and he told me first thing in the morning. It was 1530. I went to a terminal and asked an Air Force sergeant how I could get to the 109th. He told me they worked on the other side of the airfield and their company area was on the other side of the base by the hill. He told me he had a friend who might come get me if that's where I had to go and after about fifteen minutes and a cold coke an open Army jeep pulled up with a dirty looking staff sergeant at the wheel.

He yelled out, "Somebody need a ride to the 109th?"

"Thank you, I do need a ride. I'm Captain Thompson, a JAG from Saigon Support Command, and am investigating a murder that happened here about a month ago."

The Staff sergeant said, "I understand Cornelius may get a while in prison, sir."

"My job is prosecutor, and as such, I'm attempting to do just that."

"Staff Sergeant Scott Perkins, sir. I wasn't at the fight but I heard it was bloody and horrible."

"Did you know Specialist White?"

"Yea, I knew him."

I grabbed my briefcase and we started for the jeep, "Can you tell me anything about him?"

"Not too much. He was here for a couple of months and did his job. Nothing monumental. He packed chutes like most of the riggers. The 109th's a small company with a specialized job. I'll show you a bit when we get over to the hanger, but most of the guys will have gone up to the company area by now."

"What do you mean a small company?" I swung into the front passenger side.

He started the jeep and we drove off in a swirl of dust and sand out of the air field area onto a sandy hard-packed road that went out and around the perimeter of the airfield, "Most of the guys know one another and we're pretty close. Oh, we have friends coming in all the time and it's fun to see different people, like you. The excitement of what happened broke the monotony a bit but this sand, all the time sand, sand everywhere gets to you. There's not much to do. Hit the beach but after four or five times guys stop doing that. They pretty much listen to the radio or tapes and drink a lot. So you get to know who's who. Cornelius had a bit of an attitude but in the unit we all get along. Do you know him?"

There were no trees as we drove along under the hot late afternoon sun. "I just read him the charges. We're trying him for murder."

Perkins said, "Well no one wanted to cross him, that's for sure. I don't know why. It was just something about him."

"Was he in any other fights that you knew of?"

"I don't think so. Oh, there are some fights all right but most of the time it's a punch or two and everyone makes up and goes back to doing their own thing."

We were coming into a wide open area with some buildings that looked like storage areas in the rear and a big hanger facing a runway from the airfield. It all was hard-packed sand and I already was getting tired of it and grit was in my hair from the ride. I had only been on the ground for maybe forty-five minutes. "Do you know anybody who saw the fight?"

He looked at me and said, "Everyone talked about it. I think there were only five or six guys who actually were there. I think the CID talked to them but I'm not sure."

"Are they around so I can talk to them?"

"I think two DEROSed, but three are still here—Paul Spitz, Bill Ledford, and Jim Stagnitta."

Perkins pulled into a parking area next to a door towered over by the maybe three story high hanger. He beckoned me to follow him. The building had an aluminum skin over some kind of metal struts. We entered a huge bay filled with parachutes rolled up on the concrete floor in various configurations apparently ready to be rigged for air drops. Perkins told me this was the day's work and at about 0300 a couple of C-130's would pull up and a rigger crew would fit the appropriate chutes to cargo on the planes. He said the riggers didn't know where the supplies were going but would be told whether the drops were high level or low level and that's about all. They had to figure weight, mass, and level of drop. We walked among the chutes and he pointed out the various kinds and what they were used for. At the other end of the building, we came to an office. "This is my little place in the war Captain. Welcome. Excuse me, sir, while I call the company and tell the clerk you're here and need to talk to Spitz, Ledford, and Stagnitta."

As Sergeant Perkins spoke on the phone I looked around his office. It was apparent he was some kind of coordinator between the Air Force and the riggers. He had a large schedule on the wall covered with plastic and grease pencil markings indicating what was coming and when. I couldn't read it for the technical babble. He also had some pictures of what appeared his home in a snow setting. He saw me looking at it and said, "Rochester, Vermont, in the winter. We have a cabin near there and it reminds me there's another world out there other than this moonscape." I asked, "How long have you been in?"

"This is my second tour. Got shot first time around and have 215 days to go this time. Seems pretty safe here but it gets to you after a bit. I just made E-6 and have five years in. Don't think I'll stay but with the money I saved from my last tour and now, I think I'll go into computers. They look like the thing of the future. I wish I had one here but the Army doesn't believe yet. They will before long. Captain, they're looking for your guys. Let's go up to the company and I can introduce you to the old man and get you someplace to stay. Chow will be in an hour."

"Thanks Scott, that's much more than I expected."

We left the rigger area and drove again around the airfield to another road that led away and to the other side and up a hill. The views were amazing. I could feel the sea breezes as we went up and could see some islands just to the outside of the bay. They looked green and above the dark blue sea made a fantastic picture. Scott Perkins looked over and said, "It gets old fast."

We got to the company area and it was all Army. Barracks type buildings were set in neat rows with paths between. Outhouses and piss tubes told me there was no plumbing in the barracks. Some of the buildings were sand-bagged but it didn't look like much of an effort. These guys didn't anticipate an attack. I guess it was that the peninsula was pretty well protected. He pulled up to the company orderly room and I met the CO who said he had a place for me to stay and was getting the witnesses together. He said I could use his office but only if I stayed for dinner and joined him at the club on the hill after. I thanked him for his hospitality and told him I had to be at the airfield in the morning to catch my flight back to Long Binh. He said it wasn't a problem; he had to be up at 0300.

Ledford was first in. He reported with a crisp salute as I sat behind the CO's desk. I told him that wasn't necessary and to relax.

"I was at the fight, sir. I saw Cornelius run down the path to his barracks and in a minute come out, run back, and immediately start punching the Armored Cav guy in the back. I didn't think it fair because the fight wasn't over. The Cav guy knew it and was still fighting when Cornelius jumped in. Hector was pretty tough. He's the guy from the 109th who was in the fight. I saw Hector dodging some blows and about to roll out of it when the Cav guy let up. Actually, I think the Cav guy had Hector down pretty good. I then saw a lot of blood; at first I didn't know who was cut. Cornelius was still hitting him all over and I could see blood coming with each hit. One of the Cav guy's buddies then pulled Cornelius from behind off his buddy and Stagnitta jumped in to break it up too. Blood was everywhere."

I asked, "What did Cornelius do when the Cav guy and Stagnitta stopped the fight?"

"He looked down at the Cav fighter, I don't know his name, and watched him try to get up but then fall to the ground. He didn't try to get away or anything and then someone yelled to get a medic. Next thing I know top comes running in and tries to stop the bleeding but then sees it's of no use. He tells Marty Winters to take White to the Orderly room and then tries to get someone to help the guy on the ground. Top's DEROSed so I don't know what he had in mind or what happened to Cornelius after that."

"Did you see Specialist White with a knife?"

"Yea, I saw him standing there with a small knife in his hand. He had lots of blood on him and Hector got up and was bloody as well. The Cav guy passed out and when the medic finally got there, he was dead."

"How long did the medic take to get there?"

"It seemed a long time but I'll bet it wasn't more than five minutes."

"How well did you know Specialist White?"

Ledford thought a minute about his answer. "Not too well. He was in the company and everybody knows everybody else but he was black and they stayed by themselves a lot. It wasn't anything racial, it's just that they stayed together—

they would eat together and drink together and all that stuff. They never went to the beach."

"Was Hector part of their group?"

Spec Four Ledford answered, "No, Hector was Mexican and he pretty much got along with everyone, not that the black guys didn't but they had their own thing going. I can't testify to it but I think they smoked some weed and they always had special hand signals."

"On the knife that Cornelius had, had you ever seen it before?"

"I never saw that particular knife. Or at least I don't think I have. It's a rigger knife. We all have one."

"The knife White had was difficult to open. Are they all like that?" I was confused.

"Not all but when they're new sometimes it takes a while to loosen em up."

"Do you know of any fights between Specialist White and anyone else?"

"Not that I know of Captain."

I thanked Specialist Ledford and told him I would ask for him to testify at the trial. I said I would speak to him a bit more to tell him exactly what I would ask and that I only wanted him to tell the truth and if he thought of anything else to give me a call. Ledford then saluted and left. I yelled at him as he left, "What's your DEROS?"

He yelled back, "It's 126 days, sir, I'll be there."

Spitz came in next and pretty much said the same thing as Ledford but told me Cornelius made a thing about being able to open his knife fast. Spitz said he had seen Cornelius on the rigger floor show off by pulling the knife out of his pocket and whipping it open. I asked him if that was the same knife he had the night in question. He said he didn't know but he had seen Cornelius with a pocket knife that opened real fast. I then thought I might have to tell this to Phil Smith, White's defense attorney and my office mate, but wasn't sure. After all it was my idea about the knife and the premeditation and if I didn't use it for that purpose then why should I have to tell Phil something that I thought about but rejected. Maybe I should ask LTC Cassidy. Damn. I told Spitz I didn't think I would need him but just in case to stand by. I gave him my card and told him to call me if he thought of anything else. He said he would be available if I needed him.

Stagnitta came in and asked, "How do you like Cam Ranh Bay, sir?"

"It's beautiful Sarge. How long have you been here?"

"I've been with the 109th about three months but I've been in country for over a year. I extended to get this assignment. I love it here at the beach."

"What do you do?"

Stagnitta said, "I'm in charge of supply for the company. I get the chow sent in as well as all the sundry things that keep us happy and going. I also get a good bit of beach time. Some of the local ladies come in to make it nice."

"So you're not a rigger."

"No sir. I'm supply."

"OK, I understand you were at the fight between PFC Marshall and Specialist Hector Lopez."

The supply sergeant explained, "Yeah, we were all having some beer at the club and these Cav dudes get all excited because Hector starts riding them about jumping around from one place to another in the jungle. He asked if they were a bunch of monkeys going from one tree to another. Hector was having lots of fun but the Cav dudes got upset. They said they were pacifying areas. Hector said it sounded like they were fighting and not pacifying anything. The big Cav dude who was in the fight said they saw much more action than anyone around here and were actually fighting to win the war. He said they could blow away even the threats of infiltrators. It went on like that for awhile and got nastier with every beer and a lot was going down. Eventually Joe Stewart, the club NCO, told them to get out. When they left, the fight started almost immediately."

"Did you see Specialist White at the fight?"

"Yea, he was there."

"What did he do?"

"I was behind him coming out of the bar and then the fight started. All was OK until Hector hit the dirt and the other guy started hitting him while he was down. Some sand got in Hector's eyes and he had some blood on his face. I saw Cornelius run off down to the barracks. He wasn't gone more than two or three minutes. The next time I saw him he had the knife in his fist. It was hard to see exactly what it was because it was dark but I knew it was a knife. I then saw him start stabbing the guy in the back. I couldn't believe it at first but no one did anything so I jumped in and pulled Cornelius off trying not to get stabbed myself. I was too late and the guy died. It was terrible."

I asked, "When did you first see White with the knife?"

"When he jumped into the fight."

"Did you see him return from the barracks?"

"No, I was watching the fight and then I saw him make his move."

"Did he reach into his pocket or do anything like that to get the knife?"

"Not that I saw. When I saw him, he had it in his hand."

"Was it open?"

"Yea. Actually it was the blade I saw. It's a small knife but I saw the full blade, about three or four inches. He was holding it in his fist with the blade out the back of his hand, the other side from his thumb, so when he started punching he would bang his hand down and drive the blade into the Cav guy. Then he moved his hand up and swiped it across the Cav guy's neck. Blood spurted and I jumped in. The Cav guy collapsed and I grabbed White. He must have hit an artery in the neck."

I asked, "Did you ever see White open the knife?"

"I just saw him back at the fight with it in his hand."

"When you grabbed Cornelius did he still have the knife?"

"Yes sir, but I told him to drop it and he did."

I thanked Jim Stagnitta and told him I wanted him to testify at the trial and if he had anything else to call me. Scott was in the outer room when I came out and told me the CO had to go over to the air field and would be back after dinner. It was about 1830 and dinner was from 1800 to 1900 so we didn't have a lot of time. I asked to see the area where they had the fight. He rolled his eyes and said OK but we had to hurry. I took it Staff Sergeant Perkins was hungry. We walked about 250 yards from the company office and went by the company enlisted club to an area Scott told me was where the fight occurred. I asked where Specialist White's barracks was and he pointed a couple of buildings down. We walked down and entered the open bay barracks. Each bunk was casually put together; most had mosquito netting draped around the bunk area; and there were trunks along side and bags hanging at each bunk. I asked what the bags were and Scott told me they were required in case of an attack. Weapons were not assigned but each soldier was required to have a go-to bag with some stuff he could grab to take with him to hold him over during any attack. He said that was the CO's direction and it kept everyone alerted and mentally prepared to a potential threat. I asked which was White's bunk and Scott didn't know. He said replacements had come in and all White's stuff was sent to Long Binh Jail.

After dinner, Captain Ryan met me and took me in his jeep up the hill to the officer's club. It was a small shack with a wooden plank shutter across an opening at the front that was propped open by two boards, one on each side. It had a wide shelf at the opening and a lieutenant behind the shelf. Behind him was a refrigerator and open cabinets on the back wall next to the door stocked with glasses, booze, crackers, and peanuts. He grabbed a napkin and put it in front of me and asked what I wanted. There were small stereo speakers on top of the shelf and a receiver on a table next to a sink. I stood in the sand in front of the "bar" and behind me were a gaggle of chairs looking out over the bay into the South China

Sea. I ordered a rum and coke with a piece of lime for fifty cents. The view was breathtaking. That little bar of scrounged lumber with its scrounged chairs was the most beautiful bar I have ever been in. The cost of the Cuba Libra might have influenced my feeling just a little. I sat there relaxed as Ella Fitzgerald serenaded us from the bar and wondered how this beautiful country could not stay out of trouble. Cam Ranh Bay was a nice place to visit if you didn't get in an argument.

I met my morning flight and the captain said it had to go to Nha Trang before returning to Saigon. It was a short flight but we stayed for lunch. I had no idea what the pilot's agenda was but I was just a hitch hiker and beggars can't be choosers. We landed at a small airport after a short ride up the coast and I got a ride into town. On the ride, I saw many more bicycles than cars. The South China Sea beach was long and looking out you could see several islands breaking up an otherwise empty vista. Beach houses and tourist homes lined the beach to give it a resort town character. The houses were old and for the most part shabby. Still in the morning, you could see unmade beds and messy rooms inside openings across their fronts. A cool breeze wafted in from the sea.

When I got back to Long Binh I decided to hold off telling the defense about the knife. It was in the evidence bag accompanying the file and the defense had access to that. I wanted to see witnesses from the 11th Cav to get their version of the fight. The troop to which Charlie Marshall was attached was operating around the Michelin Rubber Plantation just above the small town of Dau Tieng. I arranged to catch a ride on a supply C-130 on its way to an airfield near the rubber plantation. I then would catch a supply chopper to the troop where the witnesses to the fight were currently located. I went over to Tan Son Nhut and my C-130 fell through. I heard of a Chinook going to Tay Ninh. I figured if I caught that I could get a chopper over to the Michelin Plantation.

I hitched a ride and learned Tay Ninh was a major a transportation hub. We were in the jungle near the Cambodian border and I stayed close to the air field. It was hectic and choppers didn't stay long at Tay Ninh. I quickly got a ride for the pretty short Huey jump over to the Michelin plantation. The pilot gave me some ear phones so I could hear all the chatter and he could talk to me. He was an Army warrant and apparently liked having a JAG on board. We went straight up, much higher than what I was used to and almost directly east. We then swooped down to a combat airfield, a short metal runway designed primarily for C-130's. The pilot told me to take a look out the right window. I saw a badly torn up airplane pushed to the side of the perforated runway.

The pilot reported over my ear phones in what sounded like an artificial voice with lots of static. "That baby got hit just last week. Some VC hit it with a rocket.

All the crew made it out of the burning aircraft but you can see this area is barely ours. The air crew escaped but under constant rifle fire. The C-130's now carry half loads and come in from a high altitude with little warning using a steep descent so the VC won't have much time to aim and fire."

I asked, "Can you see them?"

"No, but they're out there as you just saw. We'll keep the engine going and you'll see everyone scurrying around when we land to unload you so our time on the ground is minimal. When we land get the hell out. The flight NCO will tell you when."

As we were coming in the pilot didn't wait for his NCO and he yelled over the intercom, "Captain, get your stuff together and take off the harness. As soon as I land I'm outta here. You won't have much time so be ready."

I was the only one leaving and felt a little guilty about putting everyone in harm's way. But the pilot juiced me and when we touched I was out and running in a crouched position to the side of the metal strips that were the runway. I didn't know whether he was putting me on or not but the derelict from the previous week gave him substantial credibility and the chopper took off immediately.

I found the S-3, the squadron operations officer for my witness's troop, sitting at a camp desk on top of a sand-bagged bunker with a loaded 45 caliber pistol on his desk. He was doing paper work. I explained my business and he told me the regimental commander was about to make an inspection of that troop and they were in an anticipatory state but if I was going to get the pervert who stabbed Charlie Marshall in the back, he'd give me the Old Man's chopper. I told him that wasn't necessary. He said their mission was to push whatever enemy they could find the hell out of Vietnam and they were doing it. He said they were going to chase them to hell and back and would give them hell when they found them. The S-3 was juiced. He took me into the command bunker where everybody was jammed up with maps and radios all over the place. A few people were behind field desks looking at maps and teletype. It seemed mass confusion but I was the only one confused. We were in a sand-bagged bunker that must have reached underground. He got on a radio and told someone I was coming out for a short visit before the old man got there and to take care of me.

He said, "You'll be leaving in twenty minutes. I have you on a supply chopper going in the jungle. It's loaded with fuel bladders for the dragons so pray no one fires at you. How's that for quick action? Now go do your thing and get that little fucker."

He was wearing a sweaty green undershirt and I presumed he was a major because of his job so I moved out smartly and said, "Thanks, sir!"

Jungle Outpost   *Field Underground Bunker*

This time the chopper took me at tree top level quickly over the jungle with doors open on each side and gunners perched at the rear edges of the doors behind the biggest machine guns I've ever seen. We flew over a circle of Green Dragons in the middle of a heavy foliated jungle. The tanks had pushed down the vegetation to an area about fifty yards out from the platoon all around the circle except for one side that was close to some trees and vegetation. I could see they were taking a break. We dropped in and I made my way through about an inch of mud to an E-7 who came out to greet me. He asked if I was the JAG who was prosecuting the Marshall murder and I acknowledged I was. He asked who I wanted to see and I told him Pete Markum and Gerry Bailey, the two who were with Marshall in Cam Ranh Bay. He said Bailey was there but Markum had his foot shot off a few days before and he understood was in San Francisco at the Letterman Hospital. He took me over to Bailey's Assault Cavalry Vehicle, an M113A armored vehicle known as a Green Dragon. Lots of fuel bladders were lying around and several vehicles were attached by thick canvas and rubber hoses. A tank recovery vehicle was pulled up next to a beat up chow wagon that had a canvas awning projecting off its rear. The place was thick with mud and military gear was scattered all about. It was not what the Navy might consider ship-shape.

Bailey was on top of his Dragon boiling some water for coffee on a portable little contraption used as a stove. He was shirtless, skinny, and boasting a wide black mustache. His vehicle was parked next to a tank; I think it was a Sheridan. Its cannon was pointing at the jungle not more than a chip shot away. Each M113A had a 50 cal machine gun on top mounted behind a steel shield. The tanks were interspersed among them. A couple of guys were constructing a chain link fence in front of Bailey's vehicle that was supposed to defuse an incoming rocket to lessen its damage. I asked Bailey if we could talk. He told me they were setting up for that night and maybe two. He said the regimental commander was rumored to be coming in for a visit but he was eager to help. Most units would spiff up when the big boss comes by but this group seemed more intent on getting their act together for night protection than prettying up what by nature under the foliage was a morass. It made sense to me and no one seemed stressed out about the command visit. I figured the commanding officer must be a pretty good leader or the troops felt it more important to get their act together before the night drifted in with its attendant horror.

Armor Coffee Break   *Vietnam Army Latrine*

Bailey asked if I wanted a cup and I declined. He then told me he, Charlie Marshall, and Pete Markum got a couple of days off and decided to visit a friend at Cam Ranh Bay. He said they found a place to stay with the riggers and had a great day on the beach drinking beer and flirting with some local girls. He told me he was glad Charlie's last day was fun.

I asked him, "What did Charlie do with the 11th?"

"He was an ACAV driver and was tough."

"Tell me about the fight."

"We were drinking beer and the riggers were arguing with us about why we would move from place to place in the middle of nowhere. They didn't understand that we constantly were chasing VC and NVA troops and were doing a pretty good job of it. Just now, there are some VC units in the area, maybe within fifteen clicks. By constantly moving we keep them on the defensive and every once in a while we find some and give them a taste of democracy. With our fire power, there's no contest. The biggest problem occurs if we don't move. If we stay too long or get stuck at some river or mud hole they sneak up at night and hit us with their rockets and sappers. But this Spanish dude at the club gets a bit uppity and he and Charlie get into each other's face. The bartender tells us to get out and it seemed the entire bar emptied onto the street outside the club. Charlie hits the Spanish dude and they start having a pretty good fight. Charlie knocks him down and hits him a couple of times and then they start to let up a bit. The Spanish dude actually was a pretty good fighter. I even saw him smile at Charlie. Then this black dude jumps in with a knife and starts stabbing Charlie in the back. I'm on the other side of the fight and I move as fast as I can around to get him off but this other rigger guy beats me to it. By then Charlie's all cut up and collapses."

Bailey seemed a bit emotional so I waited for a few seconds and then asked him, "Had you seen the guy who did the stabbing before?"

Bailey composed himself and answered, "He was in the bar, sir, a black guy, and he came outside with everybody else but I noticed someone leaving the fight. I think it was him but I'm not certain, it was pretty dark. What makes me think it was him is out of the corner of my eye I saw maybe that guy start walking away and then run and go into a barracks a few buildings down from the fight. Then the next thing I know I see what seemed to be the same guy running back with his hand in a fist and then jump into the fight."

"I take it you think the guy went to get something?"

"He went to get his knife. I'm sure of it. The guy seemed to walk slowly away and then speed up like he'd made a decision. You need to talk to Pete Markum. Maybe you can call him. He got his foot shot up pretty bad a week or so ago and got air lifted back to the states. Pete saw the guy leave and come back. He told me the dude went to get a knife. It was the same guy who killed Charlie."

I told Gerry Bailey that I'd need him to testify and asked him if he minded a few days in Long Binh. He said if it was alright with the Troop commander, he'd be only too happy to come. I thanked him and said I had to get back to Long Binh as soon as possible. He thanked me and I got out of there as soon as I could. I didn't want to be overnight in the jungle in the middle of an encircled wagon train with high elephant grass pretty close on one side and the enemy not ten miles away. The jerry-rigged chain link fence seemed a weak reed upon which to lean for defense. I figured I would be more a liability to these guys than any help notwithstanding my month's training at Tigerland. I saw a bunch of choppers coming in and figured the regimental CO was about to land. The troop commander saw me and told me to stand over on the side and wait for the Cav CO to go by. He said the squadron commander's chopper would take me back to Tay Ninh while the regimental CO had dinner with the troops and conducted his visit. The Old Man waved at me after he landed and I got the hell out of Dodge.

Jungle Outpost   *Jungle Gas Station*

At Tay Ninh I hitched a ride on a C-130 going into Tan Son Nhut. The plane was empty except for a couple of other hitch hikers. We sat on hard steel seats with our backs resting on the walls of the plane and the Air Force flight engineer told us to buckle in as we took off. I twisted around to get a view and as usual it was spectacular over the jungle. The plane was making a lot of noise and we flew pretty low for where we were. I had total confidence in the flight crew; I suspect it was a defense mechanism. There were no Bloody Marys, my usual flight fortification, so all I had for courage was my enduring faith in those in charge. It was evening and when we left Tay Ninh I was soaking wet from the heat and humidity.

As we proceeded to Saigon the pilot seemed to shoot straight up. I thought he either saw or got some info of a potential rocket attack. But as we breached some clouds I saw they were of various colors and looked pretty angry. I could see some breaks in the cover with dark blue coming through but the breaks were at differing levels. The pilot climbed over the peaks and then would either swoop quickly down of his own design or be sucked down by some force of nature. As we went up and down over the clouds we also were being twisted from side to side and were zig zaging through the sky. It was not a very long ride from Tay Ninh to Saigon so the fun didn't last long. The pilot however saved the best show for last. As we turned, either on our own or as a consequence of wind tunnels, I could see by twisting around and looking out a small window a number of black clouds interspersed through an otherwise clear shot at the Tan Son Nhut airfield. I also saw streaks of lightening and felt the concussion of thunder claps. The plane took a hard turn to avoid one cloud while dropping down and turning even harder so we were almost on our side while we circled around the cloud coming in. The pilot then straightened out the plane and again we nosed sharply down and I could see through an open flight deck door the runway coming closer a bit off center to the left. He leveled off some more and swooped in with a final steep descent that ended with a sharp bump and wheels down at the beginning of the landing strip. My confidence was legitimized as we taxied the few feet to the terminal. I stayed where I was for a minute attempting to put together my briefcase and the few other things I had with me on the trip when the captain walked out of the flight deck. He was sheet white and looked like a 14 year old. I sat and watched as he limped bent over and tripped on his way off the plane. I then knew how C-130's could maneuver to land anywhere and finally I was scared.

When I got back to the head shed I went to LTC Cassidy's office. I told him about the witness in San Francisco and my dilemma about the rigger knife. He replied, "Gregg, the knife is evidence and that includes its properties. If you're planning on making it a big part of the premeditation then in the spirit of full disclosure you should tell Phil Smith what you found that might contradict your theory. Such are the travails of prosecution. Now Phil will argue that the blood made the knife more difficult to open. You might want to get something to counter that. Further, this might not be the same knife that White could flip open as easily as the witness indicated. If White refuses to testify, we may never know. You could plant that seed in the court's mind. Why didn't White have the knife in his pocket at the fight? Did he come directly from work to the club or did he change clothes. You need to check these things. Now about the witness in San Francisco. What's his name?"

"Markum, sir. I'm not sure of his grade but he's enlisted and was with the victim at the fight. I think Bailey is influenced by what Markum told him about White going to get the knife. If I were defense I could pretty much destroy his testimony especially after he admits it was dark and he really wasn't watching White carefully. It might even undercut the entire case so I have to handle him carefully. But I think Markum did see him, at least that's what it appears. Maybe I can call him."

Cassidy looked back at me and smiled. "I think a call won't do it. Under the circumstances I believe a deposition is in order. You have to take Phil with you. Now, you want a deposition because Markum might not be available but the real reason is to show Phil that Markum might be a damaging witness if he comes to trial—the wounded soldier and all that. If you get the deposition, maybe Phil will stipulate as to what Markum would say. He could be a prick and demand Markum's presence but I wouldn't if I were him and I think Phil's smart enough to realize the damage it would do. Now, if Markum's testimony is not what you think, Phil may demand his presence as a defense witness. You need to check to see what he'd say. Call the trial counsel at the Presidio and have him give Markum a visit. They will need to set up the deposition anyway. I'll give Harry Rice a call and let him know what's going on. He's the SJA there."

My first thought was a week in San Francisco and how I could drag it out. Then I thought Cassidy was a pretty smart dude and probably a pretty tough prosecutor. No wonder they pushed him to keep coming east after he fell off the wagon.

Cassidy got the Old Man to order the deposition and Phil and I got five days temporary duty, or as they say in the military TDY, to Letterman General Hospital with an allowance of $108 for room and meals. My orders told me I couldn't carry my weapon and also read, "The carrying of narcotics or marijuana is prohibited." I thought that a bit strange; I wondered where carrying weed was not prohibited in the military. I also was admonished to use government transportation, available messes and quarters. Good luck for the mess and quarters.

We flew to Guam, from there to Hawaii, and then onto San Francisco all in contract civilian airliners. We flew in our green jungle fatigues and boots with our civvies and Class B uniforms in our duffels. My boots were off quickly after take-off. We landed at the San Francisco airport and grabbed a shuttle to the Hilton hotel in the middle of town—just off Market Street. Phil and I would get the unavailability certificates from Letterman later, if at all—we really didn't care. Being back in the United States was fantastic. The streets were clean and the city organized with no pervasive smog. We checked into the Hilton with rooms on the same floor and carried our duffel bags onto an elevator. A guy in a business suit was looking at us as we got on and asked, "What are you doing, just getting back from Nam?"

I said, "We just got in but are here just for a few days. We need to do some work at Letterman and then go back."

He gave me a card and said, "Well we're having a cocktail party up on the roof at the Cityscape Bar—we have our own party room but it's pretty big. There's a food broker's convention in town and a dinner later out of the hotel but come up as my guest for a few drinks. We would be honored to have you."

I looked at Phil who nodded back. "Sir, we don't have suits but it sounds great."

"Don't worry and wear what you have on. We'll only be there maybe thirty minutes to an hour more so come as soon as you can. The group is going to a show and dinner."

"Thanks. We'll be up in a couple of minutes."

Phil and I went to our rooms and freshened up. I shaved and threw water on my face but didn't change from my fatigues. I then called Phil and asked if he was ready. He asked if we should change. I told him free booze and we'd better hurry. He said he was ready.

The Cityscape Bar looked out over San Francisco and provided a view of the city. It was at chopper height. What was better was the feeling of a real restaurant in the United States and no war. Our friend from the elevator introduced himself and gave each of us his card. He said they would be leaving soon but for us to make ourselves at home and to stay as long as we wanted. We thanked him and got a drink at an open bar—there were two, one at each end of the room. We stuck out a little in our fatigues but the food brokers were warm and hospitable. Apparently our host told them who we were and that we would be coming. As you might expect with food people, there was ample fare. We were hungry and bellied up to the table. I didn't think we would need dinner. The brokers started to leave and reiterated for us to stay and enjoy as long as we could. With the booze, I was already on my second, I felt especially warm and thankful and expressed as much. Soon Phil and I were alone and no one was taking anything away. The bartenders were gone but the bar was open. We sat down next to plates full of oysters; cheeses; globs of raw hamburger poked by onions and capers; little philo triangles filled with some wonderful chicken mixture; smoked salmon; and slices of prime rib with horseradish on little sour dough rolls. A big fruit display was in the middle of the table but it didn't appear touched and we didn't touch it. How could these guys have this and then go for dinner? The dinner must have been something else.

We had lots to do the next day and were exhausted after the trip so we left the Cityscape around 9 P.M. and went to our rooms. I saw Phil take a loaded plate with him. I fixed yet another drink and took that with me. I turned on the TV, it was the first time in almost six months I saw television, and fell asleep on the double bed still in my fatigues but sans boots.

I awakened at 6 A.M., took an alka selzer, and started planning my day. I emptied my pants pocket and the key to the office jeep padlock fell out. I had taken it with me. What a stupido! It was parked outside the office and no one could use it—I had the key. We got a ride to the airport with a friend at Headquarters Company. I used the jeep earlier in the day and never put the key back on its hook by the office door. The guys would really be pissed and I felt awful. What a start. About 8:30 I called Phil's room. There was no answer. Maybe he was in the shower. I put on some pants and went down the hall and knocked on his door. Again, no answer. He had gone without me. I guess that was proper, if it was my defense I wouldn't want the prosecutor around. I started to hustle; I didn't want Phil to be the first to speak to Markum.

Pete Markum was a Specialist Four and in an amputee ward, a large room occupied by several other Vietnam casualties. The room had lots of windows and was bright and sunny. I introduced myself and it was apparent Phil hadn't yet gotten to see Markum. He asked me if I had talked with Gerry Bailey and I told him I went in the field to see him. He wanted to know all about my visit, what the guys were doing, where they were, whether they asked after him, and what was going on. I related to him as much of what I knew and talked about my flight back through the monsoons which I don't think interested him too much. I told him all the guys asked after him and, specifically, Gerry Bailey told me to talk to him. I explained we were going to have a deposition the day after tomorrow and hopefully, we could use that in court rather than having him come to testify. He said he didn't mind going back; they were planning to fit him with a prosthetic as soon as his leg heeled, and he could be ready in about a month. That's not what the doc's told me when I called from Vietnam but I didn't want to tell him that. They were talking more like three months and that didn't include physical therapy. We couldn't keep White in pretrial that long and might lose other witnesses so a delay to trial of a few months was unquestionable.

I asked Markum how he got wounded and he answered, "We were moving through a forest of rubber trees when we got hit by an NVA ambush. We didn't know how many there were but they had lots of rockets and maybe a mortar or two. We formed up against the area of attack and laid out a welcome. A bunch of trees came down and I understand later they found six NVA bodies. We stopped and no more rockets were coming in. We were still receiving small arms fire so everybody pretty much kept down. I manned the gun on top of our ACAV and was giving bursts of 50 cal's to wherever I could see or hear gunfire. It was a pretty good gunfight before the Apaches got there. I heard something to my side and was adjusting my position so I could return fire and my foot must have been outside the shield in front of my gun because I felt a horrendous blow. It actually knocked me back away from the gun and off the track. Someone yelled 'medic' and I must have passed out because the next thing I remember was being beside the ACAV with someone messing with my foot. The Apaches rode in just over the trees soon after blasting away into the jungle which put an end to the contact. Behind them a Huey medevac hovered over us and someone dropped a cage through the rubber trees and someone hitched me up to it. The medic drugged me some but I remember being pulled through the trees and into the chopper. They took me to a hospital in Nha Trang for a couple of days and then to Cam Ranh Bay where they flew me here."

I asked how he was and he said a lot better than most of the guys there. I then asked about the fight and Charlie Marshall's murder. He told me pretty much what everyone else did but when we came to White leaving the fight after Charlie got Hector down and started punching him, he told me, "I saw the black dude. He was standing right across from me and looked pretty mad. I watched him because I thought he might jump into the fight and if he did I would too. But he put his hand in his pocket and appeared to be looking for something. Then he turned and started walking down the path between the two rows of buildings just back from where the fight was going on. I saw him walking and then start running. He went into a building and then I went back to watching the fight. It seemed that Charlie was letting up and the rigger he was fighting knew it. The guy actually smiled at Charlie. Then this guy comes out of nowhere and starts punching Charlie in the back. I could see some blood and then I saw he had a knife. A few people started going toward the fighters and I did too but before I could get to them the black dude was off Charlie and covered with blood. Charlie moved in an attempt to turn around and he tried to get up but then collapsed on the ground. The worst was a deep slash in his neck. He was pumping blood pretty bad. I felt terrible for him because immediately when I saw him I didn't think he'd make it."

I asked Pete Markum, "What kind of knife was it?"

"I couldn't see. I only saw a blade coming out of the back of his hand. He would swing it like it wasn't the first time the guy was ever in a knife fight."

"Why did he go back to the barracks?"

"I didn't know it was his barracks at the time, I just saw him go in a building on the run but I'm certain he was looking for his knife." Markum readjusted his leg as he spoke, obviously in physical discomfort.

I went over all the other things we would get into in the deposition and told him he had to cooperate with the defense attorney who would see him probably later that day. I told him the black guy was Cornelius White. I admonished him not to conjecture or give opinions but only to state the facts as he knew them. I told him it was an opinion that White was looking for a knife and he should not say that. I let him know that his testimony might be stronger if he stated just what he saw and then let the court make the inference from his deposition as to what White was looking for. I think he understood and I told him I would try to drop by again before the deposition but if I couldn't, I would see him the day after next. We thanked each other and I left to go over to the SJA office.

I met LTC Rice who lined me up with the court reporter and one of his trial counsels who helped me get the deposition going. I checked to see if Phil had been by the hotel. He was there and had left an hour ago. I presumed he was at the hospital so I caught up with him there and told him our plans for the deposition and we made plans for dinner. He told me he got a rental car and asked if I needed a ride back to the hotel. We decided to meet late afternoon. We went across the Golden Gate to the Spinnaker for dinner and my steak made the entire trip worthwhile. We didn't get steaks like that in Nam.

The deposition went off without a hitch. Markum obviously didn't like Cornelius White but he didn't say anything that would detract from what he previously told me about the murder. His fighting days were over. Phil and I got the requisite sour dough bread to eat and take back with us to the guys in the office and we looked around town and across the bridge to Sausalito. When we got back it was nearing Thanksgiving and the trial. Phil stipulated to Markum's testimony, as LTC Cassidy predicted he would, to include that Markum saw White searching for something in his pocket before he ran off looking for a knife.

Phil moved to suppress the autopsy photos. I knew it was coming but didn't anticipate the vehemence of Phil's objections. I knew they exhibited a terrible attack. I figured at the minimum, I could salvage them to rebut extenuation and mitigation. Both of us were prepared and had strong arguments but the decision was one of those that rested in the discretion of the military judge. His first look at the evidence gave me a clue I would lose. He clearly was shocked at what stood before him. Notwithstanding I felt him leaning my way when I pounded on the theme that White was vicious and the pictures showed it. Phil could see it as well and came up with a compromise. He presented the judge a diagram of a body with puncture wounds and cuts marked in ink where they appeared on Charlie's body. It was plain but showed the number of punctures and cuts without the photograph of a sliced and torn up naked body on a sterile slab. I objected but Judge Stanford quickly adopted it as not prejudicial and granted Phil's motion as modified by his offer. Phil gave the judge an out and he took it to my dismay.

Cornelius through Phil pled not guilty. My turn came first and I called the riggers, Bill Ledford, Jim Stagnitti, and Scott Perkins. Perkins testified about White's room and how it was set up. Spitz was there but I didn't call him. I called Gerry Bailey from the 11th ACR. Phil's cross didn't do much and he didn't pursue. I didn't push Bailey on his conclusion that White was going to get a knife but rather made him stick to the facts. I made it clear to the court that Cornelius killed Charlie by a knife he retrieved from the barracks. I introduced the knife and gave it to the court. I held back on my theory for premeditation that to open the knife needed some intervening thought with the idea that Phil would make a big deal about Cornelius' ability to whip it open quickly. I could come back to that later and get in my evidence that it was not the blood that made it difficult to open but the newness of the knife in the go-to bag. Spitz was available if Phil said anything. If Phil didn't, I could address the knife in closing. The court had the knife; I could tell them to examine it to determine how hard it was to open. I introduced Phil's diagram of the body and the location of the various cuts. I introduced and read the stipulation based on Markum's deposition. I figured I had proven that Specialist White had to be thinking of what he was going to do. Premeditation was weak at this point but I had it. I rested.

Phil was in a bit of a quandary. He didn't want Cornelius to testify but I made a case for premeditation so he had to pick a defensive strategy. He could go for a defense of another theory with White giving an explanation for his actions and try to get off Scot free. I had a pretty strong case so he had to factor in his chances on that. He might go the murder two route and try to get the court to buy off on a passion of the moment defense to murder one. To go for the defense of another theory he had to call White. He might even go for both defense of another and the passion of the moment which is what he did.

Phil first called an Army psychiatrist who initially testified about his credentials so he could be qualified as an expert and give opinion evidence. He then testified, "A soldier is trained in combat to fight for his unit and specifically other members. The Army drills into each combatant not to leave anyone behind. The military depends on unit cohesion and it's well known that soldiers fight more for their unit than for any other motive. A soldier in combat, for example, will fight to keep his unit intact thinking all the time about unit welfare rather than, for example, killing communists to restrain fascism from creeping throughout the world. If his comrade were in mortal peril the soldier would exert deadly force to help him and probably would act without much thought. It's not unheard of that such an action might not be remembered especially if committed in passion."

Phil asked, "What if a soldier's comrade was in a hand-to-hand fight and was on the bottom bleeding and clearly losing the fight? In your professional opinion, could the soldier, under those circumstances, act in passion in a deadly manner to defend the soldier who was about to lose the fight?"

"Yes, especially in a combat environment."

"Could a combat support setting and a fight between two soldiers produce the same result?"

"Yes, I think it could."

Phil looked at me and said, "Your witness."

"Doc, we all understand combat and the need for each other's support for protection."

"Yes, that's what I'm talking about."

"I understand that some soldiers go through agonizing ordeals that cause such emotional stress they can't remember what happened."

"Yes, that's basically what I'm saying. Frequently when the mind experiences a horrific event it will blot it out from the person's memory in order for the person to function. This happens to everybody. When something bad happens you don't want to think about it because it bothers you. You consciously place that thought out of your consciousness and think about more pleasant things. Well, if the event is really terrible, your psyche makes the decision to forget for you."

"You mean this would happen in a terrible combat encounter?"

The doc said, "We have experiences of it happening especially when a soldier's comrades are killed horribly before their eyes in a nasty firefight or attack. A soldier might have flashbacks of these incidents for the rest of their lives and might even require psychiatric treatment and possibly medication to blot out or control the flashes of the bad memory. This is a form of what is commonly known as post traumatic stress disorder."

"Are there other symptoms related to battle fatigue that might cause this?"

"This isn't a case of battle fatigue but could be a case of an action precipitated by an immediate fear of mortal danger to a friend or comrade and that might set off a passion that would not immediately be remembered."

"Do you know of similar such incidents of memory loss in defense of other cases?"

"Well, not personally."

I asked him, "How did you formulate this opinion?"

"I remember studying world war two post traumatic stress cases in medical school."

"Well, can you relate for the court some examples of incidents that might trigger such an event?"

"Basically it's mortal danger to the person being assisted under terrible circumstances."

"You mean an enemy pointing a gun at your friend in combat where people are shooting and killing one another?"

He said, "If it were an enemy who he knew would kill his buddy then it might."

"Might this apply to whenever two soldiers in the same unit had a fight?"

"It depends on the circumstances."

"Is it that the quality of the deadly force triggers the response?"

"Usually, this happens, that is the mind will cause the person to forget something composed of a trained response when there's a specific fear of mortal danger in a setting of substantial mayhem."

"So in a fistfight with some wrestling it would be unusual?

"It probably would but could still happen."

I thought I had him. "What if there was an intermittent event that removed the person from the horror of the actual mortal danger, would you expect the same result?"

He quickly answered, "Not usually, but the circumstances can always change. It usually happens when there's an immediate and continuous fear of a mortal event."

"If a fight were occurring between two members of the same unit would it have the same combat stress as combat with an enemy?"

"No. But the two in question were not members of the same unit."

"Have you actually treated Specialist White?"

"No. I was asked by Captain Smith about possibilities of memory loss and stress and he asked me to testify."

I started to get into the break between when defense of another might come into action and when it was executed but decided I might not want to hear that answer and besides that was not the doc's expertise, it was a legal question. I also didn't ask him about the level of violence; that Cornelius' vicious attack was substantially more life threatening than the fight between Hector and Charlie. I left that to the judge's instructions and the court with my closing argument. I thought I had whittled down the psychiatrist's theory as it applied in the case and with the doc not treating White felt I had enough. I smiled broadly, looked at the court, thanked the doctor, and sat down.

Phil then called Cornelius. I swore him in and Phil started his examination.

"Please state your name and unit."

"Specialist Four Cornelius White. I'm assigned to the 109th Quartermaster Company and stationed with the riggers at Cam Ranh Bay, Vietnam."

"What are your duties with the 109th?"

"I rig chutes for supplies and material delivered by Air Force C-130's. I also rig bombs. I fix them for high-level drops or low-level drops; depends on what the load master tells me is needed."

"How did you get in the Army?"

"I enlisted after high school."

"When was that?"

"About a year and a half ago?"

"Who do you have at home?"

"My mom died when I was born and her sister raise me. I don't know who my father is. My mom's really my aunt."

"When did you make Spec Four?"

"About three months ago."

Phil was finished with the opening amenities clearly designed to make White comfortable and got into it. "You heard from Captain Thompson's witnesses about an argument up at the rigger company club. Were you there and if so, would you please tell the court what happened."

"Yes sir. I was in the club. Folks come to the Bay to get some beach. Some dudes from the 11th were there and I seen them at the club. They's drinkin' beer and spoutin' how's they're the true warriors of the war. Hector and some other guys get into it wit them and they all starts yellin' at each other. Stewart, the club dude, tells them to git and the club empties. This big dude starts hittin' Hector pretty good and then they wrestle and Hector goes down. The white dude then gits on top and starts hittin' him hard. I thinks he's gonna kill him so I gits my knife from the barracks and come to help out. I's afraid for Hector and thinking just to git the guy off. I don't member much after I git back to the fight."

When he stopped talking the courtroom was utterly silent. I saw the court reporter look at Cornelius whose eyes were big and who was staring at Phil Smith. Phil broke the tension after a minute. "What's the first thing you remember after you got to the fight?"

Cornelius was very quiet. "Sir, I member being over the white dude with the knife in my hand. Someone had me by da arms and was holdin' me. I heared someone say drop da knife and I did. Dat's the first thing I heared."

"Do you remember stabbing PFC Marshall?"

"No sir. I don't remember it at all."

Phil looked at me and said, "Your witness."

I started with some of my own bullshit. "Specialist White, how did you like Cam Rhan Bay?"

"It's fine, sir."

I immediately could tell Phil had coached him well. "You said you were raised by your aunt. Do you have any brothers or sisters?"

"My family's the same as hers and I've got two sisters."

"How old are they?"

"Auriel's the oldest, she's twenty-six and married. Rosie's twenty-four."

"Do they write you?"

"I got a couple letters from Auriel."

"What are your plans after Vietnam?"

"I think I might make the Army a career."

I thought I could help him there, maybe a lifetime career. I looked over to the court in dismay and back at White. "When the 11th Cav guys were in the bar, did you talk to them?"

"No."

"Well, just what did you do?"

"I was drinkin' some beer and they was sayin' how much they did and Hector was mouthin' off to them about what we did."

"So, I take it you were drinking with Hector?"

"No, Hector was with some other guys. I was sittin' with Leroy and George."

"Who were they?"

"Leroy's a black dude from Philadelphia and George is from Sumter, South Carolina. Both are with the 109th."

"Is George black also?"

"Yes sir."

"Is Hector white or black?"

"He's Mexican."

"Does he live in your barracks?"

"He lives down the way from my barracks, maybe two buildings down."

"Does he work with you?"

"Yea, he's a rigger."

"Are you on the same shift?"

"Sometimes."

"Are you in the same work detail?"

I could tell he was getting onto my line of questioning. He answered, "Sometimes." He figured he'd better become Hector's friend.

I decided not to pursue, the court saw what was going on. Instead I asked, "Why did you leave the bar when the club manager, Joe Stewart, told Hector and the 11th Cav guys to get out of the bar?"

"What do you mean?"

I figured Phil had told him if he got in a bind to ask me to repeat the question? I asked again, "Why did you follow the fighters outside?"

"I guess I wanted to see a fight."

"Can you describe it?"

He hesitated a second too long but then answered. "Everyone likes to see a good fight."

"So how did the fight go?"

"Well the big guy hits Hector in the face after they start yelling at each other. He hit Hector first, I'm certain of that. Then Hector gets in a few licks of his own. Then they start wrestlin' and the 11th guy slams Hector down to the ground. That's when I thought he's gonna kill him."

"Who's going to kill whom?"

"Well the white guy's on top of Hector and he hits him."

"Specialist White, have you ever been in any fights?"

"Yes sir."

"Do the fighters punch and wrestle?"

"Yea."

I knew what he would say but I wanted the court to hear the scenario. "So, were the two fighters here doing anything different than what you know that other fighters do?"

"Wadda you mean?"

He wanted some time to think. "What was different about this fight than fights you were in?"

"Most of the time I was in fist fights, not wrestlin'."

"So how did those fights end?"

"Someone always jumps in and stops em."

"Have you been around fights where someone was killed?"

He thought a minute and looked around the room. "I knows some fights back home; guys got knifed and was hurt pretty bad. I think one of them didn't make it."

"Why didn't you jump in and end the fight between Hector and PFC Marshall, Specialist White?"

"They had two other dudes standing by and Marshall was a big tough guy."

I had Cornelius thinking and the court knew he was thinking. "So exactly what did you do?"

"I saw Hector bleeding pretty bad so I needed something to help me convince PFC Marshall to stop fighting. I looked for my knife and didn't have it, so I went to my bunk to get it."

"Tell me about going to your barracks?"

"It was pretty close so I ran up to the room and got my knife."

"So you ran the whole way?"

"Yea. I don't know what the dude meant when he says I walked and then ran."

"OK, when you got to the barracks, exactly what did you do?"

"I got my knife and came back."

"Where was the knife?"

Phil objected because he knew I was getting into too much thought process. He said it was irrelevant but the judge overruled him and I continued. "Where was the knife?"

"I looked for it in my dirty work pants but couldn't find it. I knew I had a knife in my go-to bag so I got that and started running back to the fight."

"What's a 'go-to bag'?"

"Just in case we come under attack which is pretty unlikely, it's a bag where we keep some stuff to hold us over for a couple of days until we get back to our barracks."

It finally hit me. "So the knife you got to take back to the fight was not the knife you normally carry to work?"

Phil objected again as irrelevant and as a question already answered. The judge said overruled and told Specialist White to answer the question.

"No, it's my 'go-to' knife."

"Was it a new knife?"

I knew the damage was done but Cornelius answered. "I don't know, the first sergeant gave it to me for my bag."

"When did you open the knife?"

"I don't remember."

"Did you take the knife with you when you went back to the fight?"

"I can't remember."

"What's the last thing you remember?"

"I member getting the knife and that's it."

I lead him a bit; I could on cross. "Then the next thing you remember is the guy holding you and someone telling you to drop the knife, right?"

"Yes sir."

"Have you ever been in a knife fight?"

"No sir."

"So you don't know how a knife fighter would hold a knife?"

"No sir."

I went over to the court and took the knife from the table in front of them and took it to the witness stand and asked Cornelius how he would hold it. Phil objected and said it was irrelevant. The judge asked us to approach. He asked what I was attempting to do. I told him the knife was very difficult to open and I wanted the court to see that it took someone who was thinking what he was doing to open it. The judge said he thought that was permissible but Phil said the witness had answered that he couldn't remember. The judge said overruled and I went back and gave Cornelius the knife and asked him to open it and show the court how he would hold it. He struggled to open the knife and finally did and held it in the palm of his hands in an innocent fashion. I thanked him, went up and took it from him, closed it and put it back on the table in front of the court.

I sat down, looked over at White and said, "That's all."

Phil came back and asked again about White's memory. Cornelius swore he didn't remember anything of the attack. Phil then brought in some character witnesses from the 109th. One was White's work supervisor, who said he knew Specialist White as a mild and peaceful person and that he didn't think he would be capable of such an attack.

Phil then rested. The judge asked if Phil or I had any suggestions for his instructions and I offered a couple on defense of another especially with the use of reasonable force as dependent on the apprehension of death or grievous bodily harm and that the test is subjective and what a reasonably prudent person might do under the same circumstances. Phil objected and the judge said he would come up with something. I felt I had a number of soldiers at the fight, none of whom expressed any danger of grievous bodily harm or death.

I argued premeditation to the court emphasizing White's decision to get the knife and I reminded the court that Specialist White was facing life imprisonment which might influence his memory more than a stressful combat incident. I didn't dwell further on that. The rest was a reiteration of the facts. What made Cornelius snap is anyone's guess. Phil presented a masterful closing with what he had to work with. He spoke of the quality of life in the Vietnam Theater and the closeness of comrades in arms.

The court was out for four or five hours and I was worried. Phil seemed happier as the time crept on. Finally, the President of the Court came out and said he wanted to ask the judge a question. The judge opened the court and the President said, "Your Honor may we wash the knife? It has dried blood on it and we're worried about changing the evidence. Can we do that?"

The judge looked over at me. "That's not a problem."

The President then left and Phil said he wanted a mistrial. The judge asked on what grounds and he said because they wanted to change the evidence. The judge denied it. The court was out another 45 minutes and came back with a conviction of murder one. After the extenuation and mitigation phase of the proceedings, the court sentenced Specialist Four Cornelius White to imprisonment at hard labor for the remainder of his natural life, reduction to the lowest enlisted grade, total forfeitures, and to be dishonorably discharged from the Army. I felt I had done all I could to avenge Charlie Marshall. Little did I know at the time this would be my last major criminal case.

Judicial Duty

LTC Cassidy's new deputy was getting upset with my frequent absences judging special courts martial; at least I thought it was the new deputy, Cassidy was a pretty sly dog and the deputy most likely was imparting Cassidy's direction. The two full-time special court judges promised by the JAG folks both at USARV and the Pentagon had just arrived but not too many JA's knew what to expect with them. The deputy called me in and told me to back off a bit and let the full-time guys start taking the load. I was doing a bunch. Already in November, I had sat on thirteen trials and my December docket was growing. I didn't think it was taking away from my duties with Saigon Support Command; after all I just got a conviction on a big case and had a pretty good record. Forsythe had DEROSed so I didn't believe I had to get permission, at least that's what I rationalized. In any event, I was told to back off; he didn't tell me to stop but told me to send any requests for my services to the full-time judges for their first refusal. I didn't realize I was undercutting their efforts but my docket was full and I had no idea what they were doing.

I still had difficulty saying no. I got calls from the 4th Transportation Command in Saigon, the 11th ACR, the 29th Support Group, and several others. As directed, I always asked if they had tried to get a full-time judge. The answer was pretty much consistent. They wanted me. Not that I was all that friendly to the prosecution. I didn't hang too many and did my best to be fair. Most of the cases were not guilty pleas but the command evidence was usually convincing and there were few not guilty verdicts. I marked that up to the good work of the command JA's and good leadership. Strong leaders didn't use military justice as a crutch. I especially was hard on guys sleeping while on guard. I heard about a unit at an isolated location upcountry that was overrun by VC due to a sleepy guard. There were substantial casualties. He got a general court-martial and the max. My thoughts were guard-duty sleeping in combat was serious by itself and didn't need casualties for aggravation. The offense was a disservice to the entire unit, whether you were overrun or not.

Drew Downes; Combat failure to obey

Sergeant Drew Downes was drafted in 1967 and reenlisted after his first tour. He was promoted quickly and his platoon leader soon realized he was a leader. He made squad leader within two months of his first foray into the jungle. His platoon leader was a West Pointer, a competent officer, and good leader. His company commander, an ROTC grad from Notre Dame was on his second tour in

Nam, the first in which he earned a Bronze Star for valor. Drew had been in country for about four months and his squad was on point on a patrol in the central highlands. The platoon leader was about a quarter mile behind and was moving slowly through the high grasses and rubber trees with two other platoons at his flank and the first sergeant, the CO, and two squads about fifty yards behind. They were projecting a small summit about two miles out to set up for the night and were moving quietly and slowly but still they were too noisy.

Drew was stripped down with most of his gear and the gear of the rest of his squad portioned off and carried by members of the platoon following behind. They didn't mind because they all had a turn at point and it was the most dangerous position in the maneuver. Drew carried a five-shot 12-gauge sawed-off shotgun. He fashioned himself with non reflective dull brown paint, a stringer of grenades, and his platoon leader's 45-caliber pistol with three clips at his combat web belt along with a canteen, knife, a cushioned ammo pack of twenty shotgun shells, and a medical pack. The lieutenant carried his M-16. The ROTC company commander told him a shotgun was the best weapon for close-in jungle fighting but he had to get it himself. Drew asked a friend going to Hawaii on R&R to buy one for him and smuggle it back. Drew used a small bungee strap to hold his fatigue pants at the bottom. He was wearing jungle boots, a green undershirt, and a dark green do-rag on his head. He had five men with him all spread out. The five had M-16's with lots of ammo clipped to their belts and otherwise were going light. They had their arms and faces, the only parts of their bodies visible, painted in jungle colors.

Chipper Dawson was about ten feet ahead of Drew. He raised his hand and signaled a stop and to get down. Drew relayed the signal to the rest of the squad. Chipper then pointed to some thick foliage moving his arm back and forth in a pointing motion with a signal that there might be a trap. Drew quietly crawled forward and saw to his right what looked like some freshly cut branches covering something. He moved around the cover and came up to Chipper. All they could hear were bird calls, insect chirping, and wind rustling some scrub trees. Chipper pointed out a clear booby trap configured with a mostly hidden wire running about twenty-five feet away from them and then up a tree. Someone had attempted to cover the wire with dirt and broken off grasses but did a poor job. Part of wire even glinted with the sunlight. Mark Glenn started to crawl towards the two but Drew held up the palm of his hand to signal Mark to stop. Chipper and Drew then heard a whispered conversation coming from out of the ground. It was Vietnamese, nasal sounds with clipped endings, and it sounded excited with a lot being said. Drew signaled for everyone to hold, got his shot gun ready, and waited to see what would happen. A VC broke from a spider hole just to the other side of the tree holding up the wire. The VC had what looked like a land mine under his arm. He covered up the area from which he emerged and started to move away. Drew signaled Chipper to come with him and crawled back to where Mark Glenn had stopped and quietly said, "Let's get outta here, they're underground and it might be a supply spot."

Drew led his squad carefully from the area constantly looking for mines or other booby traps. They saw a land mine in a small clearing that was obvious to anyone looking for danger. Mark placed crosses made of small branches at trees on both sides of the clearing so they would indicate to anyone nearby that there was danger afoot. The squad then hurried back to the main group leaving a sentry about half way to report if they were followed. Drew reported what he saw. The CO moved the company up and set an ambush about 150 yards on his side of the entrance to the VC underground tunnels. He called in air support requesting a strike to commence from the opposite direction. He reported he was unsure of the size of the enemy force and requested reinforcements be placed on alert. About 20 minutes later two Air Force F-4 Phantoms zoomed over the jungle coming from the far side while the captain waved his arms. They circled and came back shooting up the area around the spider hole with their 20 mm cannons. They made another pass and this time laid down some napalm that turned the target into a blazing inferno. We heard some muffled secondary explosions and the fire sent up lots of black smoke. We waited but no one came into our ambush zone and we couldn't see anybody around. After about thirty minutes the platoon leader signaled Drew to check out what happened. Drew's squad came out from their hastily dug holes and sneaked over to where the bombs hit. They saw a deep hole still burning that might have been a supply depot. He warned his squad of ammo that still might cook off. Drew sent Chipper back to report an all clear. The CO came up and confirmed the find. They didn't see any bodies but there were substantial war materials destroyed by the Air Force jets. Drew and Chipper got the Bronze Star for valor and each member of his squad got an Army commendation medal. Drew later was advanced to platoon sergeant and promoted. He saw a fair amount of action patrolling the area and some of his men got wounded but he had no loss of life. He and Chipper became close friends and each depended on the other in the confines of the jungle battlefield. Drew got a reputation for infighting with his shotgun but in reality, he never used it in combat. One time he used it to shoot a snake. After his first tour he and Chipper reenlisted together and both were assigned to the 199th Light Infantry Brigade. They found themselves again in the high grasses but this time closer to

Saigon. They had a pretty good officer but he stayed for only one mission. A new platoon leader, 1LT Graham Knott, took over. It was his first time in the jungle and knew it all or at least thought he did.

Waiting for Mission Brief

Knott led a couple of night missions out of the base camp to provide protective cover. This was routine duty and everyone had his turn. The platoon was to listen and report on any seen or perceived enemy activity. The patrols were more a nuisance than anything else but about every fifteenth time someone would see some activity and the platoon would report it or fight back from contact. Knott, however, thought they were great. He volunteered his platoon each week. The third time out Drew saw some bent grasses in one area and not far away some mud where it shouldn't be. These signs were not conclusive but they merited further examination. Drew caught up to Knott. "Sir, I think there is a small enemy unit ahead of us."

Knott said, "What makes you think that?"

"There's bent grass as if a bunch of people walked over it and there is a rut in the mud as if a wheel went through it."

"Is that it?"

"Yes sir."

Knott said, "We've got about seventy-five acres to cover and can't wait for signs like that. We have to move on."

"Sir, we need to be on the lookout and especially careful."

"I always am Sergeant Downes." Knott led the platoon personally without any lookouts or advance force. After all, he was an advance force.

They came to a stream flowing down toward their way and started following it through the area. It was in a ravine between two sloping hills covered with heavy vegetation. Drew kept telling the platoon to spread out and most did but some inexperienced kids bunched up close to the lieutenant who continued to plow ahead with them in the valley alongside the stream. After about a half mile, Knott signaled to Chipper to move up to the front. The hill on the right had flattened out and they were stopped by a thirty foot cliff with a little pool at its base made up by the stream flowing in the left side. Knott and his little gaggle quietly rested on a moss-covered clearing next to the pool. The rest of the column got what cover they could on both sides of the stream. They could see up the hill on their left but not beyond the cliff. The rise to their left was covered by dense foliage. Knott told Chipper to go down the stream and check out if anything was behind the cliff. Chipper looked up at the hill to his left as maybe a better vantage point from which to reconnoiter but moved out as told. He was about twenty yards around the bend when all hell broke loose.

A North Vietnamese force had set up just on the other side of the cliff in the rise above the stream. Chipper, their only target, was initially hit in the back. He dropped his M-16 and staggered. Another shot tore off the side of his head splattering bone and brain matter in a cloud of red. He died and fell in the stream, his blood coloring the water. Some of the VC then scooted up to look over the top of the cliff and started firing at Knott and his gaggle at their resting area. Knott quickly low crawled back to some rocks that provided cover to his right but three of those with him were shot, one wounded seriously. Miraculously they were not all killed.

The NVA did a poor job of setting and executing the ambush. They thought the Americans would proceed around the bend and get caught with little room for retreat which they would have if someone hadn't been over zealous and unloaded on Chipper. The NVA leader was inexperienced and his raw troops impatient. Tet used up most of the NVA's experienced troops and this was the VC leader's first action.

Drew initiated counter fire and directed his team to the rise on the left from which they were able to direct fire into the ambush and the top of the cliff. The lieutenant with Drew's covering fire sent some guys to pull the wounded into his little protected area. Drew was firing over Chipper and saw the unit's radio abandoned alongside the stream just up from the wounded. He crawled through the foliage down the hill and then broke out from it and into a run to retrieve it. He found a little ridge at the edge of the left side of the stream and used that for cover to get back to where he called for help. The lieutenant was pinned down or just hunkered down, Drew wasn't sure which. The firing slowed but the VC continued intermittent blasts both into the jungle hiding Chipper and his fire team and over the cliff at Knott's gaggle. A Magic Dragon showed up in about fifteen minutes and made a gun run using its Quad-50's to spray one side of the hill and then the top of the cliff. The North Vietnamese fled quickly carrying their dead and wounded and melting into the jungle.

Drew saw Chipper face down in the stream. He ran down to him and wiped the blood and water from what was left of his face, gritting his teeth to hold back an emotional wail. He carried him still dripping water and fluids to where the unit congregated. Drew covered Chipper with some palm fronds until the corpse was zippered up in a big rubber bag. A medic shoved one of Chipper's two dog tags up and into the roof of his mouth. There was no place for dust offs to land in the little ravine and the wounded were extracted by cage to hovering choppers, a potential target in the enemy infested area. Chipper was carried with the wounded for his trip home. Drew was shaken, broken, and more scared than he had ever been.

Knott reported back to headquarters that his fight was a success and that the NVA had lost a major battle. He estimated the VC had at least twenty KIAs. He said his platoon drove them off from a planned attack on the base camp. Drew told the CO what happened but the CO said he already had the report. He thanked Drew for his efforts and told him he was sorry his friend was killed. The wounded were medivaced out of country and four new soldiers were assigned to the platoon. A week later the CO gave Knott a mission to reconnoiter an area about fifteen clicks from the base camp as a site for a possible listening post. It would require the platoon to stay in the jungle five to seven days. He was going to support them once they got going with two platoons from another company. Knott would be in charge.

Knott called his platoon together just outside his hooch to brief them about the mission. He said they would head out the next day before noon. Drew couldn't believe the hurry and didn't feel the platoon could be any where near ready for a week's stay in the jungle in that time frame. He told Knott the platoon wasn't ready and Knott said they were going to move out at noon and if he had to stay up all night to get the platoon ready, then he was to do it. It was 1600. Drew said he wasn't going. Knott said he would go; it was an order, for him to get ready, and immediately start the preparations. Drew again said he wasn't going and turned around in front of the platoon and walked out of the briefing area and over to the first sergeant's shed.

Drew told the first sergeant that Knott was incompetent, dangerous, and said he wouldn't go on patrol with him. The first sergeant told him if he didn't go he could go to jail for a long time and it could be the death penalty; it would be disobedience to orders during war. Drew said he still wasn't going. In the meantime Knott went to the company commander and told him what happened. The CO told him to take it to battalion legal. When Drew left, the first sergeant called the battalion sergeant major and informed him what was going on. The battalion sergeant major told his boss and Drew was put on quarters, reassigned to the battalion holding company, and put in charge of work details. Charges were drawn up for disobedience to the orders of a commissioned officer and violation of regulations by the possession of a privately-owned weapon—the shot gun Drew still carried. The battalion commander recommended a special court-martial and called the brigade commander to explain his reasoning. The 199th CO told his sergeant major to have the legal clerk ensure they got the same military judge they had before. The battalion CO reassigned Knott to assistant S-4, a logistics staff position, and sent the current assistant S-4 who was in his sixth month in country to take over Knott's platoon. The platoon didn't go on the week's patrol to find a listening post.

The 199th legal clerk relayed I was personally requested to sit on Sergeant Downes' court-martial. He asked if I was available. I told him I could do it; it was easy because they were about a 20 minute jeep ride from where my office was but that they had to get a no go from the full time in-country special court judges in Saigon. In about a half hour I got a call back saying they were unavailable. I requested transportation and he said that wouldn't be a problem. They had three cases for me—the first was a wrongful marijuana possession. A company staff sergeant caught the accused lighting up in the back of a deuce and a half. The accused pled not guilty. The main issue was whether the staff sergeant had a proper reason to look into the back of the deuce and half to see what was going on. The defense counsel made a big deal about the staff sergeant not having the expertise to know what marijuana smelled like. The trial counsel countered that the staff sergeant had a responsibility to check out smoke coming from the back of the deuce and half no matter what it smelled like and when he saw the accused in the back corner of the truck with a roach between his thumb and forefinger and letting out his breath with an exhale of smoke, he could assume it was marijuana. The CID reported that what the sergeant took was, in fact, marijuana. I found the accused guilty. It was his second offense. The accused was in his tenth month, had been drafted, and had served well except for the two drug cases. I reduced him from PFC to private, gave him forfeiture of two-thirds of his pay for three months, and confined him to hard labor for three months. He would serve three months at LBJ and then the two months remaining on his tour. The time served at LBJ didn't count toward your DEROS. It was a double whammy.

The next case was absence without leave for six days. The accused went to Saigon on pass for a day and didn't return for a week. He pled not guilty and said that he went into town, met a girl at a bar and went to a place where they could be alone. He couldn't remember anything after that until the day before he came back when he found himself in a bar by himself with no money. He had no prior experiences of lost memory and there was no psychiatric testimony. I found him guilty and sentenced him to six months confinement, six months forfeitures, and reduced him to E-1. He had been in country for two months and had no prior record. If he had just said he went on a lark for a week, I might have cut him some slack but his story was too much to swallow. I didn't consider lying under oath in a court martial, whether it be the accused or not, acceptable.

Sergeant Downes was my last case. He pled not guilty to both charges. He explained his reasoning for not obeying Lieutenant Knott's orders and said it was impossible for him to get his platoon ready for a week's foray in the jungle in less than a full day. He explained the shot gun was useful in the jungle and that his previous company commander suggested he get it. He said it cost him $145 and another $15 for the shells. He said he used it with his superiors' acquiescence and they all agreed it was a great jungle weapon. I had independently heard the same thing from some infantry officer friends. We all wondered why the Army didn't provide an adequate supply of shotguns for jungle warfare. I asked him if he knew it was unauthorized and he said his old CO told him it was and that's why he had to smuggle it in country. That was a little tidbit I would have preferred not to know but it was an admission. I asked where it was and he said his company commander took it away and he didn't know what he did with it. I asked where his old CO was and he told me they had all gone home; this was his second tour. Sergeant Downes testified as to how his friend was killed. Knott testified and said he had a mission and gave a specific order to his platoon sergeant. He and Downes were at odds as to the success of the mission that killed Chipper Dawson.

It was clear that the order was legal and Downes disobeyed it. Downes attempted to show his superior knowledge of jungle warfare by his past exploits and Knott's relative inexperience and based his defense on that. Knott said the platoon was already set up for a week in the jungle and Downes didn't have much to do to get them going.

I found Downes guilty of disobedience and not guilty of the illegal weapons charge. In extenuation and mitigation it became clear why the case was referred to special court. Downes testified what he was doing, that he hadn't been in pre-trial confinement, and that he only had a few months remaining in his tour. I asked about the mission he refused to go on and he said it never happened. He told me Lieutenant Knott was reassigned to assistant supply officer for the battalion. The battalion sergeant major testified that Downes was a good leader but was under terrific pressure especially after the loss of his best friend. I sentenced him to be reduced in grade from sergeant to private and to be restricted for two months to an area as determined appropriate by the convening authority. I felt that military discipline demanded the reduction. Downes could no longer lead. Confinement would serve no purpose but he might be of use to the command. Reduction in pay wouldn't be appropriate, his pay was going to be reduced with his loss in grade, and he would be working. I never heard another word from the command or anyone else about the case, one of the toughest I had in Vietnam.

New Assignment

In the middle of December, LTC Cassidy requested me to come to his office. I thought I was in trouble. He told me LTC Carl Lector wanted to see me over at USARV headquarters and didn't say much else. I sweated that my frequent judging had been brought to the top JAG personnel folks in Vietnam. I was just a captain and of the 20 certified part-time judges in Vietnam, there were only four captains, the remainder being majors; and I had the busiest docket. I borrowed the office jeep and took off mid-afternoon. I thought about what I would say while I sat for about thirty minutes in LTC Lector's waiting room. Lector was the Executive Officer for the USARV SJA and I had heard a pretty good guy. He finally called me into his office and I was about to salute when he asked me to have a seat. He told me I was half-way through my tour and they liked to move career officers at this point to widen their experience. I didn't realize I was a career officer and felt relieved I wasn't being shipped home in disgrace. He told me they had two positions for which I was qualified. He said the 5th Mech needed a brigade judge advocate and there was a command judge advocate vacancy at Headquarters Area Command, Saigon. He said it was my choice and to let him know as soon as possible but not later than the end of the week. I thanked him and drove back to my office and told Cassidy about the offer. He said congratulations; it sounded like a promotion and great opportunity. Cassidy was a great bull shitter but I quickly realized this meant I'd be responsible for managing a legal office. Saigon rang a bell that kept ringing in my head.

I asked around about the 5th Mech and McCormick told me those guys were living and working in sand-bagged bunkers under persistent rocket attacks. He said they recently took control of the Quang Tri and Dong Ha areas from a Marine Division and were operating in conjunction with the ARVN's somewhere about as far north as you can go and be under our control. He laughed and said when Ho Chi Minh farts; they can smell it in Quang Tri. I knew Headquarters Area Command was in Saigon, a city well within our control, and Ho was not too popular there. I thought of persistent rocket attacks, sand in my underpants and constantly being dirty. I had seen guys coming in from these places and they didn't look happy. I weighed that against a daily shower in a hotel in Saigon and good Chinese restaurants. I quickly called Lector and told him it was a tough decision but my choice was Saigon. As soon as I said it I thought maybe I should have checked that out but then I remembered there was a French Sportsman Club in Saigon and the city was the Paris of the Orient. He told me I would start the 1st of the year.

Christmas

A few days later I got a call from the legal clerk for the Army Depot in Long Binh who said he had a couple of cases for which the command needed disposition and they needed it fast. He said the Depot commander wanted the docket cleared by the first of the year. I told him about the full-time judges and he told me he tried but both were unavailable—they were upcountry on some orientation visit. I asked what he had in mind. He said there were three cases—failure to repair and possession of an illegal weapon, a first-time possession of marijuana, and misappropriation of a vehicle. I figured I could fit them in while transitioning to my new job. "How soon?"

"Don't be mad sir, but the only day we have when everybody can be here is December 24th."

"That's Christmas Eve; you really want to hold courts-martial on Christmas Eve."

"We don't have any alternative, sir."

"What about waiting until the full-time judges get back in the area, they're really nice guys."

"Captain, we're under terrific pressure to get these cases disposed of before the end of the year and the old man asked for you by name. He seems to like you and he's leaving. Two of the cases have been sitting awhile. If you're not available, maybe he can call your boss."

I figured I was in enough trouble with my boss as it was on the judge issue but the personal request made me feel good. "I think I can get away but you know it's difficult to get convictions on Christmas Eve. Make sure the CO knows that."

"Sir, we need to get these off the docket."

I told him to tell the convening authority and call me back with his reaction. He called 30 minutes later and said the CO wanted the cases off the docket and didn't care what happened. Christmas in the military away from home pushes the limits of nostalgia. The mess halls did what they could but it just isn't the same. Turkey and dressing smothered with sticky gravy prepared from a recipe in an Army Manual and served from aluminum trays on a steam table in a hot and noisy open temporary building just doesn't do it. Eating the traditional meal alongside a crowd of homesick GI's smelling of musty fatigue cloth and dried up sweat is not the same as listening to my uncle cry while giving the blessing and praying for those who are no longer with us. The excitement of Santa, the smell of pine tree sap, eggnog punch while gazing at presents stuffed under the tree, Champagne later with Eggs Benedict, and then dinner at my grandparents' with even more presents and food was Christmas. Going to the office for a half day and then to my hooch to read wasn't.

Christmas Eve afternoon, I attempted to do my part to instill some Christmas spirit at the Army Depot in Long Binh. The three cases on my docket were relatively minor; an illegal weapon with no accompanying evil intent, a failure to repair from laziness along with a first-time possession of marijuana, and a misappropriation of a jeep for a ride into Saigon. The latter was for an authorized trip but there was a misunderstanding as to the use of the vehicle. The accused said he thought he had authority to look around and procedures for use of vehicles were pretty lax. It was something I could hang my hat on and remembering Billy Hucks' visit of which I could have been accused. In each case I ensured the accused understood the break they were receiving. I gave the druggie an exceptionally strong pep talk and told him about the availability of rehabilitative jungle transfers for nonconformists. There were no ornaments on the tree in my court room that afternoon but Santa arrived early and gave three scared soldiers a Merry 1969 Christmas.

When I returned to my Long Binh office Christmas parties were everywhere. The Saigon Support Command commander was making his rounds and saw me in the hallway. He addressed me as "Judge" and wished me a Merry Christmas. I didn't know he knew who I was and, other than he was one of those generals who called everyone with JAG insignia judge, maybe he did. Our office was decked in merriment and the booze was flowing but not for LTC Cassidy. I'm sure he was struggling but he kept his promise and stayed sober. I told him what I had just done at the depot and he rolled his eyes. I could see him thinking just a few more days. Christmas Eve night the chaplains in the area presented a convoked Mass. The Long Binh stadium that recently hosted Bob Hope and his contingent filled to capacity; it was more than just Catholics. It wasn't the cathedral in Saigon but when the priests in their white chasubles and surpluses went out into the aisles to serve communion, they looked from above like angels in a sea of green bringing much longed-for Peace to their homesick combatants. The next day I went to the office but did little work. Not too many came back after the noon time Christmas dinner. Everybody was reminded of the Tet offensive and the enemy's penchant for making war at the holiest of holidays.

A week later, Cassidy hosted a going away get together for me in his trailer. Lieutenant colonels and colonels each had a small living room, a Pullman kitchen and their own bath and bedroom. Even though Cassidy was on the wagon, he provided a well-stocked bar. He poured me the stiffest drink I had since the night I was first commissioned. It was my last night in Long Binh.

PART SIX
HEADQUARTERS AREA
COMMAND, SAIGON

After my decision not to work and live in sand-bagged bunkers near the North Vietnamese border, I inquired about my assignment. I found Headquarters Area Command, Saigon, known as HAC, was responsible for facilities in the Saigon area and generally the infrastructure to support the American forces in and around Saigon. It was basically a city manager operation. The command operated billets in Saigon; it supplied the mess halls and military NCO and officer clubs; it provided off-duty recreation; it was responsible for security for the area; it collected trash; it insured communications for our forces working in the city; it assigned vehicles and provided for their fuel and maintenance, although many of the commands had their own vehicles; and I soon found out it had special court-martial jurisdiction for those stationed in the Saigon area. General Creighton Abrams was the Commander in Chief of all forces in Vietnam and as such he ran what they called the Military Assistance Command, Vietnam, or MACV. MACV was a unified and combined command made up of officers from all the United States Armed Forces along with officers from our allies—Australia, New Zealand, Korea, Thailand, and the Philippines. We had special court-martial jurisdiction over General Abrams' US Army element. My boss also was the court-martial convening authority for the HAC headquarters company to whom everybody assigned to the command was further assigned, the 34th General Support Group, the 507th Transportation Group, the Regional Communication Group, the Phu Lamb Signal Battalion, the 69th Signal Battalion, the Capitol Military Assistance Command, the 1st Military Intelligence Group, the 525th Military Intelligence Brigade, and the 4th Psychological Group.

My technical chain of command would be USARV meaning I got legal support from LTC Lector and the office that assigned me. The MACV command dictated everything else. Its judge advocate, Colonel Larry Casserly, had a reputation for not suffering fools. I heard a story at the JAG School in Charlottesville that on one occasion he was so upset with a briefer he threw his phone at him. He also complained so bitterly at a major command staff meeting about the personnel officer, the G-1, who was at the meeting that the division commander relieved the personnel officer and appointed Casserly to the job. He immediately straightened up what had been a poor performing G-1 operation. Casserly was close to General Abrams which gave the MACV legal office increased status throughout the command.

Our headquarters building was an attractive French-built structure located in a compound on a busy street in Saigon. It was surrounded by a four-foot wall over which ran a chain link fence topped with angled-out barbed wire. The front gate was manned by contract Vietnamese guards. Seeing the contract guards, mostly Vietnamese papa sans, I thought one of my first priorities should be to get a proper weapon. The compound was composed of about two acres with a large structure fronted by a porte cochere and wide steps leading from that through an entry area sided by wrought iron forged artfully into attractive designs. The second and top floor exterior walls were concrete topped by tall multi-paned windows. Our headquarters was beautiful in its elegant simplicity and at one time must have provided a wonderful home to a successful Frenchman. I entered the marble floor of the expansive foyer and asked where the JAG office was. Someone pointed down the main hall to a room on the right. It had three desks with an Army executive desk in the back, lots of sunlight from an expansive window decorated with elegant wrought iron, and a high ceiling. A large wooden door led from the office to a European-style bathroom with claw footed tub, ample sink with bronze faucets, and its own ornamented window. I felt like Dorothy; "Toto, we're not in Kansas anymore."

I reported to my new boss, Colonel Bob Minor, a tall no-nonsense artillery officer. He welcomed me and explained the command and its court-martial responsibilities. He introduced me to the deputy commander, Colonel Paul Caruso, my rater. A good war-time rating is imperative to a successful military career and I had not had one as of that time because my former supervisors had not been in their positions the ninety days required. The peculiar thing about command and staff judge advocates is that they report on military justice matters directly to the convening authority and not to or through their first boss, normally the deputy commander, their rater. I had to keep the deputy happy even though I would officially bypass him on military justice matters which were the main part of my job. Cassidy gave me some advice on this when I left Saigon Support Command. He said always let the deputy know what's going on and stop by his office when you need to get the convening authority's concurrence or action on justice issues. Do not ask his opinion; just tell him what's going on. Politics are everywhere. Minor's office was upstairs and in a large office at the front of the building. There were four Quonset huts on the far side of the compound with a small parade field and stand of trees separating them from the main house. One of those housed my attorneys and clerks as well as the command court room.

Staff officers at our command stayed at the Saigon Caravelle Hotel. I hadn't previously been there. I was hoping for the Rex. The Caravelle was close to the Opera House and a couple of blocks from the Saigon River. It was a bit shabby but much better than what I had in Long Binh and it wasn't a sand-bagged bunker near the North Vietnamese border. I was supposed to share my room. When I got there, I found it basic but my room mate was not there. A few civilian clothes hung in his closet. As it turned out, he came by just once the entire time I was at HAC. He didn't tell me where he worked but said he stayed with his girl friend at a villa in the suburbs. I got to my office the next morning and met the clerks and attorneys who made up my office. One was a non-JAG attorney, certified nonetheless to practice in military courts. He had been there awhile and introduced me to the other members of the HAC staff. As Command Judge Advocate or CJA, I was their attorney. I found I also was legal counsel for the contracting officer for the Vietnam Central Purchasing Agency. This was the command that purchased for all nonappropriated fund activities—the various clubs, recreation centers, libraries, etc in Vietnam. Army Regulations required me to review each contract over a thousand dollars; there were fifteen to twenty contracts each week. I also met the Headquarters company commander who assigned me a 45-Caliber pistol and a captain's combat kit. He said that's all I was authorized. He ran a small officer's club I immediately joined by giving him five bucks.

The CJA was assigned an International Scout. It was an office vehicle but I had priority use with my own parking spot in the compound. I had a Chinese-Vietnamese secretary, a Spec Five chief legal clerk, two other legal clerks, and two full-time attorneys, one a JAG captain. He was junior to me which meant he really was junior. We ran an average of seventeen to twenty-five courts-martial each month for the jurisdiction that encompassed approximately 20,000 troops. Our work schedule was seven days a week with eleven hour duty days. I had a weekly staff meeting with Colonel Minor but otherwise my time was my own. As the CJA, I didn't act as counsel in courts-martial. My job was to advise the convening authority on the cases. If I were to prosecute any, my advice would be suspect and besides, it was against court-martial procedures.

As part of my briefings I was read into an ongoing program managed by MACV and operated by the intelligence commands and Special Forces. It was supposedly a pacification program, the Phoenix or Phung Hoang program. The State Department was responsible for pacification and Phoenix was their baby. They got General Abrams to run it. It was primarily a South Vietnamese operation and dependent for the most part on their spying and intelligence. The State Department liked that. The target was the Vietcong Infrastructure, the leadership of the communist effort in South Vietnam. The communists were killing or maiming South Vietnamese government officials, locally elected leaders, and anybody who befriended their enemies. They ran a terrorism campaign in South Vietnam that killed over 12,000 people in 1969 and 1970.

An, our secretary, told me she much preferred an older boss but I was ok. The legal clerks really kept the place going. They would receive the charges forwarded by the subordinate commanders and get the courts-martial moving. The trial counsel would usually give me the evidence he used for prosecution after his trials. There was lots of marijuana. At first I tried to give it back to the criminal investigation folks who initially had confiscated it but they didn't want it anymore. I knew of no official procedures for this so I got either An or one of the clerks, whomever was around, to accompany me into my bath room and I flushed the stuff down the toilet. I then made a memo of the date and time and we both signed it. With the number of drug cases on our docket, I ensured the plumbing at the headquarters was kept in a high state of repair.

Joe Harlan; Fame Has Its Rewards

Sergeant Joe Harlan graduated in 1968 from the School of Journalism at the University of Wisconsin. He was facing the draft. He decided against a commission and instead enlisted in the Army with a promise for assignment as a 46R Broadcast Journalist. He ended up in Vietnam where he became a disc jockey and radio announcer. The troops loved Joe as did the press corps. After a news story about him by a friend from UPI that was published in papers throughout the states, Joe gained national recognition as a first class announcer and looked forward to multiple job offers after Vietnam when he was discharged from the Army.

Sergeant First Class John Lassotovich pretty much ran the radio operations at Harlan's station. Lassotovich was responsible for the facility and the station's special equipment to broadcast all over Vietnam. Lassotovich reported directly to MACV, known as Pentagon East. He and Joe were under the command of the Commander, MACV Army Element, but technically worked for the MACV Public Affairs officer. At the station, Lassotovich was in charge. He had seven enlisted men working as producers, broadcasters, and technicians. A Vietnamese cleaning crew had been cleaning the office but funds were cut and MACV told Lassotovich to do it in-house. He published an extra-duty roster to handle the job. Each person would clean the office one day each week. Harlan's turn came up and he ignored the duty. Lassotovich asked him about it the next day and Joe said he had to attend a meeting with the Saigon press corps and didn't have time. Lassotovich said ok but I'm moving everyone down a day and it's your duty tonight. Harlan didn't answer. The following morning, the place was a mess and Lassotovich was pissed. He confronted Harlan again and Joe said he forgot. Lassotovich was upset and ordered him to clean up the office immediately. Joe said he had a program he had to get ready for and was unable to do it. Lassotovich said, "Sergeant Harlan, I'm giving you a direct order to clean up the office. You will sweep, mop, and empty the trash cans throughout the offices. Do you understand?"

Harlan smiled and looked at him and said in a deep melodious voice, "Sergeant Lassotovich, I don't believe it appropriate for me to perform those duties especially with my show coming up in approximately an hour and a half." He then turned and walked away.

Lassotovich went to his desk and called LTC Jimmy Rowe, the Public Affairs officer, and asked for help. Rowe told Lassotovich to get someone else to take Harlan's gig for the day and he'd take care of it. Rowe then called the Army Element CO, 1LT Paul Ward, and told him Harlan was refusing to perform his assigned cleanup duties and needed some persuading. Ward called Lassotovich and told him to send Joe over to report to him. Lassotovich told Joe his performance for the day was cancelled and to report to Lieutenant Ward at MACV. Joe called his friend at the press corps and told him the Army was persecuting him because of his fame and making him do clean up duties. Joe figured there would be another UPI press release and the international response would demand his improved treatment. The reporter scowled and continued his investigation of prisoner torture and abuse by the South Vietnamese Army. Harlan reported to

Ward as ordered. The lieutenant told him, "Sergeant Harlan, you have done a great job here in Vietnam and we all love to listen to your shows. I know Sergeant Lassotovich has a lot on his plate and he only requests that you help him out. I understand all he wants is for you to join in with the others and clean up the station maybe once a week. Maybe an hour's extra duty. This is a new requirement and something that's necessary."

"Sir, thank you, but I don't believe cleaning up the station is part of my assigned duties nor should it be. It's my understanding that the Vietnamese are perfectly capable and available to perform these functions and we should be using this resource."

Ward said, "I understand Sergeant Lassotovich gave you a specific order to clean up the station this morning. I also understand you didn't comply. Is that correct?"

"Sir, I was unable to because I had a broadcast I had to get ready for, but that's beside the point. I should not have to perform those duties."

Ward was exasperated. He didn't want to make it a Federal case and realized Harlan was famous throughout Vietnam. "Joe, all you have to do is sweep a bit and mop up some floors. It shouldn't take long and that's what's required. You could be court-martialed for refusing SFC Lassotovich's order. That's serious. I'm willing to give you a chance to make this go away if you agree to perform as ordered."

Joe thought, I've got them, they're afraid of me. There's no way they're going to send this to a court-martial. I'm not going to do it. "Sir, I'm not going to do it."

Ward was perplexed. He said, "Joe, don't say that now. I'm going to give you some time to think about it. If you still decide not to clean up the station, let me know first thing in the morning. You are dismissed."

Joe came back the next morning and sauntered into Lieutenant Ward's little office at MACV Headquarters. He said, "Sir, I've thought about this and there's no way this is the kind of duty that should be given radio announcers. I'm not going to do maid's work."

Ward dismissed him, and afraid the issue might escalate and the hammer would come down on him, called Colonel Rowe for advice. Rowe blew his top at Ward's failure to take immediate action and told him to call JAG and give the guy an Article 15.

Ward called me that afternoon and described his problem. He was surprised I had never heard of Joe Harlan. I sent him to Terry White, one of my legal clerks, who actually prepared the papers and told the lieutenant how to administer the nonjudicial punishment. It was Ward's first experience.

Lieutenant Ward asked Harlan to stop by his office. When Harlan knocked on Ward's door, the lieutenant smiled at him and asked the sergeant to take a seat. He referred to Sergeant Harlan as "Joe" and explained to him that he didn't have to accept the proffered nonjudicial punishment and instead could demand a court-martial. Harlan felt this was playing right into his hands. He would make a spectacle of the trial and the press would save him. Joe declined the nonjudicial punishment. Ward, now stiffened from Joe's dismissal of his offer and wary of Colonel Rowe's fury, dismissed Harlan and immediately called Lassotovich and asked him to suspend Harlan from further broadcasting which Lassotovich was more than pleased to do. The listeners were not told anything about what happened. Joe's time period was filled with a new announcer brought in from the field, Sergeant Tom Rooney, an Irishman with a special lilt to his voice that immediately was liked by everyone.

Ward called and asked what he should do. I told him we would prepare Summary Court-Martial charges but Harlan still could refuse those. Ward said if that's what I thought was appropriate, do it. We did and Harlan refused the Summary Court.

I was now pissed and prepared papers sending Brother Harlan to a Special Court-Martial with authority to put him away for six months. Colonel Minor agreed and signed the order convening the trial. I was getting the action ready when my phone rang with an urgency I hadn't heard before. It jumped as it rang on my desk. I looked around and was the only one in the office so I picked up. A deep bass boomed out what I thought was, "Gregg, this is Colonel Cassidy, what are you doing on the Harlan case?"

"Sir, good to hear from you. How's everything in Long Binh?"

Colonel Casserly, the MACV SJA and close friend of General Abrams, with an even more heightened tone responded, "Gregg, what the hell do you mean Long Binh?"

I meekly said into the phone, "Who is this?"

"It's Colonel Casserly at MACV."

Sweat beaded on my head and the AC was on high. "Sir, I'm sorry, I thought you said Cassidy." Cassidy had been my boss at Saigon Support Command. This was not a good start.

"Well what the hell's going on with Sergeant Harlan? What are you doing?"

"Sir, we offered him a summary court and he turned it down. I'm getting the case ready for a special."

"He's not yours."

"I don't understand, sir."

Casserly, realizing we were doing what we should have been, or that I was totally flustered, calmed down and adopted a different tone. He said, "General Abrams transferred him to the 101st Airborne Division up North. He asked Major General Wright up there if he could take Harlan and teach him to soldier. Wright apparently said they needed a communications sergeant at Fire Base Fury. His sweet little voice should help him be understood over the rocket fire. Fury's on a little mountain just outside the A Shau Valley and sees considerable action. A Huey was shot down near there last week with the pilot and three others killed. They think it might have been a missile. Harlan has five months on his tour and, if he lasts that long, maybe he can bring some glory to the 101st."

"Thank you, sir." I hung up and threw my file on Joe Harlan in my out basket. I called Colonel Minor and told him what happened. He said he just heard and it couldn't happen to a nicer guy. There was no more said about Broadcast Journalist Joe Harlan on the radio and no one seemed to mind. I heard later the radio station won the MACV contest for cleanest staff office.

Captured Weapons

Captain Mark Goshen, the HAC, Headquarters Company Commander, and I became pretty good friends. I drank with him at his little club and helped with some disciplinary issues and a report of survey that possibly could have held him liable for the loss of a weapon. He also got me to give a class to the company on changes to the UCMJ. This especially was good for me because it introduced me to the enlisted men at headquarters. I told Mark I didn't think the 45 he issued was of much help should we have another attack like occurred at Tet. He said he might be able to do a little better. A few days later an MP stopped by and introduced himself as Captain Hank Schaefer. Hank said he was partially responsible for the security around Saigon and heard I needed a weapon. I wasn't sure what he was up to so I remained quiet. He went on and said most weekends his MPs encounter armed sappers coming into the city and capture or kill them. At this stage in the conflict, captured weapons normally are available to anyone who can use them against the enemy.

Adventures of a Viet Cong Spy

In 1944, Dang Hai Lanh, called Lanh, was recruited by Thinh Tan Bao to join in the nationalistic push for a free Vietnam. Bao was from Hoang Hoa Tham, a village near China and was a communist. Lanh was from Na Ca in the Can Nong Province in North Vietnam near the Chinese border. The area was beautiful with verdant mountains bisected with rivers and paths. It contained many valleys with fertile fields. Lanh was twenty years old and a Buddhist. He tried the best he could to follow the Eightfold path—right speech, actions and livelihood as well as right effort, mindfulness and concentration, and finally, right thoughts and understanding. He felt life was full of suffering and his job was to fight off the many desires he had that made him suffer. He felt his problems were caused primarily by the Japanese and French oppressing the Vietnamese people. If he could make that go away his life would substantially improve and he would be on his path to happiness. Bao told him Vietnam was undergoing a major change and it was time for the people to stand up and gain their independence. Bao spoke of international Communism and how people like he and Lanh could use the same principles peoples had used in other areas of the world to gain independence. It was not so much for personal independence but for independence of the beautiful and tradition rich nation of Vietnam. Lanh agreed with everything Bao said and pledged to do all he could with right actions and commitment. Lanh was young but like his Vietnamese name street smart. Bao called him to meet with other members of his Army propaganda team. Lanh left his wife of two years, Le Dinh Cong, to tend their three acres of tea and went with Bao to the Dinh Ca Valley.

Lanh learned to fire a rifle and flintlock. In 1944, in Vietnam, ammunition was scarce so Lanh only got to shoot twice. He joined up with some other members of the team to visit two small outposts run by the French. He was now part of what they called the Tran Hung Dao Platoon. They visited the French sites, really nothing more than mud huts, pretending to be suppliers of locally made spring rolls. They spoke to a group of the Vietnamese military who were manning some little outposts and told them of their movement and what they thought would be a new beginning for Vietnam free of foreign domination. They said the time was perfect for action with the foreign wars ending and the French weak. Three days after their meeting, on December 24, 1944, the Tran Hung Dao Platoon, armed with thirty-one rifles and fourteen captured antique French flintlocks, sneaked up on the French outpost at Phai Khat. Lanh signaled to one of the guards who at the meeting said the Vietnamese at the post wouldn't resist if someone killed their leader, a French lieutenant. The guard pointed to where the Frenchman was eating his Christmas Eve dinner. Lanh sneaked up behind him with a long knife, grabbed the lieutenant's hair as he was leaning over his plate, and pulled his head back. He cut the Frenchman's throat and then pulling him away from the table stabbed him in the stomach and chest. The lieutenant died quickly and Lanh signaled the team to enter the outpost. About thirty Vietnamese military gave up their weapons and said it was necessary for them to be taken prisoners so when the French found out about the attack, they would let them return to their families. The next morning, Christmas, 1944, the platoon went to Na Ngan, another French outpost not far from Phai Khat. As the Vietnamese soldiers working for the French looked the other way, one of Lanh's friends shot and killed a French officer who was walking over to his latrine. The sixteen Vietnamese soldiers at Na Ngan quickly surrendered and gave up their weapons as "prisoners" of the Tran Hung Dao Platoon.

In early 1945, Bao and his friends, under the leadership of Vo Nguyen Giap, continued their proselytizing and recruitment. With Ho Chi Minh providing political guidance from China, in mid April, 1945, Giap and leaders from other similar groups throughout Vietnam held a conference outside Hanoi. Communist organizations from Laos and Cambodia came and gave Giap confidence that he was not alone in his efforts for independence. In mid-May, at a Buddhist Temple in Cho Chu village, he formed the Vietnam Liberation Army. Lanh marched proudly with now General Giap and was touted as a hero for his actions at Phai Khat. The Japanese still maintained control over Vietnam. Giap's Army, using communist strategy, stayed hidden and were constantly on the move. Lanh worked hard in establishing a communication network made up of the self defense or "te vu" units around Hanoi. The Japanese surrendered their World War II effort on August 15, 1945. Immediately Lanh ignited communications with the "te vu" units to enlist them and anybody else they could find to join an uprising against the Japanese in Hanoi. Giap led his Army joined in by those self defense units and marched into Hanoi. The Japanese seeing the Vietnamese Army and a mass of marching civilians provided no opposition. The victory spawned substantial communist rhetoric and Ho Chi Minh came to Hanoi from his exile in China for the independence celebrations. On September 2, 1945, Ho declared the formation of the Democratic Republic of Vietnam and assumed political control. Lanh celebrated with his comrades in Hanoi and they proclaimed the nation was now free of foreign control.

Lanh returned to the Can Nong Province and his tea operations where he proudly exhibited the medal presented by General Vo Nguyen Giap for his actions at Phai Khat. Nine months later, Dang Thi Bian, was born. She was his first and would be Lanh's only child. Lanh picked the name Bian because he believed in the communist doctrine for secrecy. He remembered Ho's seven principles for guerilla tactics—secrecy, speed, activeness, mobility, stealth, flexibility, and maneuver. By the time Bian was born, the French, unable to resist Vietnam's charms and resources and with an infrastructure for colonization in place, came in force and drove Giap and his Vietnam Liberation Army out of the Vietnamese cities and into hiding in the jungle and the mountains. General Giap sent a message to Lanh that there was still important work to be done.

Lanh didn't think he would be needed again by Giap or the communists but thought the communist methods were a good way to rid the country of the French. Lanh found Giap in the mountains and joined in Ho's guerilla activities. He participated in assassinating a number of village chiefs reported friendly to the French. He lived in the hills and was constantly on the move throughout the late 40's. He would operate sneak attacks and then with his small force would hide in mountain caves or jungle tunnels. He went back to Can Nong province to see his family only three times during this three-year period. He continued to recruit members to the effort, many staying in their villages but promising allegiance to Giap and the communist effort. The French actually helped him by conscripting farmers and others in rural areas to work on their projects for minimal wages and by heavily taxing the middle class. Their heavy-handed colonization and response to any opposition made the Vietnamese people long for freedom.

Dang Thi Bian, aged three, accompanied Cong, her mother, and a hired worker as they worked the tea farm. The neighbors weren't sure where Lanh was but many suspected. One asked Cong if he could buy her farm so he could expand his tea operations. Cong told him Lanh would be home soon and they planned to keep working the farm. On July 7, 1949, a French platoon drove up to Lanh's modest home in Hoang Hoa Tham and through an interpreter from Hanoi asked Cong where Lanh was. Cong said he was not home but went south to visit his ailing mother. The French officer stated Lanh had not paid his taxes and he had received information Lanh was affiliated with Giap and was a terrorist. Lanh's wife, Cong, without changing expression, told the man Lanh managed the little tea farm and would be away for the next month or maybe more on family matters. She said she knew nothing of his being a communist but if he were she would know and he wasn't. The Frenchman told her when Lanh returned to have him report to the French outpost and pay his taxes. He said if he didn't hear from Lanh within two months, he would come back, take control of the farm, and sell it for the back taxes. After he left, Cong broke down and cried. Bian didn't know the problem and tried to comfort the only parent she really had ever known. Cong went to a friend who had a newly married grown son living at their small home and sold them the farm. She went to the French outpost and paid the taxes. She left a note addressed to Lanh with the new owners in which she explained what happened. The note said she had gone to Binh Tan on the coast near the Song Ma River and Tran Hoa. Cong's uncle was a fisherman and lived there.

Lanh found Cong in Binh Tan but was unable to stay with her. He had to return to Hanoi where he gathered intelligence for President Ho and General Giap. Giap's forces were growing and he constantly was moving throughout the mountains. He set up supply lines that permitted him to expand his area of operations. In 1952, Giap had six infantry divisions and one heavy artillery division with which he conducted hit and run operations against the French. Lanh stayed in Hanoi and provided Giap intelligence of the French plans, and from what he learned from his contacts throughout the country, their movements. Giap obtained control over a large area around Northwest Tonkin and the Laos border area, garnering equipment and supplies along the way. The French hit back in an organized major attempt to break Giap's supply lines but Giap continued his strategy of ambush and run. His forces harried and bled the French. Giap lost numerous members of his volunteer Army but political recruiters throughout the North found an ever expanding source of recruits with every victory.

Giap's forces, now called the Vietminh, started to conduct more sizable military operations. The French intelligence determined they were training recruits in Dien Bien Phu, and decided to exterminate the training base and take control of the valley. That would give them a presence with military control in the heartland of Giap's strength. It was risky because Dien Bien Phu was 300 miles from Hanoi and support for the operation had to be by air. The plan was to get an air strip first and then set up a series of well entrenched bases to provide each base covering fire support from an attack on its neighboring base. Substantial French artillery flown in by air backed by mortar and airlifted tanks strengthened the French defenses. They then initiated heavy patrols into the country to find and destroy the communists. The French were well entrenched at the start of 1954, when Lanh sent word to Giap that he heard from his spies in the French headquarters that Henri Navarre, the new French General for Vietnam, sought approval from his higher command for the operation in Dien Bien Phu but didn't get it. Lanh reported that Navarre's initiation of the costly and risky operation without full approval presented an opportunity for the Vietminh that could end the war.

Giap was convinced by Lanh's argument and thought if he could get his artillery over the mountains close to Dien Bien Phu, he could give the French a bit of trouble. He used all his forces and whatever volunteers he could find to carry his guns over the mountains. This was a monumental effort that the French did not think could be done. Giap then proceeded to lay siege to the French positions. He concentrated his fire power, targeting one outpost at a time to undermine the French strategy of mutual support. Giap's strategy was more effective than he imagined. He first bombed the airfield rendering it unusable and eliminating the French supply network. He then went after each little outpost. After a heavy artillery barrage, he would follow up with an en mass infantry attack. The little French posts fell incrementally. The Vietminh then dug trenches in order to get closer for human assaults on the major French positions. The fight continued through the spring slowly eating away at the French force. The French suffered substantial casualties with a high desertion rate by their non-French mostly Vietnamese forces. On May 8th the French surrendered and Giap captured 7,000 Frenchmen. Five thousand of those died on the 400 mile march to China and in the subsequent incarceration. During the long march many wounded were carried through mud and rain. They slept in the mountains and jungle and lived on a handful of rice for each day's 16 mile walk. The French lost a total of 8,000 men in Dien Bien Phu and its aftermath. They also lost their fervor for further effort in Vietnam.

Lanh was considered a hero for pressing the fight against the French and for his intelligence on French operations. General Giap awarded him another medal but since he was an intelligence officer and known to many foreigners in Hanoi, it was kept secret. After the award, he went to see his family now settled in Binh Tan, about 160 kilometers south of Hanoi, and recuperated on the nearby Sam Son Beach. Lanh was thirty years old and a hero. Bian was eight. Cong had purchased a small house in the village and was working for her uncle arranging fish sales to the local markets. Giap paid Lanh an equivalent of what he would have earned with two year's of his tea proceeds, a part of which Lanh used to purchase a new boat for his wife's uncle. On July 20, 1954, the Vietminh and the French military came to a mutual agreement to cease military operations in Laos, Cambodia and Vietnam. Vietnam was partitioned around the 17th parallel into two states which would become one with an election promised in 1956. China and Russia were tired of fighting with the Korean War just over and wanted no more. They decided to use Uncle Ho and his communist friends for political action to take control over Vietnam. The United States saw the country turning communist and decided to trump the national elections. Instead of waiting for the agreed on elections throughout the country, the United States sponsored an election just in the south where they proclaimed Ngo Dinh Diem, an American ally, President of South Vietnam. The Buddhists joined the communists and many others to oppose this rule. This group initiated terrorist activities against Diem's government.

In January, 1959, Lanh went to the Fifteenth Party Plenum of the Communist Party of Vietnam. The Vietnamese communists agreed to use military force with support from the Russians and Chinese to overthrow Diem. Soon after, the National Liberation Front was formed and Lanh became a charter member. Bian was thirteen. Lanh again left his wife and her uncle's now prosperous fishing business in Binh Tan to join the fight. The family had a beautiful although modest villa at the Sam Son beach and Cong controlled the fish market in Tranh Hoa. Lanh felt it was time to make Vietnam one nation and to rid it of all foreign control. He thought the United Nations might oppose further intervention by foreigners designed to rob Vietnam of its precious resources but he didn't trust the UN. He believed being categorized a communist nation was little to pay for Chinese and Russian support to rid the nation of its shackles. Uncle Ho could deal with the communists later. Lanh thought that after all, the Geneva Accords dictated, and the parties agreed, that the nation should only be divided for two years and then overall free elections would unite Vietnam under one leader. If the Americans had not intervened, the election would certainly have chosen Uncle Ho president. The Americans worried the nation would become a subaltern of Russia and Ho a satrap. They certainly didn't understand Uncle Ho. Lanh said to himself if the pushy Americans had not intervened, Vietnam could have had the promised national elections and been free of the Americans and all foreign domination. Lanh thought if he could get rid of the American puppet, the Americans would leave and the nation would be one and independent.

Lanh left his second floor balcony overlooking the South China Sea and hitched a ride on a fishing trawler out of Sam Son. He rode down the coast to the old French resort, Vung Tau. He entered the south and began to recruit people who thought like he did. He set up an apparatus to gain intelligence and started the same guerilla tactics he found so useful against the French. His recruitment avoided the communist doctrine he used previously in the North because he believed the fight for nationalism by itself was more appealing to the people in the south. Lanh was successful, as usual, and his group of protesters and anti-Diem activists came to be known as the Viet Cong. Lanh recruited in small villages and towns. Many who joined were communists with an international agenda but many more like him were willing to sacrifice their lives just for national unity. Lanh especially was successful with Buddhists. They thought the time had come for change and joined Lanh to get rid of Diem who they considered nothing more than an American lackey. In October, 1963, Lanh sought out a South Vietnamese general whom he heard was dissatisfied with Diem. He remembered his successes with the two French lieutenants at Phai Khat and Na Ngan and thought if he could get the Vietnamese Army to back down he could kill the beast. He was very lucky.

Brigadier General Nghiem Duc Trung initially fought for the French but was careful to maintain ties with village and city leaders throughout Vietnam. He was upper middle class and his family was from the ancient city of Hue. He emphasized integrity within his command and never stole from the enlisted men and non commissioned officers even though his brother commanders of the South Vietnamese Army encouraged him to follow what they regularly did. A South Vietnamese general had substantial autonomy and control over all aspects of his men's lives, including their pay. There was little oversight, if any, and Trung was starting to become wealthy but not at the cost of his men's loyalty. He hated Diem whom he blamed for his best friend's death. His friend was a Vietnamese Army colonel and commander of a South Vietnamese regiment in the delta. It was not responding to VC action as Diem thought it should and Diem didn't trust the regiment. The colonel was assassinated and Trung blamed Diem.

Some of Trung's high ranking friends in the military didn't believe Diem understood or cared anything about the Vietnamese people. They wanted little and some felt Diem could have become a great leader but squandered the opportunity by ignoring the villages and their needs and by secluding himself to the good life in Saigon with many trips to the United States. Trung met Lanh and told him he was worried about an American backlash to a military revolt and also about who might succeed Diem. Lanh told him he would ensure the General's safety with Hanoi and it was his opinion the Americans would not support Diem against his own people. Lanh hinted the powers in Hanoi might reward the person who led the revolt against Diem with an important role in the south, maybe even temporary Presidency, until Ho could be elected. Trung recruited a few other generals whom he thought were dissatisfied with Diem. They were forming a plan but were hesitant to move forward because they didn't know who they could trust, and if they failed they knew they would be executed. But then, in the summer of 1963, Ngo Dinh Nhu, Diem's brother, attacked some Buddhist pagodas that he had heard were VC havens. Buddhist monks were upset at the intrusion of their religious sanctuary and started national protests. One monk set himself on fire in downtown Saigon. Trung felt the time was now. He spoke to his men and told them he was going to lead a group of units against Diem and take over the government. He asked if they supported him and they gave a resounding cheer. He still was afraid of the Americans. Trung was close to his

American advisor and asked him if the United States would kill him if he led a coup. The advisor said he would get back to him. A few days later an American civilian gave Trung over $40,000 to assist in his effort to overthrow Diem. On November 1, 1963, the generals led the attack against Diem. As Lanh predicted, the Americans didn't assist Diem and Diem and Nhu were captured and executed. A few weeks later, President Kennedy was assassinated in Dallas. The United States had 16,000 "advisers" to the South Vietnamese Army in Vietnam at the time.

One of Trung's friends took over as President and became a friend to the Americans. With Diem's death, Lanh sent a message to General Giap that the South was ready to be brought together with the North. Giap sent North Vietnamese regulars across the border and started operations against the South. Trung's friends, the Vietnamese generals, however, were not ready to give up control and resisted. One of them became President. The North Vietnamese attacked an American ship in the Gulf of Tonkin which prompted Congressional support for action. Johnson escalated troop strengths and support for the South. Lanh thought the Americans would learn from the French and leave. He was wrong. The Americans didn't give up but stiffened their resistance and continued to escalate military responses to the communist actions. The communists in Hanoi decided to mount a protracted campaign of small actions to wear the Americans down. Instead the United States stoked the draft and basically took over military operations against the North and the VC.

Lanh introduced the black pajamas to the VC as a uniform of sorts. The black would help them hide in the dark and the silk would quiver in the wind to take away any human profile. Lanh encouraged night action and continued secrecy. He instituted a program of terror where he would identify and kill or maim American collaborators and their families. If a village chief didn't pledge support for Lanh's VC, he was assumed to favor a divided Vietnam and became a target. Lanh worked hard and set up VC units that would attack isolated U.S. forces. He initiated many ambushes against convoys and individuals traveling the roads. Lanh owned the night. He entertained some substantial attacks on outposts but mostly let Giap's officers from the North lead those. Giap sent him rockets and other equipment but his main source was the South Vietnamese whom he would bribe with funds from the North and from which he and his VC would steal. Lanh thought that constant fear would undermine the American resolve but was worried because with every major VC effort the U.S. would send more troops and the troops were smart and well equipped. Not like the French. Lanh knew he was not the only VC leader in the south but he didn't know who or where the others were. He understood this was the communist method. Lanh operated primarily around Saigon and in the area from Saigon up to Tay Ninh. He set up regular rocket attacks at targets in Long Binh and Bien Hoa. Giap provided an unlimited supply of such rockets he obtained from the Chinese. Volunteers carried these on their backs walking most of the way down the west Vietnamese borders into the south. Lanh had a VC cadre of almost 500 full-time collaborators who continued to recruit throughout the area. He didn't know most VC individually but knew his recruits were fighting the war.

In 1967, as opposition to the war grew in the United States, Ho and Giap sent an encrypted message through a system of couriers to Lanh in which they questioned if the people of South Vietnam would join a major North Vietnamese effort against the United States. Lanh thought of the French and of Dien Bien Phu with Giap's resolve in destroying that operation and causing the French finally to surrender. He knew he could get his VC energized to assist in any large scale North Vietnamese Army attack. He responded that if the North Vietnamese regulars came in force, he could get the VC and a good many of the South Vietnamese Army to join them against the Americans. He said he thought a lot of the "chieu hoi," the Viet Cong who for a stipend gave themselves up to the U.S., would return and fight again. He said he wasn't sure whether the people in the south would band together against the Americans like the people of the North did against the Japanese in 1945 but if the operation was conducted carefully, it would engender a strong sense of national unity. Giap sent the plans for his Tet offensive and asked for Lanh's logistical help and his VC armed support. Lanh didn't have command of but maintained political control over a VC sapper battalion. He also was connected to many VC cells in the Saigon area. Giap especially needed assistance from Lanh in hiding and supporting troops and weapons coming from the North so they would be in position for the coordinated attack. Giap gave Lanh detailed dates and basically his order of battle for the Tet holiday campaign. Lanh immediately realized the dates Giap provided didn't coincide with the dates they celebrated Tet in the south. He had heard the North changed its time zone which altered their calendar while the South kept the traditional holiday calendar. He made a mental note to let Giap know there was an important variance. Giap's plan called for a simultaneous attack on eighty cities, towns, and military bases. He would make substantial use of suicide attackers especially at the American Embassy. Lanh read the message, marked his calendar in his own encrypted manner, and set up a schedule to meet Giap's request. He then burned the message.

Lanh had to get things moving. He left his Saigon apartment to attend a meeting in Cholon. He carried his calendar but the rest of his information was in his head. He walked through a suburb to where he could hire a rickshaw when three South Vietnamese jeeps pulled up alongside him. An officer grabbed him while two soldiers pulled him in the jeep and tied his hands and feet. The officer addressed him as Mr. Lanh and called him a communist VC. He then hit him in the face with a hard round short stick. It broke Lanh's nose which immediately bled profusely. Lanh saw an American with them. The soldiers laughed and the Vietnamese officer hit him again cracking his cheek bone. Someone then threw him while dazed and in shock behind the jeep's back seat. They drove to a South Vietnamese Army compound on the outskirts of Saigon and hustled Lanh into a stark aluminum building most likely built by Americans. They took him to a medium-sized room where the ARVN officer pushed him into a metal chair and a soldier tied his arms to its steel armrests and his legs to the chair's metal supports. He noticed through the fog of pain from the beating he already received that each leg of the chair was standing in a pan of water. He was scared. The officer spat, and with his short stick, struck Lanh's immobilized arm. Lanh screamed aloud as the arm was crushed by the short but stout blow. He felt faint and the officer asked him if he was a communist. Lanh didn't answer. The officer then pushed the stick into his arm's comminuted fracture and Lanh screamed from the pain and fainted. Someone threw water on him and he revived. The officer asked him if he was in the village of Bau Cua and enjoyed killing Chu Van Chinh and his family. Lanh remembered dismembering and killing Chinh's children in front of Chinh and his wife and then cutting Chinh's throat and letting his wife go so she would report what happened to traitors. Chinh had betrayed an operation causing the loss of eight VC. Lanh said nothing. A soldier took a box and hooked some clips out of the box onto his side and on the chair legs and then plugged it in. The officer told Lanh to start saying something or he would experience pain substantially worse than anything he could possibly believe. Lanh said nothing. A soldier threw a bucket of water on Lanh while the officer turned a dial on the box. Lanh's eyes saw spots before going blank and every spot on Lanh's body shivered and contracted in severe pain. He screamed in agony as each nerve ending throughout his body was set afire and then passed out.

Lanh awakened and felt as if he were floating. He realized he was drugged and could see he was on a helicopter flying over some large body of water; he thought it was probably the South China Sea. Each movement of the helicopter seemed as a wave of pain that lifted and then dropped him. He could not move his arm without severe shocks of pain running up and down his side. He was exhausted.

He tried to move his legs but felt burns all over which when touched felt like the tips of knives being thrust in the sores. He could see the officer who interrogated him through the fog. He was sitting across from Lanh with another prisoner who Lanh recognized as a VC leader from somewhere in the highlands. The officer asked the other man something Lanh was unable to understand. The other man shrugged. A Vietnamese soldier sitting next to the officer pushed the helicopter door open, reached across and grabbed the bonds around Lanh's chest, pulled him out of his seat, and threw him out the door. Lanh was forty-four and had been away from home for nine years.

When Lanh didn't show for his arranged meeting, one of his lieutenants went to his apartment but saw South Vietnamese police in the building and left. He made some inquiries but was afraid for his own safety to delve too deeply. He sent a message to Hanoi that Lanh was lost. Giap told Ho and the two felt they should keep silent at the hero's loss because they were uncertain how much the South and the Americans knew about Lanh. If they understood him to be a major VC leader, all his acquaintances would be in peril. Giap sent an NVA brigadier general to Sam Son beach to see Cong. He brought her flowers and told her that due to Lanh's sacrifice she would receive an annuity for the rest of her life. Cong had not seen Lanh in almost three years and had not really lived with him for nine. She was sad at his death but a part of her had known he would never come back. She felt he would experience a much more comfortable role in his next life and celebrated that.

Bian was twenty-two and worked at the fish business. Her great uncle died in a monsoon while fishing off the coast and her mother now owned and operated the fishing fleet that provisioned markets almost all the way to Hanoi. Bian had heard all the laurels about her father and with her mother's business acumen and success, felt she could do anything. She wanted to follow her father's footsteps and go south but her mother adamantly forbade it. Over the next year Bian heard about the Tet offensive and how it lost countless North Vietnamese lives and didn't win any major battles. She also heard about heightened dissatisfaction in America with its Vietnam War. She had always felt her father's emotional support and presence. She knew he lived a dangerous life but believed he was invincible. She missed him and now had an empty void in her life that her mother spending more and more time on the business was unable to fill. Bian had to do something. She talked to some people who had been to Saigon and one told her about a friend connected to the resistance. His name was Long and he was known to hang out around Chanh Hung, the Saigon Fish Market. Bian went into her savings and in late 1969 sneaked away from Sam Son. She stowed on a trawler going south and followed her father's path but only as far as Ninh Hoa. She took a bus from there to Da Lat and then south to Saigon. She went to the fish market and asked around for Long. No one knew him. She came back the next day and asked some people. One man asked what she wanted with Long. She said she was from a fish market near Sam Son and wanted to talk about an expanded market. He said to wait. About an hour later the man came back with Long. She asked if she could discuss a business proposition. Long invited her to dinner and after that Bian told Long she wanted to help. He said, help what? Bian then offered her services to the Viet Cong.

Bian was attractive and from experience with her mother's business, could do secretarial work. She could type and understood filing and general office procedures. She couldn't speak English so Long told her to apply for a job with the South Vietnamese Army. She filled out the paperwork and was told to go to the Army compound for an interview. When she got there, the unit had gone to the delta for operations and the personnel officer, still at the camp, told her to return in six months. Then Long invited her to join him on a mission.

The two drove out of Saigon on a motor scooter and traveled north to Cu Chi. They pulled off Route 1 about three kilometers from Cu Chi, hid their scooter, and followed a small trail through some high grass and scrub trees where they met up with a small band of pajama clad men. The VC gave her two rockets to carry and they all walked through the jungle to an American compound being used as the Headquarters for the 25th Infantry Division. One of the VC told Bian he participated in the Tet attack against the base.

He bragged, "We had about twenty comrades with us that night. Most had satchel bags. We tried to do it all at one time but our watches must have been off. Some threw their bags over early and the base started shooting off flares. The rest of us kept on schedule anyway and, at midnight, we blew up the fence at one place and ran into the compound throwing our bags wherever we saw some good targets. I could see a number of trucks loaded with supplies and other equipment burning. I threw mine at a small building that I thought held weapons but it tuned out to be a bathroom. I hid for two days under a building and then walked off the compound with a group people who were working there."

Bian's group was worried about patrols but hid in the brush around the compound and didn't see any. Three had AK-47's. They carried four land mines and six rockets. They buried the land mines on the trail and crawled through the night to where they could hear the compound's noises—motors running, doors closing, music from some radios, and murmurings of distant conversations. One of the men whispered, "There is barbed wire and a low mound just ahead. It's closely guarded. When we fire the rocket, the Americans will send up flares to see who's there, so stay low and in the shadows. A comrade who works in the kitchen on the base told us there's an ammo dump not too far from the perimeter. He sometimes comes with us but couldn't make it tonight."

They showed Bian how to fire the rocket and where she should aim. She pointed it to an area close to where the men pointed and pushed down hard on the button. It fired with a terrific blast. Smoke enveloped her and her friends. As promised a flare was shot into the sky but it was away from their cover, so they kept low and quiet. The group then started firing off the other rockets and immediately beat a hasty retreat into the high grasses away from the resulting cloud of smoke. As they were crawling out several flares went off immediately above their position. They laid low until the flare was extinguished and started to move but then another went off. Bian was worried the Americans would come and wanted to get out of there but Long told her to stay still. Eventually, the flares stopped and the group crawled through some swampy grasses to the path Long and Bian came in on. The Americans never came out of their compound. The group went through rice fields and across flat land to a village called Xom Giong, made up of houses elevated to avoid floods during heavy monsoons. The group was met by a friendly farmer and his wife who fed them a dinner of rice and pork. They stayed the night together. Bian made love to Long and the next day the two returned to Saigon.

About two weeks later Long said he had another mission for Bian. This time she had to go it alone. She would take a satchel charge and throw it in an American motor pool in the Saigon suburbs. If she encountered any guards she was to shoot and still throw the satchel. She then was to get out of the area as quickly as possible. Bian wore black pajamas under a colorful ao dai. They gave her an AK-47 with two loaded banana clips and a small canvas bag. The satchel had a shoulder strap and when she was ready to throw it she first had to pull an igniter cord just inside. Long told her she had to go that Friday night. Bian got ready and Long gave her the equipment. She strapped the rifle so it was flat on her back and fitted it under her ao dai. The ao dai was flimsy and didn't do a good job of concealment but it was better than nothing.

About 2300 Bian set out for the motor pool. She canvassed it the day before so she knew the guard's location and the best spot from which she could toss the bag. She figured she would hide behind a vehicle across the street, get her weapon ready, pull the cord when the road was clear, and then run across and toss the satchel over the wall. She would then shoot the guard or anyone else who came after her and run through an alley across the street and to a small trash area where she could hide the rifle and get back to Long's room where they would celebrate like they did outside Cu Chi. She walked with purpose down a busy street and was about to cross a bridge that would get her to a side street on the way to her target when she heard a man yell at her. She didn't understand what he said but knew it was some kind of order. It sounded like a cough. She got scared but continued on when she saw another American soldier pointing a rifle at her and yelling the same thing. The second soldier was just across the street. She turned around and a banana clip fell out of her pajama pants pocket. She reached for it and the ao dai lifted up exposing the AK-47. The soldier across the street started yelling at her and she started to run. The American at the foot of the bridge then shot her in the back, the bullet going through Bian's rib cage and exploding into her heart. Bian never made her 23rd birthday. The soldiers called in the incident and their shift officer came and confiscated the weapon, the two banana clips, and the satchel charge. Bian's body was taken away and buried without ceremony in a common grave near the city dump outside Saigon. Long was killed through a Phoenix operation a few weeks later. Cong never knew what happened to Bian and spent the remainder of her life searching for her daughter.

The following Monday, Hank Schaefer brought me my longed for protection—an AK-47 with two banana clips. He told me they killed a girl attempting to blow something up somewhere in the area. He said it was amazing, almost every weekend they capture or kill a VC crossing that bridge. I placed the rifle and clips in the bath tub next to my office where they stayed, unused, for the rest of my tour.

Billeting; Musical Chairs

Colonel Minor requested I come up to his office. I grabbed a note pad and immediately hit the wide marble stairs in the entry hall of the former French residence, two at a time, turned at the top and hustled down the wood paneled corridor into his reception area. His secretary told me to go right in; the colonel was waiting for me. Lieutenant Colonel Horn, the provost marshal, Lieutenant Colonel Plant, the procurement chief, and Lieutenant Colonel Curran, the personnel officer were in the room. "Glad to have you here Judge. We've got a problem. We just leased a hotel in town and need it desperately because the owner of the Rex advised us we can no longer use his hotel for our folks. We got a good deal at the Regency and want to move the personnel who have been staying at the Rex to the Regency,"

I said, "OK sir, what's the problem?"

My boss continued, "Well we need to vacate the Rex in five days and fourteen Vietnamese families refuse to leave the Regency. They say they have a right to stay because they have been living there over a year or something like that. We have most of the people from the Rex relocated but we need the 14 rooms."

Colonel Plant, the procurement officer, piped in. "The lease with the Regency says it's their responsibility to relocate the civilian families in the hotel and clear it out."

Colonel Horn said, "The lease already started, it's our place now and the Vietnamese refuse to move. We have mostly military in the Regency now. There may be a few U.S. civilian employees and I can't guarantee their safety with numerous Vietnamese coming and going at their whim. I set up a barrier with MPs yesterday to keep out the civilians but the people complained to the State Department and the Embassy called Colonel Minor and told him to stop. I suggested we move their personal effects out on the street but now the local press is watching and we have to be gentle."

Colonel Minor looked over at me. "Gregg, we needed the rooms at the Regency and we need them yesterday. The Embassy called and asked me to remove the MPs and not to enter the rooms occupied by the Vietnamese."

I really didn't think a heavy-handed approach was the best way to get this thing sorted out. I knew the Vietnamese saw us as a cash cow and any opportunity to get some American dollars was an opportunity to be embellished. I could see the tenants making a big deal in the local press of anything we did. "Sir, I don't know the Vietnamese law on this but if it's anything like US law and the occupants had more than a day-to-day rental agreement, which it appears they do, the landlord is supposed to provide adequate notice. Aside from the contract ramifications, the tenants might sue for damages in a Vietnam court which means in all likelihood, they would win. Maybe a meeting with the tenants, the landlord, and a Vietnamese attorney might help. At least it would show we're thinking of their welfare. There's a Vietnamese attorney at MACV JAG and I can ask Colonel Casserly if we could borrow him for the meeting."

"That sounds like a good plan. We might have to play musical chairs with those still at the Rex but I hope not. Keep me informed Judge and let me know if you need my help. For the time being, keep the MPs in the Regency lobby, double their presence in and out of the building and if anyone asks tell them I said so. But tell the MPs not to interfere with the tenants coming and going. I also don't think we should be buying these nice folks anything fancy. Keep me informed."

Colonel Casserly, the MACV JAG, at my request, made Mr. Huy, a Vietnamese attorney employed at the MACV JAG office, available for the meeting. Casserly, as usual, seemed to know what was going on and clearly anticipated my call. I spoke to Huy on the phone and he told me the tenants had a claim against the owner of the hotel because they were permanent residents and came under a different category of tenant in Vietnam than a mere hotel visitor. I got the firm impression he considered us mere visitors. He said the owner would need to arrange for a new place for each family and was responsible for moving their personal effects. He advised the move shouldn't be too bad because the furniture was furnished by the hotel and the Army could assist in moving the personal stuff if the tenants agreed. I called Plant and asked if he minded if I called the hotel owner and discussed the problem. He said if I thought it wouldn't undercut the contract, it was ok with him. I asked if there were any funds available if the new residence for the families cost more than what they were paying at the Regency. I was attempting to cover all contingencies. He said he wasn't paying for their housing and I had to agree with him but hoped it wouldn't go to a Vietnamese court. I could see down the pike the State Department arranging for an Army payment in accordance with local custom. Easy for them; it wasn't out of their hide.

The next morning I picked up Mr. Huy at MACV and we drove to the Regency. Colonel Plant was already there with a captain from his office. The hotel owner, Mr. Minh, and approximately twenty other people who I suspected were the permanent resident families were milling around in the lobby. A few were sitting on folding chairs obviously set up for what looked like a very formal meeting. The military is very efficient. When Huy and I arrived, Minh started speaking to the group in Vietnamese, and according to Huy, explained the circumstances and that they had to move. Mr. Huy then addressed the group and I think told them Vietnamese law only required Minh to find them a new place in the same price range and to pay for their move. At least that's what he said he was going to say. The tenants didn't have an attorney present but Huy leaned over and whispered to me two members of the Saigon press were present. After Minh spoke, Colonel Plant said he could help move any of the families if they wanted. When Plant was finished and Huy explained what he said in Vietnamese there was general shouting and commotion with everyone attempting to speak at the same time. When the commotion was over and everyone quieted down, Mr. Huy walked over to my chair. "They didn't like the place Minh selected for their new home. It's another of Minh's hotels but it is not supposed to be as nice as the Regency."

I asked the Vietnamese contract lawyer to MACV, "Do you have any suggestions of what we should do?"

Huy said something in Vietnamese to the owner, Mr. Minh. Minh nodded and said something to the families. Huy then answered me, "You could look at the new quarters to see if they are compatible to those at the Regency and, if you decide they are, the families will go there but, if you decide they're not, you go with me to find something compatible. Any costs at the new place are not to exceed what the tenants are paying at the Regency."

Thanks Huy, now I was really in the middle of things. "What about our offer to move the families?"

"That's not an issue. They will move themselves and would rather the Army not be involved. We will not have to pay anything on that."

I figured they were probably taking half of Minh's hotel with them. I finally realized they understood they had to move and soon; it was just a matter of where. I told Colonel Minor what I was doing and, again, he requested me to keep him posted.

Mr. Huy asked Minh to go with him and me in my Scout to see Minh's other hotel. I asked Minh if he would show me a room or two at the Regency so I had something to compare. Huy said he had to go to the bathroom. Minh accompanied me in an elevator and pushed a button for the third floor. When we got off Minh smiled at me. "Captain Thompson, I would like you to be my guest at Rex for weekend. I provide you entertainment and number one comfort."

I felt a bit trapped in his hotel alone on the third floor. "Mr. Minh, I think we need to take care of this situation before we do anything else."

He walked down the hall and opened a door. "This is room occupied by Army officer. He at work. The family rooms compare."

I looked in and there was only one bed and the room was similar to what I had at the Caravelle but it also had a small sofa, a little refrigerator, an easy chair, and a wooden desk with a desk chair. It had a built-in closet and an adjacent bath room with tub but no shower. "Are the rooms the families occupy similar to this?"

"Captain, the rooms are same. Tell me what you need and I fix you up this weekend or whenever you want."

He had a white shirt open at the neck and I grabbed the front of it in my fist and pulled the smaller man over to me. "Mr. Minh, I don't like being tempted with a bribe. The only thing I can say right now is that your other hotel had better be nice." I then let him go, turned my back, saw the stairs, and went down in a hurry. My face felt hot and I knew it was red. I wanted to settle down before running into Huy again, so I stopped and took a few deep breaths. I felt used and violated.

When I walked into the lobby as Minh was just getting out of the elevator. He said something to Huy in Vietnamese and went into his office. Huy said, "Mr. Minh told me something has come up and he cannot go with us. He's going to provide us a hotel to look at. I will take you there."

"You might tell Minh to give us a couple of alternatives."

"It's not necessary. If his hotel is not suitable, I know of several others."

I looked away and Huy went into Minh's office. I didn't know whether Huy was in cahoots with Minh or not. I now felt I couldn't trust anyone. Plant had left and now I didn't feel comfortable looking around Saigon under these circumstances. Huy came back in a few seconds, said he had the address, and we should go.

We went out to the Scout and I told Huy I had to go to my office first to get some papers. He said they were waiting for us at the hotel. I told him they could wait. We didn't talk on the 15 minute ride back to HAC. When I got there I excused myself and got Captain Darrell Morgan, the only other JAG in my office, to come with us. I wanted a friendly witness to whatever spectacle was about to occur. I had a sinking feeling that Hue, the hotel owner, the tenants, or someone was trying to set me up. It just didn't feel right. I introduced Morgan to Huy and the three of us proceeded to the Hotel Liberty in silence. It was an older building about four stories high. The lobby was ratty and there was no elevator. It smelled of sour vinegar. I asked the clerk if we could see a room and he bowed profusely. Huy stayed in the lobby as Darrell and I walked up a flight of stairs. The hallway was dark and an old man was sitting on a wooded stool at the second floor landing. He looked at me and Darrell and then looked down. The clerk opened the first door on the right and I went in. It had unpainted dark wood walls with a wooden chair rail around the room. A flickering light bulb dangled from the ceiling in one corner and a table lamp stood in another. There was no bathroom. The room had a scary-looking dusty old armoir, leaning crookedly as if it had missing feet on one side, for a closet along with a sorry double bed with a sagging mattress and two hard chairs. A wooden chest with drawers had two folded skinny towels with a small naked bar of soap on top. I understood why the families were making a ruckus.

When Darrell and I got back to the lobby, Huy said, "You didn't like it did you?"

"Why did you bring us here? This obviously is not the same caliber hotel."

"You're the judge and it's your call."

"Mr. Huy, please don't waste our time. Do you know a hotel similar to the Regency where we can give these people adequate housing?"

He formed a sinister smile. "I know just the place."

I followed his directions and we traveled across Saigon. We came to a busy street in a semi industrial area. There was a fair amount of exhaust fume smog but that could be found throughout the city, especially when a bus or little motorcycle van went by. The Hotel Solaris was in a block with a small market on the same side as the hotel and a barber shop next to that. The hotel took up the rest of the block on that side of the street and it had balconies across the front of each of its five stories. On the other side there was an attractive little park with trees set geometrically around well laid out paths. The sporadic patches of grass seemed well tended. The rest of the park was hard packed dirt. The park was surrounded by a chain link fence. I smelled a hint of disinfectant in the lobby like a toilet that has just been cleaned with Pine Sol. A clerk sat at a desk jutting out from the wall so you faced him as you entered the room. There was a light on the desk and a vase of fresh flowers. There were two small elevators and some easy chairs in an informal setting. The carpeting was worn but the floor well swept. Huy spoke to the clerk in Vietnamese and this time went with Darrell and me as we looked at a third floor room. It was adequate and although the furnishings didn't look as new as the Regency's, the room was about a quarter larger than in the Regency and the bathroom was similar to what I had in my office but without any fancy faucets. The hotel looked at one time to have been very nice. It certainly was adequate and comparable to the Regency.

"Is there a price differential here, Mr. Huy?"

"Normally, this hotel would cost a bit more but the owner is a friend of mine and I told him our problem. He is willing to let 14 rooms for a year at the same price the families have been paying at the Regency. He promises not to raise the rent for a year and then not more than 10%, and maybe not at all."

I was afraid to ask how close a friend the owner really was. "Mr. Huy, I believe we have a solution. I would like to tell the families my decision."

"I can do that if you want."

"Thank you but I feel it's my responsibility. I also need to call Colonel Minor. Let's go back to the Regency."

When we got back it didn't take the families long to congregate. I told them of the Solaris and that I felt it would be acceptable to them. Several nodded and I got the impression they knew. They moved the next day and we got all our people out of the Rex although a couple of the Rex tenants got to stay there a few extra days. Colonel Minor especially was happy. I wondered what I was missing at the Rex the coming weekend.

Bart Johnson; a Deadly Game

Colonel Minor again called for me. This time it was it was just the two of us. "Sit down judge. A papa san was shot a few days ago walking down a small path near one of our leased apartment buildings. He was killed. We have the lease on the apartments and use them for contract employees currently working on a water processing plant for the 4th Transportation Command. The old man's family is upset and they seek reparations. The Embassy asked me to investigate. I asked the CID to look into it and they learned that after work our tenants would go up on the roof and drink beer. They also would shoot some privately-owned rifles and pistols off the roof through trees behind the hotel. Apparently they just shot at random targets like at branch or piece of trash up in the foliage. The CID got statements from some of the tenants and that's what they say. The CID report says the path where the old man was walking goes across the back of the apartment building through the trees from a small village about a quarter mile away to a market just on the other side of the hotel. The resident statements are that they have seen local people walking down the path. It's clear that the night of the murder a Mr. Bart Johnson was firing a 22-rifle off the hotel roof. I've got the CID report but before sending it to the Embassy, I'd like you to take a look at it. I want to try the bozo for murder."

"Sir, at first blush it sounds like negligent homicide or some type of manslaughter but normally we can't try civilian contractors."

"Well we told the Vietnamese police and they're not interested. They say it's a matter for us; they don't want to try Americans in their courts." He gave me the file and I said I'd get back to him.

Bart Johnson was a master electrician on the water plant contract. He was making $22 an hour but with substantial overtime scheduled at $30 an hour. He was on a personal services contract with a water purification subcontractor for the major U.S. contract developer in the Saigon area. Bart's deal was for four months, if not extended, and he anticipated over $25,000 for his efforts with no costs for housing or meals. In the United States for four month's work, Bart would be lucky in 1970 to make six thousand dollars.

The CID report determined Bart shot the old man. He admitted he was shooting off the roof the same night the man was killed and no one else shot their weapons that night. They made no comment about the civilians being in possession of privately owned weapons. Johnson made a statement that denied seeing the man on the path and denied that he had ever seen anybody walking behind his apartment building. He admitted he had seen a path but his statement is that he thought it was abandoned.

The papa san was shot with a 22-caliber bullet. It pierced his brain and the brain hemorrhaged killing him while he lay unattended and unseen on the path. My first question was whether it was a negligent homicide or the more serious involuntary manslaughter. The investigation didn't conclude there was any sufficient evidence of Bart's intent to kill, or for that matter that there was any thought of killing, so a more serious crime was not apparent. If the negligence was simple, then negligent homicide was an appropriate charge. Maximum sentence under the UCMJ is three years for negligent homicide. If the negligence was "culpable" then involuntary manslaughter was appropriate and the maximum sentence under the UCMJ is ten years. A lawyer is supposed to know the difference between simple and culpable negligence but it's not always clear which is why we have trials. In my reports of survey I had some experience in this area. Simple negligence was stupid. Gross negligence or in the criminal sense, culpable negligence, is real stupid. I was not convinced Mr. Johnson didn't know the path was being used. It wasn't overgrown but could clearly be seen at its entry into the woods. Maybe Bart didn't see someone walking down the path that evening but he should have known someone could have used the path and he was not able to see if they were on it or not when he shot his rifle. That inability to see when using a deadly force, in my mind, clearly was stupid and negligent. That the weapon was deadly and could seriously injure or kill gave a high degree of care in its use.

A lawyer looks at the forseeablity of the act. If the actor might foresee that his action could kill someone, to continue the action is culpable. The degree of forseeablity might be a matter for sentencing. If he saw a man entering the woods and shot anyway it would be culpability that might warrant a tough sentence. I didn't think Bart saw the man on the path walking in the woods. I did think he shot with the knowledge that someone might be there. He, or a reasonable person, could foresee that a person would walk down that path from a village to a small store. He might not be as stupid as the person who shoots knowing someone's in the area but he's still culpable because he recklessly shot into an area that he could foresee people might be walking. All that, however, would be applicable only if we could court-martial him. Even though I prosecuted the PX civilian employee at Long Binh, this case didn't involve any military personnel and the individual worked for a civilian contractor. It would be difficult to show he was "serving with or accompanying an armed force" which is first necessary to make the person subject to the Code. The other part for jurisdiction was the time of war issue. I remembered LTC Cassidy's reaction at our conviction of the PX employee and his feeling that the case wouldn't stand. It was my determination we couldn't prosecute. The states at home didn't have jurisdiction and the Federal government had no authority to prosecute a civilian for an offense on foreign jurisdiction so Bart wouldn't be prosecuted when he went home. The South Vietnamese Government had an overall policy not to prosecute Americans no matter what the crime. Bart Johnson was going to skate, something the UCMJ keeps from happening to military personnel no matter where they are. I figured all we could do was bar him from the post exchanges, our facilities—mess halls and residences, and maybe send him home. I suggested first we get his passport. I wrote it up and sent my memo to the boss.

Colonel Minor asked me to take the report to the Embassy. I met with the Embassy in-country counsel and one of his State Department lawyers. They agreed with my analysis. The State Department took Johnson's passport and arranged for his transportation to San Francisco. In effect, Bart Johnson was deported from Vietnam. I don't know whether the Embassy paid reparations to the old man's family but I hope so.

Wilborn Brown; a Spy of Sorts

We had an AWOL from Headquarters Company, 519th MI Battalion that caused Colonel Minor to swallow about half a bottle of Tums and still feel upset. Wilborn NMI Brown, Jr. was a graduate of Tufts College and not able to evade the draft. In the military NMI means no middle initial. They can't stand non conformity. He was 6'3" and weighed 200. He had no real problems with the military in the first half of his tour. The command recommended his promotion to Spec Four with about six months to go in country and accordingly, he was promoted. Will was smart and got into military intelligence where he was assigned to the 519th. They assigned him to counter intelligence. Counter intelligence runs numerous programs to keep our operations secure and secret thereby subverting the enemy from garnering information about us and what we do and intend to do. It's not guarding the perimeter and performing military police duties but rather mounting operations to thwart or mislead the enemy's intelligence efforts such as giving off false radio signals and publicizing security efforts by all personnel. The "loose lips sink ships" publications are counter intelligence. Brown was assigned an undercover job where he'd go into Saigon and present himself as a weak or discontented character who might be willing to do something to hurt the Army. He was supposed to find out who was recruiting spies against the U.S. and how they were doing it. His success in this endeavor is how you look at it. Will apparently felt his shenanigans in Saigon were successful, at least to him, in that they allowed an alternate function to what an Army Spec Four normally would be expected to do in a war zone. He may have gotten the VC to watch him for awhile and therefore not watch or otherwise go after someone more susceptible to their efforts. He thought that a minor success. He wasn't making the Army a career and realized Spec Four was as high a grade as he could expect so he had no incentive to put himself in harm's way. His job was dangerous but he saw a number of other Americans living well in Saigon with no apparent connection to the military or means of support so he didn't feel threatened.

Will got a cheap room at the New Martin Hotel. It was a dive in the midst of a thriving gypsy market where everything imaginable was for sale. Anything from used and smelly tee shirts to iced French Champagne to fly ridden pastries to boys or girls was available. Things were bought and sold from carts in the gutters, from wobbly tables on the streets, and from sinister characters in darkened alleys. A proprietor would sit in a little metal chair or squat over his goods usually set out on the side of the street. Many sellers stood around and squawked their wares to passers by. The better shops were in squeezed in shacks protected by ramshackle bits of corrugated metal, scrap aluminum, and torn canvas. You could buy a marijuana cigarette for one dollar MPC. You could change money and sell anything you could buy at the PX for a substantial profit. There was always a brisk market for whiskey, cameras, stereos, small men's Levis, cigarettes, toiletries, and children's clothes. If you were authorized PX privileges and didn't have much to do, you could make a lot of money buying and selling stuff from the Post Exchange. That is if you didn't get caught by military police. It was a very active and lucrative Black Market.

Brown figured he could work the market, buy a funny cigarette or two, and hang around to see if someone would be interested in him and his help in some nefarious military activity. In a week no one asked where he was stationed or with whom he worked. He did have a good time observing what was going on although he was a bit lonely. He met a couple of Americans who obviously were AWOL but none wanted to talk about their status or how they lived. It seemed they would take orders from a papa san here and there and go to the PX, buy some stuff, and make their deliveries. None were selling the stuff themselves. Will thought it might be too risky working with the papa sans so he sold whiskey at a premium and kept a record of each transaction in a little note book so he wouldn't get in trouble.

His room at the New Martin Hotel was the pits and after a week's profits, Will decided he could afford something a little better. Ostensibly going to the PX in Long Binh, he stopped at an Army office in Saigon and called his handler, Staff Sergeant Clyde Patterson. "Sarge, I've set up a liquor store at the market. It's going pretty well but I'm running out of ration cards. Can you get me some more?"

"I think we can arrange that. How about ten more to start?"

"That sounds pretty good Sarge, I think with my profits, I can afford a better place to stay. The New Martin really sucks."

"Ok. Find a new place to stay but report it in and, at a minimum, report in each week. Do you understand, and lay off the weed." Before he left the company area Patterson told him, "An MP named Watson is working the area in uniform. He's another member of our unit and undercover with the MPs. Send any messages through him but only him. Of course, you still can call."

Will moved to the Crystal Hotel where he had his own bathroom and clean sheets. He continued to sell whiskey and found scotch did best. He made $10 each transaction and expected to sell three to four bottles a day. He would change the dollars for MPCs making even more money. Will quickly went through the new ration cards. Each was good for three bottles of spirits and three bottles of wine each month. Will found the wine didn't sell very well and stuck to spirits. He figured he could exceed making what Patterson expected and live better with the extra money. He went to the Bien Hoa and Tan Son Hut airfields and begged unused ration cards from departing troops. The ration cards were the key. He found unused cards in the trash at the airport. If they had an unmarked whiskey block, he'd hit the jackpot. The PX clerks checked off the cards but rarely checked Will's ID against the card's true owner. If they did, he'd say he left his ID in his hooch. He tried buying more than three bottles saying he was purchasing for a unit party at a small PX on Long Binh and the clerk told him his buddies had to accompany him. It worked better if he got in a big line and didn't say anything. He wore his uniform to the PX and the airports and then changed back to civilian clothes to sell his stuff. He knew he'd need to change his product to avoid serious suspicion from the exchanges and the MPs hanging around the air ports. Will then met a girl.

Lauren was Australian, beautiful, and a photo journalist. She bought a bottle of Cointreau, an orange flavored liqueur that she said she preferred on the rocks. He paid $5 for it and sold it to Lauren for $12. Will was intrigued by her Aussie accent and struck up more than a casual conversation. They had dinner in Cholon and ended up at her place, an attractive apartment on the top floor of a three story building around the corner from the Rex Hotel. It was in a pretty nice part of town. Lauren shared the apartment with another Australian but had her own room. They drank some of the Cointreau which, with the rest of the wine and booze he had with dinner, gave him a cloudy buzz. When he was leaving that first night he and Lauren kissed on the landing and it turned into a fiercely passionate embrace with Will losing all sense of propriety. Lauren invited him back in. Her room mate was out. He played, stayed, and ended up moving in some of his stuff from the Crystal. Lauren wanted to know more about the Saigon underground. Will was eager to please and Lauren was eager to express her gratitude. She drove a small Peugeot and took him to Long Binh. They went to a PX where he bought her some perfume. She wanted some background pictures for a story she was doing and he said it was ok but not to include him. He showed her around Long Binh but asked her not to photograph the Long Binh Jail. Lots of soldiers seeing a "round eye" were anxious to see her and she accommodated them all capturing their stupid poses. He never revealed his undercover status. He met Margaret, her room mate, who immediately flirted with him. She was prettier than Lauren. Eventually Lauren wanted to see the Crystal Hotel and how he did what he did. Will was embarrassed about the hotel and finessed that but suggested that he move full-time into the apartment. He said he would help pay the rent. He signed out of the Crystal and moved in with Lauren and Margaret. Lauren told him not to worry about the rent but he could help with the groceries. She went with him to the market just once.

Lauren was not in the afternoon he moved his stuff to the flat, but Margaret, the room mate, was. He didn't know what Margaret did and didn't ask. She got him a Foster's and positioned herself next to him in the living room on a soft creamy pink sofa. As she sat down she looked into his eyes and he noticed the tip of her tongue slip out of her mouth and wet her top lip. She smelled of lilacs. She pressed her thigh against his as she positioned herself on the couch. He sipped his beer and, as they were talking, she placed her hand on his leg. Before he knew it, Margaret moved her hand up his khaki pants and brushed his pants zipper lingering her fingers and pushing down just a bit. He felt his heart beat faster. He got harder and was scared they would be caught. She looked him in the eye while grabbing him over the top of his pants. She rolled her eyes and gently massaged him up and down and then looked down and pulled open his zipper. He felt blood course throughout his body as he popped out. She grabbed it lightly. He leaned over and kissed her deeply, heightening the excitement. She pulled away rubbed her cheek against his penis and kissed it. She then took it in her mouth. He was afraid Lauren would come into the apartment and throw him out. The excitement of his being caught with the mid day sun shining in was especially erotic. Margaret taught him things to do that he had never seemed possible. She was on top of him when he finally exploded and it seemed her movements sucked out his entire loin. When finished, she walked naked into the shower and he wondered what he had gotten himself into. He looked around the apartment and saw Lauren's camera equipment hanging on a chair and her note books scattered on the floor by the entrance to the bathroom. There were several spent film cartridges spilling out of an open bag dangling from the chair. He was a day late in contacting Sergeant Patterson but figured it could wait.

This part of Saigon was pretty nice-tree lined streets and European style buildings. It was Sunday-morning quiet. There was a French market on the corner and Will bought some camembert cheese and imported sausage. He found a tin of smoked duck that looked good so he bought that along with a baguette and a bottle of wine. Lauren was there when he delivered the groceries and greeted him with a big smile. She knew. Margaret was on the sofa wearing a flimsy robe. While smiling at Will, she moved her legs apart causing her robe to open. Lauren put together the meal, lit a few candles in the apartment, and the three shared the meal and each other for the next month. Will didn't report to Clyde Patterson but continued selling PX goods constantly rotating his product to avoid suspicion. He likewise rotated the ladies frequently having them together. He supplied marijuana he got from the market and the three partied frequently.

Patterson got worried at Will's failure to report in so he sent one of his guys to see what was going on. He found Will at the market, caught his eye, and signaled to meet surreptitiously. He asked if Will was all right and Will said he had something going on and couldn't talk. He told Will to call in when he could, that Patterson was upset. Will still didn't call. Twice emissaries from Patterson left messages to call Patterson at the Crystal which Will ignored. The weeks turned into a month and then some. Lauren and Margaret seemed to be spending more and more time together, sleeping in Margaret's room and going out together during the day and often at night. On one occasion Lauren brought another guy into the apartment and took the young, officer-looking guy into Lauren's room where Bart had his things and had been sleeping. Will didn't like it because he had his stuff there. He said something and Lauren said he could have come in and joined them. Margaret finally told Will that she and Lauren had finished their work and had to go back to Sydney. They said it was fun but he had to leave the apartment when they did because it was on a long-term lease with a publisher in Australia who had another tenant coming in. Will decided it was time to see Clyde Patterson.

Sergeant Patterson made Will wait outside his office for over an hour. He then called him in and asked, "Specialist Brown, you've been out of contact, status unknown, for over two months and now you just show up. I asked you to keep in touch and sent a message to let me know what you were doing. I hope you have something to give us. What happened?"

"I met up with a couple of girls from Australia and one in particular seemed suspiciously interested in me. I felt this was the feeler you told me about and I encouraged the relationship, even moving in with her and her room mate for a time, but they returned to Australia. There names were Lauren and Margaret."

Patterson felt he was being set up. "Did you get any other contacts? What did you do all this time?"

"Most of the time I kept up my cover and played the market. I moved around a bit and rotated my stock. I had lots of Vietnamese customers, a few French, and even some Americans apparently living in Saigon. Nobody else wanted to meet me or try to get me involved in anything."

Patterson started thinking it was time to make a case. "You were required to keep an accounting of your sales. Where is it?"

Will thought a minute. "The girls must have taken it. When they left I had to get out of the apartment and my stuff was in Lauren's room. She had lots of note-books lying around and she must have grabbed mine by mistake when she packed up to go back to Australia."

"Well how much money did you make and where is it?"

Will handed over a fat manila envelope. "I cleared $942. It's both dollars and MPC. I used some of the profits to pay for taxis back and forth to different bases. One time I ran down to Vung Tau to see if I could sell some stuff there. It didn't look too good. I hadn't been there before and the exchanges on Long Binh were starting to get suspicious."

Patterson looked Will in the eye and with a raised voice said, "I'm pretty upset you never called in. I can't believe you couldn't at least try to make contact. You were on military bases by yourself and surely could have gotten something to us, especially if you had anything, even two Australian girls. But it seems you didn't have anything. I'm considering charges of violation of directions and orders. Your failure was more than just a poor job. I actually think you went absent without leave when you failed to call in the first time. You had no authority to be away after that. If you had something going, I can't see it. You're dismissed and not to leave the company area. I'll let you know what we plan to do. Do you under-stand?"

"Yes Sergeant Patterson."

"Lieutenant Colonel Marden wants to see you. I think he was concerned with your being away so long without reporting in. Report to him when you leave. Do you understand this or do I have to have someone accompany you to his office?"

"I understand and I'll report right now."

LTC Abe Marden, the 519th Commander, had been monitoring Spec Four Brown's activities since Patterson reported at a staff meeting that an undercover agent was two weeks late in reporting in. Marden sent a team to see what Will was doing. They followed him to the girl's apartment but didn't want to interrupt what could have been a valuable operation. Marden appeared furious, especially since Brown brought in no new intelligence for his two month effort and possibly because he considered Brown's operation no more than a frolic. When Brown reported, he told him to get a defense counsel; he was charging him with being absent without leave.

Marden called Colonel Minor, my boss, and told him he wanted Brown's head. I had advised Minor about command influence and he knew he had to tread softly in justice matters but that didn't hinder Colonel Minor from getting pissed. He hated people trying to work the system to their benefit and to the detriment of everybody around them. He called me. "Gregg, you're going to get court martial charges from the 519th on a Specialist Brown. It's an AWOL case but I want you to check it carefully to see if there's anything besides a two-month AWOL that we could charge him with. Let me know what you come up with."

Wilborn Brown's case was a charge of two months AWOL with a recommendation for a general court-martial. I knew that wouldn't fly and after reviewing the file felt we'd be lucky to get a conviction for AWOL. The command never dropped Brown from the roles or annotated their morning report that he was missing or absent. After all he was undercover and they knew where he was most of the time he was gone. There was a hint of drug usage but no drugs were found and Brown was not observed smoking weed and wasn't talking. Brown's log allegedly was stolen. Any Black Market activity was part of his cover so that couldn't fly unless we considered that when he departed from his undercover operation and went AWOL, the Black Market activity wasn't protected. The problem with that is we had no record of any activity and it was too complicated. Patterson and Marden made their decision to let the operation run. That their guy decided to turn it into a sex frolic with a couple of Australian bimbos was something they allowed to continue and I didn't think we could get a conviction and besides, if we lost on that, we were in peril of losing the whole damned thing. I figured the AWOL might fly with a good prosecution argument and a technically-minded judge and we should leave it at that. I told Colonel Minor what I was thinking and he said he didn't like it but agreed it was the safest way to go. We decided to go for a special court that could give Brown six month's confinement for the two month absence.

Darrell Morgan, the JAG in my office, prosecuted and Frank Carlucci, from the 4th Transportation Command, a non-JAG attorney certified to act in courts martial, defended. USARV sent Richard Green to judge the case. Green was a JAG Captain and part-time judge, like me. Darrell stopped by after the trial and told me Brown pled guilty. I was astounded and immediately thought we might have an issue of inadequate counsel with Carlucci permitting him to do that. He then said the judge, after hearing Brown's story, reduced him to Private First Class and gave him a $200 fine. I controlled my anger and asked what happened. He said the judge was influenced by Brown graduating from college and answering the draft for two years. Brown said he was going to get out of the military as soon as he could and was not all that familiar with military protocol. He said what Brown did while AWOL was never brought up. It didn't sound right to me but at this point I was a messenger boy. I stopped by our new Deputy Commander's office on the way up to tell Colonel Minor what happened and the Hispanic Deputy told me, "Geez, for two hundred dollars, I go AWOL for two months in Saigon." If he only knew what he could be doing during the absence.

Colonel Minor was furious. "He found him guilty didn't he?"

"Yes sir. The judge has to go over the elements of each offense before accepting the plea and get the accused to admit to each one. He accepted the plea."

"Who's the judge? What's his story?"

"Richard Green and he's from the Da Nang Support Command. I don't know him. USARV assigned him for this case only. Darrell told me they didn't get into Brown's activities while AWOL. It sounds very peculiar but at least we got a conviction."

The colonel said, "I don't want that judge coming back to my command."

"Sir, that's out of my control. USARV assigns the judges and I'm not a player other than to let them know your displeasure."

"Please do that and I'll contact USARV."

Colonel Minor sent me a copy of the letter he sent Colonel Irv Peterman, the USARV SJA. It requested Captain Richard Green not be assigned any more cases in Headquarters Area Command. Minor called me back to his office. He got up and closed the door. I thought I was really going to get it. "Gregg, Abe Marden just stopped by and told me some things about the Brown case. I think you need to know what happened. It's classified information. Colonel Marden was upset when he learned Brown didn't report for three weeks. He thought he might have gotten into something over his head and might be in danger. Marden checked out the apartment where Brown was staying and found it was leased by an international consortium in Hungry that sent a parade of different people to stay for short periods in Saigon. The girls with Specialist Brown were Russians, not Australians. We're pretty sure we knew what they were doing in Saigon but the State Department had control. The Embassy and their folks had an eye on them even before they met up with Brown. They followed each girl at different times and the girls took pictures of our facilities and ports but apparently there's nothing we can do about that. They wanted to see who the girls contacted and what the contacts did. They asked Marden to let the thing play out to see what would happen. Wilborn Brown was in a nest of spies and didn't even know it. At least he was honest about where he was. Brown came closer to breaking into the Russian spy network than the CIA or State department had with their folks watching the apartment for almost a year. Everybody was excited and then Brown blew it by being totally clueless as to what was going down. Brown's naivety probably opened the door for him. It's too bad he paid more attention to what's in his pants than to what he was supposed to be doing."

"Wow! Did they set up the guilty plea and the sentence?"

Minor replied, "I don't know. I suspect so because it just doesn't compute. I know the MACV Intel folks have close relations with the CIA so I wouldn't be surprised but nobody's telling me anything."

"Sir, nothing in this country is ever what it seems."

"That's an understatement Gregg. Keep up the good work."

He walked me to the door, opened it by pushing it back against his wall, and I left.

Norbert Smith; A Bribe

I was in my office one afternoon, alone, working on a nonappropriated fund maid service contract. The contract was designed to provide our tenants maid service "of a quality equal to that rendered in first class hotels." Enlisted personnel had to pay 1200 piasters and officers had to pay 1450 p. With the official exchange rate at 125 piasters for a $1 military payment certificate the monthly charge came to $9.60 for enlisted and $11.60 for officers. If the tenant illegally changed his money on the street, he'd pay about $4 a month, depending on the rate he negotiated. The maids, among other things, would wash and fold your laundry, starch and press your fatigues, and shine your boots. While reviewing a provision about what to do if one of the maids was found looking through a soldier's stuff, a young man in civilian clothes entered my office. The guy introduced himself as Norbert Smith and told me the following story:

"*I'm an agent for the Wells Fargo Bank and work in Saigon. I came from West Virginia about two years ago and live in the suburbs in a former French villa with four other Anglos who also work in Saigon. The villa's surrounded by a concrete wall topped by broken glass and some sharp metals. We keep the front gate barred and locked. I got here just before Tet and heard fighting but stayed in the villa with my house mates and a couple of our help and we weren't attacked. We have two Vietnamese security guards, two maids, and a cook. Last Friday night, after dinner, one of my house mates and I decided to play poker over at the French Tennis Club. It was Poker Night at the Club. I got five grand cash from a hidden stash in my room from previous winnings and put it in a money belt hidden under my shirt. I kept $150 in my pocket for drinks, tips, and whatever.*

"*It was high stakes poker and who was there varied each week. Friday, two Vietnamese men, maybe in their 50's; a German; my room mate, Freddie; me; and another American, probably a contractor, made up the table. I didn't do well at first—I lost about a grand, just didn't have the cards, and when I bluffed it didn't work. But then my luck changed and I started to win. Once you start winning, the bluffs work. I got my grand back and then some. We played until almost 1:30 in the morning. One of the Vietnamese lost a bundle and wanted to pay in piasters. We argued over the exchange rate but I didn't have any choice in the matter. I felt cheated. Freddie and I compared our winnings and I came out ahead with maybe $750. Freddie lost $450 and that wasn't bad for Freddie. He rarely wins.*

"*Freddie wanted to go home. I was still juiced from my win so I told him to take the car; I'd catch a cab later. He dropped me off at a bar down on Tu Do Street. I got a good reception especially for the late hour and took a couple of girls to a rear room. I was there about an hour. I drink when I play poker and had some more at the bar so when I left, I was a bit wobbly. I started looking for a taxi and didn't see any so I started walking up to the Rex where cabs hang out at that hour. I remember going out into the street but not much after that. The first thing I then know is waking up at the 3d Field Hospital with my naked butt hanging out of a hospital gown. My money belt was gone. I hurt all over. A nurse saw me awake and immediately came over and asked how I was. I felt terrible and asked how I got there. She said some MPs found me in a gutter unconscious and brought me in. She told me they took me to the emergency room and the ER technicians examined me to see if there were any injuries other than my head wound. She said the chart says the medics saw a money belt with some dollars sticking out under my shirt and told the MPs who hadn't yet left the hospital. Apparently one of the MPs looked into the belt. She said the police confiscated my money. She said they wanted to talk to me when I was feeling better and wanted to find out who I was. My wallet and the cash in my pants were gone. They let me out of the hospital after lunch.*

"*I went to the MPs and told them they had some of my stuff from the night before. They asked who I was. I said they didn't know my name because I had no*

ID the night before when in the hospital but I gave it to them just the same. An MP Lieutenant came out from an office behind the desk sergeant and said they had a report about a mugging on a John Doe from the night before. He asked if I was the John Doe and I told them I guess I was. He told me hospital orderlies found my money belt with 315,000 piasters, $2,000 MPCs, and $2,850 in greenbacks. He said that was strong evidence of illegal Black Market activity, the money changing kind. Accordingly, they confiscated the belt. He said if I had any questions to see you. So here I am. I'd like to get my money back."

"Mr. Smith you tell an intriguing story but you have to admit 315,000$ Vietnamese, $2,000 MPC, and $2,850 in greenbacks in the streets of Saigon in the middle of the night certainly smacks of money laundering or black marketeering. It's even a presumption. While you're not technically bound, there are administrative procedures the MP office runs to see about returning any funds you can prove were obtained legally. Surely you know that after being here two years."

"You can't play in the poker games at the Club unless you have dollars."

I said, "Apparently, the Vietnamese man played and he didn't have any dollars. You said he paid his losses in 'P'."

"Is there any way I can get my money back without all the bureaucratic crap?"

"You can appeal to the Commander of the MP Detachment but it doesn't look good."

He wagged his head and looked down and said in a lowered voice. "Captain, I have a proposition. If you get my money back, I'll split it with you."

I felt my face start to heat up. "Excuse me?"

He repeated a little louder, "I'll split it with you if you can get my money back."

I got up, walked to my door, and along the way before I opened it looked at him hard. "Get out of my office. I don't take kindly to bribes. Maybe we can't try you here but I can sure make your life hell before you're expelled from the country. Get out."

He left and I shook. The thing is I was tempted. I was pissed to have been placed in that spot. Then I thought maybe he was working for the CID and trying to set me up. Problem is that clearly was entrapment. On the other hand they wouldn't try me for that kind of stuff; they would drum me out of JAG and probably my commission, so entrapment wasn't even at issue. I decided to call Colonel Minor; I had to tell someone. "Sir, Captain Thompson. Got a sec?"

"Always for you, Judge."

"Some civilian came by a few minutes ago and tried to bribe me. Apparently he was mugged but when he got to the hospital, the MPs found a lot of greenbacks and piasters in a money belt. They confiscated it and he said I could have half if I got it back for him."

"You too. He's already offered the MP Detachment Commander the same thing. It's pretty clear there wasn't a poker game. He's probably made tons on the Black Market. I have a call into the Wells Fargo manager and I'm suggesting sending him home."

I felt a little better but then thought of how I could have gotten the money out of the country. "Thanks boss." I hated being tempted.

The Sergeant Major Consortium

I didn't have much contact with the Command Sergeant Major. He stayed close to the Old Man and attended the weekly staff meetings but rarely said anything. I met him but he never asked for legal assistance or had any legal issues. He DEROSed about two months after I arrived as Command Judge Advocate and his replacement, Command Sergeant Major Ted Mabry, came in from the United States Pacific Command, commanded at the time by Admiral John S. McCain, Jr. PACOM reported directly to the Chairman of the Joint Chiefs of Staff and had overall responsibility for our theater of operations. Mabry was the senior sergeant major for a three-star Army staff officer at PACOM and his assignment to a colonel at a much lower command was highly unusual. Mabry was in his mid-forties, smart, good looking, and fit. Admittedly, U.S. Army Headquarters Area Command was in Saigon and pretty good duty compared to what could be in Vietnam but nevertheless, and even though I thought HAC should be a general officer command, it was a big drop in Mabry's status to go from a three-star to an O-6.

CSM Mabry stopped me in the hall and introduced himself. "Judge, I'm about to go on R&R to Australia and wondered if you have a minute?"

It was a bit unusual because hardly anyone ever goes on R&R when he first gets in country. He must have convinced someone his tour in Hawaii was hardship and he needed a break. I couldn't believe Colonel Minor would authorize it but apparently he didn't object. I thought maybe he wanted a power of attorney or an update for his will. "Welcome to HAC Sergeant Major; we're glad to have you here. You know we're all set up at our legal assistance office in the Quonset huts out back to do wills and powers of attorney. I can take you out there if you'd like."

"I was thinking of something more confidential than that. Can we go to your office or can I have an appointment?"

Bells went off and I felt a lack of trust permeating from good ole Ted Mabry who now seemed more slick than smart. "You know Sergeant Major that my primary client is the HAC commander and I can't discuss personal justice or disciplinary issues with you. If you're working on something for the boss, that's another matter and I'd be glad to discuss it with you."

Mabry said, "I just wanted discuss a few things and thought we could make it hypothetical."

"Maybe you should speak to one of my lawyers. If you'd feel more comfortable I can set you up with an appointment with an attorney at USARV or maybe at MACV."

"Thanks judge, but no thanks." He then stalked off.

Ted went on his R&R to Australia and I didn't see him for the next three weeks. I'm glad I didn't let him suck me in. Ted was involved in something over my pay grade and something that ended up over Colonel Minor's as well.

Mabry went on his R&R to Australia and bought beef for a consortium of his sergeant major buddies headed by the Sergeant Major of the Army. They in turn sold the beef to Army nonappropriated fund activities in Vietnam for their clubs and restaurants. Nonappropriated fund activities are programs for the military funded through participation by its military users, the soldiers and authorized patrons. They receive no direct funding from Congress and meager support from appropriated activities, the operational activities of the military departments. Funds come from exchange profits and other monies generated by clubs, guest houses, and nonmilitary activities set up for the benefit of the soldier. The Sergeant Major of the Army got together with his buddies and some civilian entrepreneurs to control money making military operations. They would target lower and mid-level enlisted personnel working as club and restaurant managers, food service operators, and morale and welfare managers to request goods and services for their operations. They used bribes, personnel rewards such as R&R paid trips, or threats of poor assignments and bad ratings to get them to comply with the consortium's requirements.

In Mabry's case, they asked the club manager to provide the command fund purchasing office a narrow and specific requirement for beef and to request its delivery within a tight schedule. The consortium consequently was the only bidder who could meet the requirements. Few bidders could expect a profit with the stringent requirements and the published expected price range. AJAX Enterprises, the sergeant majors' consortium, bid near the top of the range and agreed to meet all the published requirements and specifications. In actuality, the consortium's company couldn't perform at its offered price and didn't plan to. But the club manager wouldn't complain. The club would get a product although not what the contract called for. Instead of the premium beef, AJAX planned to supply select beef, two grades down, with a smattering of premium so an examining Army veterinarian, if any was around, could examine the delivery shipment and mark it acceptable. If a vet was scheduled for an inspection, the club manager would accompany him and ensure he just examined the premium portion of the order. If there was a problem, the sergeant major would bribe the vet and if that didn't work, get him reassigned. The sergeant majors had substantial power throughout the Army and the Sergeant Major of the Army was using it. Delivery times and methods such as air conditioned shipping containers kept at specified temperatures would not be enforced. Because of the war, the contract called for the nonappropriated fund to absorb any losses of product within the war zone, as described and referenced in the contract by a 1965 Executive Order, which included as part of the war zone, the adjacent waters a few miles off the coast of Vietnam.

Mabry's trip to Australia was paid by the Army as an R&R trip. He arranged purchases with meat purveyors in Australia controlled by the Corsican mafia. The mafia managed an Australian beef market controlling the production of the beef, its butchering, and all in between to include shipping. They agreed to arrange the shipments Mabry requested and to provide shipping documents referencing the sales to AJAX at false prices. Mabry arranged an alternate set of books to protect his investment and ensure deliveries. The mafia took advantage of AJAX to unload its overstocked standard and commercial grades of beef. It saved its premium grades for Corsican mob controlled restaurants in the Far East, such as the San Francisco Steak House in Hong Kong. AJAX and its consortium would profit grandly as would the Corsican mob. Enough was left over to bribe the club managers and any other officials who might get in the way. If a club manager didn't seem interested or rebuffed an offer, he'd be reassigned. The clubs would serve hamburger and expected to lose money.

The Corsicans got Mabry to agree to purchase kitchen equipment for any restaurants in clubs operated by nonappropriated fund activities from its company. Mabry said he could do that. They discussed other Mafia operations but Mabry made it clear he didn't have authority to go beyond beef purchases and new kitchen equipment. The sergeant major's work took him two days. He had the rest of his R&R week off. The mob set him up in an attractive villa adjacent to Manly Beach, a short ferry ride from Sydney. The mafia threw in as a surprise a young Australian maid. He had the time of his life.

Not long after Mabry's return, I was reviewing my daily feed of nonappropriated fund contracts when one in particular stood out. It was a contract for exclusive delivery orders that gave AJAX Enterprises, a Delaware corporation with offices in Northern Virginia, the franchise for the sale of premium beef to clubs and nonappropriated restaurants in Vietnam. There were two American style restaurants in Vietnam run by the fund. They were designed to give the troops a feeling of home while at war. I was surprised at the extent of the projected sales and that we were buying just premium, "restaurant-quality" beef that was to be cut into filet mignon, New York strip, T-bone, porterhouse, rib eye, and club steaks. The cost was substantial but I'm a lawyer, not a food buyer and I don't know how to run a restaurant. I thought from experience that most of the beef at the clubs certainly was not "restaurant quality" and hoped for an improvement. I figured maybe the club managers determined the better beef would encourage more to pay the extra amount for a good steak. I certainly would. Most of my meals were at mess halls in the Saigon area and free but I needed at least one meal a week at a commercial or club restaurant to maintain my sanity. The contract delivery schedule seemed a bit queer. It almost made air freight mandatory to meet the delivery window from the placement of the order to its acceptance at the club. The cost didn't reflect that. I figured the club managers and AJAX must have such an experience that AJAX would always have the beef in transit in anticipation of the orders. The minimum expected orders as estimated in the contract certainly would give such a conclusion. The requirement for refrigeration seemed appropriate but the slim margins of temperature tolerance seemed oppressive. I wondered who would monitor this. I thought maybe the examining vet could tell. I certainly didn't think the fund was going to baby sit the beef while in transit. I looked at my staffing cover sheet to see if any vet had reviewed the specs and they hadn't. I made my approval dependent on such a review and the vet's chop. There was a vet nearby in Long Binh so I didn't think that would be too onerous a burden for the purchasing office. The thing otherwise seemed legally sufficient. It had all the appropriate boilerplate and everybody but the vet reviewed so I signed off. At the time, I knew nothing of Mabry's shenanigans.

About a month later at the Monday morning staff meeting Colonel Minor said something about procurement fraud that caught my ear. I believe he was mostly directing his comments to Lieutenant Colonel Plant, the procurement chief. Minor related there was a massage parlor on the Long Binh compound that recently was a focal point for the relief of a USARV brigadier general. He said it had sinister underpinnings and wondered if we had a massage parlor within our nonappropriated fund activities. He said the massage parlor was supposed to be part of the NAFI in Long Binh and the post actually built the facility but no money ever came into the fund. Colonel Plant said he didn't think we had anything like massage parlors and Sergeant Major Mabry piped up that we didn't. Minor said to keep an eye on this kind of thing and let him know if there was anything like that in the command. I figured it was a CYA, cover your ass, by the Old Man because Saigon had numerous massage parlors that catered to the military and Tu Do Street was full of bars with Boom Boom girls who loved the American GI.

I thought it was a good time to try the Steak House Restaurant run by our NAFI and asked the two lawyers who worked with me if they wanted to get some good steaks for dinner. We went into town and the restaurant was decorated as a fancy steak restaurant but it wasn't very crowded. We grabbed a table and looked at the hand written menu. There was no steak on the menu. It had hand written what was touted as the "Best American hamburger in Vietnam" along with spaghetti with meat sauce and numerous other ground beef offerings. The guys started razzing me about a great steak and I was getting pissed. I asked for the club manager. Sergeant First Class Cal Keiser appeared and asked if he could help. I said, "Sarge, this is supposed to be a steak house and you don't have any steak. What goes?"

"Sorry sir, but we get our beef from Australia and the ship bringing it in hit a mine last week and lost refrigeration. We lost the entire shipment and have had to serve hamburger."

I remembered that the contract just called for prime meat. "Where'd you get the hamburger?"

"That's from our freezers. We had some left over from a previous shipment. It was the first shipment from AJAX."

It seemed odd because I remembered when I reviewed the contract I was surprised the contract didn't call for ground beef. "Was the hamburger from the Australian supplier?"

"Yes sir. That's the only beef supplier we have. They have an add-on that included some lamb chops but we don't have them yet. All that we ordered went bad when the ship hit the mine. I heard they had to throw the meat overboard. The ship was only slightly damaged."

"Sergeant Keiser, on the previous shipment, did you get hamburger or steaks?"

"Sir, I'm not sure. You would have to speak to the chief cook about that and he's not here. Is there a problem or something? I understand your frustration at not having steak. We're doing the best we can in a war zone and things happen."

"Thanks Sarge. Maybe I'll give the cook a call. What's his name?"

He thought longer than he should for his chief cook's name. The club manager should know who his chef is. "Sir, I would rather you not bother him. I'll speak to him and you can call me tomorrow. If I may ask, where are you stationed?"

I told him I was the Command Judge Advocate at Headquarters Area Command and my companions were attorneys there. We ordered hamburger and it was not the best American hamburger I had in Vietnam. In fact, it was sorry and the French fries sucked. The salad wasn't bad and the lemon meringue pie was great but for five bucks a piece and the promise of a good restaurant quality meal we were disappointed. With no steaks, we had beer instead of wine. I thought to myself when leaving I'd never go there again.

The next day Sergeant Major Mabry popped into my office. "I understand you heard about the ship with our steaks hitting a mine the other day."

I considered his calling the steaks "our" steaks and wondered what his proprietary interest might be. "Yes Sergeant Major. We went over to the NAFI steak house last night and they didn't have any steak. Their shipment apparently fed the fish in the South China Sea."

"I understand the ship hit a mine."

That also made me wonder. "It's strange that a mine could cause the refrigeration to go out but not do any other damage to the ship. I'm thinking that maybe we should get an investigation going. As I remember from the contract, the troops will have to pay for the loss of the product. A shipment of prime cut steaks is expensive. I should probably get the Navy to check it out. I have a friend in Navy JAG who might get something going."

"Do you really think that's necessary, sir. I mean the Navy's got a lot on its plate, and to do an investigation about some lost meat, well it might be a waste."

"Sergeant Major, when that boat came into the war zone, we bought the product. It wasn't cheap. We paid substantially for restaurant quality beef. I'd be a lot happier if there's someone who could tell me how a mine can knock out refrigeration and not have any serious damage to the ship other than ruining our beef. It doesn't make sense. I think an investigation is time well spent. Something else bothers me. I can't understand why the steak house is serving hamburger from steaks that were left over from the first shipment. Hamburger wasn't a part of that contract. It just doesn't make sense."

"Oh, I think the steaks were gone. That hamburger undoubtedly came from the mess halls to keep the Steak House open. I'm sure they did a trade or something like that."

"That's not what the club manager told me. He said they made the hamburgers from frozen steaks from the first shipment from AJAX. And they were terrible. Sergeant Major, something's going on and I'll need your support with the Old Man to protect the soldier's funds. Can I count on you?" It seemed he was down playing the thing and I wanted to put his feet to the fire. I remembered the firm as AJAX. His response surprised me.

"Sir, I really think you should leave this alone. It would be best for you and the entire command if you let this go. I suggest you seriously think about it. You do like it here don't you?"

I felt a not so vague threat and the hairs went up on the back of my neck. I could feel my face redden and quickly thought I'd better calm down or no one would take me seriously. "Is the ship's issue why you came to see me or do you have other business?"

"No sir. This was just a courtesy visit."

I didn't want to bother Colonel Minor with just anything yet but thought if I were to ask for a Navy investigation, I'd need his ok and besides he told the staff to tell him if we thought something strange was going on. I called his secretary and asked if he had some time to see me. She said he would be out all day but had some time in the morning. I felt that gave me a chance to sleep on it and also to calm down a bit. Further, I hadn't called Keiser back and figured I'd better get my ducks in a row. I was glad Minor wasn't in. Already I was jumping the gun.

I called Keiser mid-morning and he wasn't in. I called back just after lunch and he still wasn't in. I asked when he was going to be back and the lady said in about an hour. He wasn't in after the hour and I decided it was time for a ploy. I got An, my secretary, to call the Steak House and ask to speak to the manager about a possible waitress position. I told An if the person answering the phone said there were no jobs, to say that she had worked in Australia and her boss there told her to call him. She made the call and started speaking Vietnamese. In a minute she handed me the phone. In a second or two I heard Sergeant Keiser say, "Did you need to talk to me?"

"Sergeant Keiser, this is Captain Thompson from HAC JAG. I'm the one who spoke to you last night about the restaurant not having any steak. I've been trying to get hold of you."

"Yes sir. I've been terribly busy. I'm sorry I haven't been able to get back to you."

"Did you call Sergeant Major Mabry about my visit last night?"

I heard silence on the other end of the phone. "Yes sir, I was trying to find out if you were who you said you were."

"It seems that the sergeant major doesn't think it's a big deal to lose a shipment of beef. You're almost out of business, what do you think?"

"No sir, no sir. Of course, it's terrible for the restaurant. Our customer numbers are down and we're losing money. The board of directors for the fund may close us down."

I decided I would get to why I called. "Sarge, what did your chef say about the hamburger?"

"Sir, that's my mistake. I was all wrong last night. The chef got the hamburger from a friend in one of the mess halls in Long Binh. All the steaks from our supplier are gone."

Obviously, the sergeant major formulated a better story. I guess I could check who gave him the beef but certainly no one would admit to that kind of scavenging. I thanked him and hung up.

I checked with the procurement office on the AJAX file and found out they cleared the contract without getting the vet's chop. In effect that nullified my chop. The contracting officer nonetheless executed the contract. The entire project seemed like a cluster fuck. There is no vet chop and no evidence in the file that a vet inspected the first shipment. The contract is for premium quality steaks and the shipping times are unreasonable unless there is presumption of an order with procurement experience which might be ok but the contract was just starting. The club made a second order before receipt of the first that certainly suggested a full house which wasn't evident from my experience. Then a mine hit the ship and knocked out the refrigeration so the second order had to be thrown overboard. No telling what was in that order but I'll bet it wasn't all premium restaurant-quality filet mignon. There was no other known damage to the ship. The damage occurred just as the ship entered the combat zone so the fund had to pay. Sergeant Major Mabry seemed in cahoots with the club manager and the food at the restaurant sucked.

I saw Colonel Minor at 1030. Before we started Minor asked CSM Mabry who sat just outside Colonel Minor's office to check with Headquarters Company to see whether there were sufficient 45-caliber rounds for a limited terrorist event. He said to check personally and let him know ASAP. I saw Mabry get up and leave the command suite.

"Sir, something peculiar is going on with the NAFI steak contract. All the steaks were lost due to a mine that hit the ship transporting them just as the ship entered combat waters. The refrigeration unit was the only thing damaged by the mine blast and I'm thinking maybe a Navy investigation might be in order.

Under the contract in place, NAFI has to pay for the shipment once it enters the combat zone.

"Gregg, I'm on the NAFI board and we've been looking at the steak house for some time. It's been losing money and its management is substandard. We encouraged Sergeant Keiser, the Club Manager, to get a better supplier awhile back and the new supply contract just began. I heard about losing the shipment by combat action but hadn't heard the damage was focused just on the refrigeration unit." He got up from his desk and closed his office door. "I don't think a Navy investigation will help other than to find outright fraud and these guys are too smart for that. We didn't have any representatives on board the transport and there's little we can do. It was a civilian vessel. As far as the first shipment being unacceptable, the club manager is the contractor's representative and he accepted the shipment so we're stuck. I had some concerns of my own when I heard about the mine. A third shipment is on its way and should be in Saigon within the week. I have a veterinarian on standby to examine the meat and the port director is supposed to call me when the ship asks for berthing. I've been working with Colonel Plant on this and if the meat doesn't meet the contract specifications, the contracting officer will terminate for default. Now you need to keep secret what I'm about to tell you. I've suspected someone's involved with contract fraud with the Steak House. It was strange you chopped the contract and we're watching the contracting officer who has handled the action."

"Sir, I gave a chop but conditioned it on a veterinarian signing off on the refrigeration temperature range and inspection schedules."

"That makes sense. Someone must have removed the chop from the file."

"Sir, you know the Sergeant Major visited Australia when he first got here. He has access to all staff communications and he's been bugging me about the contract."

The colonel didn't say anything, just looked out the window.

"Sir, I went over to the steak house a week or so ago and had a terrible meal. I checked into it and Sergeant Major Mabry jumped into my knickers right away. He's obviously close to the club manager."

"I didn't authorize the R&R; I was at a briefing in Hawaii. I inquired about it when I got back and the Sergeant Major told me it was an exception; that his family was in Australia for a church assembly and he asked the acting commander to get his R&R in advance so he could attend. I'll let you know what happens. We'll not request any Navy investigation at this time."

LTC Plant called me the following week and told me the steak contract was terminated for convenience and the Nonappropriated Fund Board for Vietnam was closing the Steak House Restaurant. He told me the action was reviewed by NAFI headquarters in Washington. I heard nothing further from the Old Man on the matter. It wasn't long after that when reports of the Sergeant Major of the Army being involved in contract fraud started making the news.

Freedom Bird

My DEROS was down to three days and I had my ticket home. I was so short you could barely see me. I was going to the Army Claims Service, then at Fort Holabird in Baltimore, my home town. My office gave me a warm sendoff and I briefed my replacement on the command idiosyncrasies. I gave him the AK-47 in my bathtub with its banana clips. I hugged An and wished all well. Colonel Minor presented me a Bronze Star medal for service and told me one day he expected me to be a leader in the JAG Corps. He considered me a lifer and thought that was a compliment.

As I flew away on my Freedom Bird, I remembered the time I looked out the window at Fort Polk watching the guys who had just returned from Nam. My decision to become an Army lawyer in the shadows of Tigerland cost me two more year's military service and taught me war was hell. I spent my year in the fog of war and learned what warfare could do to its participants. Wilbur Enoch learned early to cultivate friendship through an alternative lifestyle. In Vietnam he was a hero but when tempted by his senses fell into what he thought would make him important and loved. He didn't know he was a pawn. Marcus Jackson was a nice kid but he was segmented by race. He wasn't a racist but Vietnam gave him every opportunity to be one. He was fortunate it was the military and not some Southern prosecutor who held him responsible for his actions. His little group of pot smokers certainly did not act with murderous intent. His tragedy along with Bobby Kichener's was the racial divide in Vietnam that mirrored the divide in the United States at the time. Ed Bond was troubled from birth. In a war zone he was a ticking bomb that exploded after folding two pair. Colonel Farrell Jordan wanted to be a man of decision and independence in his new Green Beret command. He was no John Wayne. When pressed by his superiors about an important decision he'd made without top cover, he lied. The fog of war blurred his vision. The superiors, to get even, clothed the resultant criminal proceedings with a specious intelligence classification. When the press found out, the "adult leadership" at the Pentagon and White House snuffed out the retribution.

I could see through the fog those who would take advantage of people they could and those who cut corners. Such low life's blossom in the fog especially when money is plentiful. Major Ted Westerfauel and his boyfriend lived on the edge. The Major had no problem feeding his desires with sales for the enemy's benefit. Charlie Long who took poor Harry Schaeffer to the rear of the barracks took advantage of Harry's mental impediment. Freddie Walker could handle pressure but not combat. The pressures between civilian life, even as a 911 operator, are different from combat and let nobody tell you otherwise. David Boone, the civilian PX manager, took advantage of what he thought was an opportunity for an extra buck. He lost his job and, but for an undeclared war, his freedom. Cornelius White, the rigger, epitomized the danger of weak character in a climate of legitimate killing. An argument over who might be doing the most for his country turned into a senseless death. Then there was Drew Downes. He was the prime example of a tough and smart jungle fighter ruined by a raw leader's incompetence. Many complain of fragging by draftees, even saying that's the reason the draft didn't work. They don't know the whole story. It wasn't just the poor leaders who were susceptible to being cleansed from the battlefield, but as everyone involved with Freddie Walker knew, if there was a serious threat, there were many ways to neutralize it.

As we flew over the Pacific I thought of Joe Harlan and wondered if he made it. Joe didn't really understand the military. A person's grade and rank trumps a job in almost all military settings. Lifers understand that. Wilborn Brown certainly had a good time. He didn't realize he was close to breaking a spy network and becoming a success. As it was, he accepted failure. Ted Mabry and his sergeant major buddies played the fog well. They maneuvered like a planter's wart into the Army bureaucracy. A Congressional investigation finally cut out their malignancy.

I wondered what would have happened if I had accepted Norbert Smith's bribe and taken up Mr. Minh on his offer of a weekend away from it all. I wondered why I didn't sneak the AK-47 into my foot locker and send it home as war booty. The fear of losing what was so dear to me, my legal profession, was a principal reason, but I wonder if my principles by themselves were enough. What if I knew I could get away with it? Did the fog of war cloud my principles? A moot question; but haunting in its possibilities. After all, it obscured the principles of many others much stronger than me.

Today, Vietnam is a beautiful country with an economy based on capitalist principles ruled by a national communist government. It depends heavily on tourism with its beaches on the South China Sea still the most beautiful in the world and capitalist investors infusing billions to reap its benefits. Another invasion of foreigners with stuffed wallets appears on its way. What would have Dang Hai Lang have thought?

South China Sea and Coast of Vietnam from the Freedom Bird

Statistics

The National Archives, Statistical information about casualties of the Vietnam Conflict, prepared by Theodore Hull, Archives Specialist, Electronic and Special Media Records Services Division December, 1998; Revised 12/02; 8/05; 2/07 are as follow:

See also http://www.archives.gov/research/vietnam-war/casualty-statistics html#state.

2,594,000 Americans served in South Vietnam during the war years (January 1965 to March 1973). Between a million and a million point six served in combat or close combat support.

Peak number in country at any one time was 543,482 on 30 April 1969.

58,156 Americans died in Vietnam; 47,359 from hostile combat action.

303,704 Americans were wounded in action; 153,329 required hospitalization.

25% serving in Vietnam were draftees. Draftees accounted for 30.4% of those killed in combat. Of the volunteers, no one knows how many signed up for another year's commitment to get promised jobs.

97% of Vietnam Era Veterans were honorably discharged. Of those 97%, the author believes well over 99% are proud of their service.

Racial deaths and participation closely reflected the racial composition of the United States at the time.

7,484 women served in Vietnam of which 6,250 were nurses. Eight women were killed in action.

Army had 38,209 deaths.

Marines had 14,838 deaths.

Air Force had 2,584 deaths.

Navy had 2,555 deaths.

The North and Viet Cong estimate their losses at 1,100,000 killed in action, 600,000 wounded, and over 125,000 captured.

The South Vietnamese Army had 223,748 killed in action and 1,169,763 wounded.

South Korea had 4,407 killed in action and 17,060 wounded.

Australia had 469 killed in action and 2,940 wounded.

Thailand had 351 killed in action and 1,358 wounded.

New Zealand had 55 killed in action and 212 wounded.
Web Site Maps:
http://www.nexus.net/%7E911gfx/vietnam.html
http://www.nexus.net/%7E911gfx/NVNmap.html
http://www.rjsmith.com/topo_map.html
http://www.chairborneranger.com/images/longbinhmap.htm
http://www.vnbd.com/map.htm

LTC Annie Ruth Graham; a lifer

Posted on the internet by her niece is the letter from LTC Annie Ruth Graham, an Army nurse, written at Christmas, 1967. LTC Graham died the following August. She was a lifer. God bless her.

"Greetings! This Christmas finds me a long, long way from North Carolina. I arrived in Saigon on 18 November and almost immediately departed for Tuy Hoa (pronounced Too-ey Wah) where our hospital (400 bed) is located directly on the beach of the South China Sea which is perfectly beautiful but quite treacherous. All buildings here are tropical type and the hospital is cantonment style. It is monsoon season now so we have torrential rains at times. The climate is quite humid but the nights are really rather pleasant. Getting used to my new outfit (tropical fatigues, jungle boots, and "baseball cap") is not as "exciting" as in World War II but I'm quite sure I'll manage to survive it all! Our nursing staff consists of 59 nurses (12 male) who of our enlisted personnel seem very well trained and apparently have been doing an excellent job. The tour of duty here is 12 months so I plan to be home for Christmas next year. I hope you have had a good year and that your Christmas is filled with joy and the New Year with more happiness than you could possibly wish for. Hope, too, that everyone will pray for peace. Love, Ruth."

978-0-595-71918-1
0-595-71918-X

9 780595 485093